D1105552

IT
HAPPENED
AT THE
FAIR

Center Point
Large Print

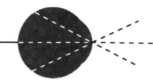

**This Large Print Book carries the
Seal of Approval of N.A.V.H.**

IT
HAPPENED
AT THE
FAIR

DEEANNE GIST

CENTER POINT LARGE PRINT
THORNDIKE, MAINE

This Center Point Large Print edition
is published in the year 2013 by arrangement with
Howard Books, a division of Simon & Schuster, Inc.

The text of this Large Print edition is unabridged.
In other aspects, this book may vary
from the original edition.
Printed in the United States of America
on permanent paper.
Set in 16-point Times New Roman type.

ISBN: 978-1-61173-718-9

Library of Congress Cataloging-in-Publication Data

Gist, Deeanne.
It happened at the fair / Deeanne Gist.
pages ; cm.
ISBN 978-1-61173-718-9 (library binding : alk. paper)
1. Inventors—Fiction. 2. Teachers of the deaf—Fiction.
   3. World's Columbian Exposition (1893 : Chicago, Ill.)—Fiction.
   4. Large type books. I. Title.
PS3607.I55I8 2013b
813′.6—dc23
                                                    2012043058

To my PIT Crew
(Personal Intercessory Team)

Julie Ashton
Victor and Kendra Belfi
Lisa Gettys
John and Pat Kane

who committed to daily stand in the gap for me as I labored to fill five hundred blank pages with the first draft of *It Happened at the Fair*. Your support, encouragement, and unfailing diligence made the most difficult part of the process an absolute delight. I love you, admire you, treasure you, and thank you.

AERIAL VIEW OF THE 1893
WORLD'S COLUMBIAN EXPOSITION

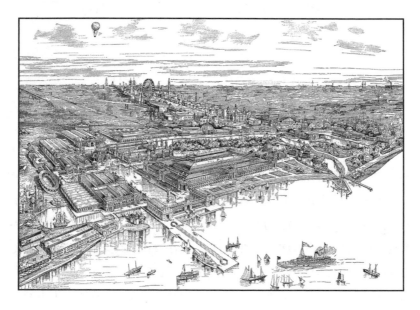

" 'Do you know where it is?' Cullen asked. 'The fair is huge, over six hundred acres according to the guidebooks. "Over that way" could mean yards or it could mean miles.' "

To view a map of the fair, go to
www.DeeanneGist.com/WCEmap.pdf

ACKNOWLEDGMENTS

This year I celebrated thirty years of marriage with the love of my life, Greg Gist. As a young man, it was his fantasy to have a woman who would one day stay at home, raise his children, cook his meals, and be his helpmate. Well, I've definitely stayed at home, helped raise the kids, and even managed to cook a few meals. It's the helpmate part that I seem to struggle with the most.

You see, I have ideas. Lots of ideas. And over the years, I've tried to turn those ideas into realities. I've done chain letters, Amway, 900 numbers (remember those?), started an antiques business, produced and manufactured parenting products, dabbled in journalism, and ended up settling into this profession of novel writing—all from the comforts of home.

I'd always seen Greg as being, well, tolerant of my many escapades. Until now. As I reflect on our thirty years together, I realize he has been way more than tolerant—he's been downright supportive. He has done more than his share of carting kids to and fro, of hiring a housekeeper to free up my time, of blessing me with a lovely and comfortable home—as well as my current office, with floor-to-ceiling windows in front of me and floor-to-ceiling bookshelves behind me—of paying for all the aforementioned ideas (all of which have cost him not a little bit of money), of sharing his frequent-flyer miles, of bringing me flowers "just because," of putting up with my eighty-hour work weeks when I'm on deadline, of giving up football games to sit through very, very long award ceremonies, and of taking charge of the household while I gallivant around the country to conferences and events.

So to you, my beloved, wonderful, handsome man, I say thank you. Thank you for being an incredible father, an amazing provider, a wonderfully romantic partner, and a staunch supporter of all my wild ideas. I love you so, so much. Happy anniversary, my sweet.

CHAPTER 1

Cullen's eyes swelled to mere slits, his roughened cheeks itched, and a sharp line separated the raw skin on his neck from the skin protected by his shirt. It had happened every planting season for his entire twenty-seven years and it would happen for the next.

He yanked off his gloves, shirt, and undershirt, worked the pump, then stuck his whole head beneath the water. The icy stream stung and soothed all at the same time. He dared not dither, though. Those cotton seeds rode on the breeze and any exposed skin would begin to itch within a day's time.

Rearing up, he combed his fingers through his hair. Water drizzled down his back, mingling with the sweat collecting between his shoulder blades. The hinges on the back-door screen squeaked. His stepmother clomped out, her plump body listing with the weight of the pail she toted.

"You ready to throw that out, Alice?"

She nodded, dirty water sloshing over the sides of the bucket. "I've got it. You get on inside. You know better than to be out here without a shirt on."

"A few more minutes won't hurt." Taking it from her, he retraced his steps, tossed the pail's contents, and pumped fresh water into it.

She stood at the door, her back holding the screen open. Her auburn bun sagged, as streaked with muted white as a song sparrow's wing. "Come on," she said. "Ya look a fright."

Pulling off a boot, he glanced inside. His father already sat at the head of their hand-hewn table, shaking out his napkin. Three plates balanced across its slightly slanted surface. The table had been Cullen's first attempt at making a real piece of furniture. He'd presented it to his mother on his eleventh Christmas, prouder than any rooster in the henhouse.

By the time he realized her other table was not only level but also nicer, she'd already passed away. She never let on, though—just stroked it as if it were made of mahogany and asked Dad if he didn't think it was the grandest table he'd ever seen. Dad would give Cullen a wink and agree that it surely was. To this day, Cullen didn't know what had happened to their good table.

"Ya gonna stand out there all day or *cm* in so we can eat?" Dad tucked a napkin into the collarless neckline beneath his bushy black beard.

"Coming." Dropping his boots outside, he stepped in, plucked an undershirt from the wall peg, and pulled it over his head. At least his arms and chest still held a healthy glow. Two strips of startling white skin dissected his coppery torso, delineating the spots where his suspenders rode. Going shirtless during the plowing was not a problem, it was the planting, weeding, and harvesting that bothered him most. "Smells good, Alice."

The door banged shut behind her. "Made ya some bean *kttl* soup."

He suppressed a cringe. Bean kettle soup. Again. It was the third time in as many weeks.

Shrugging into a shirt, he secured the buttons, snapped his suspenders into place, scraped back his chair, and froze. A letter from the National Commission of the World's Columbian Exposition sat beside his plate. "What's that?"

Dad scratched the back of his head, fluffing his wiry curls, the same black color as Cullen's.

"Yer the reader in the family," he said.

Cullen jerked his gaze to Dad's. "Why's it addressed to me?"

Alice plopped a cast-iron pot on the table. Dad handed her his bowl.

"It's been opened." Cullen lowered himself into his chair, being careful to keep his hands clear of the table and envelope.

"I had Luther read it to me," Dad said.

If the store clerk had read it, then the whole county would know of its contents by now. Everybody but Cullen, that is.

"What did it say?" he asked.

Alice served up bowls for the three of them.

"Accordin' to *Lthr*, it said you've been accepted as an exhibitor at the World's Fair."

11

He wheezed in a breath, his swollen airways in as bad a shape as his face. "An *exhibitor? Of what?*"

"An automatic fire sprinkler system."

A prickling sensation began behind his eyes. "How did they find out about my sprinkler system?"

"I told 'em." Dad took a spoonful of soup, chewed the ham, and swallowed.

"Told them? How?"

"I sent in an application fer ya."

The headache that had danced along the edges of Cullen's skull began to make inroads. "You can't read or write well enough to do that."

Dad shrugged. "Got me some *hlp* from the preacher."

Cullen started to rub his forehead, then stopped when he encountered tender skin. "And why would you do a fool thing like that?"

"Watch yer mouth."

"I want to know why, Dad."

He leaned his chair back on two legs. "I found the World's Fair ad for exhibitors underneath yer mattress last spring when I took it outside fer Alice to beat clean."

Moisture began to collect on Cullen's neck and hairline. "So what? The entire world's been reading about the fair since it was awarded to Chicago in '90."

"The entire world ain't hiding it under their mattress."

"I wasn't hiding it. I just, I don't know, didn't have anyplace else to put it." Even to his own ears, his excuse sounded feeble. "Besides, I forgot all about it."

"I looked at it again when I got *hm* today. Its edges are frayed and it's been opened and closed so many times the paper is splittin' along the creases."

Cullen placed his arms on both sides of his bowl. "Look, Dad. I'm a farmer, just like you. Just like Granddad. And just like Great-Granddaddy before him. A little boy who mourned the loss of his mother rigged up that stupid thing."

"A little boy who became a man overnight."

"It's nothing but a toy."

"Ya spent years perfectin' it."

Cullen fisted his hands. "And it didn't help one iota when I spent heaven knows how much of your harvest money installing it in the cowshed. The thing still burnt straight to the ground and very nearly caught the barn on fire."

"Ya fixed that when ya added them fusible joints."

Cullen slammed his fist, rattling the dishware and causing Alice to start. "I'm not going to the World's Fair, Dad. I appreciate the gesture. I know your intentions are good. But I'm not going. Especially not now. It's the planting season, for crying out loud."

Dad's chair thumped to the ground. "Don't ya *thnk* I know what time o' year it is? I may not read so well, but I can sure tell the difference in the seasons."

Closing his eyes, Cullen tried to calm himself. But his pulse was ticking, his breath was coming in spurts, and the prickles behind his eyes had turned into hammers. "You're missing the point. I meant no insult."

"Then at least give me enough credit to see when a fella ain't cut out for farmin'. Look at ya. Ya can't see in the spring. Ya can't breathe in the summer. And ya can't *hrdly* stay standing during the harvest. Never have, never will. You know it. I know it. And yer mama certainly knew it. Why do ya *thnk* she spent so much time givin' you all that book learnin'? So you could hide ads under yer mattress while ya killed yourself in the cotton fields?"

Cullen surged to his feet. Dad made it to his just as fast.

Alice rapped her spoon on the table. "*Sit down.* Both of ya. I spent all day on this soup and if ya don't eat every last bit, I'm gonna make nothin' but mush for a month of Sundays."

A bird preparing for nightfall landed on the windowsill, pecked at the curtains, then took off with a chirp. One of the dogs out front barked, the others responding in kind.

The tension eased from Dad's shoulders.

"Beggin' yer pardon, Alice. We'll be glad to sit down. Cullen, tuck yer napkin in."

He sat, stuffed his napkin in his collar, then shoveled mouthful after mouthful of the soup into his mouth. The sooner he finished, the sooner he could escape to his room. He was reading *The Farmer's Encyclopedia* and had just gotten to the section on tongueless plows.

He could feel Dad's gaze but refused to acknowledge it. Swallowing was an effort, though. He cursed himself for even saving that ad. He didn't know why he had. He certainly didn't expect anyone to ever find out about it.

Heat began to rise up his neck. Had Dad told Luther about the ad? Did the whole county know about it?

Dad cleared his throat. "Luther said the folks runnin' the fair turned away all but a third o' the applicants. That to be chosen is not only a *grt* honor for ya but for all o' Mecklenburg County."

He kept his head down. "I'm not going."

"I'm asking ya, son. Fer me."

Dropping his spoon in the bowl, Cullen whipped up the envelope, yanked out the letter, and shook it open. He skimmed it, quickly finding what he was looking for, then held it up for his dad. "Did Luther mention exhibitors are responsible for the costs of transporting, handling, arranging, and removing their exhibits?"

"He did. He also said them fair folks weren't chargin' ya fer the space."

"Even still, do you have any idea how much it will cost just to transport the equipment?"

Dad scratched his chin beneath his beard. "Seein' as the railroad will let ya carry a hundred pounds fer free, I reckon it shouldn't cost ya nothin'."

"Nothing but the packing crates, the fare to and from, my room for six months, my meals for six months, a suit that fits, city boots, extraneous expenses, and who knows what else."

Dad raised his brows. "Since ya seem to know so much about it, maybe ya oughta be tellin' me how much it costs."

"I have no idea."

"Well, I do. Somewheres around three hundred dollars."

Alice took a quick breath.

"Then why are we even discussing this?"

"Because I already paid it."

Alice whipped her head toward Dad.

"Paid it?" Cullen's body flashed hot, then cold. "Are you out of your mind? No. That's, that's . . . crazy."

"Well, it's all arranged. Marty down at the train station took care of it fer me."

"Where did you even get that kind of money?" It wasn't his business, and under normal circumstances, he'd never have had the gall to

16

ask. But these weren't normal circumstances.

"I had a little tucked away from when the cash was rollin' in back in '90 and '91."

"A little?" Cullen's lungs quit working. Try as he might, only a quiver of air would go through his pipes. "That's a whole year's harvest," he rasped. "It's way too much. And you know it. Especially with cotton prices as shaky as they are right now."

"Pshaw. We're fine."

Alice pushed back from the table, her expression tight, her movements jerky.

Cullen grabbed the napkin from his neck. "Well, I'm not going. You'll have to tell them you changed your mind."

Dad took a deep breath. "Life's an unsure thing, son. You know that firsthand. Sometimes, ya just got to *rch* out and grab it, right by the tail."

"What about the crop?"

"Dewey's boys said they'd hire on."

Cullen's jaw slackened. "You've already asked them?"

"Ayup."

"What about Wanda? We're supposed to get married."

Dad studied him. "Ya set a date?"

"Well, no, but we're going to. And it'll be sooner rather than later."

Dad folded his napkin in half, then in half again. "Forever's a long time. A few months on the front end or the back end won't make much difference."

"We're not talking about a few months. We're talking half a year. We're talking the planting, the weeding, and half the harvesting. We're talking clear to November."

Dad hooked his thumbs in his suspenders. "I know how long the fair runs."

His nostrils flared. "What if I went all the way up there and nobody wanted it?"

"Then ya can come on home and be a *frmr*. You'll be no worse off than ya are now."

"You'll be three hundred dollars poorer! The economy is in a mess and farming is as unreliable as a woman's watch. I had no idea you even had a cushion like that. The last thing you want to do is spend it on something so frivolous." He paused. "I can't take it, Dad. It's too much. I'd never forgive myself if it was all for nothing."

"I'm gifting it to ya."

Alice slammed a coffeepot onto the stove.

"I'm gifting it right back," Cullen said.

Dad dragged a hand down his face. It had been a long time since the two of them butted heads.

"I know you mean well, Dad, but children are always saying stupid things. Things like, 'I want to be a sheriff when I grow up' or 'I want be the president' or," he lowered his voice, " 'I want to be an inventor.' It means nothing. It's silly talk."

"Not if that's what they're destined to be."

Feeling all the bluster leave him, he allowed his shoulders to slump and played his final card. "I'm going deaf, Dad. Even if I manage to find investors, once they learn I can't hear like a normal person and that I belong in an asylum, they'll withdraw their offers."

Alice twisted around, her face stricken, her hands crinkling her apron.

Dad's eyes narrowed and his jaw tensed. "Yer not goin' deaf and ya don't belong in a madhouse. So maybe you have a *lttl* trouble hearing every single word a fella utters. Ya get by just fine."

"When things are nice and quiet I do, but it's getting worse. Especially if there are other—"

Dad held up his palm, effectively stopping him. "Madhouses are fer crazy people. There's nothing wrong with yer think box. You're more book smart than over half the county."

"Nobody cares about book smarts once they find out there's something wrong with you. Just look at Ophelia Ashford. She went blind after staring at the sun and her parents shipped her off to Blackwell's lickety-split."

"Miss Ashford's parents are the ones who should be locked up, not her. But quit changing the subject. I've already wired them folks up in Chicago and accepted their invite. I've found ya a boardin' house and paid fer yer room— nonrefundable, nontransferable. I'm not asking ya anymore. I'm telling ya. It's why yer mother learned ya. You may be able to let all her hard work—her *life's* work—go fer nothing, but I'm not." Lifting up one hip, he pulled a ticket and a bulging envelope from his pocket, then slid them across the table. "Yer gettin' on the Richmond & Danville in one week's time. Yer goin' to Chicago. Yer stayin' at a boardin' house called Harvell. And yer gonna give this thing a chance. The best chance it's ever had. I'll see ya in November."

The anger simmering inside began to bubble again. He could not believe this. Swiping up the ticket, the money, and the letter, he stood. "Fine. I'll go. And I'll fail, like I always do. Then I'll come back and we can put this thing to bed once and for all."

CHAPTER 2

Ｈow much longer before ya finish?" Wanda asked, batting at a bug flying about her head.

"I'm almost done." Cullen threaded a bolt on an animal-powered treadmill he'd rigged up. "I just want to make sure this is still working for your mother before I leave."

One of Wanda's sisters burst out the back door, tagged her brother on the run, and bounded down the porch steps. "Yer it!"

"Am not!"

"Are too!"

The twins sat cross-legged in the yard, reciting nursery rhymes and keeping time with their hands as they slapped their thighs, clapped once, then each tapped the other's palm. Inside, the baby's cries sliced through it all, the open windows offering no buffer.

Wanda tightened her lips. "I *stll* cain't believe yer not gettin' back 'til November."

"Me, neither."

"I don't know what all the fuss is over. Who cares about some dumb world's fair?" Pulling loose the strings of her sunbonnet, she yanked it off her head, mussing her blond hair. "And who cares about some old explorer who discovered America four *hndrd* years ago?"

Pausing, he glanced at her. Even in the fading

light, he could see the irritation snapping in her eyes.

"Lift that lantern for me, would you?" he asked.

Tossing down her bonnet, she grabbed the lantern.

He tightened the bolt he'd threaded. "The celebration of Columbus's discovery is just an excuse for us to show the world how far we've progressed in the past four hundred years and for them to show us how far they've progressed. Ever since the Paris fair in '89, we've been itching to do something bigger and grander than the Eiffel Tower."

"Sounds ta me like it ain't nothin' more than a big ol' peein' contest."

Grinning, he set down his wrench and straightened. "I guess that's not too far from the truth." He curled his tongue against his teeth and whistled for the dog. "Cowboy! Come here, fella. Get on up here and let's see if she's working again."

The black-and-white border collie bounded across the yard and onto the treadmill, activating the flywheel, which moved the walking beam up and down, which then pumped the churn dasher attached to it.

The back door opened again. "Charlie!" Mrs. Sappington called, stepping onto the porch. "Oh, Cullen. Ya fixed it."

Pushing the brake lever, he stopped the

treadmill and let Cowboy jump off. "It was no problem, ma'am. Your new churn's just a little shallower than the last. All I had to do was drill a hole closer to the fulcrum."

She smiled, her round cheeks rosy from the warmth of the kitchen. "The *prblm* wasn't drillin' the hole. The problem was knowing the exact spot ta *drll* it in. I sure do 'preciate it."

A boy with scuffed knees and short pants clomped up the steps. "Ya call me, Ma?"

"It's yer turn in the bath *wtr*. Come on, now."

Cullen put the tools back in the box, then stuffed it under the porch. He'd put off seeing Wanda as long as he could. Not only to give his face time to settle into some semblance of its former self, but also because he'd had a thousand details to see to before leaving. His train pulled out in the morning, though, and it was time to pay the piper.

"Finally." Wanda stomped off toward the smokehouse, the lantern in her hand swinging like a church bell, her hips doing the same. He followed, taking a moment to appreciate her cinched-in calico frock, which hinted at curves beneath. It would be her company, however, that he'd miss the most.

"I don't like it anymore than you do," he said. "But Dad left me no choice."

"Ya could've told him no," she snapped.

"I did."

She whirled around. "Ya could've meant it."

He took the lantern from her. "I did mean it. But he'd already laid out a great deal of cash, none of which I could get back. I tried."

"But it don't make a lick o' sense. Yer a farmer. What's yer dad thinkin'? That he can dress ya up in purty duds, send ya up to Chicagy, and turn ya into John Edison?"

"Thomas Edison. And no, yes, maybe. But you're right. The whole thing's ludicrous."

Her lips began to quiver. "I don't want ya to go, Cullen."

He grabbed her hand and squeezed. "That makes two of us. I'm sorry, Wanda. I really am."

"Will ya . . ." She took a shaky breath. "Will ya marry me afore ya go?"

Releasing her, he leaned back. "I can't. There's no—"

"I knew it!" Spinning, she stumbled down the path, her shoulders starting to shake.

Die and be doomed. What a convoluted mess.

She pushed into the smokehouse and slammed the door. It was the only place quiet enough for him to hear above the ruckus her siblings made.

The crickets silenced momentarily, then started right up again. He forced himself to move forward. But marry her? Tonight? The thought had never even occurred to him. And if it had, he'd have dismissed it out of hand.

Taking a fortifying breath, he stepped inside

and closed the door with a soft click. The over-whelming aroma of smoked ham, pork shoulders, and bacon stifled all his other senses, bringing with it a rush of well-being. He and Wanda had spent many an evening in here talking about every-thing from the stunts they'd pulled as youngsters to the kind of house they'd one day live in.

But in all that time, he'd never once mentioned the World's Fair advertisement he kept. And why should he have? It was nothing. Just a promotion piece from a grandiose event that was in every newspaper from here to kingdom come. It had nothing to do with him. Nothing to do with her. And nothing to do with the life they'd mapped out for themselves.

Until now.

Meat hanging from the rafters like overgrown bats cast gruesome shadows on the bricked walls. In the shed's center, Wanda stood with her back to him, head down, shoulders limp. As least she wasn't crying. Not out loud, anyway.

Easing up behind her, he set the lamp down and turned her around. "Come on, now. I'm the only one around here who's supposed to have swollen eyes and puffy cheeks."

With a *humph,* she swiped a cuff beneath her nose. "Ya don't have puffy cheeks."

"Only swollen eyes."

"Not them, neither. Ya got the prettiest eyes I ever seen."

He hooked a tendril of hair behind her ear. "Only when I look at you."

Tears began to pool. "I know ya can't marry me tonight. It's just . . . when are ya gonna marry me? Lavelle and Billy John done fell in love, married, and had a little one in less time then it's taken us to set a date. My friends, they're . . . they're startin' to poke fun at us. At me."

Protectiveness welled up inside him. "Who's poking fun at you?"

"Everybody."

"Who, everybody?"

She waved her hand in a dismissive gesture. "It don't matter. What matters is that it's time fer a date. We got to have a date afore you leave."

He looked around the smokehouse, seeing everything, noticing nothing. The two of them had been best friends since the day his mother died. Wanda had stood outside the mill same as everybody else. But instead of watching it burn to the ground, she'd watched *him* watch it burn as he screamed for his mother and had to be held back by Wanda's father.

He'd been twelve. She'd been seven. But he'd never have made it through the following years without her. He loved her. Always had. Always would. When her braids had been released and twisted up in a bun, everybody assumed the two of them would wed. And they'd assumed it too.

He didn't recall actually asking her. It just seemed the natural way of things, though he'd never been in any great rush.

"Yer awfully quiet." Her voice bounced around the conical roof.

He shrugged. "I'm not sure what you want me to say. What am I supposed to do? Just pick a random date?"

"Random's all right with me if it's all right with you."

"Well, it's not all right with me. A lot of thought should be put into it. We don't even have a place to live yet."

"We can stay here while ya build a place. Pa said so."

She'd talked to her father about it? Before she'd talked to him? "We're not living here. I'd never be able to hear over all the noise. It would drive me crazy."

"What if we have a passel o' little ones? They gonna be too noisy fer ya too?"

He frowned. "Are you trying to start a fight?"

"No, Cullen. I'm trying to get a date. There's four Saturdees in November. Pick one."

His jaw began to tick. "I've had just about enough of people painting me into corners. I can handle only one corner at a time. Right now, I have to do this World's Fair trip. When I get back, we'll pick a date."

She tightened her lips. "Well, I'm sorry. I didn't

know pickin' a date would make ya feel like you'd been painted into a corner."

Sighing, he dragged a hand through his hair. "That didn't come out like I meant it."

"What exactly did ya mean, then?" She propped a hand on her waist. "Do ya even want to marry me?"

"Of course, I do."

"Then what are ya waitin' fer?"

"I told you. We'll set a date when I get back."

She worried her lower lip. "What if ya meet some fancy city gal up there?"

He rolled his eyes. "I'm not meeting anybody."

"Ya don't know that."

"I do know that."

"Well, I think havin' a date will make it a little harder fer yer eyes to roam."

"My eyes won't roam."

"Prove it."

He blinked. "What?"

"Prove it."

"How?"

"Let's have our weddin' night. Right here. Right now." Reaching up, she began yanking pins from her loose blond bun.

He tensed. "Stop that. For the love of Caesar, we're in a smokehouse."

"I don't care." Pins clattered to the floor and sailed across its bumpy surface.

He grabbed her wrist. "I care. I'm not taking

you on this filthy brick floor in a smelly smokehouse where any one of your family can bust in."

Breaking free of his grip, she continued what she was doing, her arms hiked up, her chest heaving.

He spun around. "I'm leaving."

"No!" Scrambling up behind him, she launched herself onto his back.

He took an involuntary step forward.

She wrapped her arms and legs clear around him, hooking her ankles across his stomach, her wrists across his neck. "Please, Cullen." She moved against him in an effort to secure her hold.

He sucked in his breath. "No, Wanda."

She refused to let go.

He pried her feet loose, only to have them hook again when he reached for her arms. Back and forth they went until he lost his balance and they both tumbled onto the unforgiving brick floor.

He immediately rolled to the side. "Take the deuce, are you all right?"

Instead of answering, she pressed herself against him, kissing him as passionately as she knew how. But it was a maiden's kiss. She had no idea there was any other kind. And that was his undoing.

A rush of love and protectiveness surged through him. Wrapping her close, he took control and for the first time taught her how a man kisses a woman.

She blossomed against him, pressing forward when he pulled back, her hands traveling everywhere. "Please, Cullen."

'He captured her wrists and brought them to his lips, then released her and stood.

She propped herself up on an elbow, her chest lifting with each breath. "Everybody does it, ya know. No one can believe we've been together this long and not done it."

"The same 'everybody' who's been making fun of you?"

No answer.

"Maybe it's time for a new set of friends."

She tossed her head, the last of her pins tumbling free. "Are ya worried ya might get me with child?"

"Among other things."

"If that were to happen, I could just go up to Chicagy and we could be married up there."

"That's not going to happen because I'm walking you back to the house. Right now."

Still, he didn't go help her up. The more distance he kept between them, the better.

"Then when can we have us a weddin' night?"

"When everything's official."

"And when will everythin' be official?"

"The last Saturday in November." There. He'd set a date.

Pushing herself to her feet, she plowed her hands into her hair and lifted it before allowing it to spill down her back and over her shoulders.

Sweet heaven above, it went clear beyond her hips.

Swallowing, he forced his eyes to meet hers. He wouldn't be walking her anywhere. Not when she looked like that. "I'll see you in November, Wanda."

Her face collapsed. "Can I come up to see ya, at least? We could tour the fair together."

"You'd have to have a chaperone."

"Not if it were our weddin' trip."

Much as he wanted to comfort her, he stayed where he was. "Even married, it'd be too costly. The room Dad rented is on an all-male floor and is big enough for only one person. No refunds. No transfers."

Biting her lip, she crossed her arms beneath her breasts, hugging herself.

"I'm sorry," he said. "The time will pass before you know it."

He strode to the door and reached for the latch, her words stopping him.

"That sprinkler system won't bring yer ma back."

He bent his head. "I'm not doing it for her. I'm doing it for Dad."

He stepped out the door, then closed it behind him as gently as he could.

31

GRANDSTAND AND PLATFORM IN FRONT OF THE ADMINISTRATION BUILDING

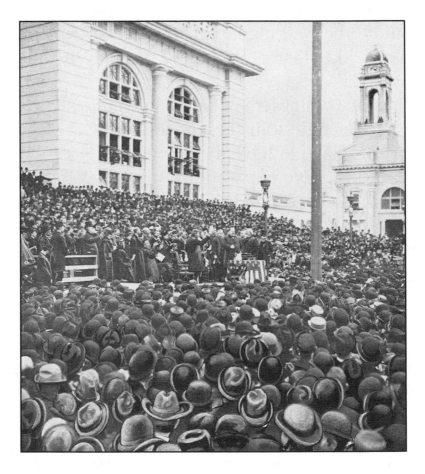

"As soon as President Cleveland touched the key, every engine and piece of machinery in the entire fair would be set in motion."

CHAPTER 3

Cullen flipped up the collar of his overcoat. Its gray wool blended in with moisture-laden clouds and offered a mite of protection against the raw winds. But in truth, he hardly felt the cold. He was still angry with his father. Still feeling guilty about the money. And still wishing he and Wanda hadn't parted with an argument.

The only good news was Chicago didn't have a cotton seed in sight and for the first time since the planting started, he enjoyed deep, cleansing breaths. Between that, healthy skin, and the energy of the people, he couldn't help but be caught up in the excitement of the World's Fair's unveiling. Chicago might have many-storied buildings, roaring streets, and whirring cable cars, but all memory of it faded when Cullen beheld this temporary fairyland, this "White City" that his country had raised up seemingly overnight.

Crowds poured into the park like a stream of lava, overflowing all boundaries. People of every nationality and every age swarmed over the pier, across the viaduct, and onto the lakefront, all pressing toward the platform he stood before.

He'd been reading articles about the fair for three years now, but its magnificence was still a shock. The crowds coming to commemorate

Columbus's discovery would indeed find a New World. Only this one would be of iron, electricity, and American ingenuity.

His fire sprinkler display, assembled and ready for onlookers, was like an ant among a city of giants—insignificant and easily overlooked. He had no prayer of competing against the monumental exhibits in Machinery Hall. But even that mighty building, with all its wonders waiting to be explored, would stand empty a while longer. The people here—more than half a million, if the projections proved accurate—had come to catch a glimpse of their president, Grover Cleveland, as he pressed his finger on the magical button that would bring their fabricated world to life.

As an exhibitor, Cullen had entered the park early and claimed his spot long before the public gained admittance. His landlady had told him she and her boarders were going to gather in front of the platform Cleveland would be speaking from. So he'd posted himself at the very hub of the plaza, or "Court of Honor" as it was called, surrounded by architectural wonders on every side.

Before him stood the Administration Building, its mighty gilded dome towering above its neighbors. It served as the sun around which all other buildings orbited. Its immense proportions and attention to structural detail left no doubt that this fair would glorify not only science and industry but also beauty and art. Even in the gray light, its dome seemed to glisten.

Today, however, its entrance was blocked by a temporary grandstand and stage, along with a line of uniformed Columbian Guards, so named for the Columbian Exposition. The intimidating force had been handpicked for their height, physique, character, and ability to serve and protect. At the moment, they formed a human barrier between the crowd and the presidential platform just ten feet away.

Cullen sized up the guard facing him. He was the same height as Cullen, though the black pompon on his cap gave him a few more inches. Five horizontal stripes of black braid dissected his blue coat like cross ties on a railroad track, shiny brass buttons spiking their centers. The guard's attention swept over the crowd and touched the structures that formed the first ring of the galaxy encircling the Administration Building.

In the week Cullen had spent preparing his exhibit, the layout of the Court of Honor had become so deeply ingrained in his mind that even if he closed his eyes, he could see all the guard perused. To Cullen's left stretched Machinery Hall—his home away from home for the next six months. To his right was the Electricity Building with Edison's seventy-foot Tower of Light inside. Behind him, an abyss of mud extended to an avenue a city block wide, with the epic

Manufactures Building—reputed to be four times larger than the Roman Colosseum—on one side and the Agricultural Building on the other. Between the two lay a miniature lake known as the Basin. Blue, white, and yellow gondolas glided across its surface, giving it a Venetian flair, their cheery colors striking a bright note in the foggy mist.

Beyond the Basin, a peristyle—where each state of the Union had its own column and sculptured figure—formed an open barrier between the park and Lake Michigan. Gray gulls wheeled and rode cork-like on the water, quarreling with the ducks that paddled there. Breakers charged the wall, flinging up their white spray as if they too wanted to see the festivities.

He scanned the faces of the men and women pressing around him. No sign of Mrs. Harvell. Instead, he saw old men with snuffboxes, young men with their best girls, women with babies in their arms, men wearing rubber raincoats, and young girls in gay attire.

Voices rose in distress as thousands of feet continued to trample through the muck. A man tried to wrench his stuck galoshes out of the mud, only to have his foot come free, leaving the rubber boot behind, its sides quivering. The hems of ladies' skirts gave them endless anxiety, either having to be lifted or face getting damp and soiled.

It was a good thing Wanda hadn't come. She'd have been frightened by all the sights, the sounds, and the very thought of being at the center of tomorrow. Still, he missed her, and it was only May 1st. November had never seemed so far away.

Someone from behind accidentally shoved him into the Columbian Guard.

"Steady, there," the guard barked.

Straightening, Cullen mumbled an apology and glanced over his shoulder. Being a full head taller than most, he was able to see over the profusion of black derby hats and lacy women's confections filling every available inch between him and the Basin. He had no prayer of finding Mrs. Harvell among them. The bobbing heads formed a human mosaic and spread clear back to some curved bridges, then across those bridges and on to the Manufactures Building on one side and the Agricultural Building on the other.

Balconies, porticos, and roofs blossomed with spectators. The peristyle held moving figures thick to the right and left of each column.

In spite of the wind, men climbed up ropes and improvised ladders to the dizzying pinnacles of Machinery Hall. They slid into perilous places on the dome of the Agricultural Building and stood in every nook of the Administration Building, hugging its statues, turrets, and parapets.

Cullen shook his head. Two years ago Jackson

Park had been nothing more than morass and sand barrens. Today it held an entire city of stupendous buildings made of hastily constructed shells sprayed with a white, Alhambra-like veneer made from plaster of paris. For the sake of the men now clinging to its towers, he hoped the plaster of paris held.

A fluttering on the northeast corner of the Administration Building caught his eye. Looking up, he watched as the president's blue flag, with white eagle and stars, shook itself frec. President Cleveland had arrived at the park.

Cullen's cheer joined the ones around him, and a single ray of sunlight pierced the clouds, bringing another round of cheers. Within ten minutes an opening directly in front of the Administration Building heralded the president, members of his cabinet, the presidents of the fair, a descendant of Columbus, and a few government officials. But Cullen's attention was completely captured by President Cleveland.

He was almost as tall as Cullen and a lot rounder around the middle. A silk hat somewhat the worse for wear covered his balding head, while his famous mustache covered his mouth.

A mighty bellow rose alongside Cullen's whistle. As the president moved within earshot, the man beside Cullen shouted, "How are you, Grover!"

The great man smiled, walked boldly up the

platform stairs to a plush leather chair reserved for him, and sat with confidence. The notables bunched up behind him, surveying the sea of humanity before them.

An orchestra burst into the "Columbian March." Its notes caught between the facades of the two palaces and sent a rebounding echo down to the peristyle. In the excitement, the crowd pressed forward.

Locking his knees, Cullen leaned back, struggling to keep from being pushed into the guards.

He might as well have argued with a cyclone. Standing as he was at the vortex where all currents joined, it was only a matter of seconds before he and those next to him were shoved forward, sweeping away the once-formidable blue line of Columbian Guards as though they were fragile reeds.

The mob poured into the previously empty space. The eager hundreds behind jostled forward, and an overwhelming force carried the blockade up to the very edge of the platform. A guard grabbed Cullen's shirtfront and slung him back, but nothing could check the human stampede.

A woman several yards away held up her little one, shrieking to the people in the grandstand to save her baby. Another woman trapped against the rails fainted.

"Help!" a feminine voice cried out.

He spun around. All he could see was the beribboned green hat upon her head being jostled from side to side as men pushed past her with cruel elbows.

Her tiny gloved hand shot up, fanning a dainty handkerchief of surrender. "Guards. Someone. *Please*. I—I can't breathe!"

The music thundered, whipping itself into a crescendo.

Cullen used his height, his breadth, and his outrage to battle his way toward her. An elbow slammed into his back, knocking the breath from him yet propelling him closer to her.

Ignoring the stinging blow, he strained ahead, a salmon swimming upstream.

Her arm and hat wrenched sideways, her cry of pain searing his ears.

"For the sake of Peter," he shouted. "Someone help her!"

But his words were lost in the jumble.

Her arm wilted, the handkerchief slowly disappearing from sight.

"No! Don't faint!" He willed her to hear him. "They'll trample you!"

He made a herculean rush forward, and then he was there. She'd stayed on her feet, but her face was white and drawn with terror.

He opened his arms as wide as he could. "Quickly. Come here."

She pitched herself against him, then lifted her

chin, resting it against his chest. "My ankle. I've twisted it."

Nodding, he clamped her safely against him, then looked around, easily able to see over the quaking mass. A woman to his right invaded the benches reserved for reporters. Crawling onto a bench and then a table, she grasped the rails of the grandstand and hiked a leg to mount it.

One of the correspondents pulled her back down by her skirt, causing her to fall and break his table. Cullen felt his outrage bubble again, but he already had his hands full.

Some excited men in the crowd tried to calm those around them by battering them with umbrellas. Other men laughed at being thrown about and managed to get in a few gasping cheers, having no idea it wasn't a speech they hailed but the chaplain's prayer.

It was the women, however, who suffered the brunt of it. They screamed, they struggled, they disappeared from view. He'd never realized the destruction a crowd could cause. He kept glancing at the platform, expecting the chaplain to put a stop to the mayhem below. Instead, he simply stepped back and welcomed the next speaker.

The woman in his arms began to buckle, drawing his attention. Not only had her face lost color, but her lips had become pale. With each passing minute, the pressure around them grew worse. He had to move her before she passed out completely.

Crouching over, he touched his lips to her ear. "I need you to hold on to my neck. I'm going to carry you to the press section where there's more room."

The scent of rosewater wafting from her neck contrasted sharply with the smell of panic coating the air.

She shook her head. "You can't."

He frowned. Did she doubt his strength? Though her coat covered the specifics, he could feel a very slender form beneath it. "You're tiny as a mite."

Bunching her hands around fistfuls of his jacket, she slowly pulled herself up, straightening her one good leg. Up, up, up she rose until the tip of her head reached the bottom of his chin.

He lifted his brows. She might be thin, but she was quite tall for a woman. Still, he leaned down and easily swept her into his arms, then began to press forward. With each step toward their goal, she gave a tiny yelp of pain and drew up her knees, then squeezed her eyes shut and clamped her teeth about her lips.

This wasn't going to work. Her ankle was too exposed. Even standing still, it was abused by the push and pull around them.

"I'm going to set you down for a minute," he said, lowering her legs.

She nodded.

He supposed he could sling her over his shoulder, but that would be not only indecorous, it would still leave her ankle unprotected.

Scanning the area, he caught the eyes of two massive fellows with hair so blond they looked as if they had no brows or lashes.

Cullen jerked his head in a come-here motion. "This lady is hurt," he shouted. "I need your help."

The larger of the two blond giants frowned. "*Snakker du norsk?*"

Cullen blinked, unsure if his hearing was acting up or if the man had spoken in a Scandinavian tongue. "Help. This lady needs help."

The Vikings forged their way to him.

Releasing one of his arms from around the woman, Cullen pointed to her, then pantomimed hoisting her up into the air.

The men grinned, clearly game for the challenge.

The woman's eyes widened, the first bit of color flooding back into her cheeks. "Wait—"

Cullen shook his head. "Just keep yourself as stiff as you can and put your arms across your chest."

"No, you can't just—"

Grasping her shoulders, he lifted her up. One Viking took her waist, the other her feet. She gave a quick cry and buckled her knees.

"Careful," Cullen shouted, pointing toward her ankles with his head. "She's hurt."

Nodding, the bigger blond swooped up her dragging hems and clamped his large hands around her calves. The woman squealed in shocked surprise.

The three of them raised her high above their heads and began to make their way toward the press benches. Cullen gave a savage yell, forging a path where before there had been none.

He glanced again at the stage, noting a pretty young woman with graceful gestures reciting a poem about Columbus seeking guidance in the sea and sky. If the distressed cries of the wounded distracted her, she gave no sign of it.

President Cleveland sat with quiet dignity, hands threaded across his belly, but his eyes were alight as they tracked the progress of Cullen and his Viking comrades. Cullen gave a helpless shrug and winked.

A hint of smile lines touched the president's cheeks, and he gave an almost infinitesimal nod of his head.

Finally, they made it to the press section. The men carefully lowered their cargo into Cullen's arms. She frantically clasped her hands about his neck for support while he thanked the two men.

The Vikings moved back through the press of bodies, heading toward another woman in peril.

Director-General Davis had replaced the young

poet, but the few who could hear his words weren't listening. All attention was on the cavalrymen who, Cullen was relieved to note, rode through the crowd, making way for the ambulances that followed. A detachment of Fifteenth Infantry cleared a space where the wounded could be taken.

The relentless pressure that had first caused the trouble eased, and the panic slowly subsided.

"You can put me down now, sir. There's room enough here for me to stand."

Cullen glanced down, having almost forgotten he held her. "What about your ankle?"

"I can stand on one foot."

"It's no hardship to hold you."

"You're very kind, but it's really not necessary."

An outburst erupted from the throng, a wave of enthusiasm sweeping over them. Grover Cleveland had risen and approached a flag-draped table. The only thing on its surface was a velvet case made in three decks. Secured to its top deck was a golden telegraph key. As soon as he touched the key, every engine and piece of machinery in the entire fair would be set in motion.

The woman tugged at Cullen's neck. Without taking his eyes from the president, he released her legs, bending carefully until her feet touched the ground.

"You okay?" He had to place his mouth against her ear to be heard above the roar.

Nodding, she released his neck and lifted one foot like a dainty flamingo.

He pulled her back against him. "Lean on me. If you get too tired, just say so and I'll pick you up again."

Removing his silk hat, Cleveland smoothed a hand over his head and waited for the applause to subside. Finally, he raised an arm. The unconscious murmurs of the multitude hushed. Every man, woman, and child stood still to hear the words of the president of the United States.

"I am here to join my fellow citizens in the congratulations which befit this occasion." Standing erect and calm, he gazed out on the scene, his voice loud and strong, his words succinct.

Whistles and whoops reverberated throughout the Court of Honor. Hundreds of squawking seagulls flew over, then dipped themselves in the lagoon.

"Let us hold fast to the meaning that underlies the ceremony, and let us not lose the impressiveness of this moment."

With the completion of every sentence, the crowd punctuated it with thunderous applause. Cullen's heart swelled with patriotism and pride.

"As by a touch the machinery that gives life to this vast exposition is now set in motion, so at the same instant let our hopes and aspirations awaken forces which in all time to come shall influence the welfare, the dignity, and the freedom of mankind."

Securing the woman with one arm, Cullen whistled and whipped off his hat, swinging it in the air, just like acres and acres of like-minded citizens. A hundred thousand handkerchiefs appeared, fluttering in the breeze like a sudden fall of snowflakes.

With an exaggerated flourish, Cleveland pushed down the golden telegraph key and set off a chain reaction.

Old Glory, whose silken folds had been bound, whipped open to catch the razor-sharp breeze. A massive cheesecloth veil fell from a ninety-foot gilded figure of the Republic posing in the waters of the Basin. A halo of electric lamps illuminated her crown. Her uplifted arms held a staff of Liberty and an eagle with wings spreading over the court.

On the roofs and towers of the surrounding palaces, seven hundred flags and streamers unfurled in an explosion of color. Whistles of steam launches in the interlocking lakelets and canals drowned out the boom of a cannon aboard a man-of-war in the lake beyond the peristyle.

A flock of snow-white doves was set free to circle over the waters, and the national salute of twenty-one guns paid tribute to the occasion. The lilt of chimes from Germany's building rode along the coattails of the breeze. Electric fountains shot streams of multicolored water high into the air, rising and falling, spinning and whirring, all in a lyrical dance of pink, yellow, sea green, and violet dewdrops.

Playing bass to this hallelujah chorus was the roar and hum of innumerable engines beginning to ripple throughout the grounds.

The crowd quieted, momentarily awed into stillness, before letting out a cheer that lasted minutes. Then, like a lightning bolt fracturing the sky, they broke apart and dashed in a thousand directions, hurrying to take in the wonders set before them.

The 1893 World's Columbian Exposition had officially begun.

COURT OF HONOR AND GRAND BASIN AS VIEWED FROM THE PERISTYLE

"The layout of the Court of Honor had become so deeply ingrained in Cullen's mind that even if he closed his eyes, he could see it."

1. Agricultural Building
2. Machinery Hall
3. Administration Building
4. Statue of the Republic
5. Electricity Building
6. Manufactures Building

CHAPTER 4

Packed as they were at the hub of the crowd, it was going to be a while before Della and the man supporting her could move from their spot. And with each passing moment, her embarrassment grew. Propriety had had no voice when she was hemmed in on all sides and fear overtook her. Though she'd blamed her distress on her ankle, it was the other that had led to her panic.

But now that she was beside the press benches, she had much more room to breathe. Since she was on one foot, her rescuer circled round to face her, still holding her elbow.

"How are you feeling?" he asked.

"Much better. Thank you."

Rarely did she have to look up to meet a man's gaze. But this gentleman was a good head taller than most, and frightfully broad about the shoulders.

"I don't believe we've properly met." His brown eyes took a quick survey of her. "I'm Cullen McNamara, of Charlotte, North Carolina. How do you do?"

She slid her eyes closed, then girded herself with bravado. He was simply a guest at the fair. It's not as if she would ever see him again. All she had to do was pretend she hadn't hurled herself into his arms and held on for dear life. Then, in a few moments' time, she'd be free of him.

"How do you do. I'm Adelaide Wentworth of Philadelphia."

Whipping off his hat, he released her arm and made a bow. No bald spot hiding under that hat. A head full of thick black hair.

"Pleased to meet you," he said.

"And I, you. Thank you very much for coming to my rescue. I'm certain my ribs would have cracked in two if I'd stayed there another minute."

"It was my pleasure."

Warmth rushed up Della's neck and into her face.

Biting his cheek, he held back a smile. "Perhaps a poor choice of words under the circumstances. I meant nothing by them."

"No offense taken." She scanned the crowd, trying to gauge how much longer she'd be stuck.

"Do you see the members of your party?" he asked. "If you describe them to me, perhaps I can spot them over the crush and call out to them."

She cast about for an answer. He might be her rescuer, but he was also a complete stranger. So she didn't care to tell him she'd become separated from her fellow coworkers during the madness. That would inevitably lead to more questions. And if he found she was an exhibitor, he'd most likely discover where she worked.

She could explain they'd all planned to meet other lodgers from their boardinghouse, but then he'd want to know which one and he'd discover where she stayed. No, the less he knew, the better.

"I'm afraid I was separated from my friends long before the crush began."

He cocked his head to the left. "I'm sorry? You were what?"

"Separated from my friends," she repeated.

"Did you have a rendezvous point, by any chance? Or a particular destination that was first on your party's list?"

To lie or not to lie? Her father had filled her with all manner of frightful tales about unescorted women whom men preyed on.

"The Holland Mill," she blurted.

"What's that?"

"A replica of an Amsterdam mill from the turn of the century, where Blooker's Dutch Cocoa Company serves hot chocolate."

"Excellent. Where is it?"

"Oh, over that way." She whirled her hand in a southeasterly direction.

He glanced toward the Agricultural Building. "Do you know exactly where? The fair is huge, over six hundred acres according to the guide-books. 'Over that way' could mean yards or it could mean miles."

"Farther than yards, shorter than miles."

He cocked a brow. "You have no idea where it is, do you?"

She stiffened. "I most certainly do. You walk between the Agricultural Building and Machinery Hall, then on past the Stock Pavilion to the South Pond. And they have excellent cocoa, I'll have you know. I've sampled it myself."

Humor filled his eyes. "The fair just opened, Miss Wentworth. When exactly have you had time to sample the cocoa?"

She realized her mistake at once. Only exhibitors had been allowed entrance up to now. "I had some this morning, before I came to listen to the opening ceremony."

He made no attempt to hide his smile. Deep laugh lines. Straight teeth. Sparkling brown eyes. The man was handsome in every sense of the word.

"I'm impressed," he said. "A trip to the cocoa shop and a place at the front of the crowd. I had to stand in my spot for over three hours to secure it."

"Oh, look." She pointed toward the Manufactures Building. "The crowd is starting to move."

He glanced over his shoulder. "So it is."

"Well, I thank you again for your help, Mr. McNamara. I'll leave you to find your group."

He hesitated. "What about you?"

Alarm bells began to sound in her head. "Oh, I'll be fine. Besides, won't your friends be looking for you? Your wife, perhaps?"

"I don't have a wife just yet."

"I see. Have you no friends, then?"

His smile returned. "Nary a one. And I don't know about Philadelphia, but in North Carolina we don't abandon our womenfolk. We make sure they get safely to where they're going." He held out his elbow. "Shall we test that foot of yours or would you prefer I carry you to Blooker's?"

The fact of the matter was, her foot hurt like the devil, and her other leg was becoming fatigued from supporting her entire weight. "I think what I'd really like to do is go to the Rolling Chair Company. I'm afraid I'm not going to get very far on this ankle."

He immediately took her arm. "Perhaps a visit to the ambulance corps would be better."

Allowing him to support some of her weight, she shook her head. "The women they're attending are no doubt in much worse shape than me. I don't want to bother them."

"I insist."

She hesitated. At the Rolling Chair Company she'd have a chair boy as guide and escort, so she'd have no need of Mr. McNamara. But with the ambulance corps, she'd be alone and he might very well decide to stay with her.

"No, really," she said. "The Rolling Chair Company would be best. My friends will be wondering about me otherwise."

"I'll go tell them what happened and where to find you."

"No!" She took a deep breath. "No, you've been inconvenienced way too much already."

"It's no trouble. Now, shall we go see what the doctor says?"

He took a step forward, then halted immediately when she took a hop.

"You can't put any weight on it at all?" He looked at the hem of her skirt but of course couldn't see her ankle.

She shook her head. "I've tried several times."

Without a by-your-leave, he bent over and swooped her up again.

"Mr. McNamara, I—"

"No arguments, Miss Wentworth. It's very possible you've broken that ankle. Now hold tight while we make our way to the ambulance corps."

She frantically looked around, praying her coworkers had left. She had no desire to explain to them or anyone else what she was doing in this man's arms—again. She needed to get rid of him as quickly as possible.

He maneuvered past a chair boy repairing a wheel on his now empty chariot and a couple studying a map of the grounds. When they reached the sectioned-off area for the wounded, he leaned over to place her in an empty invalid's chair.

"No, no." She stiff-armed the side of the chair.

"No need to put me in one of these. I'm not an invalid, I just have a bruised ankle."

He straightened, still holding her in his arms, his face very close. A whiff of his mint shaving soap touched her nose.

"That's what the chairs are for," he said. "People who, for whatever reason, can't stand on their own two feet."

"Just put me on the ground, Mr. McNamara. I'll be the judge of what I can and cannot do."

After a slight hesitation, he put her down. She grabbed the handle of the invalid's chair for support.

"I'm going in search of a nurse," he said. "If you get tired, sit down."

She watched him weave through women on stretchers and children on pallets before he flagged down a nurse. No sign of anyone she knew, thank goodness.

Moments later, he returned to her. "You may have to wait here a while. They're awfully busy. But that's probably just as well. It will give me time to get to Blooker's, tell your friends where to find you, then bring them back. Are you sure you don't want to sit down?"

"Quite."

He sighed. "Very well, then. What do your friends look like?"

Warmth filled her cheeks again. "Really, you needn't—"

"No arguing. They must be beside themselves with worry."

She swallowed, trying to decide if she should continue pretending or tell him the truth. Would a nefarious man offer to go collect her friends for her? But if she told him the truth, she sensed she'd never be free of him.

Men are wily creatures, her father had said. *Just because they look respectable doesn't mean they are. You must be on your guard every moment.*

"How many are in your party?" he asked.

Though there had been three of them, she decided to round up. "Four."

"You and three more women?"

As long as she was padding her story, perhaps she should add some men to the mix as well. "Um, men."

His brows shot up. "You're here with three men?"

She flushed. Maybe she'd overshot it a bit. "No . . . yes. I mean, two men, one woman."

His expression began to cloud. "Those men left you alone? In a crowd this size?"

Oh, crumbs. She hadn't thought of that. Sighing, she rubbed her head. What a tangled mess. "Our separation was my fault, I'm afraid. I was, um, late finishing my cocoa and I was supposed to catch up with them. But the truth is, I didn't count on all these people—none of us did. Anyway, I never did find them. That's why I made my way to the front. I was looking for them." She blinked, impressed with her ability to fabricate a somewhat coherent tale on such short notice.

Unfortunately, he grew more fierce. "That is no excuse whatsoever. They never should have left you. Period."

She opened her mouth, but had no answer that would suffice. And after all, why should she defend the fabricated men? Shame on them for behaving so poorly. "You're quite right, now that I think about it. What a very ungentlemanly thing to do. I shall talk to them about it forthwith."

"Not until after I give them a word or two of my own." He jammed his hat on his head. "Now don't move. I'll be right back with your *gentlemen* and lady friends."

He strode off, then turned around and came back. "What do they look like?"

Her heart began to soften. He couldn't possibly be a man of poor ilk.

And acts of kindness, girl. You've always been susceptible where that's concerned. I don't care if the fellow's offering to swim the Atlantic for you. Do not trust him.

Her father was an alarmist. She knew he was an alarmist. Still, he was fifty-one. She was twenty. He was a man and therefore very acquainted with the gender. She, however, was a woman. An inexperienced woman. So if in doubt . . .

"I'm sorry. What was the question?" she asked.

"What do they look like?" he repeated, his impatience with her "friends" lacing his words.

"Look like?" She glanced to the side, frantically trying to come up with something specific but vague. She certainly didn't want to describe her coworkers. "The men are in overcoats. The woman . . ." She thought of a delicious outfit she'd seen in the milliner's shop window at home. "She's wearing a big red hat with a giant, fabulous bow at the back. Lots of red feathers at the front. It matches some red velvet trim on her jacket and skirt. The skirt is made of a—"

"Their names?"

"Names?"

"Yes. I think I'll be able to spot the lady easily enough. But it would help if I knew their names."

"Um, Misters Biggs and Glenn, along with Miss Cate." All were cousins on her mother's side.

Spinning around, he stormed off. She almost felt sorry for her cousins. Except there were no cousins. No one at all to fit the descriptions she gave.

If he was a bad man, he was getting what he deserved. If he wasn't, if he truly was a Good Samaritan, he'd be giving up his precious time at the fair to run futile errands on her behalf. She tried to console herself with a reminder of all the exhibits he could see between here and Blooker's.

Except he wouldn't be stopping at any of them. And when he failed to find her "friends," she had no doubt he'd come right back here. When he did, she had no desire to confess all.

How exactly would she tell someone who'd saved her from being crushed, carried her to medical personnel, and gone to collect her friends that she thought he might have ill designs toward her person? She couldn't. Wouldn't.

Signaling the chair boy who'd finished his repairs and was heading back to his station, Della quickly engaged him to take her to the building where she worked, which was a good mile in the opposite direction of the cocoa shop.

MACHINERY HALL

"Taking a fortifying breath, Cullen plunged into the cavernous building with walls higher than the Temple of Zeus."

CHAPTER 5

Cullen jogged across the Court of Honor, splattering mud with each step. The sounds of engines coming from Machinery Hall reached him clear over here. He only hoped that during the goose chase he'd just given up on, he hadn't missed the crush of people who'd undoubtedly slipped into the Hall while waiting for the court to thin out.

He'd never found Miss Wentworth's friends, and by the time he returned to the ambulance corps, they'd moved everyone to an infirmary. After he'd located it between the Horticultural and Children's Buildings, he discovered his patient was long gone, and the nurse was too harried to recollect her.

He hoped Miss Wentworth's party had caught up with her or she'd retired to her hotel. Either way, it was going on three o'clock and he'd yet to make an appearance at his booth.

He might not have a chance of selling any fire sprinkler systems, but he at least had to try. He'd promised himself he wouldn't return home with empty pockets. He needed to make back every penny his father had spent on this venture, no matter how daunting that task appeared.

Rushing up the wide marble-like steps, he ignored the six large statues frowning at him from atop Machinery Hall's entrance, the names of prominent inventors carved into their shields. He wasn't worthy of being in this structure, which was built in their honor, and even the sculptures knew it.

Dragging the soles of his boots against the boot scraper, he dislodged as much of the mud as he could, then opened the massive wooden door.

A deafening sound knocked him back a step. He couldn't believe the engines for lighting the fair, powering its exhibits, and running hydraulics were really so loud. Or maybe the noise came from the countless booths inside presenting machines for everything known to man. Whatever it was, the cacophony was almost beyond human tolerance. Still, it was where he'd spend ninety percent of his time over the next six months, so he'd best get used to it.

Taking a fortifying breath, he plunged into the cavernous building with walls higher than the Temple of Zeus. His booth was tucked in a far corner, clear at the other end of the seventeen-acre building.

He'd read that two of White Star's cruise ships could fit lengthwise into the building. But to him, it looked as if three train houses had been plopped down side by side. There were no interior walls, only pillars, giving an open, airy feeling to the place.

The Hall wasn't as crowded as he'd hoped it

would be. He trusted the noise wouldn't keep people away indefinitely. He passed a huge block of booths with agricultural implements, locomotives, saws of all sizes, and woodworking machines, then slowed as he approached the match factory. Its machines cut hundreds of matches at a time, then dipped them into an igniting substance before dropping them into boxes, which were cut, folded, and labeled right before his eyes.

Tucked along the back wall, printing presses were hard at work, their clanks, whirs, and bangs making vibrations beneath his boots. It was all he could do not to cover his ears while he walked by. It looked as if he'd have to get used to it, though, for they were only a few booths down from his.

During setup, only the automatic platen press had been running. Of all the automatic devices man had invented, it was one of his favorites. The eighth wonder of the world, as far as he was concerned.

Spotting it, he slowed. A fella about his dad's age shut it off and said a few choice words to it.

"Trouble?" Cullen shouted.

The man wiped his hands on his ink-stained apron. "This blasted thing is jammed again. It's *nthng* but a—"

"What's it doing?" Cullen stepped up next to him, taking a closer look.

64

"The blower isn't *wrking*, so the suction arm can't pick up the paper."

Cullen had seen the letterpress running several times over the past week. A blower fluffed up a stack of paper, causing the top sheet to rise. Then an arm with suction-cup clippers applied a vacuum to the sheet and carried it to the press.

Studying the device more closely, he made a slow walk around it. "Looks to me like you might have two problems."

"Two *prblms*? That's all I need."

Cullen gave him a sympathetic smile. "You have any extra tubes?"

The man shrugged. "Sure. *Smwhr* around here."

"Well, this one has a crack in the rubber." He pointed to the tube. "That's part of the problem. The other, if I'm not mistaken, is you have a relief valve open." He tapped the valve. "I think that's supposed to be closed."

The man scratched his jaw. "I believe you might be right."

"Well, try those two things. If it doesn't fix the problem, call me over and I'll see if I can find anything else."

The man stuck out his hand. "Abel Tisdale."

"Cullen McNamara. I have an automatic fire sprinkler right over there." He indicated it with his thumb.

"Automatic?" Tisdale made a face. "The bane of my *exstnc*."

65

Cullen laughed. "I'm afraid that's where everything's headed these days."

"*Unfrtntly*, I think you're right. I appreciate it, son. I'll do what you *sggstd* and if I run into any more snags, I just might take you up on your offer."

"It'd be my pleasure." His mood lifted briefly, until he entered his tiny booth and reality intruded once more. He was wedged between a shiny red fire wagon on his right and an elaborate fire escape cage on his left. The cage moved up and down a ladder while its operator wound a crank. There wasn't a single visitor at this end of the building.

"Has it been this empty all day?" he shouted to the operator.

The fellow took a cotton ball out of one ear, but left its mate in the other. He looked to be a few years younger than Cullen, but he couldn't tell for certain. Bright red curls covered his head and freckles most of his face.

"What's that you said?" he asked.

Cullen held out his hand. "I'm Cullen McNamara of Charlotte, North Carolina."

The man's eyes lit. "Me, too!"

"You're Cullen McNamara?" Cullen asked.

He laughed. "John Ransom. Our farm's a few *mls* north of Garibaldi Station, just across the county line from you."

"Is that right?" Their handshake held. It was

good to meet someone from home. "Our farm's due west of Charlotte. Close enough to get to town when we need to, far enough to get some peace and quiet when we want it."

"I could sure use some *peez* and quiet right about *nw*." John was on the short side, but what he lacked in height, he made up for in brawn.

"Have they talked about rotating the running of machines to help cut down on the noise?" Cullen asked.

John shook his head. "That wouldn't be practical. Ya can't ask an interested customer to come back *tmrrow* because today's not your day for demonstratin'."

"Well, we've got to do something."

"The girls at the Crowne Pen Company said we should all go to the Woman's *Bldng* and take lip-readin' lessons in that school for the deaf they have."

They glanced a few booths up at Crowne Pen Company's exhibit, where the entire process of gold-pen manufacturing could be seen. Attractive salesladies stood behind plate-glass cases filled with souvenir fountain pens. Three of them smiled and waggled their fingers.

Saluting them, John leaned toward Cullen. "I told 'em I just might pretend deafness if it meant I could spend all day in the Woman's *Bldng*."

Chuckling, Cullen clapped him on the shoulder. "So what brings you to the fair, John Ransom?"

"I work at a firehouse here in *Chcgo* and was chosen to serve on the fair's fire brigade. Durin' my off-hours I display hoses, nozzles, and couplings and give *flks* a ride in the escape cage over there."

"I thought you farmed in Gaston County."

"Gave it up." The red curls on his head shook with each word. "I hate farmin'. It was supposed to be in my blood, but I loathe everything about it. The plowin', the *anmls*, the uncertainty of the crops. All of it."

Cullen slipped a hand into his pocket, his fingers brushing across a watch inside. It had been a wedding present from Cullen's mother, and his father had given it to him before he left.

Pulling it out, he clicked it open and closed. Open and closed. "So you just quit? And moved clear up to Chicago?"

"Yep. 'Bout broke my daddy's heart."

Open, closed. Open, closed. "Why Chicago? Why a fireman?"

He grinned. "Chicago was where I ran outta money and got *hngry*. And who wouldn't wanna be a fireman? There's nothin' like conquering a fire or savin' folks' lives. It's a lot more exciting than pushin' a plow, I can tell you that. What about you? The boys and I have been lookin' at your *sprinkr* all mornin'."

Cullen glanced at his booth. It consisted of two free-standing walls joined at the corner and covered with a latticed ceiling. A huge hole had been cut into each wall, revealing pipes and nozzles. Spigots popped through the ceiling. Labels with long descriptions had been glued to various parts.

"It's nothing, really. Just a device my dad wanted me to display for him."

"You invented it, though, right?"

Cullen nodded.

"I'm impressed, and kind of surprised. It seems like a mighty funny thing for a *farmr* to do."

He shrugged. "I've always been handy with anything mechanical. For years, folks would bring me everything from broken watches to disabled farm equipment. With the money I earned, I bought a few tools, read a few books, tinkered in the barn, and, well, that's the result." He waved a dismissive hand at his exhibit.

John whistled. "Well, show me how it *wrks*."

Cullen walked him to the booth. He'd barely begun when a couple more men from the booths to his right sauntered over.

John greeted the one closer to him with a slap on the shoulder. "Cullen, this is Frank Garvey of Company Seven, and that there is Ed Bulenberg with *Gnrl* Fire Prevention of Chicago. Boys, this is Cullen McNamara. He made this *sprnklr* here."

Bulenberg scoffed, his brown hair thin, his expression petulant. "I've seen one of these

69

automatic systems before. They're completely unreliable."

"Where'd you see one?" Cullen asked.

"In a theater. The thing caught fire and the sprinkler pipes never opened up. A total waste of money."

Cullen nodded. "They probably oxidized. That's why I made this one so the fusible joint has no contact with the water until the solder joint severs."

"Your *sprnklr's* automatic?" John asked. "It can turn on by itself?"

"It can." He showed them how it worked.

Bulenberg didn't outright contradict him, but it was clear the man had a distrust of automatic sprinklers in general and Cullen in particular.

"I don't know why *vrybdy* thinks they have to come up with a machine to replace jobs only a man can do." Bulenberg leaned over and spit. "There's only one way to use a *sprnklr* system. Have somebody turn it on, then wait for the fire brigade to arrive."

"Nothing will replace the fire brigade." Cullen looked over the system. "But if the fire is at night or the worker's away from the sprinkler's lever, this one's designed to keep the fire under control until the trucks arrive. Still, those manual ones have worked for years. I'm here only because my father asked me to come."

A couple of businessmen approached to see

John's escape cage. John stuffed the cotton back in his ear and returned to his equipment, as did Frank and Bulenberg.

For the next five hours, only a dozen people wandered by, three of whom allowed Cullen to explain his system. None were all that interested, though. Once the supper hour had come and gone, not a single person ventured to the back corner of Machinery Hall, interested or not.

Finally, closing time arrived, and one by one, the vast machines were silenced. Picking up his hat, Cullen headed toward the front.

"Wait up, McNamara."

Cullen turned, allowing John to fall into step beside him.

Yawning, John placed his hands on his head and twisted from side to side. "That was a *lng* day."

"It sure was."

"You have any nibbles?"

"Nary a one," Cullen said. "What about you?"

John shrugged. "We're not really trying to make sales. We're just here to show the progress America's made in firefighting."

"That must take a lot of pressure off."

"It does." John screwed up his face. "You know what I *thnk* you need?"

"What's that?"

"You need to do a demonstration. You know, build yourself something small—like a shed.

Then install your *sprnklrs*, set the shed on fire, and let your system put it out. I bet that would sell you some."

"You're probably right," Cullen replied. "But I can't imagine the commission granting permission for something like that. Especially with these white palaces as flammable as they are. One stray spark could wipe out half the park."

"I don't know about that. You ought to *lk* into it. The least you could get is a no."

"I suppose."

John elbowed him and lowered his voice. "Look there. It's those gals from the Crowne Pen *Cmpny*."

Cullen scanned the aisle, then saw the women admiring some scarves the textile machines had woven throughout the day.

"If I didn't know better," John said, "I'd *thnk* they were waitin' on us. Or you, anyway. They've been eyeing you all night."

"I doubt that," he said.

"Oh, yeah? Well, maybe you better take another look, my friend."

Sure enough, one of the blondes spotted him from the corner of her eye, then quickly whispered something to her friends.

"You *wnt* to see if they'd like to go into town?" John asked.

Smiling, Cullen shook his head. "I'm too tired, I'm afraid."

"Ah, come on. You ate only a boxed supper. You've gotta be *hngry*."

"All the same."

John gave him a suspicious look. "Don't tell me you got a *grl* back home or somethin'?"

"Afraid so."

"Well, I'm *srry* to hear that." He perked up. "Or maybe I'm not. All the more for me to choose from." Tipping his hat, he headed toward the women. "See ya, *McNmra*."

"Goodnight, John."

Rather than passing by the girls, Cullen cut across an exhibit and over to the next aisle. No sense in borrowing trouble.

OBELISK OUTSIDE MACHINERY HALL

"Vaughn guided him toward the South Canal,
where a replica of Central Park's obelisk sat."

CHAPTER 6

One week turned into two. Then two into three, and Cullen was no closer to selling a sprinkler system now than he had been when he burned down the cowshed back home. His serious visitors either already used non-automatic sprinklers and couldn't justify the expense of updating or were distrustful of an unproven system such as his. There had been one man, though, an owner of a cotton-waste warehouse, who'd been intrigued and had come back twice. But he mumbled, and Cullen simply couldn't hear him. He'd had to ask the man to repeat himself two or three times after each sentence. In the end, the man had thrown up his hands in frustration and gone to Bulenberg's booth instead.

Ever since, Bulenberg made a habit of standing in the wings, then deftly swept Cullen's customers to his manual sprinkler exhibit as soon as they left Cullen's booth.

Gazing into the distance, Cullen now stood beside his exhibit tired, frustrated, and worried. The noise hadn't let up, and his ears rang so badly, he decided he'd rather put up with cotton seed. At least when he farmed, he was accomplishing something.

He'd written Wanda every night, but he couldn't say much since she couldn't read, which meant someone who could would have to read the letters to her. Turned out that someone was none other than Thomas Hodge. Farmer-boy extraordinaire and Wanda's closest neighbor.

Hodge took great delight in penning her return letters. He inserted his own editorial comments and not-so-subtle barbs, even going so far as to write that the only thing Cullen was worse at than inventing worthless contraptions was romancing a woman.

No wonder it took you so long to set a wedding date, he'd written. *Poor Wanda actually yawned through your last letter.*

Wanda? Who did he think he was, calling her by her Christian name? Did he call her that to Wanda's face? And just what did Hodge expect? That he'd spill his heart, only to have Hodge read those words out loud to Wanda? Not likely.

So his letters remained dry and stilted, and Wanda's had become increasingly so. Was she embarrassed by his lack of flowery words? She'd never expected them before.

He tried not to think about it. There was no point in trying to figure out a woman. They were illogical, inconsistent, confounded creatures, and Cullen didn't know why God thought He'd been doing Adam a favor.

Yet Wanda's latest letter had given him something totally unexpected to worry about. Hodge had not-so-casually revealed he'd been in the mercantile when Luther refused to sell to Cullen's dad on credit. Hodge offered a hollow expression of condolence, then made a point of saying he'd told Wanda he never had that problem.

But none of it made any sense. Cullen didn't even know his father had been buying supplies on credit. And even if he had been, how could Dad's credit be used up when he had money stashed away? Cullen fired off a letter home asking about it, but it would be a while before he heard back.

The one bright spot these days was the camaraderie that had developed between John and him. Nothing could get that fellow down. No matter how bad the news on the stock exchange, no matter how slow it was in the Hall, he'd always come up smiling and take a front seat next to the bandwagon. In the evenings, when the Hall was dead and a number of machines had been turned off, he'd regale Cullen with tales of the adventures he'd had once he left farming. Cullen wondered if he'd ever been that carefree.

Maybe. A long time ago. When Mama was alive and sat by the hearth telling him and Dad stories of the days before the War. Or when she'd read *Robinson Crusoe* and *The Three Musketeers* to them and answered his endless questions with patience and a smile.

Cullen shook his head. He'd never lacked for questions back then. Did snakes have eyelids? Did the sun have a shadow? How old was the universe? Who thought up math? What are the sun's rays made of?

He sure did miss those days.

A middle-aged man with a cane walked straight toward him, making direct eye contact. Uncrossing his arms, Cullen slowly straightened.

"How do you do?" The man held out a hand. "I'm Lawrence Vaughn, owner of Vaughn Mutual Insurance *Cmpny*."

"Cullen McNamara, of Charlotte, North Carolina."

Leaning on his cane, Vaughn rested his other arm against a portly belly and studied Cullen's system through tiny round spectacles without earpieces. His cropped white hair made a ring beneath an expensive derby hat. Cullen would bet there wasn't much hair, if any, were Vaughn to remove that hat.

Having become more succinct with his presentation, Cullen covered the basics within two minutes.

But then one of the larger printing presses started up and began spitting out newspapers. The noise level increased tenfold.

"Did you *vntin ddds*?" Vaughn asked.

"I'm sorry?" Cullen said.

"Did you *vntin ddds systm*, I said?" Vaughn's shouts were barely audible.

Cullen nodded, hoping he'd asked if Cullen was the inventor.

"As *mngr* and owner of Vaughn *Mtl*, I'm *alwys tryg* to *ncurag* business owners to *adpt* the most up-to-date *apprts* for *extngshing* fires. Our *cmpny* has long *prtstd* against high rates of insurance *chrgd* by the fire offices—*spclly* for *mll* owners."

Something about insurance rates and up-to-date fire equipment, maybe.

"Do you have any insurance *cmpnies offng rdcd prmms* to *bsnss* owners who install your *atomtc sprnklr* system?"

Something about installation. Since no one had installed his system, he figured the answer was no. "Not yet, sir," he shouted.

Vaughn tucked a thumb into a pocket on his vest. "Well, I'll *tll uwht eyd* do."

"I'm sorry?"

Vaughn smiled. "It's *ld* as the *dckns* in *hr*, isn't it?"

Cullen nodded, having no idea what he'd just confirmed.

Vaughn pointed to the door closest to them. "*Lts* go *otsd*."

Cullen followed Vaughn to the side door. The noise level dropped dramatically the moment they stepped out, but Cullen's ears continued to ring.

"It's *abbuva* in there," Vaughn said. "I don't know how they expect us to conduct business, do you?"

"No, sir." He stuck a finger in his right ear, trying to open it up, but of course it did no good. "My ears are ringing fit to be tied. I'm still having trouble hearing you, even out here."

"Well you'd better figure *smthng* out, son." Vaughn drew down his eyebrows—the only bit of brown hair he had left. "One of my board *mmbrs* saw your display last week and asked me to speak to you. We're looking to pick up more policyholders. And you're looking to sell sprinklers. What if the two of us did a bit of back-scratching?"

"In what way?"

"The board is toying with the idea of offering reduced fire insurance premiums to anyone who buys your *sprnklr*."

"What kind of discounts did you have in mind?"

"We haven't decided. But if you sell a lot and they do well, we'll encourage our current policy-holders to purchase the system too."

Like a fisherman who felt a gentle tug on his line, a rush of energy with a good dose of skepticism put him on alert. "That'd be wonderful, sir."

"How *mny* have you sold so far?"

Keeping his face free of expression, Cullen held his line steady, recognizing a precarious hold when he had one. "None so far."

Vaughn tapped his cane. "You need to get *bsnss*

80

owners and mill owners interested. That noise in there is a problem, though."

Cullen gave the man a wry smile. "The fellow in the booth next to mine said us exhibitors ought to go over to the Woman's Building and have those teachers of the deaf show us how to lip-read."

Instead of laughing, as Cullen had expected, Vaughn straightened, eyes widening. "That's not a bad idea. You know, McNamara, you ought to do just that."

"Oh no, sir. I was merely joking. I couldn't possibly—"

"I'm serious." Grasping Cullen's arm, Vaughn guided him toward the South Canal, where a replica of Central Park's obelisk sat. "Don't you see? You'd have a leg up on everyone else. While they can hear only every fourth or *ffth* word, you'd be able to 'hear' them all."

"Well, maybe, but what about the men I'm speaking with? How are they going to hear me?"

"They won't need to. Between the *dsply* you have that shows a behind-the-wall look at your system and the in-depth signs explaining the functions of each piece, well, all you'd have to do is point and demonstrate."

The two of them stopped in front of the obelisk, its Egyptian hieroglyphics faithfully duplicating Cleopatra's Needle in New York. If Cullen had been able to lip-read, he'd have been able to answer the cotton man's questions and would most likely have made a sale. Still, lip-reading lessons would cost money. Money he didn't have.

Slipping a finger behind his collar, he loosened it a bit. "Sir, I just don't see how I could do as you suggest. How would I have the time? I can't be sitting in a classroom with deaf children and simultaneously be here selling my sprinkler."

Vaughn placed both hands on his cane. "No, I don't suppose you could. And you'd look *rduloos* sitting in there with all those children."

The gentle lapping of the canal blended with the murmur of those around them. A rolling chair guided by a uniformed man in blue whizzed past them, zigzagging in and out of the crowd.

"What about after supper?" Vaughn asked.

"What about it?"

"The teacher could tutor you in the evenings."

Cullen shook his head. "I'd have to leave my post."

"No one's going to come looking for business deals after supper. Evenings in the park will be filled with sightseers and *yung* lovers. It would be the perfect time."

Suppressing the urge to argue, he decided instead to confess his main concern. "I'm afraid I wouldn't be able to pay her what she's worth."

"Oh, I'm sure you'll think of something—an innovative man like you." Vaughn waved his hand in a dismissive gesture. "No one said the road to *sccss* was easy."

A tiny bead of sweat sprang out along Cullen's hairline. He wasn't innovative. He was a farmer. A farmer from North Carolina who had no business being here. But he couldn't say that to Vaughn, not when his offer would sweeten the pot for potential customers.

Vaughn lifted a brow. "I'd say my proposition is *wrth* it, wouldn't you?"

Cullen found himself nodding. Earning his dad's money back was worth it. Worth whatever was required of him.

"*Excllnt*." Vaughn popped open his pocket watch. "You'd best head over there now. The school day's almost complete, and you'll want to catch one of the teachers before they all leave."

Ignoring the tightness in his chest, he shook the man's hand. "I'll get right on it, sir."

KITCHEN GARDEN IN THE CHILDREN'S BUILDING

" 'This is our Kitchen Garden,' the woman said.
'It is devoted to teaching little girls how
to become good housewives.' "

CHAPTER 7

It had been another day for goose chasing. The deaf school wasn't in the Woman's Building but in the Children's Building. And of all the attractions at the fair, Cullen couldn't think of any other he'd rather skip more than the Children's Building. What possible interest would he have in looking in on a bunch of kiddies whose parents had checked them at the door?

Joining a small group of visitors, he followed a middle-aged tour guide in severe black who droned on about pink medallions decorating the wall and a life-size mural of *Silver Hair and the Three Bears*. The guide was exactly the kind of woman who'd placed him in the corner of a schoolroom for hours at a time before his mother had taken over his schooling.

He sighed, wondering if stiff expressions and a steady monotone were prerequisites for all teachers. He certainly didn't fancy having to spend hours of his free time with one. At least he wouldn't have to put up with any mocking, whipping, or corner sitting.

The guide led them to a room in the southwest corner of the building. "This is our Kitchen Garden. It is devoted to teaching little girls how to bcm good housewives."

With a name like "Kitchen Garden," he'd

expected plants, pots, and topsoil. Instead, forty or so girls in spotless pinafores occupied themselves with house chores. Some swept the room with miniature brooms. Others crawled on hands and knees, scrubbing the floor. Several bent over tiny washtubs in an effort to make dirty little dolls look white as snow.

"Now make sure the hems are turned the *crrct* way." A woman wearing a frilly apron and cap walked down a line of pint-sized mussed-up beds.

Little girls turned the mattresses and punched them into a degree of softness, then spread pristine sheets and bright blankets on top. The tucking-in process showed they'd been well taught. Not a one made a hasty boardinghouse tuck but instead produced corners exactly like Alice's.

His guided group continued on, passing through a noisy kindergarten class for young children, a playroom for school-age children, and a wood-carving class for the older ones. In the library, the guide boasted that nearly every volume had been autographed. Stockton, Kipling, Longfellow, Alcott. He noted, however, that *Billy Butts the Boy Detective* had been left out of the collection.

Finally, they arrived at the deaf school. The guide stopped outside the door, pinched her lips, and waited for stragglers to catch up.

When all had gathered, she folded her hands.

"Behind these doors is a *dmnstrtn* of the Pennsylvania Home for the Training in Speech of Deaf Children Before They Are of School Age."

Cullen blinked. Was that the name of their school? What idiocy. Some woman obviously thought that up.

"The entire school of twenty pupils picked up and moved from Philadelphia to *Chcago* for the duration of the fair so that people could see firsthand the important work being done. The emphasis of their program is to teach the deaf to speak and lip-read through observing and imitating the process of vocalization. It is the school's *ffmm* belief that if these children are treated the same as hearing *chldrn* and they are surrounded with hearing and speaking *only*—no sign language—then when they are grown, they will function in society as equals and no one will ever know they are deaf."

Cullen stilled. Was that true? Could a person learn to lip-read so proficiently that he could lose his hearing and no one would be the wiser?

Looking at the doors leading to the classroom, he reminded himself that even if the woman inside was the worst kind of tyrant, he needed to stick it out anyway. For the sake of earning that money back, if nothing else.

"You are lucky," the guide said, "for the teacher you are about to see is the very best. She *ggdduuaadd* first in her class from Alexander Graham Bell's School of Oratory and received a personal recommendation from him."

He nodded. That was who he wanted then. The best.

The guide pushed open the doors and indicated they should enter with a swoop of her arm. Inside, a group of very young tots sat in chairs arranged in a semicircle, their feet dangling high above the floor. The teacher, her back to the visitors, squatted in front of a youngster with blond ringlets springing from her head like clockworks gone amok.

The teacher took the little girl's hand and placed it against her cheek, nose, and throat. "*Nnnnnn.*"

The tot furrowed her brows in concentration. "*Wwwwwww.*"

The teacher shook her head. "*Nnnnnnn.*"

"*Ddddaaaa.*"

Leaving the tot's hand where it was, the woman placed a finger behind the child's front teeth, gently tapping them. "*Nnnnnnn.*"

"*AwNnnnnnn.*"

"Yes!" She placed a soft kiss on the girl's head and received a beaming response.

From the back, the teacher didn't look like a high-strung old maid. Her light brown hair was silky and in a soft twist. Her neck, long and slender. Her waist, small and delicate.

She stood. Up, up, up she went.

His mouth slackened. It couldn't be.

She turned. And the impact hit him full force. He'd only seen her in a coat. But now there was nothing obstructing his view.

Her green skirt and white shirtwaist showed off a slender figure with curves in all the places they should be. For the first time, he noticed her delicate facial features. Blue eyes. And bright smile.

Until she saw him. The smile froze.

He said nothing. Did nothing to betray his surprise.

She was not so guarded. Shock, bewilderment, then horror played across her face.

The guide cocked her head. "Miss Wentworth? Did we startle you?"

Shaking herself, she turned her attention to the guide. "Yes. I mean, I guess so. I was very focused." She plastered on another smile, but it wasn't the natural one of before. "Welcome. We were, um, just about to finish up."

"Well, carry on," the guide said. "Pretend we're not here."

Miss Wentworth's gaze collided with his, then she turned quickly about. "Can you welcome our guests, children?"

She spoke the words as if she were teaching a normal group of children. He'd expected her to speak more slowly and methodically.

"Good day," they chorused, though the enunciation was slurred and nasal.

"Lovely," she said. "Now let us finish our lifters."

Walking to her chair, she smoothed her gown beneath her as she sat. "Remember, *lift* the tongue to the top of your mouth." She demonstrated.

The children mimicked her and he felt his tongue touch the back of his teeth.

She picked up a napkin off a table next to her. "All together now . . . Napkin."

"*Nobin.*"

She held up a nickel. "Nickel."

"*Ninkl.*"

She went through a dozen more items and praised them effusively even though their words were warped versions of the real ones. Finally, she led them in a prayer. The children didn't close their eyes, though. They clasped their hands and watched her lips. He bowed his head.

"Blessed be thy holy name, O God, and blessed be thy mercy forever. Amen."

The woman beside him touched a handkerchief to her eye.

"You may line up now, children." She held an open palm toward the door. "Mrs. Rosenburg will take you to the playground."

The students jumped from their chairs and scrambled to do their teacher's bidding. At the door, a young woman wearing a white apron and cap escorted them out.

"The playground on the roof is our next stop as well," the guide said. "This way, please."

His group left, but Cullen stayed behind in the sudden quiet.

Miss Wentworth clasped and unclasped her hands. "You're going to miss your tour."

"I went on it only so I could come to this room."

She blanched. "How did you find me?"

"Find you?" He frowned. "I didn't, though I spent a good bit of that afternoon looking."

"But you did find me . . . because you're here."

He shook his head. "I was looking for the teacher of the deaf children. I had no idea you were she."

"Oh." She looked about the room, before finally returning her gaze to his. "Did you have a question for me?"

"Yes. Where did you disappear to that morning?"

She swallowed. "No, I meant did you have a question for the teacher of deaf children?"

"I did." Flipping back his jacket, he slid his hands into his pockets. "But first I have some questions for you. Did your friends ever find you?"

She picked a nonexistent speck from her skirt. "It's Mr. McNamara, correct?"

"Yes."

"Well, Mr. McNamara, I'm afraid I have a

91

confession. It's been on my mind ever since opening day, and I'll be glad to get it off my chest." She paused. "I, um, have no friends."

He blinked. "None at all? I find that hard to believe."

"No, no." Her eyes were the clear, clear blue of an ocean. An ocean with mysteries beneath its surface. "I have friends, of course. It's just, none of them are here. At the fair. Only the other teachers I work with."

He allowed that to sink in. "Then it was the other teachers who were at the cocoa shop, not two men and a lady in a large red hat?"

She swallowed. "No. No one was at the cocoa shop. I made that up."

His lips parted. "Why?"

She wouldn't meet his gaze. "I don't know. I guess because we'd just met and I didn't really know you and I'd been separated from my coworkers and my father is just sure I'm going to get myself into trouble because I think everyone is like me."

He struggled to keep up. "And what are you like?"

She shrugged. "Simple."

He doubted that. No female was simple. "So anyone who isn't simple needs to be avoided?"

Sighing, she touched her fingers to her head. "No, I meant, you know, *simple*. At face value. They are who they appear to be."

He was still confused. "Did I do something to offend you?"

"No, no. Not at all. You were very gallant. I don't know what I'd have done if you hadn't come to my assistance. That's why I've been feeling so bad, the way I lied to you and all."

Good. And well she should. He couldn't believe the time he'd wasted on her behalf. "Where did you go?"

"Here. I came here straightaway."

He looked at her hem. "How's your ankle?"

"Oh, fine. Perfectly fine. It was sore for a few days, but I wrapped it. It's all better now." She took a deep breath. "I'm sorry. Very sorry."

He scrutinized her. If teachers in his day had looked like her, he wondered if he'd have been so quick to let Mama take over his schooling. "Do you whip the children at the front of the classroom when they're bad?"

She gasped. "What? *My* children? Certainly not. Whatever gave you that idea?"

Yep. He'd have definitely been more hesitant to leave. "How do you keep them in line, then?"

"I don't know. They don't act up all that often."

"And when they do?"

She shrugged. "I suppose I might have them sit by themselves for a few minutes. Take away a privilege of some sort. Was that the question you came here to ask? How we discipline the children?"

"No. I wanted to ask if you'd teach me to lip-read."

"You?" She took a step back. "I couldn't possibly. You'd disrupt the entire class. Not to mention you'd look ridiculous. What would our visitors think if they came in and you were sitting among the children?"

"I didn't mean here. I meant privately. I'm looking for private lessons."

"Out of the question."

"Why?"

"Because . . . I have no time. My school day is completely full."

"What about the evenings?" he asked. "You could teach me then. You just said you didn't have any friends."

"No. I'm sorry, but the answer is no." Spinning around, she began to move a chair from the semicircle to the wall.

He moved the ones at the opposite end until they met in the middle.

"Is it because you have to stay with the children until bedtime?" he asked.

"No, there are night nurses who take the children once the school day is over."

"Then your nights are free."

She picked at her nails. "I really—"

"Please," he said. "I'm a quick study."

"Why do you need to lip-read?"

"I have an exhibit in Machinery Hall. The noise

94

is excruciating. I can't hear a word anyone is saying. If I don't do something, then all the time and expense I went to in order to get here will be wasted."

Her eyes widened. "You're an exhibitor?"

"I am."

"Of what?"

He hesitated. "An automatic fire sprinkler."

"What's that?"

"Nothing of importance."

"Obviously it is or you wouldn't be exhibiting it at the fair."

He glanced about the room. The walls were adorned with paintings depicting various ways to entertain deaf children. Little girls with cherubic faces played house and dolls. Rambunctious boys explored the outdoors and sailed toy boats.

"Mr. McNamara?" she asked.

He pulled his attention back to her.

"What exactly is an automatic fire sprinkler?"

"It's a series of pipes installed in ceilings. They have spigots that automatically open up and spray water when a fire starts."

"How do they know to do that automatically?" Her tone held genuine curiosity. Curiosity he didn't intend to satisfy.

"It's rather complicated," he said.

She lifted a brow.

"Feel free to come by Machinery Hall and see

for yourself, if you'd like. I'm in the very back, left-hand corner."

"Perhaps I will. It sounds marvelously inventive, and think of all the lives and property it would save if every building had one. You must be doing very well here. Congratulations."

He decided not to bore her with the details and instead pointed to a circle of five chairs in the back. "Where would you like those?"

"By the window, please."

He placed them against the wall. "Will you help me?"

"I'm afraid I can't."

"Why? Are you still distrustful of me?"

"No, it's not that."

"Then, what?"

"It takes a long time to learn to lip-read." Smoothing a tendril up the back of her neck with quick efficiency, she tucked it into her hair pouf. "Years, in fact. It's not something I can teach you in a few lessons. And I really don't have the time."

Years? Surely she exaggerated.

"Your evenings are full, then?" he asked.

"I plan to see the fair in the evenings. But it doesn't really matter anyway, because I wouldn't want to spend all my free time teaching someone who can hear perfectly well."

He rubbed his eyes. Only his family and Wanda knew about his hearing. The topic was entirely too inflammatory for knowledge of it to be bandied about. Entrusting his secret to a virtual stranger was not to be borne.

"I could be your guide," he said. "To the fair, I mean."

She gave him a small smile. "I truly am sorry."

Letting out a long breath, he looked at the tips of his boots. "The truth is, Miss Wentworth, I do have difficulty hearing."

Total silence. He peeked up at her.

She'd narrowed her lips into thin lines. "How *dare* you pretend about something like that."

He straightened. "I'm not. It's true."

"Really, Mr. McNamara. We have stood here and conversed for the last twenty minutes. At what point, exactly, were you unable to hear me?"

"That happens sometimes. For one thing, it's perfectly quiet in here. No background noises whatsoever. I also hear certain people better than others. Your voice is at a perfect pitch. I can hear every word. But the tour guide who showed me in here? There were several words I couldn't catch, and I had to guess what she was saying by context."

She started to the door. "The answer is no. Good day, sir."

Catching up to her, he encircled her arm. "Wait."

She wrenched it away.

He quickly stepped in front of her, blocking the door. He needed these lessons. He hadn't sold a single system. Vaughn's offer might be just the carrot he needed to close a deal. Furthermore, if what the tour guide said was true, this wouldn't just help him at the fair, it would help him the rest of his life. "I'm not the one who's been concocting falsehoods, Miss Wentworth. I believe you hold that honor."

Gasping, she took a step back.

He gave no quarter. "You are the first person outside of family whom I have ever shared my plight with. The noise in Machinery Hall is simply my excuse. I am losing my hearing, especially in my right ear. It started a little over a year ago and has worsened over time. I would never lie about something like that. Never."

Her gaze zigzagged as she looked into both his eyes. Surely she could see the truth there.

"Mr. McNamara, I really—"

"Don't say no." He took a step closer. "What if my hearing continues to deteriorate? What if I lose it altogether? Do you have any idea how frightening that prospect is? And if lip-reading really does work, if I can learn to do it so proficiently that I can get along no matter how . . . how deaf I become, then I still have a chance at living a normal life. Please, Miss Wentworth. Please."

With each sentence, her expression softened.

He scrambled for any other enticements he could offer. "You can still see the fair. There's no reason we can't do our lessons out and about, is there? It's not as if there are any written assignments. Am I right?"

"That's correct," she said, her voice dropping and making him strain for the first time. "There are no written assignments."

"Well, there you are, then. And when you think about it, it only makes sense that we do our lessons in the park. With me able to hear you so well, I will need others to practice on. What better place for that than the fair?"

Still, she hesitated. "It takes years to master."

"Then there isn't a moment to spare."

"I wouldn't even know what to charge you." She clasped her hands in front of her. "Besides, I highly value my time off."

He couldn't spend any more of his father's money. There was little enough left as it was. "I'm sorry to say, I don't have sufficient funds to pay you. Acting as your guide is the only compensation I can offer. Everything I have in the world has been sunk into the fair. If I don't succeed, I'll . . . well, I have to succeed. And in order to do that, I need those lessons."

Looking at everything but him, she shifted her weight from one foot to the other.

"You said you didn't have any friends here," he continued. "A woman on her own amid such a crush of people can be in a great deal of danger. You've already seen that for yourself."

Bowing her head, she pinched the tucks along the waistline of her skirt. "I'm not completely alone. I have my fellow teachers."

"Whom you could easily be separated from, just like on opening day. Your father was right. If you were my sister or loved one, I'd want you to have a proper escort. I could be that person for you. In fact, I could be that person for all of you. Invite the other teachers along. Then you could all take turns tutoring me. And perhaps, when the fair is over, if my exhibit is a success, I could compensate you then."

Her fingers flattened, smoothing down all the pleats at once. "I suppose I could ask them."

"Of course you could."

"Would we get to pick where we go?" she asked. "What buildings and exhibits we see?"

"Absolutely." He held his breath.

Her shoulders wilted, her eyes closed. "Very well. I will speak to them about it."

For the first time, a wave of hope washed through him. "Thank you. Can I call on you tomorrow, then?"

"Not here." The first sign of humor touched her face. "Since we both know where Blooker's Dutch Cocoa Company is, why don't we meet there? Say, about four o'clock? I'll give you an answer then."

He smiled. "Excellent. I'll see you tomorrow."

FORESTRY BUILDING

"Having lived in Philadelphia all her life, Della craved an opportunity to learn about forests and meadows in other parts of the country."

CHAPTER 8

When Della's school had been asked to hold classes at the fair, she assumed the entire faculty would stay together in the same boardinghouse. But Chicago was so booked, they'd had to split up. The three teachers had been assigned to Harvell House. Della had been given a tiny room on the women's floor, while Maxine and Hilda shared a larger one at the opposite end.

At least the brownstone row house was within walking distance of the fair. Miss Garrett, the director, had to travel seven miles to and from on the train.

Sitting in the front parlor, the three of them studied guidebooks and maps of the fairgrounds trying to select the building they wanted to tackle next. Della pushed aside a leaf dangling from the potted tree beside her, exasperated with all the paintings, busts, plants, whatnots, peacock feathers, vases, and prints crowding the room. The mauve and navy diamond-print carpet butted up against the silver and red floral wallpaper, making her eyes cross every time she looked at them.

"What about the Forestry Building?" she suggested. So far they'd made it through only the Palace of Art and the Fisheries Building. Having lived in Philadelphia all her life, she'd only seen the countryside as a child during short visits with her grandparents. She craved an opportunity to learn about forests and meadows in other parts of the country. The Forestry Building would be the perfect opportunity.

"They don't have a restaurant," Hilda said, her triple chin smashed against her neck as she studied a guidebook. Her thinning white hair provided glimpses of a pink scalp. "I say we go to the Mines Building."

Maxine wrinkled her nose, her black hair pulled loosely into a snood, her spectacles tipping sideways. "Not that one. Who wants to see a bunch of minerals, ores, and metals when there's so much else to see?"

"But it says the restaurant there is similar to the one Dr. Henderson Hayward operated at the Centennial Exposition in '76." Following the words with her index finger, Hilda read the endorsement aloud.

Maxine listened, her head tilted in contemplation. "That does sound tempting. Perhaps we could eat there but go elsewhere for touring. The Transportation Building is right across from it. What do you think, Della?"

She shrugged. "The Transportation Building sounds good. It's just I hate to keep spending money on food when we're provided with dinner here."

Hilda glanced up, her expression appalled. "But

the food is my favorite part. We'll never again have an opportunity to sample meals from world-renowned chefs or from faraway places we've never heard of."

"I guess I'd just rather spend my time and money elsewhere."

Maxine looked at her over the rim of her glasses. "Like where, Della? We're not allowed to wear anything fancy or extravagant to work, so you don't need clothes. Our room and board is provided for us in Philadelphia, so you don't need money for that. And if you end up getting married, your husband will take care of all your worldly needs. So why not spend a few coins on the World's Fair? Heaven knows we'll never attend another one."

But those meals didn't cost a few coins. They cost a lot of coins. Still, she remained silent as Maxine and Hilda planned out their week according to the restaurants they wanted to eat at first, then the exhibits that most interested them. Finally, they folded up the maps and stacked the guidebooks.

"You're awfully quiet this evening." Hilda grabbed the arm of the blue settee, shifting her girth into a more comfortable position. "Is something the matter?"

Della took a deep breath. "Actually, I had an unusual visitor today."

"Oh, dear." Maxine laid a reassuring hand on

Della's knee. "Did one of the tourists challenge you about what we're doing with the children?"

"No, nothing like that. This man is an exhibitor and stopped by the classroom at the end of the day. He would like us to teach him to lip-read— after hours, of course."

"Is he deaf?" Hilda asked.

"Not yet, though he says he's been systematically losing his hearing over the past year."

Maxine rolled her eyes. "What does he think? That he can learn the vowel and consonant families and instantly lip-read?"

"Something like that." She brushed a hand across her skirt. "I told him it takes years to master, but he still asked for the lessons."

"Poor man." Hilda's brows crinkled, her puffy cheeks sagging. "That must be very frightening. How old is he?"

Della lifted her shoulders. "I don't know—late twenties?"

"A young man, then."

"Yes."

"I assume you told him no." Maxine's eyes were magnified behind the lenses of her spectacles.

"I tried, but . . ."

"Oh, Della." Maxine's voice rose. "Don't tell me you said yes."

"No, I just didn't say no."

Hilda tapped her thumb on the armrest. "How much did he offer to pay us?"

Della swallowed. "All of his funds are tied up in his exhibit. He offered to be our guide in the evenings—a protector, of sorts—then pay us at the culmination of the fair once he's had a chance to make some sales."

"Of all the ridiculous things." Maxine scooped up her guidebook and stood. "I'm turning in, ladies. I'll see you in the morning."

"Good night," Della said.

"I'm right behind you." But Hilda didn't so much as budge.

Maxine's serviceable boots clicked softly on the entry-hall floor, then became quieter as she went up the wooden steps.

"You're thinking of doing this, aren't you?" Hilda had become a bit of a mother hen, offering an ear when Della needed advice and a shoulder when she needed solace.

She looked down at her hands. "I was considering it, yes. I'd hoped you would too."

Hilda gave a long sigh. "I'm sorry for the man's troubles, but he's not asking us just to give up our evenings. He's asking us to give up a chance of a lifetime. A chance to see the Chicago World's Fair."

"He said we could do our lessons while viewing the fair. I thought we could perhaps alternate working with him throughout each evening. That way, we could still see the fair and help him too."

"He'd change the entire dynamics of our group. We wouldn't be able to talk freely. And he'd try to take over our itinerary."

"No," Della shook her head. "I made it very clear that we'd pick the exhibits. He readily agreed."

"Of course he agreed. He wants us to say yes. But no man is going to be led around by three women. Not for five months, anyway. And that's what it would take. If he is to receive any benefit at all, he'd need lessons every single day, even Sundays." She gave Della a sympathetic look. "This isn't like taking in a bird with a broken wing, my dear. This is a man we're talking about."

Her throat began to thicken. She hadn't realized how much she'd counted on Hilda's support. "You're saying no?"

Her voice gentled. "I'm saying no."

Della bit her lip. "Do you think it would be inappropriate for me to say yes?"

"You mean, by yourself?"

She nodded, the idea beginning to take hold. She'd be able to pick the exhibits. She wouldn't have to eat at any restaurants. And she wouldn't have to turn in at eight o'clock simply because the other two women were the early-to-bed sort.

Hilda frowned. "What do you know of him?"

"His name is Mr. McNamara. He's from the Carolinas, if I remember right. He's invented an automatic fire sprinkler and is exhibiting it in Machinery Hall."

"Are you sure?"

"He invited me to go and look at it. He said he's in the back left-hand corner. And . . ." Her voice dwindled.

Hilda lifted a brow. "And what?"

"And he's the same man who rescued me from the crowd on opening day."

Her lips parted. "The one who carried you over his head?"

"One of them, yes."

"I thought you didn't tell him who you were."

"I didn't." She lifted her palms in an I-give-up gesture. "He was just as surprised as I was. The last thing he expected to find was me. He had no idea I was one of the teachers."

Though Hilda had never married, she was a hopeless romantic. When Della had first told them of her savior, Hilda had clasped her hands together and pressed them against her heart.

"Well." She straightened, a sparkle entering her eye. "I daresay you owe him one. And I feel sure he'd be quite the gentleman. After all he did for you, you can hardly refuse him, can you?"

"My thoughts exactly."

POSTAL EXHIBIT IN THE GOVERNMENT BUILDING

DOG SLEDGE

PONY EXPRESS

POSTAL CAR

"Full-size dummies took him back in time to the cowboy and mustang of the Pony Express."

CHAPTER 9

Standing at the fair's postal counter in the Government Building, Cullen waited as a clerk checked to see if he'd received any mail. The fair was due to open in thirty minutes, so no one else was about. He basked in the quiet. So different from Machinery Hall.

Every method of mail carrying, from an old stagecoach to the latest postal car, played out before him. Full-size dummies took him back in time to the cowboy and mustang of the Pony Express. A mountain carrier in snowshoes stood across from a bullet-riddled coach that had twice been captured by Indians. His favorite display, though, was the dog-sledge and team, so lifelike he expected to hear the dogs bark at any moment.

The clerk returned, and a surge of pleasure shot through him when the man handed him a letter, not from Wanda, but from home. Finally. He tore it open, then flipped to the second page to see that Reverend Roebuck had penned it for his father. The more he read, though, the slower he walked, giving no notice to a giant globe of the United States, land grants from colonial times, or a procession of wax figures clad in army uniforms. He pushed out the south door and made his way to Machinery Hall by rote as he reread the letter.

Dad owed the Charlotte merchant two hundred

dollars, which he couldn't pay, so they'd refused to give him any more credit. Cullen let his hand fall for a minute. What was Dad thinking to spend three hundred on sending him to the fair when he owed two hundred to the merchant? What happened to that cushion he'd talked about?

Shaking out the letter, he picked up where he'd left off. Dad didn't want him worrying. He'd gone to the bank and borrowed a thousand dollars. The only reason he was even saying anything was because Cullen had asked. Dad promised it was nothing to fret over.

Nothing to fret over? He borrowed a thousand dollars and didn't want Cullen to fret over it? He rubbed his mouth. A thousand seemed awfully excessive. Still, it would pay off the merchant debt and leave them with eight hundred to go toward taxes, seed, mortgage, supplies, and expenses. Or it should have. But it hadn't.

He turned to the next page. Dad had been required to pay some interest off first. Interest of four hundred dollars, in addition to the two hundred in principal.

Cullen frowned. The interest shouldn't have been that high. Something wasn't right. He'd write Reverend Roebuck and ask him to check on the interest rate. In the meanwhile, Dad still had four hundred dollars left. It wouldn't be enough come the end of the year, though.

He sighed. Dad had always handled the money.

He couldn't read and write so well, but he was good at numbers. Besides, it was his farm. Since Dad had never brought up the subject of money, Cullen hadn't felt all that comfortable asking. But just because he hadn't asked didn't mean he was unaware of the price of cotton or how many bales they'd produced. The number he hadn't had was how much Dad spent. Evidently, quite a bit. Enough for him to need to borrow a thousand dollars.

He rubbed his eyes. If the cotton prices held and they had a good year, they should make four hundred—three hundred at the worst. And with the way the economy was going, he probably should count on the worst.

Tucking the letter back into the envelope, he climbed the steps of Machinery Hall. Dad's four hundred and the harvest's three hundred would leave them about three hundred short. Earning back the money Dad had spent on sending him to the fair was no longer just a goal, it was a necessity. He'd ask Mrs. Harvell one more time if she'd let him leave early and refund his money for the days he had left. But he didn't have much hope of that happening. No one was parting with his money right now—not after the National Cordage Company had gone bankrupt the first week of the fair.

It might have been the company's own fault for trying to corner the market, but the fact was, it had overspent, incurred huge debt, and used up all its cash to pay investors. Everyone was still waiting to see what the fallout would be, but whatever it was, it would be big and it would affect the whole country. No, Mrs. Harvell was a shrewd woman. She'd not be refunding anything.

BLOOKER'S DUTCH COCOA COMPANY

"A Dutch maiden wearing wooden shoes and a gaudy dress curtseyed to Della."

CHAPTER 10

Della had never taught an adult before, and certainly not a man. Knowing she'd need to establish a professional teacher-student relationship, she'd dressed in the most matronly suit she had. Beneath her coat she wore a somber black skirt and bolero. She felt sure it added at least four years to her twenty.

Weaving between the Machinery and Agricultural Buildings, a short, red-faced man pushed a rolling chair into her path. She quickly jumped aside, then followed its progress. In its seat was the man's rather large and portly wife, with a young tot in her lap. Two little girls in their Sunday dresses sat on each armrest, holding tightly to their mother. A young boy, not quite old enough for school, sat on the mother's feet, dangling his legs over the footrest.

Good heavens. They certainly were making the most of their forty-cents-an-hour chair rental.

Rousing herself, she continued down the pathway. A woman staggered out of the Agricultural Building, squinted into the light, and propped a hand on her waist. "Well, of all the confounded messes. Whoever planned this fair made it so whenever you come out of a building, you ain't anywhere nearer anything in particular."

Her husband pulled a Rand McNally map of the fair from his coat, and the two began to puzzle over it. Della could certainly sympathize. She'd become lost in the Court of Honor alone. No telling how many times she would turn herself around before the fair's closing date.

Then she remembered Mr. McNamara would be with her much of that time. Perhaps he had a better sense of direction than she did.

Just past the obelisk, a crowd converged on a set of wooden stairs like sand in an hourglass, all heading for the elevated railroad that ran throughout the grounds. She skirted around them, then glanced up at the four-car train screeching to a halt and rattling the scaffolding supporting it.

She paused for a closer look. No cloud of smoke, nor any of the familiar chug and belch of a steam engine.

She studied the crisscross of cables above it.

"Marvelous," a man close by breathed.

And indeed it was marvelous. The train was powered by electricity.

Shaking her head, she hurried on, holding her breath so as not to smell the cattle, horses, swine, and sheep in the Livestock Exhibit and gave no pause for Germany's outdoor exhibit. Blooker's was straight ahead.

The clumsy old tower was a replica of a long-standing Holland windmill built at the beginning of the century. But instead of grinding meal, the giant blades now powered a chocolate grater. Just thinking about it made her mouth water.

Pushing open the large wooden door, she waited a moment to let her eyes adjust. A rich chocolate aroma enveloped her, along with warmth from the cheery fire. She removed her gloves and unbuttoned her double-breasted jacket. Mr. McNamara had yet to see her.

His coat lay draped over an empty chair beside him. His hat rested on its seat. He conversed with a rosy-cheeked Dutch maiden wearing wooden shoes and a gaudy dress. With one hand she balanced a tray of cups of steaming cocoa. Her other hand rested on a cocked hip. Throwing back her head, she laughed at something he said.

Della zeroed in on her lips.

"I am named after my mudder. Trudel . . ."

Della couldn't read her last name—something Dutch that started with a *z* and ended with a *p*.

"Strudel?" he asked.

Again the girl burst into giggles. "Nee, nee. Not Strudel, Trudel."

Mr. McNamara smiled, putting into play his laugh lines and dimples. The girl was so captivated her tray began to tilt.

Reaching up, he steadied it.

"May I guide you to a table, miss?" A Dutch maiden dressed in the same manner as Trudel curtseyed to Della.

"Yes, please. My party is right over there."

Their approach captured Mr. McNamara's attention. He rose, his smile broadening. Trudel eyed her with interest.

"Miss Wentworth, you came. Allow me to take your coat."

Tucking her gloves into her pocket, she turned her back. His fingers slipped inside the shoulders of her jacket, then slid it down her arms.

"Thank you," she murmured.

He held out her chair. "The lady would like a cup, please, Miss Zonderkop."

Trudel placed the cocoa on the table and moved on while he pushed in the chair. Draping her coat on top of his, he took the seat to Della's right.

"Have you been here long?" she asked.

"Not very."

"Well, I hope the wait hasn't been too boring."

He gave her a quizzical look. "Not at all. I did discover Blooker's has reproduced not just this tower but also the miller's living quarters as well. It's right through there."

Taking a sip of cocoa, she glanced toward the open door he indicated. "Perhaps that could be our first stop."

He stilled. "Then you'll do it? You'll give me the lessons?"

"I suppose so."

He glanced at the door. "Where are the other teachers?"

"They respectfully declined. They didn't want

to spend the entire summer and fall tutoring you, I'm afraid."

He picked at a snag in the table. "Learning to lip-read really will take that long, then? The entire five months remaining?"

"It'll take much more than that, but this will at least give you a start." Truth was, she wasn't completely sure how to go about the lessons. Should she give him an overview or just start at the beginning? "How far we advance will depend on how quick a study you are. Shall I give you a little test?"

He straightened. "A test?"

"Just to see how much lip-reading you already do."

He glanced about the room. "Whose lips should I try to read?"

"Mine."

"But I can hear you."

She smiled. "I'm going to mouth some sentences. You will be awarded five points for each one you read correctly. Ready?"

He nodded.

What time is it?

He stared at her mouth, studying it. And continued to study it long after she'd finished the sentence.

"Mr. McNamara?"

He looked up.

"Do you know what I said?"

"Oh! Um, no. I . . . say it again." He returned his attention to her mouth.

Where are you going?

"Where are you going."

"Good. Five points. Here's the next one. *Let me help you with that.*"

Again, an intense stare. An examination, really. As if he were trying to commit the formation of her lips to memory.

She sighed. "You're trying too hard, I think. Just relax."

He gave her a look of complete bafflement.

Her heart softened. "It's all right. That was probably too long a sentence anyway. Try this one. *It's over there.*"

He slid his chair back a bit.

"Do you have trouble seeing up close?" she asked.

He shook his head.

"It's okay. Please don't be distressed. I'm going to add a bit of sound this time. Not much, just a tiny bit. All right?"

Clearing his throat, he wiped his hands against his trousers. "No, no. Don't do that. I was . . . distracted. That's all. I'm ready now."

She didn't argue, but added the slightest sound to her sentence. *"Please sit down."*

"Please sit down."

"Excellent." She squeezed his arm.

He jerked it back.

Embarrassment flooded her. She hadn't meant to touch him. It was simply habit. Touch was one of the main sources of communication with the deaf. And since the children she taught lived at school with no vacations or visits home, she found they craved the hugs, love, and touches a mother would give.

"I'm sorry," she said.

He swallowed. "No, I am. I was, um, concentrating. It startled me, is all."

"I'll not do it again."

"Yes, no." He closed his eyes. "How many points do I have?"

"Ten."

"Out of how many?"

Goodness, did he have trouble with math as well? "Twenty-five."

"Let's do some more."

She took a sip of cocoa, though it had cooled considerably. "Just a few more, then."

He nodded.

Won't you come in?

"Won't you come in."

"Very good. Fifteen points."

I had a very nice time.

He snapped his gaze to hers. "I had a very nice time."

His tone had deepened. She smoothed the napkin on her lap. She hadn't meant it literally.

"Go ahead," he said.

121

I'll have to leave soon.

"You do?" he asked.

She smiled. "No. There are fifty questions in this battery of exams. None of them mean anything. They're just for me to assess your skill level."

"I see. Are we going to go through all fifty?"

"Not today. Now, what did I say?"

"That you'd have to leave soon."

Close enough. *"I'd like a cup of coffee."*

"I don't know. 'I'd like' were the first two words."

"That's right. Try this one. *Where do you live?"*

"On a farm just west of Charlotte."

"You're a farmer?"

"Yes."

"How strange. You don't look like a farmer."

He gave a small smile. "I left my overalls at home."

Smiling back, she folded her hands in her lap. "I see. Now try to remember these aren't real questions. You're simply to repeat what I say."

"Sorry. I keep forgetting."

"It's okay. One more. *I'd like to go out for lunch.*"

"You'd like to go out for lunch."

"No." She sighed. *"I'd* like to go out for lunch."

"That's what I meant. I just . . ."

She placed her napkin on the table. "Well, I think that's enough for now."

"How many points did I get?"

"Thirty-five."

"Out of how many?"

"Fifty-five."

Pausing, he looked to the corner of the room, then returned his attention to her. "That's only sixty or so percent. A failing mark."

So he could do math. "It's all right. That means you have nowhere to go but up."

He leaned back in his chair. "I bet your students love you."

Touching the watch pinned to her shirtwaist, she rubbed it between her fingers. No one had ever said that to her before. Her students were still young and learning to speak. Every word was a challenge. Compliments were not something they thought of or expended any energy on. Her director was overworked and had no time for such niceties.

"I couldn't really say." The thought filled her with warmth, though. "I certainly love them."

"I imagine you do." A long lock of his hair had escaped its Brilliantine and curved down against his cheek. "Shall we go see how millers lived in 1806?"

She glanced at the door leading to an old-fashioned parlor, sitting room, and kitchen. "I'd love to."

COLONNADE OF THE FORESTRY BUILDING

"Darkness had set in, leaving only moonlight and street lanterns to guide them to a set of benches facing the water."

CHAPTER 11

The cool outdoor air felt good against Cullen's hot skin. Staring at a woman's lips for extended periods of time was going to take some getting used to. They'd left Blooker's, passed the other windmills on exhibit, and now strolled along the South Pond in the direction of Lake Michigan.

"Have you been to see the Cliff Dwellers yet?" Miss Wentworth pointed to a giant cliff of red rock.

"I haven't. It almost looks as if Colorado imported an entire mountain for the exhibit, though, doesn't it?"

"It does." She paused, then pressed a gloved fist to her mouth, her eyes widening in delight.

"What?"

Look, she mouthed.

He scanned the mountain-like structure but found nothing to warrant her reaction. Huts with windows and doors had been carved into the sandstone, duplicating an ancient city of the Mancos Cañon Indians. Out front two gray donkeys brayed and squealed, swishing their skinny tails.

Finally, he spotted a group of nuns in full habit climbing over a high, treacherous trail. "An adventurous bunch. Are you a hiker, Miss Wentworth?"

"I don't know. I've never done it before."

She was a city girl. He'd forgotten. "Would you like to give it a try?"

"Perhaps."

"You don't sound too convinced."

She studied the rocky footpath. "My ankle is fully recovered, but I'm not sure it's up for a hike just yet."

Nodding, he tipped his hat to a group of ladies going the opposite direction. "You be sure to tell me if you need a rest."

"Oh, no. I'm enjoying the evening air very much, thank you."

All the same, he slowed their pace. They passed a crude log cabin displaying a moonshiner's still from Kentucky, which had been captured by revenue officers. A cider-like vinegary smell clung to the air.

"So how is it a girl from Philadelphia ends up being a teacher of the deaf?" he asked.

She shrugged. "I've always wanted to be one."

"Your entire life? From the day you were born?"

"Well, no." She wrinkled her nose. "I guess since I was about ten or so."

The scent of fresh bread replaced that of sour mash whiskey. A country maid in her best bib and tucker stepped from a French bakery, reminding him of home. Of Wanda. He wondered what she would have thought of nuns climbing a mountain of rocks.

"What happened when you were ten?" he asked, pulling himself back to the conversation.

"A family with a deaf child moved in next door to us. She used to sit beneath a tree and watch the rest of us race around the garden. So one day I went over, placed my straw hat on the ground, and scratched *H-A-T* in the dirt. From there we progressed to full-blown lessons complete with flash cards."

A smile tugged at his mouth. "And did it work?"

"It did." Her brows furrowed. "But that fall, she became ill, and the family moved away. So I began teaching my dog instead."

Missing a step, he gave her a sharp glance. "Your dog?"

"Yes. I checked out every library book on sound that I could. I studied how people use their lips, tongue, and voice box. I learned how ears are able to hear. And then I tested it out on my dog."

They were walking past an inspiring reproduction of the Ruins of Yucatan, right down to walls covered with vegetation and stones that had "toppled off," but he found himself much more intrigued with the woman beside him.

"Your dog?" he asked again.

She nodded. "First I taught her to bark for food, then growl. Once she became really good at it, I stuck my hand in her mouth and pressed on her throat—in different places, of course."

"Of course."

"Each place I pressed made a different sound. And before long Gypsy was able to say, 'How are you, Grandmamma?'"

His smile grew wide. "Your dog can say, 'How are you, Grandmamma?'"

She gave him a sheepish look. "Well, it sounds more like, '*Ow-ah-oo, gamama.*'"

He laughed. He couldn't help it. But instead of being offended, she returned his smile. Two dimples blossomed on her cheeks, the one on the right quite a bit deeper than the one on the left.

Since their destination was the Forestry Building, he took her elbow and cut between the Anthropological and Dairy Buildings. He'd expected an unpleasant odor from that last quarter, but as it advertised a restaurant inside, he assumed the building held dairy products and machines, not the actual cows.

Finally, they reached the Forestry Building. Tucked in the southernmost corner of the fair, it fronted Lake Michigan and attracted a much thinner crowd.

He took a deep breath, absorbing the sound of tiny waves thrumming the embankment and the slightest scent of fish floating on the breeze.

"The building isn't covered with the white . . . what do they call it?" she asked.

"Staff. It's a kind of glorified plaster of paris. And you're right. There aren't even any nails or metal in this one. The entire thing is built of wood and held together with wooden pins."

"It's a wonderful change," she said, her smile once more intact.

He assisted her onto a two-story veranda, its giant pillars formed by tree trunks grouped in threes.

"Look, the bark's still on the trunks." She pointed to one grouping, then noticed a plaque attached to its centermost trunk. "And they've listed each type of tree with the place it came from. These are from Missouri."

"What are they?" he asked.

White oosh, she mouthed.

"White . . . ash?"

"White oak. A person puckers their lips when they make a long *o*. Like this." She made a small round opening with her mouth. "*Ooooo. Oooooooak.* Now you say it so you can see what it feels like."

"Oak."

"Did you feel yourself pucker?"

This was not going to work. "What about *u?* What shape is it?"

"Same one. See? *Un*ion. *Cu*cumber. *U*niverse."

"And the *e?*"

"That's a smiler. Eat. East. Teeth. But I start with the puckers—long *o,* long *u,* and double *o*."

"What's wrong with the smilers? Can't we start with those?"

"No. The puckers are always first because

they're easiest to spot in the middle and at the end of a word."

"How long before we can move to the smilers?"

"That depends on you. The quicker you learn to pucker, the sooner we can move ahead."

Suppressing a groan, he led her inside. Numerous states and several countries showed off specimens from their forests. Minnesota displayed a block of cottonwood hewn from the first tree planted in Minneapolis. Washington's booth held a mammoth disk of cedar that twenty people could stand on at once.

He hesitated a bit before the section reserved for his home state of North Carolina. As a boy he used to roam the countryside and come home with swollen eyes and throat. It had been filled with almost every variety of evergreen and deciduous tree displayed in the booth. Still, he followed her in. A few minutes shouldn't hurt him any.

"Oh look, Mr. McNamara." Removing one glove, Miss Wentworth beckoned him, then ran her hand along a settee woven of branches and knots. "It's been varnished, but is otherwise entirely natural."

"It looks like rhododendron limbs. They bloom just in time to celebrate the Fourth of July and in every color you could imagine."

She tested the seat with her hand before trying it out. "Do you think it would hold both of us?"

In order to find out, they'd have to sit awfully close. "If it doesn't, I'd hate to be the one to discover it." He cast about for something to distract her with. "Look there. I believe that's a project I read about in the papers."

Offering her a hand, he assisted her from the settee and forced himself to ignore the smoothness of her skin. Upon reaching a gallery of photographs, she absently pulled her glove back on.

Wanda's hands were as rough and calloused as his, but they were good hands. Worthy hands. He pulled up a picture of her in his mind. Brown eyes, sweet smile, lots of curves. He clung to those memories, refusing to make a comparison between the two women.

Anyone, man or woman, would notice Miss Wentworth's blue eyes, her heart-shaped face, and her peach-colored lips. Well, maybe not the lips. He noticed them only because he'd been forced to study them all night.

"What is this?" Miss Wentworth pointed to a picture of a huge building with scaffolding.

"It's a grand castle called Biltmore. It's near Asheville. The papers said the youngest Vanderbilt is having it constructed. For the surrounding property, he's hired the same man who land-scaped Central Park and who also turned this park from a swamp into the grounds that we currently stand on."

She peered more closely at a photograph of barren, overworked terrain. "He'll have his work cut out for him if he's to make that look anything like Central Park."

"It's to be a planned forestry program. The first in America."

"Interesting."

By the time they reached the last booth, hours had passed and they'd yet to do more than practice the long *o*. They exited Virginia's section through a hollow segment of a sycamore tree, stopped by the coat check, and stepped out onto the verandah again.

Darkness had set in, leaving only moonlight and street lanterns to guide them to a set of benches facing the water.

He opened her coat, dipping it so her arms slid easily inside the sleeves.

"I'm afraid we're going to have to be a bit more disciplined with our lessons, Miss Wentworth."

"I was just thinking the same thing. I became so caught up in all those wonders, I totally forgot our purpose. If it's not too late for you, we could sit out here for a few minutes and do some work on your vowels."

"Will there be enough light?"

"If we sit on that bench over there." She indicated a bench with a splash of lantern light touching its wooden slats.

Settling onto it, they faced each other, her knee

brushing his. He sat up straighter, putting another inch between them.

"I'm going to say a list of words with the long *o* sound." She cleared her throat. "Watch for the pucker. Sometimes it will come at the beginning, sometimes at the end, and sometimes in the middle. The middle ones are the hardest, so you have to be on your guard."

He nodded.

"Only." Her voice was soft, but audible.

"I heard you."

"Did you? Even over the waves? That's wonderful. I thought you had difficulty when there's background noise."

"I usually do."

The moon's reflection cast a burnished ribbon across the lake's rippling surface. *Noise* was too harsh a word for the push and pull of its current.

"It's your voice," he said. "As a whole, I hear women better than men. But you, I hear very distinctly."

She nodded. "I'll mouth them, then."

For the next ten minutes he watched her lips and tried to read them. He'd never really noticed the nuances of a woman's lips before. Did they all have such distinct Cupid's bows?

"What did I say?" she asked.

He scrambled to think of a word with an *o* sound. "Ogle."

She shook her head. "Rosy. Watch for the

pucker. Every time you see it, insert a long *o* or *u*. Like *slogan*. See how my lips pucker in the middle? *Slogan*."

"I see."

"Good. Now watch for that. Let's try again."

For the next several minutes, he forced himself to view her lips as independent objects, as if they weren't attached to a flesh-and-blood woman. Until she formed a kiss.

He pressed himself against the armrest. "I don't know that one."

"Of course you do. Watch."

Looking him right in the eye, she formed another kiss.

"Say it out loud." His voice sounded hoarse, even to his own ears.

"But you were doing so well. Let's try it with a sentence. And watch my entire expression if you can. That sometimes helps."

Her lips began to move. He knew the minute she used it, but he couldn't fathom what word in the English language looked like a kiss.

"I'm sorry," he said. "I just can't tell."

Sighing, she tilted her head, a tendril of hair slipping free and swirling in the lake's breeze. "*Scoop*. I was saying *scoop*."

"Right." Jumping to his feet, he pulled out his timepiece. "Look at the time. I had no idea it was so late. I'm afraid we'd best be heading back."

"Sit down, Mr. McNamara."

"What?"

She threaded her hands together in her lap. "Sit down. I'm the teacher. I say when we're through."

"It's almost ten o'clock." He turned the face of his watch toward her.

"Sit. Down."

After a slight hesitation, he sat on the edge of the bench.

"Thank you." She reached into a hidden pocket of her skirt and withdrew a folded piece of paper. "I've written a list of pucker words. You are to stand at the mirror every morning and night and say each word out loud. Pay particular note to the formation of your lips."

He shot to his feet again. "I am not going to stand in front of a mirror and practice puckering my lips."

"Well, of course not. I don't want you to do anything with your lips. I want you to speak in a normal fashion without elaborately mouthing the words. That's very important."

Pulling his gloves on more tightly, he avoided her gaze. "Fine. Is class dismissed?"

She remained silent. When he couldn't stand it anymore, he looked at her.

She indicated the bench with her eyes.

He sat.

"I'm perfectly happy to forgo these lessons." Her voice was calm, not at all agitated. Simply matter-of-fact. "If you don't want to do this, I'll gladly bow out and we'll both have our evenings free."

Dragging a hand over his face, he took a deep breath. "I'm sorry. I'm not a very good student. At least, that's what my teachers always told me."

"I'll not put up with any more outbursts." She handed him the paper.

He took it, then tucked it into his jacket. "Listen, I've been thinking about what you said. About how long it takes for a person to learn to lip-read. And now I can see why. So that makes me wonder if maybe I shouldn't learn the language of signs as well. Just in case I go totally deaf before I master lip-reading."

The longer he spoke, the stiffer she became. "You must never, ever use sign language. It would brand you as deaf and different."

He shook his head. "I'd use it only at home, with my family. They know about my plight and don't condemn me for it."

"Even still, it's too risky. It is critical that you blend in with everyone else."

He knew she was right. In a society obsessed with United We Stand, Divided We Fall, anything and anyone who was the least bit different was to be avoided at all costs. At best, he'd be labeled an imbecile, at worst, he'd be thrown into an asylum like that poor Ashford girl.

"I would only use it temporarily," he said. "Until I became proficient at lip-reading."

"It takes years to become proficient. You cannot use sign language for years without someone finding out."

"I don't live in the city the way you do. I'm a farmer, and the only people I see day in and day out are family."

Frowning, she tilted her head. "I thought you were an inventor. Aren't you here to sell your fire sprinklers so they can be manufactured for businesses all over the country?"

He let out a soft laugh. "That's nothing but a father's dream for his son. I'm here only out of respect for him and because he insisted. As soon as the fair's over, I'm going back to North Carolina, where I'll live for the rest of my life on a farm in the middle of nowhere. And I'll need to know how to sign."

"What if your fire sprinklers become a success?"

"What if they don't?"

"I still wouldn't be able to teach you to sign."

"Then you are condemning me to a world of silence and isolation. Because I can't possibly learn what I need to in five short months."

Her face became stricken. "It goes against everything I've been taught," she whispered, forcing him to strain.

"And what have you been taught?"

"That our aim is to be as natural as we can with the deaf. That we must treat them as if they can hear. That we shouldn't do anything to single them out. We shouldn't raise our voices or make exaggerated movements with our lips. And certainly, under no circumstances, should we make hand gestures of any kind."

He studied her. So passionate. So sure. Yet so wrong. "It's a shame you feel that way. I've always thought the language of signs to be a beautiful thing."

Her eyes widened. "You've seen it used?"

"When I was an adolescent, I worked one winter as a news butch for the Norfolk & Southern Railway, which ran from Charlotte to Norfolk. I sold newspapers, candy, sandwiches, whatever my customers needed." He smiled, remembering the freedom he'd experienced at earning a wage all on his own. "One of the regulars on my route was a deaf man. He and his wife would sign to each other the whole trip. I was fascinated, so each day, as I waited for the train to return to Charlotte, I walked to the Norfolk library, pulled a book on sign language, and taught myself the alphabet."

She touched a gloved hand to her lips. "You know the alphabet signs?"

"Yes. Just the alphabet signs, though, not all the word gestures. And I was never so proud as when I asked that man, with my fingers, if there was anything on my tray he'd like to purchase."

"What did he do?"

"He pretty near bought me out. Best day of sales I ever had."

Her face softened. "He sounds like a lovely man, but I'm afraid those days are gone. Society has changed since then."

"Not as much as you think. What I didn't realize at the time was that I'd unintentionally offended a great many of my other customers by catering to someone 'abnormal.' And they let me know it in no uncertain terms." He watched a gull soar up from the water, then disappear in the blackness of the sky. "I never spoke to the deaf man again. With my fingers or otherwise."

She bit her lip.

"I've regretted it my whole life. I'd give anything to do that over." He pierced her with his gaze. "Will you teach me? Will you teach me the other gestures he used? Because he hardly ever used the alphabet. Only for proper names and such. I couldn't find any books about those other gestures."

She swallowed. "I'm not supposed to."

"We could go someplace private. I've heard the Wooded Island has plenty of places that would shield us from curious eyes."

She rubbed her temples.

"I'll make you a deal," he said.

She gave him a wary look. "What kind of deal?"

"How many lip movements are there?"

"There are three vowel families and eight consonant families," she said.

"What about this, once you've introduced the vowel families and, oh, let's say, three of the consonant families, you teach me a set of hand gestures."

She worried her lip.

"I won't tell anyone. Promise." He kissed his finger and crossed his heart.

She drummed her fingers. "I'd expect you to do your mirror exercises twice a day, every day from now until you have become proficient."

He balked. He couldn't imagine doing such a ridiculous thing. He also couldn't imagine being so hard of hearing that lip-reading would be his only way of understanding conversation.

After a slight hesitation, he nodded. "Very well. I'll practice."

"I'll know if you've done them or not."

He hesitated. "How?"

"By your progress." Her eyes reflected the lantern light, flickering with intensity. She gathered a handful of her skirt.

He helped her to her feet. "Then we have a deal?"

"You won't tell anyone? Not a living soul?"

"Not a living soul."

After a strained moment, she let out a sigh. "All right, Mr. McNamara. All the vowel families and three of the consonant."

Pleasure spilled through him. He held out his elbow. "Thank you, Miss Wentworth."

CHICAGO 1893

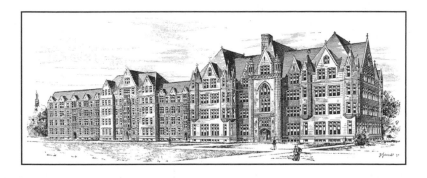

"He looked at the floor, disconcerted to know
her room was directly below his."

CHAPTER 12

Cullen splashed water onto his face, chest, and arms, grabbed a bar of soap, scrubbed all over, then splashed himself again. The mirror above the washstand blurred as water dripped from his eyelashes.

"Scoop." It didn't look at all the same when he said it. "Scoop."

He swiped the water from his eyes. "Loop. Snoop. Poop."

Padding to his nightstand, he toweled his hair and stared at her list. Her writing was different from his. Less smooth. More fussy.

"Smooth." Grabbing the paper, he walked back to the mirror. "Smooth."

He repeated every word she'd given him. All fifty. Could she hear him? He looked at the floor, disconcerted to know her room was directly below his. He'd not realized she lodged at Harvell House too. It had been a shock to them both, but when he'd insisted on walking her home and she finally revealed where she lived, it explained why they'd been at the front of the crowd on opening day. Both had been looking for Mrs. Harvell and her group.

He'd never been to any of the house meals because he asked Mrs. Harvell to box up his breakfasts and suppers. Fortunately, she offered half-board to the exhibitors staying at her house, which meant no lunches. It had allowed him to recoup sixty-six dollars of his dad's money.

Still, he'd not told Miss Wentworth his room was above hers. He simply walked her up the entry-hall stairs and touched his hat when she indicated which door was hers. Once she was safely inside her room, he continued to the top floor. Shaken. And feeling guilty, though his dad had picked out the boardinghouse and neither of them had anything to do with room assignments.

A breeze fluttered the lace coverings at his window. Was her window open too? Were her curtains the same flimsy fluff as his? Folding the list, he returned it to his nightstand and picked up his Bible. A letter from Wanda was stuck in the pages of Proverbs.

Pulling it out, he fingered its edges, comforted to know she'd touched them too, until thoughts of Hodge intruded.

He closed his eyes. "I'm sorry, Wanda," he whispered, for it was a slippery slope he walked and he knew it.

He tried to reread Wanda's letter, but every time he came to a word with a double *oo,* a long *o,* or a long *u,* he stopped and tested it on his tongue. Tried to imagine what it would look like. Yet his imaginings didn't conjure up his own lips saying it but Miss Wentworth's.

He pinched the top of his nose. What would

Wanda's lips look like if she said it? But he couldn't summon something so specific. He wished he had a picture of her, but she'd never had one made. Folks in his part of Mecklenburg County didn't have the money for such frivolities.

Frustrated, he thumbed through Proverbs, looking for a nugget of wisdom.

Whoso loveth instruction loveth knowledge,
But he that hateth reproof is brutish.

Was that how he looked to Miss Wentworth? Like someone who hated reproof? He didn't hate reproof—well, maybe he did. But that wasn't why he'd tried to end his lesson so abruptly.

He reread the verse. "Whoso. Reproof. Brutish."

Putting a finger in Proverbs, he closed the book and walked to the mirror. "Whoso. Reproof. Brutish. 'Whoso loveth instruction loveth knowledge, but he that hateth reproof is brutish.'"

He would never be able to lip-read all that. But then, he'd been taught only one motion. Maybe if he persevered, gave it a chance. Still, he'd need to hold himself apart from Miss Wentworth. He and Wanda had set a date. The last Saturday in November. He'd set it because she feared some city girl would turn his head.

He swallowed. Wanda was a lot wiser than he gave her credit for sometimes.

HORTICULTURAL BUILDING

"In the center of the rotunda,
like a diamond in a most ornate setting,
stood a mountain with a collection of tropical
plants covering its majestic slope."

CHAPTER 13

I thought we'd start at the Horticultural Building." Tugging on her gloves, Della stepped out of Blooker's and headed toward the Court of Honor.

Mr. McNamara kept pace beside her, offering up no opinion. They'd met at the cocoa mill again. She had a cup of hot chocolate with her boxed supper. He had no drink at all.

"Originally, I thought to start at the Electricity Building," she continued. "But then I reminded myself you're a farmer and you probably have very strong opinions about electricity."

"And why is that?" he asked.

She looked at him, startled. "Well, because of all the controversy over how confused plants are going to get if we set up electric lampposts along our streets. I mean, how will the plants ever know when to go to bed?"

A smile hovered around his mouth. "I imagine they'll figure it out. And we farmers, as a rule, don't have a lot of lampposts in our fields, so it shouldn't be too much of an issue. If it's the Electricity Building you want to see, I'm happy to follow along."

She waved her hand in a circle. "No, no. I'm sure you'd much rather go to the Horticultural Building. What farmer wouldn't?"

"Indeed."

She pointed to little whirling machines sprinkling water over a soft lawn of grass. A fat robin hopped about, playing in the manufactured raindrops. "Look, someone else has invented a sprinkler system too."

"So he has."

They skirted a circular basin filled with pink and white water lilies releasing sweet perfume and approached the domed facade of the Horticultural Building. On either side of the walk, magnificent fields of crimson, orange, and salmon-colored blooms were sullied with giant pots of stiff, awkward cactuses. They were as tall as two men combined and had short stumpy arms. Their small, yellow star-shaped flowers must have been stuck on by Mother Nature as an afterthought, for they didn't at all look as if they belonged.

Inside, Della came to a complete stop. "Heaven on earth, would you look at that."

Pansies. The dainty flowers stretched as far as the eye could see and in every color imaginable, making a vast, scroll-like design. In the center of the rotunda, like a diamond in a most ornate setting, stood a mountain with a collection of tropical plants covering its majestic slope. A trickling waterfall beckoned with a song of freshness.

"I've been practicing my words," he said.

She blinked, pulling herself back to the present. They were standing before the most wonderful display of foliage that has ever been seen in the history of the world under one roof and all he could say was he'd practiced his words? She'd have thought a farmer would be moved to tears by such a spectacle.

"Would you like to quiz me?" he asked.

She stared at him in disbelief. "Now?"

"Well, sure. We have a lot to cover, and I don't want to get caught again at the end of the evening without accomplishing what we set out to. So I figured we could start with a review and move to the smilers or something."

She raised a brow. "It's been one day. Are you telling me you've mastered all fifty words in one day?"

"Well, maybe not all fifty, but a good percentage of them."

She wished she'd never agreed to this. She worked nonstop with her students, and though she loved them and her job, by the end of the day she was ready for a break. Especially here at the fair.

The first week she hadn't been able to explore a thing because of her ankle. Then these last two, she'd been touring with Hilda and Maxine. The truth was, though, they'd wanted to see exhibits that were at the bottom of her list and to continue to spend money at restaurants when they could acquire boxed suppers from Mrs. Harvell. To make matters worse, the students and other faculty members were their main topics of conversation until Della could hardly wait to escape for the night.

It didn't take her long to realize the benefits of having Mr. McNamara act as a guide. Of course, that was before she knew they were both staying at the same boardinghouse.

Her father, ever concerned about her, had given her a plethora of articles and essays on the dangers a woman might face. To him, knowledge was the most powerful weapon she could wield. He'd have found Mr. McNamara highly suspect.

"Go ahead," he said. "Try me."

Sighing, she mouthed, *School.*

"Pool," he said.

Uniform.

"Humorous."

Marigold.

"Mexico."

She lifted a brow.

He smiled. "How did I do?"

"I said *school, uniform,* and *marigold.*"

His smile wilted.

She pointed toward the west side of the building. "There's an outdoor exhibition of green-houses and gardens that sounded interesting, so let's head in that direction first."

They walked through endless corridors filled

with specimens of fruit, wine, seeds, and garden machinery. Throughout it all, she tried to remember to mouth the pucker words. His recognition much improved until she realized he wasn't even looking at her. He was filling in the blanks on context clues alone.

"If you want to become proficient," she said, "you're going to have to watch me when I speak."

You'd have thought she'd asked him to arm wrestle Paul Bunyan, his expression was so appalled. Still, she could sympathize. Although the displays had become a bit monotonous to her, he was probably so enamored with them, he didn't want to chance missing something. Perhaps she should take him someplace he'd find less distracting. Someplace a man might not be all that interested in.

The displays of laces and embroideries in the Woman's Building might be just the thing or, better yet, the shoe exhibit, with countless varieties and grades of footwear. She smiled. She'd have to look again to see which building housed it.

A crowd ahead of them gathered around a thirty-foot tower made of California oranges. The intoxicating aroma made her stomach growl.

"Look at me," she said.

He turned his attention to her, his brown eyes wary.

How many oranges do you think there are? she mouthed.

"Did you say, 'how many oranges'?" he asked.

"Yes. How many oranges do you think there are?"

He examined the tower. "I'd guess—"

"Don't say it out loud." She picked up a scrap of paper by a ballot box and handed it to him. "Write *your* name, address, and guess. If *you're* correct, they'll send *you* a box of navel *oranges*."

"You mouthed *your, you're, you,* and *oranges*."

She smiled. "Very good. I'll fill out one too."

By the time they made it to the outdoor exhibit, the sun had set, its light having been replaced by electric bulbs. She carried on a one-sided dialogue for the most part, continuing to use as many pucker words as possible.

"I just can't get *over* all these plants," she said. "I'm *assuming* they're some kind of exotic spice, but they almost look like weeds, don't they?"

When he didn't repeat the pucker words, she glanced up at him and paused. "Mr. McNamara?" Clasping a portion of his sleeve, she pulled him beneath one of the hanging light bulbs. "Are you, is your, what's the matter with your eyes? They're all puffy."

He shrugged. "I'm fine."

She circled around in front of him, grabbed his lapels, and centered him so she could see better.

"My stars and garters, you're not fine at all. We need to get you to the infirmary right now."

"I don't need an infirmary."

She headed toward the exit, then turned when he didn't follow. "Come on. It's right around the corner from here."

"I know where it is. I went there on opening day to see if your friends had found you."

Her lips parted. "You didn't."

"I did."

"I'm terribly sorry."

"I've forgiven you."

"Thank you. Now, come on." She again headed for the exit. "Clearly you've been bitten by something. Heaven knows what it could be. No telling what foreign spiders and insects are hiding amidst these plants. I have a sister who swells up like a balloon when she's stung by a bee. Everything puffs up, her air is cut off, she can't breathe, and she turns blue." She charged out the door. "It scares the living—"

At the sound of the door slamming behind her, she turned. He wasn't with her. Her pulse rocketed. Had he fainted from lack of air and she'd not even known it? Lifting her skirt, she raced back inside. "Mr. McNamara! Mr. McNamara!"

"Yes?" he answered from behind her.

She screamed.

He jumped.

"Heavens." She placed a hand over her heart.

"You scared me. Are you all right? Didn't you hear me calling? Do you feel faint? I thought you'd—"

"*Silence.*"

She stilled.

"Of course I heard you. The entire fair heard you."

"Then why didn't you follow me?"

"I did. I was right behind you."

"Yes. Well, we need to get you to a doctor."

"I do not need a doctor. This happens all the time. I just need to get out of these greenhouses." Grabbing her elbow, he propelled her through the door and out onto a deserted landing by a statue of William Penn. The greenhouses were behind them, the back entrance to the Horticultural Building in front of them. Distant sounds of laughter and calls of vendors drifted on the breeze.

He released her.

She rubbed the spot he'd grasped. "What do you mean it 'happens all the time'?"

"Just exactly what it sounds like," he snapped. "It happens all the time."

She couldn't see his face, only his silhouette. "Are you trying to tell me that plants make your eyes swell?"

Silence.

A great unease filled her. "Mr. McNamara, are you or are you not a farmer?"

"I am." His words held a sharp edge. As if he'd gritted his teeth.

Clearly he was lying. And if he was lying about that, he could very well be lying about everything. Even his trouble hearing. Could her father be right after all?

"You must think me the most gullible woman on the face of the earth." Backing up a step, she surreptitiously grabbed handfuls of skirt and petticoat, inching up their hems. "Our deal is off. Good night, sir."

Spinning around, she took off at an all-out run.

"Miss Wentworth!" He hesitated a beat, then chased after her.

All she had to do was make it to the end of the building and around the corner, then race to the main boulevard. Once there, she'd find plenty of people to help her.

He was gaining quickly.

Too late, she realized she should have just run back inside the Horticultural Building. Renewing her efforts, she pressed toward the end of the building, his footfalls gaining ground. He caught her arm in a firm grip.

Screaming with every fiber of her being, she whirled around and kicked him in the shin as hard as she could.

He immediately let go, his expression one of complete shock.

She wasted no time in finishing her run to the

street. The boulevard was deserted. She couldn't believe it. Where was everyone?

Her side began to ache, but she ignored it and ran toward the Court of Honor. Glancing over her shoulder, she saw him standing at the edge of the boulevard watching her. Shivers ran up and down her arms. She didn't turn around again.

HORTICULTURAL BUILDING, EAST ENTRANCE

"All she had to do was make it to
the end of the building and around the corner,
then race to the main boulevard."

CHAPTER 14

Cullen waited for Della on a bench in the entry hall of Harvell House. He knew she hadn't beat him home because Mrs. Harvell had instituted a new system for her boarders. The woman had grown tired of waiting for everyone to return at night so she could put out the lantern. As a result, she'd decided to leave a list of names by the front door. Each person was to draw a line through their name when they arrived. The last person in was to extinguish the lamp.

Miss Wentworth's was the only one left on tonight's list. He couldn't decide whether she hadn't returned because she realized he'd be here or he should worry that some misfortune had befallen her.

If some nefarious type had tried to waylay her, he had no doubt she'd give him more than he'd bargained for. His shin still stung from her blow. But he'd let her go at the first sign of protest. A man bent on mischief wouldn't be so quick to give up his prize.

He pressed a cold washcloth against his eyes. Of all the buildings to tour, why did she have to pick that one? He'd known what was going to happen the moment he set foot inside. But what could he have said? The deal was she picked the sights.

So he'd kept his mouth shut and hoped for the best. And he just might have gotten away with it if it hadn't been for that last hour in the greenhouses.

He supposed he could understand her disbelief, but it never occurred to him she'd think he was misrepresenting himself. And now, how was he supposed to prove to her he was a farmer? He had nothing in his room that even hinted of his occupation other than the pair of denims he'd worn on the train up here. There were Wanda's letters, of course, but he wasn't about to show her those—not with Hodge's comments inserted between every other sentence. And even without Hodge's remarks, her letters would prove nothing other than the fact that Wanda lived on a farm.

The handle on the door made a slight rattle.

Removing the washcloth, he slowly sat up.

Inch by inch, the wooden door creaked open until it was wide enough for her to see the list. A breeze whooshed in, sending the paper up into the air. It floated back down to the floor in a slow pendulum motion.

He heard her mumble but was unable to catch her words.

Finally, she poked her head inside, glanced up the stairs, then stepped in and closed the door with the greatest of care.

She couldn't see him in the shadows. Had no

idea he was there. If he said something, she'd most likely scream and wake up the entire house.

Which left him with three choices. One, make his presence known and risk a scream. Two, sneak up behind her and cover her mouth—which was not typical farmer behavior. Or three, do nothing and deal with it tomorrow.

But if he did nothing, she'd have all day to imagine the worst and he'd be found guilty without due process. No, he needed to confront her now and do his best to convince her of his character.

She tiptoed to the paper and returned it to the table. When she bent to draw a line through her name, he slipped up behind her, grabbing her waist and mouth at the same time, then immediately swung her clear of the table. The last thing he wanted was for her to kick over the lantern and have a repeat of Mrs. O'Leary's cow.

She screamed into his hand, jabbed him with her arms, kicked him with her feet, clawed him with her nails, bit into his palm, then tried to butt him with her head.

"Stop it," he hissed. "I'm not—*umph*—going to hurt you. I just want to—*ooph*—talk."

She flailed and thrashed, then hooked her foot behind his calf and slid it up to the bend in his knee, then tried to bring him to the floor.

He tossed her up for a second and clasped her waist again. "Stop it, Adelaide."

"Wnwooooo!" She grabbed his little finger and tried to bend it backward.

He tightened his hold. "I'm not going to hurt you. I just want to talk to you."

She reared back, barely missing his chin.

"My name is Cullen McNamara. I'm a farmer in Mecklenburg County, North Carolina." He stopped to take several deep breaths in between her struggles. "Certain plants and weeds have made me swell up and break out in hives for as long as I can remember."

Her strength was beginning to fade, praise God.

"Think." He gave her a shake. "That's the whole reason my father sent me up here. He's scared to death I'm going to drop dead in the middle of a cotton field."

She stilled.

He took several more breaths. "So he got this grand idea to send me to the World's Fair because . . ." More deep breaths. ". . . he thinks every business owner in the world . . . will be falling all over himself . . . to buy my sprinkler system."

His poor lungs, he thought. They just could not handle plants, seeds, and Adelaide Wentworth all in one night. "But no one wants the sprinklers . . . and I'm not going to drop dead . . . because if I were, I'd have done it years ago."

His arm protested against her dead weight, but he didn't dare set her down yet. Closing his eyes, he leaned his forehead against the back of her head. "I really am who I say I am. I swear on my mother's grave."

She gave a slight nod.

"Are you going to scream?"

A slight shake to the left and right.

"I'm going to remove my hand."

Another nod.

He carefully peeled his hand away but kept it close in case she screamed.

"Put me down," she gasped.

"Are you going to run?"

She didn't answer.

He took that as a yes. So he walked them toward the bench, his legs bumping hers and tangling in her skirts.

She clutched his arms. "Put me down, I said."

"Hush, not so loud. I just want to sit down. You've worn me out." He sat, bringing her with him.

She slapped at his arm. "Let me go," she hissed, her voice quiet. "I'm on your lap."

Leaning his head against the wall, he closed his eyes. "Hush. Just be quiet and be still for one second so I can catch my breath. Please."

With a huff, she waited, then thrummed her fingers on his arm. "How long do you need? I thought farmers were supposed to be strong, what with all that shoveling of hay and digging of rows and pushing of plows."

He held out his free arm. "Grab my upper arm."

"What?"

"Just grab it."

She did.

He flexed his muscle.

The thrumming stopped. Twisting slightly, she placed one hand beneath his arm, then smoothed down his jacket with the other. "I'd have thought it'd be a lot bigger."

Sighing, he picked her up, plopped her beside him, stripped off his jacket, removed his cuff, and shoved up his shirtsleeve. Once more, he flexed.

Her eyes widened. "Good heavens, that's huge. Are they both like that?"

Rolling his eyes, he flexed his other one but didn't fool with the sleeve. He felt ridiculous.

She reached over and poked the bare one, then squeezed it and cupped it with her hand.

He looked at a point just over her shoulder and ignored the fact that she smelled like roses, her hair was completely disheveled, and her lips had parted in fascination.

Finally, she leaned back.

"Do you believe me now?" he asked, lowering his arms.

"Lots of men have muscles."

He slid his eyes shut. "Ask me any farming question you want."

"How do you milk a cow?"

He opened one eye. "That's kind of hard to explain without the cow."

She looked up at the ceiling. "How tall does cotton get?"

"About up to here." He raised his hand.

"Really?"

"Yep."

She frowned. "That doesn't prove anything. I bet lots of North Carolina boys have seen a cotton field."

Shaking his head, he pushed down his sleeve, then stalled as a thought occurred to him. A thought so disquieting, he almost dismissed it out of hand. Almost.

"There is one way I could prove it." He lifted his gaze to hers, his Adam's apple bobbing. "But I'd have to remove my shirt."

She pushed herself against the back of the bench. "I don't need to see any more of your muscles. Besides, that wouldn't prove anything."

"What if you could see the white lines where my suspenders lie when I plow with my shirt off? Only a farmer would have markings like that."

She hugged herself with her arms, her eyes darting from one thing to another. Her leg began to bounce up and down. "You're just saying that because you know I would never, *ever* ask a man to do such a thing. It would, I'd, my father would die of a heart attack if I gave you permission to do that, and you know it. So you're hoping I'll just say I believe you without making you prove it."

He said nothing. Just stared at her.

She glanced at his chest, then back up at him.

He didn't flinch or look away, but hoped to high heaven she'd take his word on it. Removing his shirt was the last thing on earth he wanted to do. What would Wanda say? How would he ever be able to justify something like that to her or even to his own conscience?

Please, God, he thought. *Don't let her ask me to take off my shirt. Let her believe me.*

Covering her face with her hands, she went very still.

Was she praying? *Please, let her be praying.* 'Cause if she was praying, surely God would tell her not to ask him. Surely He'd make her believe him.

Finally, she lowered her arms, grabbed her knees, and looked him square in the eye. "Prove it."

CHAPTER 15

This was her father's fault. All of it. If he hadn't filled her with the fear of God and made her read all those articles and told her all those horrible stories, she wouldn't be sitting here, in the entry hall of Harvell House, asking a man she'd known for what amounted to three days to take off his shirt.

She could not *believe* this was happening. She'd agonized about it all evening, ever since she'd run away from him. What if, just what if, he was telling the truth? What if he really was a farmer who was going deaf and whose eyes swelled up every time he went in the fields? Because if he was and she refused to help him, what on earth would she say when one day she stood before the Almighty and He asked her why she'd turned away one of His very own?

Then, just about the time she'd convinced herself to go back and apologize, she stopped and asked what if, just what if, he *wasn't* telling the truth? What if he wasn't a farmer and he wasn't going deaf and he had wicked designs on her person? What then? According to her father, terrible, awful, horrendous things that weren't even worthy of being verbalized would happen to her.

So she needed to know, once and for all, if

Cullen McNamara was a farmer. Because if he was telling the truth about that, then he was most likely telling the truth about everything else. And what better way to prove it than with sun marks from long hours in the field?

And what better way for a wicked, immoral man to trick her into believing him than to ask her to do something no decent, God-fearing woman on the face of the planet would ever do? She was so mortified, she almost hoped he was wicked, because then she'd be justified in the asking.

But if he wasn't, if he really was a farmer going deaf, how in the world would she ever look him in the eye again?

Prove it. Her words hung in the air like the suspended wooden sign outside Harvell House, flapping in the wind.

He reached for his tie, seesawing it back and forth until it loosened. His eyes were trained on hers, begging her to stop him. To halt this nonsense.

The question was, Why? Because he was as mortified as she, or because he was a perverse, despicable degenerate?

She pressed her lips together. *Prove it, Mr. McNamara,* she thought. *You're going to have to prove it.*

He grabbed one end of the silk tie and pulled, the swish of its release loud in the empty hall.

Lifting his chin, he removed his collar and set it on the bench beside his tie.

Next came the suspenders. They weren't black, like her father's, but red. Red like a wicked man would wear. A tremor went down her back. She'd have to get ready to yell. If there weren't some very clear, very visible suspender marks, she needed to scream her head off the minute he removed that shirt.

He hooked one suspender with his thumb and pulled it down, then did the same with the other. They lay like wilted flower stems on either side of his hips. There was nothing left now but the buttons.

He used only one hand. She always used two when she undid her buttons.

His hands were big. And rough. Rough enough to scratch her when he held them over her mouth. She reached up and touched the chapped places around her lips.

His hand stalled, then continued pushing button after button through the holes with quick flicks. When he'd undone all the ones above his trousers, he leaned onto his left hip and pulled out the tail of his shirt, then leaned on his right and did the same. His shirt parted the least little bit, giving her glimpses of his undershirt.

Every fiber in her being screamed to have him stop. To close her eyes and just take him at his word. But whoever heard of a farmer who swelled up like that? It was unfathomable.

He released the final button and whisked off his shirt.

His arms were huge, powerful. Even without his flexing them. And his chest. Land sakes. Every dip and swell was clearly defined beneath the tight cotton undershirt.

Her mouth went dry. "Wait."

He let out a slow sigh of relief.

She stood. "I'm going to stand on the steps. And if you don't have the markings you've claimed you do, I just want you to know, I'll bring this house down with my screams. Don't think I won't."

"Oh, I believe you, Adelaide. I have no doubt you'd do just that."

She lifted her chin. "My name is Miss Wentworth."

"That may be, but I think it's fair to say we're way past the formalities."

With much more bravado than she was feeling, she crossed the entry hall and went halfway up the first flight of steps before turning around.

Pushing himself up by his knees, he walked to the foot of the stairs. "Are you going to be able to see me from there? Because if it's too dark and you can't see and you let out a holler, we're going to have a lot of explaining to do. And it'll be you who takes the worst of it. My hand will get slapped, but you—you'll be thrown out on the street and will, in all likelihood, lose your job."

The thought of her job and the reaction of her fellow teachers and landlady hadn't even occurred to her. If he didn't have the markings and she screamed, how on earth would she explain why he was half-naked?

"It's not too late to change your mind," he said.

It was the wrong thing to say. Straightening her spine, she narrowed her eyes. "Do not try to intimidate me, Mr. McNamara."

Shaking his head, he rubbed his neck. "You may as well call me Cullen. Now, can you see me or not?"

"I think I can." She moistened her lips. "Yes, I'm fairly certain I can."

Turning, he retrieved the lantern and set it at his feet. "I'm going to take off my undershirt, then I'm going to lift up the lantern right quick so you can see. So don't start screaming until you give yourself a chance to have a good look. All right?"

She gave a quick nod. Her legs were trembling, her pulse was thrumming, and her stomach felt downright ill.

He pulled his undershirt out from his pants, the muscles in his arms flexing and shifting. Then he crossed his arms in front of him, grabbed the hem of his undershirt and pulled it up and over. Before she had a chance to see anything, he whisked up the lantern, holding it high.

Blood rushed through her veins. He was magnificent. As beautifully formed as any sculpture on the entire grounds of the fair. She squeezed the stair rail. Would his chest have the same texture as his arms? For his skin was different from hers. Not coarse exactly, nor was it smooth. Just . . . different.

She took a step down.

He took a step back. "Can you not see?"

Oh, she could see. She could see just fine. Dark hairs dotted his sun-kissed chest, and two white stripes traveled from his shoulders to his waist as if they'd been painted there by God.

"Miss Wentworth?"

She couldn't breathe.

"Adelaide?" His voice held a note of panic. "Please tell me you can see. They're on my back too." He spun around.

Her lips parted. The width of his shoulders was at least twice the width of his waist. And all his muscles shifted when he lifted the lantern higher.

He looked over his shoulder. "Can you see them?"

She could see exactly where they intersected, then split again.

"Yes," she whispered.

He lowered the lantern. His shoulders relaxed. He slowly turned around.

Still, she didn't move.

"Adelaide?" His voice had dropped, a hint of warning in it.

She pulled her gaze from his chest to his eyes. But she couldn't see them, not with the lantern hanging down by his legs.

"I'll see you tomorrow evening for your lesson," she said.

He gave a nod.

She scratched the stair rail with her finger. "How are your eyes?"

"Much better."

"They looked as though the swelling had gone down quite a bit. It was hardly even noticeable, in fact."

"Yes. This was nothing."

"Do they sting?"

"They'll be completely back to normal by morning."

"I'm glad." Turning, she went up one step, then paused. "No one calls me Adelaide anymore."

He said nothing.

"Della. They call me Della."

Not a sound.

She looked over her shoulder. "Good night, Cullen."

His Adam's apple bobbed. "Good night, Della."

USS *ILLINOIS* EXHIBIT

"Moored to its landing, as if it had just arrived from a long battle, was the USS *Illinois*, apparently afloat. But nothing at the World's Fair was what it appeared to be."

CHAPTER 16

The hour before the park opened was Cullen's favorite, but he had only about twenty more minutes before Machinery Hall started its machines. And he'd have to be there when it did—even if every visitor nodded politely, then stopped at Bulenberg's display and listened as he launched into an extensive discourse on the merits of manual sprinkler systems and the evils of automatic ones. Each presentation culminated with a dramatic pull of a lever, at which point his sprinklers would open up—though, of course, no water came out. Cullen had nothing so showy in his presentation, for the only thing that could open his spigots was an actual fire.

A brisk breeze off Lake Michigan's shoreline ruffled his newspaper. Tucking his watch back into his pocket, he readjusted himself on the bench and scanned the generous sweep of smooth promenade sloping down to the water's edge. An egret flew inches above the lake, its reflection distorted by the rippling surface.

Beyond it, a curved pier extended into the water. Moored to its landing, as if it had just arrived from a long battle, was the USS *Illinois*, apparently afloat. But nothing at the World's Fair was what it appeared to be. In reality, the *Illinois* was no more than a brick battleship resting on a substantial foundation of piling and heavy timbers.

Still, he'd have given anything to have toured its berth deck and afterdeck, its main deck, search lights, and battery of guns. Instead, he'd had to suffer through a tailors' exhibit, with murals depicting every form of dress attire from Adam and Eve on up to today's modern styles, a Belgian exhibit with dainty shawls, lace curtains, and dress goods, and a French exhibit where an entire wedding party of wax figures showed off the latest in bridal fashions.

It would have been the perfect time to bring up Wanda. But he wasn't at the fair to reveal his personal business to his lip-reading instructor. He was at the fair to sell sprinkler systems and keep the farm afloat. In order to do that, he needed to be able to communicate with the buyers. To soothe their fears about trying something new. To convince them his way was better than Bulenberg's. And to keep any other roadblocks—like going deaf—from entering the equation.

Just yesterday, Vaughn had stopped by to check on his progress—not only on the sprinklers but on his lip-reading. The insurance man had a vested interest in Cullen's success. The more clients he won, the more policyholders Vaughn had the potential of winning as well. So Cullen had put as positive a spin on it as he could. But the fact was, he needed to accelerate the pace of his lessons, even if it meant going to a shoe exhibit. A *shoe* exhibit.

For hours Della had exclaimed over shoes of alligator skin, buffalo, and horsehide. Wooden shoes, spiked shoes, and shoes with upturned toes. Velvet-lined shoes, scented shoes, and dainty shoes with a ridiculous number of buttons.

When they'd finally seen all the shoes and he thought they could leave, she began to examine a wall with hundreds of watercolors depicting every style of footwear worn by every blasted race for the last three to four thousand years.

He sighed. The only thing worse than studying all those exhibits was studying her lips. Yet she'd been a ruthless taskmaster, insisting he do just that. It was, after all, why he'd been accompanying her.

His progress had been painfully slow. Though she'd taught him shapes for all the vowel families and one of the consonant families, he was a long way from mastering them. Mouth movements, it turned out, were very minute actions—some more minute than others.

So much depended on whether speakers were facing him, facing away, or looking to the side. Whether their lips were thick or thin. Whether they had mustaches, beards, or both. Whether they were from the North or the South. Or even from America.

With women, he had to be particularly careful. It made them uncomfortable if he stared at their mouths for any length of time—except for Della, of course.

Still, after the fiasco in the entry hall, he'd done his level best to think of her as nothing more than his teacher, a nonperson almost. When he was with her, he kept plenty of space between them, touched her only if absolutely necessary, and limited his conversation, as much as he could, to nods, yeses, and ahems.

That worked fine when they were together. But he found himself thinking about her much too often when they were apart. Last week, John had caught him grinning for no apparent reason. Cullen had had to come up with a quick explanation or face telling John what he was really smiling about—Della and the way she'd taught her dog to talk.

He felt a smile tug at his mouth even now. Who'd ever heard of such a thing? And she'd been so expressive, her face changing as if she were an actress on the stage. He supposed he shouldn't be surprised. Facial expressions were a crucial part of communicating with the deaf. But he still found himself charmed by it.

A heron waded into the shallow surf just a few yards away. It jabbed its beak into the water, then pulled up a fish. He envied the bird and wished his meals were as easy to come by. It had been quite an adjustment to forgo his noon meal. Even Alice's bean kettle soup was starting to sound good. But if things were as bad as the papers claimed, he'd need to continue to save every coin he had.

He glanced at the headlines again. The Erie Railroad had gone belly-up, the Milwaukee Bank had suspended trading, and the New York Stock Exchange was threatening to close. Three more sizable railroad companies were barely hanging on. And forty-eight banks had failed in the last two weeks—forty of them in the South.

He rubbed his mouth. John still pestered him about setting some kind of shed on fire, then letting his sprinklers put it out. But a demonstration like that would cost money. Money he couldn't afford to spend. Yet he had to do something. If he didn't, he risked the merchant back home calling in his father's debt. And with the bank holding their mortgage, there wouldn't be a thing they could do about it.

There were already two million Americans out of work, with nowhere to go. He didn't want his family adding to their numbers. He wasn't even sure how many systems he needed to sell, though. It all depended on the size of the building and if it was a new or existing one.

He gazed out over the limitless water. In the far distance, one of the fair's whale-back steamers began to plough in his direction, its deck black with people. People coming to see this City of Delight, when all the while, the rest of the country was facing the worst depression it had ever seen.

"A glove-making machine converted
tanned hide into pairs of buttoned kid gloves,
all stitched, perfumed, and packed."

CHAPTER 17

Della couldn't believe the noise level in Machinery Hall. How did Cullen stand it? She began her trek toward the back left-hand corner, hoping she'd be able to find him within this monstrosity.

She wished she had blinders on. Every exhibit beckoned like a siren's call. Finally, she could stand it no longer. A loom weaving two dozen silk ribbons drew her. Its finished fabrics passed to an apparatus winding them into rolls. A woman darted between machines, stopping at one, correcting a fault, then setting it back in motion amid an endless array of threads.

Della forced herself to move on. She looked back and forth across the aisle as if she were watching a tennis match. A knitting machine produced yards of fabric, which transformed itself into undergarments. A glove-making machine converted tanned hide into pairs of buttoned kid gloves, all stitched, perfumed, and packed. Wood pulp became rolls of paper. Cocoa became bonbons. Gold and alloy became fountain pens.

And then she spotted him, wedged between an ornate fire wagon and an elaborate fire escape cage. He spoke to two gentlemen, pointing to the ceiling of his display, then making motions with his hands. One man inspected a spigot while another asked a question.

Cullen cocked his left ear toward him.

He wants to know about the spacing of the pipes. She willed him to hear her inner thought as she continued to read the man's questions and the two of them continued to struggle through the conversation.

The gentleman finally became too frustrated to continue. He and his companion stepped away. Another exhibitor motioned to them, giving them a steady sales pitch as he escorted them to his display. Cullen rubbed the back of his neck, then looked up at her approach. An expression of pleasure flashed across his face before quickly being replaced with polite interest.

"Hello," he shouted. "What brings you here in the middle of the day? Is everything all right?"

She smiled. "You needn't shout. I can read what you're saying."

"What?" He cupped his left ear.

Touching his arm, she went onto tiptoes and leaned in. "You needn't shout! I can read what you're saying!"

He nodded. "Lucky you."

"I came to tell you the children are practicing for a parade, so I've been given the afternoon off."

"What?"

"I've been given the afternoon off!" Goodness.

Her voice would be gone if she had to keep this up all day the way he did. "I thought I'd come see your sprinkler system!" She pointed to his display. "Can you show me how it works!"

"My sprinkler system?" He'd reverted to shouting.

She put a finger over her lips. "I can hear you."

He bounced the butt of his hand against his forehead in an oh-yes-I-forgot motion. Directing her to his display, he began to tell her about it.

His entire countenance changed. His eyes lit up, his expression became animated, his speech became so fast she had to touch his arm. "Slow down! You're talking too fast!"

His brows lifted. "I thought you could read what I'm saying."

"I can! But I also want to look at what you're pointing to!"

He squinted his eyes and cocked his head with a questioning tilt.

Leaning in, she repeated herself.

He nodded and slowed down.

The design was really quite simple and made perfect sense. Water pressure within the pipes forced a valve against a flexible diaphragm. When fire melted a solder joint, the water caused the valve to move outward until the diaphragm burst and a deluge of water poured out. She couldn't believe he hadn't sold one to every person who'd seen it. If she were a business owner, she'd certainly have bought one.

"How much are they?" she shouted.

"Depends on the size of the factory or warehouse."

"It's brilliant!"

He stared at her. His expression wasn't exactly blank, but not totally puzzled, either—something in between.

"I said, 'it's brilliant!' "

"Yes." Again, a semibaffled look. "I heard you. Thank you."

She smiled. "You're welcome." Glancing about, she spotted a side door. "It's terribly loud in here! Can we step outside?"

He studied her lips. "Outside?"

"Yes!"

Offering her his arm, he guided her through the door.

Blessed relief. "Oh my goodness, that was horrible. I don't know how you stand it. Are your ears ringing?"

"They are."

"So are mine." She searched his face. "I'm worried, Cullen. Extremely loud sounds like that can hurt your hearing, especially if the noise continues for a long time. And once you lose it, you won't ever get that portion back."

He sighed. "I don't know what I can do. I have to stay in there."

"Then you'll need to put some cotton in your ears or something."

"I can't do that. Then I won't be able to hear anyone at all. That's why I need the lip-reading lessons so much."

"What am I saying now?"

She mouthed *April*.

"April."

Teeth.

"Teeth."

Provide.

He squinted. "The pucker was in the middle, then a lip biter right after it. Do it again."

Provide.

He shook his head. "I don't know."

"Provide. I said, 'provide.' Still, that was very good."

"I've a long way to go, I'm afraid."

"True, but I think we can move to the next consonant family now."

He studied her. "That will be our fourth consonant family. Does that mean you'll teach me a set of hand gestures?"

She sucked in a breath. "Oh . . . I'd hoped you might have forgotten about that."

"I haven't."

"No, I don't suppose you have." She worried her lip. "Very well, we'll do that today. And then, as a reward, let's take the night off. No practicing puckers. No introducing peekers. Just one night viewing the fair—and you get to choose what we see."

She expected him to jump at the chance, especially considering the exhibits she'd subjected him to.

Instead, he looked down while opening and closing his pocket watch several times.

"I don't mind the practice," he said finally. "And I've been looking forward to learning the other consonant families."

"And we'll get to those tomorrow. But the truth is, I'd like a break. So today, I'll teach you some sign language and then we'll see whatever you want. How does that sound?"

No smile. No sign of excitement. She shook her head. He was such a serious student.

"Don't you ever do anything for fun?" she asked.

Tucking his watch away, he studied four sculpted lions guarding an obelisk in the South Canal. "Not usually."

She touched his arm. "Let's have some fun today, Cullen."

He gave her a sharp look, but she didn't withdraw. Every student needed to be rewarded at certain milestones.

"Why don't you quit early too?" she suggested.

"I have to be inside."

"No one's even in there. The place is like a cemetery—albeit a noisy one."

"I'm sorry. I really need to stay."

Her shoulders slumped. "All right. But you still choose what we see tonight, okay?"

He swallowed. "I suppose. If that's what you'd like."

She smiled. "That's what I'd like. Same time?"

Nodding, he turned to go.

"Oh, wait." She touched the watch pinned to her shirtwaist. "My watch quit working, so if I'm a little late, that's why."

He frowned. "What's wrong with it?"

"I don't know. It simply quit at ten-thirteen this morning, yet it's completely wound."

He held out his palm. "May I?"

"Of course." She unpinned it and handed it to him.

Turning it over in his hand, he ran his nail down the seam and popped it open, then examined its inner workings. Without a word, he removed a pocketknife from his trousers, and with a few adjustments, the gears began to turn again.

"That should do it." He closed it back up and handed it to her. "You'll need to set it again. It's . . ." He checked his watch. "Two-thirty-six."

Her lips parted. "Thank you. How did you know what was wrong?"

He shrugged. "I like to take things apart and put them back together again. Watches are among my favorites."

"Well, I appreciate it very much." She reset the

186

time, then smashed her chin to her chest while trying to pin it back on. She hated this latch. It was so hard to secure.

"Need some help?" he asked.

She looked up. "Do you mind?"

"Not at all."

She tilted her head to the side to give him more room. Furrowing his brows, he leaned in close, the now-familiar scent of Brilliantine wafting around them. She'd never noticed his eyelashes before. They weren't short and stubby, nor were they long exactly. Somewhere in between.

His fingers and knuckles brushed against her, sending a rush of chills across her skin. She sucked in a quick breath.

"Excuse me," he mumbled, a hint of red touching his cheeks.

Finally, he finished and pulled away. His eyes, a rich dark chocolate, connected with hers. She kept very still, hcr mind bcrcft of words and thoughts.

"I'll see you at the cocoa shop at four." His voice held a thread of unease and something else, something she couldn't quite put her finger on.

She hadn't meant to embarrass him. "Yes. I'll see you then. Thank you for fixing my watch."

Touching the air where his hat would be, he slipped back inside. The noise trumpeted through the open door, then diminished again as it clicked shut behind him.

• • •

"Who was *that?*" John asked, pulling cotton from his ears and leaving his post by the fire escape cage.

Cullen cupped his mouth. "Remember when I told you Vaughn insisted I take lip-reading lessons?"

Crossing his arms over his chest, John nodded, his carrot-colored hair clashing with the red firemen's shirt he wore.

"Well, that's my teacher."

Eyes widening, John glanced toward the door where she'd disappeared. "*Thnk* she'd have any objection to having two *stdnts?*"

"You want to learn to lip-read?"

"No." He wobbled his eyebrows.

Cullen shook his head. "It's all work, John."

But that wasn't entirely true. Despite his best intentions, their conversations over the past few weeks had become less one-sided. But he'd had no choice, not when she asked him endless questions about his family, his farm, and all the inventions he'd come up with over the course of his boyhood and adolescence. He'd only answered questions she specifically asked and kept those answers as succinct as possible, but she'd responded in kind and he found himself enjoying not just their conversations but also her. He'd come to know her far better than he knew most of his friends—except for Wanda.

That was the one thing they hadn't discussed. He hadn't kept Wanda a secret on purpose. He'd just tried not to encourage Della's questions. And she, of course, had never asked about that particular topic. At this point, he wasn't exactly sure how to bring it up. What would he say? *Oh, by the way, I have a woman back home that I love very much and whom I plan to marry on the last Saturday in November.*

No. It was irrelevant. It had nothing to do with him and Della. She'd been making small talk only so he could practice his lip-reading. And he'd been trying to keep things impersonal. For all he knew, Della had a man back home whom she planned to marry.

The thought gave him momentary pause.

"All work?" John asked. "Oh well, truth is, I wouldn't have come even if it weren't."

Cullen studied his friend. "And why is that?"

John tapped a clod of dirt on the floor with his boot. "'Cause there's a gal over at Crowne Pen Company who's caught my eye."

"Oh?" Cullen looked at the booth. The sales-girls were busy talking to each other. "Which one?"

"Miss Carpenter. The one in the rust-colored *gwn.*"

"The orange dress?" he asked.

John smiled. "Yeah. She's a real beauty and . . . well, I don't know, mighty special, I guess. You ought to *cm* out with us one of these nights."

"Maybe I will." Cullen pulled his attention away from the women. "So, how was your shift at the firehouse?"

John made a face. "We had to *answr* our third fire call to the Cold Storage *Bldng*."

"The one with the ice-skating rink?" he asked.

"Yeah. The iron smokestack *rnning* up its center ends several feet short of the tower, leaving nothing but wood in the hood of the cupola."

"That's insane. Why haven't they fixed it?"

"Our *chf* has lodged a formal request, but nothing's been done yet." He dragged a hand down his face. "It doesn't take us long to put the fires out. They're more annoying than *nythng* else."

"Because there have been so many?"

"Because it's a heck of a *clmb* up to the top of that thing. And then once we get there, we have to drag hoses up with our ropes." He grinned. "At least I'm *fghtng* fires, though."

"So you are."

A group of ladies approached John's booth. Perking up, he excused himself and scurried over, helping them into the cage. Giggling and flashing their fans, the women squealed as he lifted them to the top. Once they descended, they begged him to put on his helmet. He was all too happy to oblige.

"If you think taking your potential clients outside is going to thwart me, you're *mstaken*."

Turning around, Cullen tried to keep his expression blank. Bulenberg. He'd claimed to be twenty-five, but his face was as smooth as a baby's backside. Cullen would bet he wasn't a day over nineteen.

Over the course of the last two months, Cullen had watched him. Tried to read his lips. Tried to figure out what it was he said to keep his visitors so long in his booth.

Maybe it was simply a matter of hearing. Bulenberg could hear. Cullen couldn't. And for every minute they politely stood in Cullen's booth, they'd linger in Bulenberg's for three more.

"I don't know what you're talking about, Bulenberg."

Sneering, the boy pointed toward the door Cullen and Della had stepped through. "I saw you. You showed that lady your system. She was very enthusiastic, then you whisked her out the side door so I wouldn't have a chance to talk to her. Just like you did that insurance man."

Cullen lifted his brows. "You think a woman wants to buy my sprinkler system?"

"Don't act all innocent. She's probably here with her father or something and will go running to him with tales of your sprinklers."

Cullen harrumphed.

"Roll your eyes all you want, McNamara. But the truth is, we're two months into the fair and you haven't sold a *sngl* one. And taking candidates out the side door won't stop them from eventually coming to me." Bulenberg looked him up and down. "Maybe you'd best run back to your farm where your mechanical 'genius' is better appreciated."

He could squash him with two blows. But he wasn't sure what the commission's views were on that, and he couldn't afford to be dishonorably discharged.

Instead, he stared. Hard.

"I think your bark is worse than your bite, McNamara."

"Care to find out?"

Tsking, Bulenberg returned to his booth. "Just don't try it again or I'll come right out there with you."

I'd like to see you try, Cullen thought. Still, he wished he could afford that demonstration. All of the fair's exhibits had finally been installed and completed, so the commission might be open to a new query. But he couldn't afford the materials, so why waste their time and his?

WOODED ISLAND

"They meandered down winding paths,
every bend bringing new delights."

CHAPTER 18

Della and Cullen cleaned up their dinner boxes, then left Blooker's Cocoa House.

"I thought we'd go to the Wooded Island for our hand gestures," she said. "I believe you said there were places where no one would see us?"

He nodded. "That's what I've been told."

"Well then, let's see what we can find."

The canals and lagoons cut the Wooded Island off from all main thoroughfares. The only way to reach it was over high-backed bridges every bit as beautiful as the Parisian ones she'd seen in lithographs.

Guarding the one they now crossed was a statue of a grim-faced Indian, his sinewy, muscular body not unlike that of the man beside her. She closed her eyes, indulging for a brief second in the image that thought conjured up.

At the peak of the bridge, Cullen paused, turning them toward the rail. He said nothing, but he didn't need to. On every side they were surrounded by palatial architecture, beautiful vistas, and marble-like sculptures. The colossal appearance of the buildings made them seem like mountain ranges, dominating and belittling everything around them. She couldn't imagine anything but the New Jerusalem surpassing it in beauty.

Sadness crept over her, for in another four months, this would all be a deserted stretch of low-lying ground. Before the first rendering had occurred, before the first nail had been hammered, the decision had been made. Instead of continuing in perpetuity, come November, the entire fair would be torn down and destroyed.

Suppressing a sigh, she watched a blue gondola glide by, maneuvered by two Venetian men whose olive skin seemed even darker against their colorful costumes. The boat's narrow prow cut through the crystal lagoon waters, its keel barely touching the surface. Gold ornaments and velvet hangings dragged lazily behind it in the water.

She would love to ride in one. The vantage point had to be spectacular. But they were way too expensive for her purse.

"You ready?" he asked.

Stepping back, she allowed him to guide her onto the island. How quiet it was. Only the sound of distant music, the ripple of waves, or an occasional whispering couple broke the solitude.

They meandered down winding paths, every bend bringing new delights. Bubbling fountains called out to birds. Glimpses of swans, ducks, and pelicans could be caught along the sedgy banks, while beds and beds of flowers flooded the senses. Even the lagoon's wind was soft, barely shaking the petals of larkspurs, daisies, sweet

195

williams, and marigolds. A teasing breath of roses tickled her nose, though she'd yet to see any.

Cullen opened a low gate. Flowering honeysuckles trailed along its borders, releasing a new medley of sweet odors. But it was the perfume of roses, now strong, now faint, that captured her attention. Grass-bordered paths brought them closer and closer, and then she could see them. A wall of velvet color. The garlanded fence of roses stood a good eight feet high.

They slipped inside its labyrinthal design and came upon little trees covered with red and pink varieties. Low showy bushes held dozens of yellow ones, deep golden hues at their hearts. Some roses tumbled about recklessly and some leaned against little sticks, holding up one pristine blossom. There were other flowers too, but the roses upstaged them all.

Cullen led her to a bench. "Will this be all right? We'll be hidden from view unless someone comes right up on us."

She looked around. It was a dead end in the labyrinth. Roses, grass, and cool earth surrounded them. Slices of sunbeams slipped through openings of the garlanded fence, dappling her with warmth.

"It's lovely." Smoothing her skirt beneath her, she took in her surroundings. She loved roses. It was the scent she kept in her satchet, the scent she dabbed behind her ears, the scent she washed her body with.

By degrees, her attention was drawn from the brilliance of nature's bounty to the splendor of the man beside her. His long legs stretched out in front of him, ankles crossed, toes gently tapping. He slouched back, one elbow on the armrest, one elbow on the back of the bench, his arm dangling between them.

"Cullen?"

"Hmmm?"

"How is it that a farmer decides to invent an automatic fire sprinkler?"

He gave an almost imperceptible shrug of his shoulder. "Too many hours behind the plow with nothing else to think of, I suppose."

Several yards away, a brown songbird bathed itself in a gurgling fountain.

"Oh, I understand how you might have thought of the system," she said. "But very few people take their dreams and turn them into reality."

"I'd have been a lot better off leaving it in the dream phase."

Tilting her head, she studied him. His face gave no clue as to what he meant.

"Why do you say that?" she asked.

He squinted into the distance. "Because it's true."

"Why?"

"It's a long story."

"So give me the short version."

He blew out a puff of air. "I drew up the schematics when I was eighteen or thereabouts. Once the harvest was in and winter came, I began experimenting. Built a prototype. Installed it in our cowshed. Set it on fire—and the whole thing burned to the ground."

Her eyes widened. "Did your parents know you were going to do that? Were the cows inside?"

Drawing up his mouth in disgust, he shook his head. "It was my dad's idea. He's always given me more credit than I deserve. We hauled everything out, including the cows, then put a torch to it. So stupid."

She slowly straightened. "Is that the same system you have in Machinery Hall?"

He gave her an exasperated look. "Of course not."

Raising a brow, she waited, but he offered no more. Barely suppressing the urge to roll her eyes, she folded her hands in her lap. "Then where did the one in Machinery Hall come from?"

"I made it."

"I'm aware of that." She tapped her thumbs together. "I'm wondering what you did between the cowshed and Machinery Hall."

A slight smile touched his mouth. "It was a simpler time back then. Farming was booming and had been for fifteen years. So Dad wanted to hire some fellows and send me off to Boston where many of the best inventors and scientists lived." A distant quacking of ducks filtered through their wall of roses.

"I refused, of course," he said. "I'd go only if I could pay for it."

"And did you?"

He nodded. "I had this steam engine I'd built. I made money going from farm to farm threshing clover, hauling loads, cutting cornstalks, sawing wood, grinding feed, and whatever else they'd pay me for, all with the help of my steam engine."

"And then you went to Boston?" she asked.

"And then I went to Boston."

She smiled. "And you experienced marvelous success, then brought your product to the World's Fair." It was a statement more than a question.

"I failed miserably and returned home by year's end with my tail tucked between my legs."

Her lips parted. "What happened?"

"I made a bargain with a piano-factory owner. If he'd let me sleep in his basement, I'd install my system in his factory."

"Did something happen?" She bit her lip. "Did his factory burn down?"

"Not right away. His factory had my second attempt at a sprinkler system. Since then, I've improved on it even more. Much more."

"In what way?"

"In every way. My third attempt consisted of a

perforated distributor with a brass cap soldered over it, but it wasn't very sensitive because the fusible joint had contact with the water inside. So then I made a similar one, but the distributor was a rotating slotted arrangement. My last attempt is the one I have now. I hollowed the base to separate the solder joint from direct contact with the water inside and changed the pipe connect to a male half-inch thread."

She had no idea what he was talking about, but for the first time he began to show animation in his face. He was still slouched on the bench. Still had his elbow on the back of the bench with his arm hanging between them. Still had his ankles crossed. But the toes of his shoes tapped each other with a rapid beat and his face had come to life.

"Did you reinstall it in the piano factory?" she asked.

"I'd planned to, but before I could, I accidentally started a fire with my chemicals. It quickly spread. The sprinkler system—which by then I'd discovered had problems—didn't work. The whole thing burned to the ground."

She took a quick breath. "Was anyone hurt?"

"No, praise God. But he lost everything. His entire inventory."

Two birds played chase by the fountain, diving, then soaring, then wheeling to the left.

"I'm sorry," she said.

"Not as sorry as I am. Anyway, he sent me packing. I went back to farming and have been there ever since."

"What about the new system? Did you ever install it anywhere?"

With a pained look, he shook his head. "Only some sheds I'd tested it on in Boston."

"It worked, though."

"Like a beauty."

During the entire tale, he'd hardly looked at her. She'd hardly taken her eyes off him.

Smoothing up the hair at the nape of her neck, she faced forward. The toes of his boots continued to tap. With each movement, his thighs shifted ever so slightly. She gave them a surreptitious look. They were huge. Almost the size of her waist.

Images of his body bared from the trousers up again flooded her mind. The breadth of his shoulders, the bulges along his chest, the flatness of his stomach, the mountain of muscle when he'd flexed his arm.

She'd relived those moments a thousand times. When she broke her fast. When she told the children stories of knights and princes. When she slipped under her covers at night.

Neither of them spoke of it. Ever. Both acted as if it had never happened. The only measurable change was the use of their Christian names.

Did he think of those moments the way she did?

Did he think of her at all other than as a means to an end?

If he did, he never gave her any indication of it. He touched her only if she needed assistance, then immediately released her. He never stood closer than he should. His fingers never brushed her accidentally. He never watched her when he thought she wasn't looking.

Yet she was attuned to his every move, subtle or otherwise. She thought of him constantly. She looked forward to their evenings with great anticipation. She took extra care with her toilette.

All for naught. Even now, he didn't fully extend his arm on the bench, nor did his trousers touch so much as a smidgen of her skirt.

She turned her head and looked at him. How could he not feel the undertow? It was as if the gravitational pull had moved from the center of the earth to the center of him.

Yet she could do nothing. Only men had the privilege of acting on their feelings. Females had to wait. And wait. And wait. And then it seemed as if the only men who did act on their feelings were the ones who were the least appealing to her.

Just once, she wished she were a man. What freedom. What luxury. What fun. For if she were allowed the privileges of a man, she'd take his hand and bring it to her lips.

Of a sudden, his toes stopped tapping. His body

tensed. With deliberate casualness, he removed his elbow from the bench and drew his feet in.

She continued to stare. She might not have the freedom to act on her feelings, but she could do her best to prod him along.

Clearing his throat, he sat up, then rested his elbows on his knees.

Still, she stared.

He clapped his hands together, the sound loud in the quiet of the garden. "So what's the first thing you'd like to show me?"

You'd be quite surprised, she thought.

He took a cautious glance at her over his shoulder. "Would you like me to go through my alphabet?"

She snapped together her first two fingers and her thumb.

He slowly sat up. "Does that mean no?" He snapped his fingers and thumb together.

With a nod of her head, she made one knocking gesture with her fist.

A corner of his mouth lifted. "And yes." He knocked in the air.

"Only once." She demonstrated. "You knock only once when you say yes, and your fist is in the *a* position."

He tried it.

"Very good. Let's do it *again.*" She held one palm up and brought four fingers from her other hand down onto it. *"Again."*

"No, yes, again." He did the signs perfectly.

"That's right." She resituated herself on the bench. "Now, I'm going to teach you some vocabulary words, then we'll make some sentences with them."

Within half an hour, he could use the language of signs to say many of the basics, including, *Hello. It's nice to meet you. My name is C-U-L-L-E-N. What's your name?*

"This is much easier than reading lips," he said.

"Yes, but you must remember not to use it in public."

"I'll remember."

"Now you say something." She put her hands in her lap.

What do you do?

I'm a teacher.

He gave a quick shake of his head. "I understood 'teach.' What was that last thing you did?"

"It's the sign for *person.* You'd be far more familiar with the way men gesture when they refer to females." She drew an hourglass with her hands. "In the language of signs, you do the same thing for *person,* but without all the curves. Just two straight lines." She demonstrated.

One side of his mouth curved up. "I like this one a lot better." He made an hourglass.

She raised a brow. "That's not a real sign. This is female." She touched her thumb to her chin then brought down her hand. "But we digress. 'Teacher' is what I was signing. *Teach,* then *person.*"

His smile grew. He signed, *You-are-my-teach* and an hourglass.

Her cheeks warmed. Her mind went blank. She couldn't think of one new gesture to show him. "That's probably enough for now."

Placing his fingers near his lips, he moved them forward and down in her direction, as if he were blowing her a kiss. *Thank you.*

She gave a slight nod.

His face sobered. "I mean that. I'll be very careful with this knowledge."

A restless bird chirped from one of the vines, its green leaves softly stirring in the faint evening air.

Thank you, she signed.

A loose pink rose tumbled toward him. Instinctively, he swooped it up, then cradled it in his palm and examined it with a startled expression. Looking up, he extended it out to her.

She cupped her hands. Placing one of his below hers, he rolled the flower into her hands, barely shaking off the curled petal of the fullest-blown rose in all the garden.

CHAPTER 19

*D*on't think about her, he chanted to himself. Shucking off his clothes, he prepared for bed, then stood in front of the mirror. His suspender lines were fading but still visible. Pushing aside all other thoughts, he went through the puckers, smilers, and wides, then the pinchers, lip biters, and lifters three times each. He tried not to notice her handwriting or to think he was touching something she'd touched first.

Determinedly, he shifted his thoughts to Wanda. Sitting in bed, he wrote a long letter to her about the buildings, the exhibits, the statues, and the people. He told her about the wax figures in bridal attire, the tailors who'd taken credit for Adam's and Eve's leafy coverings, and the shoe with turtles' claws protruding from its toes. He told her of his concern over the struggling economy and how a great many of the exhibitors were having trouble enticing customers, not just him.

He went through her two most recent letters and marked out all of Hodge's comments, then reread the letters without them. They offered lukewarm responses to what he'd seen at the fair, and then her frustration with his father for making Cullen go in the first place. She told of a neighbor whose farm had been taken away by the bank, then blithely went on about things she'd done to prepare for their wedding.

Last, she brought up the smokehouse. Nothing overt that Hodge would be able to detect, but certainly enough for Cullen to read between the lines.

> I went to the smokehouse today to fetch some bacon fer Ma. I lingered there, letting my eyes look at all that meat. It smelt mighty good. So strong. Made me light-headed fer a minute. Whenever I play hide-and-seek with the youngins, that's where I go. It's my hidin' place. Especially at night.

Then, as with every other letter that had passed between them, she ended it with her devotion to him and her deep, undying love.

Closing his eyes, he placed it against his nose. But there was no flowery scent, nothing that might bring images of her to mind. Of course, the only scent she wore was that of lye soap. But even that would have provided him a bit of comfort. Folding the parchment in half, he re-creased the edge and slipped it into the sturdy envelope.

Guilt hovered along the periphery of his mind. Something had happened tonight on that bench with Della. Something strong and elemental that

207

he needed to avoid at all costs. He placed his head in his hands. He loved the signs. Couldn't wait to learn more. But that island, that garden, that tucked-away bench was a dangerous place. Especially with the way he'd been feeling.

Tucking Wanda's letter beneath his pillow, he blew out his candle and slid his feet under the covers. Lord willing, he'd dream about her instead of the woman who'd infiltrated every corner of his mind during the day and, more recently, during the night.

COLD STORAGE BUILDING

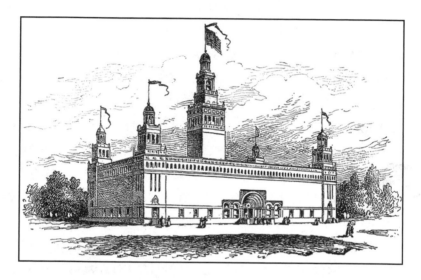

"Tall parapets stood on each of its
four corners, topped with flags snapping in
a northeasterly direction. A steeple-like tower
three times the height of the parapets rose
from the roof's center."

CHAPTER 20

Cullen's height allowed him to see over the heads of the crowd as Dr. Jastrow, in the name of psychology, administered various tests on Helen Keller. The laboratory-like room held a variety of instruments, books, tablets, and charts. The tolerant young lady stood at the front of the room and made no complaints when Dr. Jastrow applied instruments to measure the sensitivity of her fingers and palm, had her feel a series of wires and rank them in order from roughest to smoothest, and had her speak Longfellow's "Psalm of Life" as rapidly as possible with her fingers, which fascinated Cullen.

But what captivated him most was the method by which she "listened" to Dr. Jastrow's instructions. She arranged her hand against his face in a way that somehow allowed her to feel his words. Yet an explanation of this was never given. The scientist was way too busy scribbling notes about the results of his tests.

When Miss Keller had completed her sign recitation, Dr. Jastrow announced she had formed nearly seven letters per second, undoubtedly the utmost capacity for any sign reader to read.

The crowd clapped in approval, and Miss Keller immediately smiled. Cullen realized with some amazement that shc'd felt the vibrations of the applause.

Leaning down, he whispered to Della, "Were you able to follow along as she signed Longfellow's 'Psalm'?"

"It was very fast. If I hadn't been familiar with it, I'd have struggled, I'm sure."

Her hat was larger than what she normally wore and matched a white, lacy gown he'd not seen before. Rows of tiny ruffles graced her upper sleeves, then formed a V-shape across her chest. With every movement, every breath, they gave a subtle flutter. Beneath them, the gown hugged her waist and hips, much like the hourglass shape he'd made with his hands.

The crowd began to chatter as they waited for the next test.

"Is that a new gown?" he asked.

She glanced up, surprise and pleasure touching her face. "It's not new. I've just been saving it for the warmer weather."

"It's very becoming." And it was. So different from her typical skirt and shirtwaist. Made him think of the seaside, laughing children, and elegant women.

The crowd quieted as Dr. Jastrow made his concluding remarks.

"Before we dismiss, we have another distinguished guest I'd like to briefly introduce you to. Considering he is best known for inventing the telephone, you might not be aware he is also a long time advocate for the deaf. Please welcome Dr. Alexander Graham Bell."

Exclamations and applause accompanied Dr. Bell's approach. Shaped much like a cracker barrel, he stepped to the front and tugged on his vest. A head of puffed-up white hair matched a large white beard.

"Thank you." He told of his delight with Helen Keller, briefly spoke of his deaf wife, then revealed his grave concerns about the use of sign language. Last, he mentioned his course for teachers of the deaf at the Boston University School of Oratory.

"As a matter of fact," he said, "one of my graduates is here at the fair instructing young deaf students in the Children's Building. If you've not been to their exhibit, I suggest you make it a high priority. And be sure to ask for Miss Adelaide Wentworth—a name to pay attention to as we strive to liberate the deaf through lip-reading and stamp out sign language once and for all."

Della flushed with pleasure. Cullen assumed Bell hadn't seen her in the audience, otherwise he most likely would have pointed her out.

As the crowd broke up, she touched Cullen's arm. "Come. I want to introduce you to Dr. Bell."

He pulled back, his gaze shooting to the front.

Dr. Bell, whose name was carved on one of the tablets above Machinery Hall, was holding a lively conversation with Miss Keller and her teacher, Miss Sullivan. "He's a bit occupied right now, and I don't think he realizes you're even here."

"That won't matter a bit." She waved her hand in a dismissive gesture. "He came by the Children's Building to see me and has promised to introduce me to Miss Keller at some point. May as well be now."

Clearing his throat, he took a half step back. "You go ahead. I'll wait just outside the door."

Her face wilted. "You don't want to meet them?"

"I, I wouldn't know what to say."

"What about, 'How do you do. So nice to meet you'?"

He immediately thought of their sign-language lesson in the rose garden. She'd taught him those phrases. Her hands moving in a beautiful panto-mime. Graceful, supple hands that had become way too alluring.

He continued walking backward and indicated the exit with his thumb. "No, you go on. I'll be right outside the door. Take your time."

She looked to the front of the room, then back at him. "You're sure?"

"Positive." Turning, he quickly joined the rest of the crowd.

She didn't make him wait long, and her excitement over meeting Miss Keller was infectious. "She's been given special permission to touch some of the exhibits so she can 'see' them—even the African diamonds. And she's so sweet, Cullen."

"She spoke to you?"

"She did."

"And she put her hand on your face while you were talking?"

"Yes, it was—"

Ringing gongs, piercing whistles, and the clattering of hooves blasted them from behind. "Clear the track!"

Cullen grabbed Della by the waist and swung her to the edge of the thoroughfare.

Big, powerful horses leaped by pulling a fire engine, its driver half-crouched in the seat. Swift hose carriages, rattling hook-and-ladder trucks, well-secured water towers, and patrol wagons loaded with firemen followed close behind.

"That's John's battalion," Cullen said, pointing.

"What?"

Nearby guards shouted themselves hoarse warning pedestrians to move out of the way. Boys in blue who hawked guidebooks hurried from their posts in the wake of the engines.

Grabbing Della's elbow, Cullen quickened their pace. "John's on duty today."

"John?"

"John Ransom. The fireman who works the booth beside mine. I've told you about him."

She nodded. "I remember."

"He's so proud of the work he does. It would please him to no end if he found out I saw him in action." He stopped suddenly. "Is that okay? I know you said you wanted to go to the Midway Plaisance."

"It's fine. We can always go afterward." Gasping, she pointed. "Cullen, look."

Turning around, he scanned the horizon. The Cold Storage Building's central tower had a small jet of flame dancing about its head.

"This will be the fourth time that tower's caught fire," he said.

"The fourth time?" She studied it for a moment. "It doesn't look too serious, does it?"

"No, it looks more like a flame that comes from the chimney of a rolling mill." He quickly guided her through the Court of Honor.

A second alarm sounded. Buildings began to empty. Passengers in gondolas urged their crews to change their course and follow the crowd. Curious fairgoers spread the word—the smoke-stack of the Cold Storage Building was on fire.

Releasing her elbow, he clasped her hand. "Hold on tight. I don't want to lose you. All right?"

"All right."

By the time they reached the Cold Storage Building, streams of people poured around every corner. Straight ahead, a company of firemen in red shirts uncoiled hoses from their engines and wagons in a nonchalant manner. If it weren't for yellow flames in the cupola, Cullen would have assumed the department was out on dress parade doing a demonstration for the crowds.

He scanned the men, finally spotting John. "There he is." He pointed. "The short one. See him?"

She furrowed her brows, then smiled. "Yes. I think so. He has a number one on his helmet?"

"Right. All the boys in Company One do."

Another group leaned a five-story ladder against the roof of the building.

Tall parapets stood on each of its four corners, topped with flags snapping in a northeasterly direction. A steeple-like tower three times the height of the parapets rose from the roof's center. On its side, huge painted letters spelled out "Hercules Ice-Skating Rink." Above it a railed ledge. And above that, the fire.

Della touched his sleeve. "Who's the man in the white helmet?"

"That's Chief Murphy. He and Chief Swenie are in charge of all the fair's battalions."

"Fitzgerald," Murphy shouted. "Go up to the cupola with Companies One and Two and we'll hoist some hoses to you. If the fire gets too hot, there are lifelines hanging on the west side of the tower."

Cullen glanced at the left face of the tower. Painters' ropes hung from a ledge near the top all the way down to within a few feet of the roof.

"Pshaw," said Fitzgerald. "We'll put this one out just like we did the others."

Companies One and Two headed toward the building's entrance, John becoming lost in their midst.

"There's a winding staircase inside," Cullen explained to her. "They'll have to climb clear up there with their axes, ropes, and everything."

"What about the ice-skaters?" she asked.

"The rink was listed in the paper as one of this week's closed exhibits. It was having mechanical problems, I think, so there shouldn't be anyone in there other than a few guards, carpenters, and engineers. They'll evacuate at the first sign of trouble, if they haven't already."

On the ground, Chief Murphy slung a coiled rope over his head and shoulder, then mounted a ladder that stretched five stories high. His men followed suit. The moment they reached the roof, they secured their ropes to cornices and called for hoses and more ladders.

The crowd swelled. Columbian Guards in blue-braided uniforms began to push them back in order to make room for the firemen.

Cullen glanced at Della. "You stay close. The crowd is starting to grow."

"I will. And we're right here at the front. Plenty of room."

He thought he'd have plenty of room on opening day too. This group didn't compare to that one, but even so, he didn't want to subject her to anything like that again.

A loud cheer erupted from the crowd.

Cullen glanced up at the building. Black silhouettes of about thirty firemen appeared on the uppermost ledge of the tower just below the cupola and fire. John was easy to spot, short as he was. Kneeling down, he began to haul up a hose attached to a painter's rope. The man beside him let his rope down.

The flames consuming the crown of the tower grew. Pieces of blazing wood dropped inside the inner walls of the tower.

As there was scant room to work, one of the men fastened his hose to the balcony with a rope before bringing up another one. Cullen marveled at their calm confidence. The ledge was a good hundred feet higher than the roof. The only thing between them and a ten-story drop was that bit of cornice molding along the edges.

John captured a hose, released it from the rope, and stood in readiness, as did several others. One of them cupped a hand around his mouth and shouted to Chief Murphy. Cullen wondered if he was their leader, Fitzgerald.

"Cullen," Della gasped. "Look."

He followed the direction of her finger. Trails of smoke slithered through crevices around the painted "Ice-Skating" sign. Unease began to creep through him. Something below John was on fire. He hoped it didn't block the winding staircase the men had planned to descend.

Chief Murphy leaned over the edge of the roof. "A hundred-twenty-five pounds, boys," he shouted to the engines on the ground.

At the command for water, the crowd whistled and waved their hats. But Murphy's back was to the tower, making him unaware of the new menace. *Turn around,* Cullen thought.

Finally, he did. Pandemonium struck as he and the crowd caught sight of the increasing smoke underneath the men. Firemen on the roof shouted to their comrades on the tower. Spectators screeched their warnings. The men on the ledge either didn't hear or shrugged it off.

Leaning over, Cullen put his mouth close to Della's ear. "There are numerous escape lines hanging from the tower to the roof below. And look." He pointed to Engine One on the ground. "They're almost ready for action. They'll pump water up before you—"

A deafening explosion cut off his sentence. Flames and thick rolling fumes erupted from a portico halfway up the tower, igniting its staff-covered walls.

Women screamed, their shrieks rising above

the roaring and crackling of the flames. Della slammed her hands over her mouth. Cullen sucked in his breath, gooseflesh skittering down his spine.

The firemen on the roof who had shouted warnings mere seconds before stood frozen in silent shock.

Through a veil of smoke, John and the men in his company scurried back and forth on their prison ledge, looking for a means of escape.

Above them, the dome burned furiously, its cupola white with heat. Below, the portico blazed on all four sides, each archway a seething, open furnace door.

There would be no getting down the staircase, for the interior of the tower emitted black smoke streaked with cyclones of flame. Escaping down the painters' ropes, however, would mean sliding right through the fire before reaching the other end.

A third alarm sounded. Columbian Guards shouted at the crowd across from them who blocked the thoroughfare, then urged them to make way for more engines.

Chief Murphy barked an order to the men on the ground. They sprang to the hook-and-ladder wagons, then began the slow process of hoisting big ladders up to the roof.

Cullen swung his attention back to John. There was no time. Not near enough to wait on those ladders. And even if they could get them up, they wouldn't be anywhere close to ten stories high.

One black silhouette grasped the hose he'd tied to the cornice and swung over the balcony.

Not a sound issued forth as the crowd held its collective breath.

Fire enveloped the man momentarily before he shot down to the bottom of the hose, then made a short leap to the roof. His clothes were on fire, but fellow firefighters rushed to assist him.

A roar of approval shook the ground as hope sprung anew.

"Was that John?" Della asked.

Cullen shook his head. "No, he's in the middle." He pointed. "See him?"

"Yes."

Thousands of voices called to the men, begging them to slide.

Go, John, he urged. *Go.*

But he and the other men hesitated. And in those precious seconds, a gust of wind swept flames around the hoses, melted the rubber, and burned them in two. They coiled down like dead snakes, then disappeared into the fire.

The hair along Cullen's arms and neck rose.

In a black knot, John and the others clustered about one man. By his gestures, it was evident he was issuing orders.

Cullen looked at the painters' ropes, still intact. *Go,* he begged. *Quit talking and go.*

Before his thought was complete, the lines of the ropes began to part like cotton string in a gas jet. Their lengths, unable to withstand the heat, disintegrated to a scant few feet.

He groaned, hardly aware of the crowd doing the same. Della pressed herself against his side, the fragrance of roses intermingling with the smell of smoke. He encircled her waist with his arm.

Please, God, he thought. *Get them down safely.*

With great caution, one by one, they turned and crawled around the balcony to the west side, the flames almost touching their hands and feet. There was no hurrying, no panic. Every man waited his turn.

John insisted another go before him. Then another. And another. Until he was at the end of the line.

Anger surged through Cullen. He knew he shouldn't begrudge the men in front of John. He knew why John had let them pass. He was unmarried. Had no children. And was the least among them.

But Cullen wanted him down. Selfish as it was, he wanted his friend off that blasted tower.

The multitude stilled during the men's perilous journey, then cheered on its completion. But the men were no better off there. The flames had worked their way upward all around the tower.

They would have to make a choice. Either leap a hundred feet to the roof or let flames consume them.

CHAPTER 21

Cullen had managed, with a herculean effort, to suppress thoughts of his mother, but now it was impossible. He'd come over only to watch John put out a fire he'd conquered three times before. Never had Cullen dreamed a tragedy of this magnitude would unfold.

Once again he was twelve, standing helpless outside a mill in Charlotte as fire engulfed every door, every window, every possible means of escape.

She'd gone in to give a blanket she crocheted to a man whose wife had just had a baby. Cullen had been thrilled to be free of her supervision, only too anxious to break away and run to the blacksmith's. The man would often allow Cullen to work the bellows, and he'd raced off, never thinking it would be the last glimpse he'd have of his mother.

A deep, aching pain crushed him in a vicious grip. His throat began to close.

"Look!" a man shouted, bringing Cullen back to the present.

He made himself take a deep, calming breath, laced though it was with smoke.

A silhouette on the tower stripped off his helmet and spun it down to his companions on the roof. It was a mute appeal for those below to make one more effort at a rescue. Another helmet joined his.

Several firemen on the roof picked up a hose. The crowd cheered, but Cullen remained silent. He'd seen fire engines before. Knew the limitations of their hoses.

The jets activated. A thin stream of water lifted its head, barely reaching two-thirds of the way up.

Della moaned. The man beside them cursed. Cullen withdrew inside himself. He didn't pray. He didn't cry. He didn't feel.

Closer and closer the men huddled. One broke free of the rest, pushing his way through the band of comrades. He grasped one of them by the hand, then yanked him forward and threw his arms about his neck.

Brothers, Cullen thought. John had said two of the men in his company were brothers. And now they said their good-byes.

The self-imposed shell around Cullen's heart began to fracture.

One after the other hugged their friends on the ledge. They ruffled John's helmet, grasped his shoulder, squeezed him close.

Tears streamed down the faces of the firemen on the ground. The crowd prayed and cursed in turn. Della openly wept, her face drawn with horror.

Firemen on the roof frantically whipped off

coats, vests, and even trousers to form a make-shift catching net.

Clanging ambulances and multiple fire engines tore the crowd asunder. Panic-stricken guards struggled to form lines and keep the people back. British soldiers, Russian soldiers, and French marines in disordered uniforms all materialized out of the throng. Without needing direction, they faced the mob and forced an opening where before there had been none.

The crowd cheered the soldiers and every new fire engine that came from the city.

Incoming horses shone with white lather, barely able to pull their engines to the finish line. Groups of firemen, guards, hospital guides, and ambulance attendants met them with canvas cots, stretchers, and stoic expressions.

People from all over the world in a dozen languages bemoaned the fate of the men on the tower. Positioned as he was, Cullen could see the fear and disbelief on the faces of the truckmen just arriving.

Would his sprinkler system have prevented the tragedy? He wasn't sure. He'd not tested it for explosions like this. But it might have helped. Perhaps bought just enough time for John and the others to slide down those ropes.

One of the men on the tower disentangled himself from the tight knot their group had formed. Reaching down, he grabbed a rope.

No, Cullen thought, for the line had been burned and couldn't be more than fifteen feet long.

The fireman went over the edge, slid down the rope, and dangled at its end for what seemed a lifetime.

Cullen tensed. The crowd didn't move. Not a sound could be heard other than the crackling flames licking the man's feet.

Cullen glanced at John and realized the fire blocked his view. He and the other men made large gestures with their hands, as if asking one another what had happened to the man who still held on mere feet below them.

Raising his knees, the man on the rope propped his boots against the wall, then sprang away from it, releasing the rope at the same time. He cartwheeled through space, his outline sharp against the whitewashed wall.

The people sent up a roar of hurrahs.

The firemen below scrambled to follow his trajectory with their net.

The man ripped right through it, rebounded off the roof, then settled in a heap.

The sound of impact could be heard even over the fire. The crowd jumped at the crash. Confusion ensued as everyone spoke at once. Then, when realization hit, shrieks, cries, and curses abounded.

Cullen slid his eyes closed.

Della shrank into him and turned her face away.

He needed to get her out of there. "Let's go."

She shook her head, tears streaming down her face. "We're not going anywhere in this crowd."

Sure enough, they were packed in from behind. Even if they made it to the opposite edge, the guards weren't letting anyone past the barricade.

"Are you okay?" he asked.

She swiped her tears. "Yes. I can't watch, though."

Before he could gather her close and shield her from the tragedy, the woman in front of them crumbled. Extending his arms, he barely managed to catch her before she hit the ground.

"Make room. Quickly." Della nudged those around them until they opened enough space for him to lay the woman in.

"Are you okay?" he asked Della.

Nodding, she crouched down, then removed the woman's hat and loosened her collar. He stood back up, relieved Della had something to temporarily occupy her mind.

The men on the tower crowded around the rope, assuming it would carry them to safety.

"No!" Cullen shouted before he realized he'd spoken out loud.

Della jerked her head up.

He tried to mask his distress but felt sure she could see it.

Swallowing, she returned her attention to the unconscious woman on the ground.

A second man slid down. Caught unawares by the shortened length, he plummeted like a leaden ball through the fire, then right through the thin roof and into the caldron of flames below. He'd scarcely let loose of the cord when another skimmed down, his flight ending as he lodged into debris on the roof.

Too fast to count, firemen skated down the cord with heart-rending regularity. As each figure appeared outlined against the tower, Cullen's gut clenched.

Men sobbed and averted their gazes. Women clung to posts and supports, hiding their faces in their hands, then screaming whenever a groan from the crowd announced another had dropped.

All had taken the plunge but four. Standing, they huddled together, John still among them.

Cullen didn't know whether to rejoice or be even more horrified, for he knew the men finally realized what had happened to the others.

The woman on the ground recovered enough to sit up, but not stand. Della handed her a fan, then went from her to another who'd fallen to her knees with hands clasped, screaming hysterically.

Cullen followed closely behind Della, offering his help, but she shooed him away. Still, he kept her within arm's length. He didn't want to lose her in the crowd, especially under these circumstances.

The space cleared by the guards continued to fill with patrol wagons and ambulances from the city. Fire engines chugged and pounded. Yards of hose lay in zigzagged rows. Men from the hospital service grouped around little red banners. A layer of soot and horror frosted it all.

It didn't seem real. Had it just been yesterday he and John laughed over some joke? Had it only been this morning when John nudged him again about a demonstration of his system? That he stopped just short of saying his feelings for the Crowne Pen lady were becoming serious? Was the woman in question even here, or was she still in Machinery Hall, blithely unaware of the tragedy unfolding?

A child sobbed. Hushing him, the mother held the boy's head against her neck, bouncing, rocking, and crying with him. Cullen thought about the families of the firefighters. The wives, the children, the brothers, the sisters, the mothers, the fathers who had no idea their loved ones would not be returning home.

It was too much. Too much to take in all at once.

The flames grew more savage, fanned by the wind and fed by the combustible material that made up every building in the fair.

White powder from the plaster covered the people, the ground, the buildings. Billowing black smoke blotted out the blue sky that had been crisp and clear just thirty minutes before.

John and the three remaining men began to rig up a line, tying one burned remnant of rope to another, but its length was still far too short. They secured the knotted rope to the ledge, and the first man clambered over. He dropped straight down. The second came down sideways. The third just outright jumped.

John was the only man left.

Cullen couldn't breathe. Tears poured down his face. He thought of the sisters John had told him about. He'd been the only son, yet he had left farming to strike out on his own.

Grief squeezed Cullen's heart. Who would tell John's family? What was John thinking right now?

As if sensing the question, John threw his pocketbook to a comrade on the roof, then pantomimed a handshake. All alone and silhouetted against the tower, he clasped his own hand, then struck his heart. A clear message of deep affection for those who would survive him.

Cullen swiped a sleeve across his eyes and questioned God. Again. How could He let such atrocities occur?

His mother's image flashed before him. Had she died of asphyxiation or from the flames themselves? Had she tried to send him and his father a parting message? Had her last thoughts been of them or of horror?

The tower began to rock. Grasping the flaming rope, John calmly lowered himself down and dropped from its burning end.

Cullen pressed a fist against his mouth.

The tower lurched, toppled, and broke in half, collapsing in a rush of flame, smoke, and debris. The sound was like nothing Cullen had ever heard before. Surely no volcanic explosion had ever been louder.

The force tossed John into the air, before releasing him to plunge toward the roof.

Bowing his head, Cullen sobbed. Della was there in an instant, offering quiet reassurance. Going up on tiptoes, she slipped her arms about him and pulled him close. Burying his head into her shoulder, he gripped her tight, squeezed his eyes shut, and continued to weep.

For John. For the firemen. Their families. His own mother. And for himself.

CHAPTER 22

Within an hour, the entire building collapsed in a tremendous gust of flames. Firemen fought the monster. Wagons whisked away bodies. The stench caused Della to gag and look anywhere but to where ambulance attendants rushed around with blood-splattered faces.

The Terminal Station was now in plain view over the blazing ruins of the Cold Storage Building. Trains had ceased running, and the fair stables just west of the tracks had burned down. The hotels over the fence, however, remained intact, as did the rest of the fair.

Though the crowd had begun to disperse, it would still be a while before she and Cullen could get through. She rested her head against his shoulder, still trying to grasp what had happened.

Placing a hand on his chest, she looked up. "Cullen?"

He pulled his gaze from the final ambulance leaving the park. White powder sprinkled his hat and jacket. Soot clung to his face, accentuating the lines beside his eyes and making him look older than he was.

He smoothed her hair from her face. "Where's your hat?"

"I gave it to someone to use as a fan."

Slipping her hand into his, she intertwined their

fingers and gave him a soft squeeze. "I'm sorry about John."

Water rushed to his eyes. "Me too."

Her heart grieved. So much loss. So much tragedy. What if it all could have been avoided?

"Your sprinklers would have prevented this, wouldn't they?"

"I don't know. They would have been able to handle the initial fire in the cupola, but that explosion . . ." He shook his head. "They wouldn't be able to withstand an explosion."

"What about before the explosion? When we saw the smoke? They would have opened up then, right? And perhaps put out whatever it was that caused the explosion?"

He sighed. "I don't know. They certainly wouldn't have hurt. I'd like to think they would have given John and the other men a bit more time to escape, but I just don't know."

"I think they would have made a tremendous difference. A life-and-death difference."

"Maybe so." He sighed. "Maybe so."

A fireman shouted something indecipherable to another as they continued to fight the heap of burning embers. At least it looked as if they'd finally taken control of the blaze.

Cullen brushed some of the powder from his sleeve, then offered her his arm. "Let's go home."

Such simple words, yet so many men would not be going to their homes tonight. Her heart ached for them, their families, their friends, and their comrades.

She placed her hand on his arm, then paused to take one last look at the burning heap. On the east side, a fireman tried to work around a crippled statue of Christopher Columbus, which still held the world in its hand. Just a few weeks ago, she had waltzed by the sculpture with hardly a glance. It now listed at a forty-five-degree angle.

Another fireman tossed a rope over it and dragged it to the ground. The blaze devoured the staff, exposing its wooden foundation. A few moments later, the navigator for whom the fair had been named was buried in a mass of smoldering timbers, alongside an undetermined number of heroes.

CHAPTER 23

M y mother died like that."

Della snapped her gaze to Cullen's, but he wasn't looking at her. He was simply walking, staring into the distance, as if he'd not said a thing.

"Trapped on a tower?" she asked.

He shook his head. "Trapped in a fire."

They exited Sixty-Fourth Street, then drifted in the direction of Harvell House, their steps slow, their hearts heavy.

"When?" she asked.

"In '78. I was twelve."

She said nothing. Just waited. Carriages traveled in double columns, filling the avenue as people left the park. But other than an occasional call of a driver or the clopping of horses' hooves, there was no sound. No hum of happy conversations. No friendly shouts. No hawking of wares. Only stunned silence.

"It was summertime, and we'd gone into Charlotte for supplies," he said. "She stopped by the cotton mill. I headed to the blacksmith's. He'd been teaching me his trade and would sometimes let me operate the bellows."

She tried to picture what he must have looked like as a boy. Barefooted, with sun-kissed skin and trousers rolled up to his knees, perhaps.

"When the fire bell rang, the whole town poured into the streets, me included. I'd been running toward the billowing smoke for a good minute before I realized it was the mill. But even then I wasn't worried. I knew my mother would have gotten out."

White powder fell from their clothing, leaving a trail behind them. Smoke obliterated all sunlight, though they could still see.

"The owner of the mill kept the windows tightly closed so the humidity wouldn't weaken the cotton fibers. The air inside was so thick with cotton dust and lint, you could hardly see or breathe. That's why I wasn't with her. Cotton dust makes me break out in hives."

She still couldn't fathom a cotton farmer whose body rejected the very crop that provided for him.

"Sad thing is," he said, "the mill had a sprinkler system."

Her lips parted. *Please, God,* she thought. *Not one of his.* Then she remembered he'd been much older when he tested out his first one on the cowshed.

"It was a manual system," he said, "and the operatives weren't able to activate it. I don't know why, but they weren't. Some of the folks on the ground floor made it out, but cotton is highly flammable and the windows were sealed. The people on the second floor didn't stand a chance."

She swallowed. "And your mother was on the second floor?"

"She was." His voice didn't rise or fall or crack, but flattened into a monotone. "The hook-and-ladder carts arrived, of course, but even with their steam engines throwing water onto the building, there was no saving it."

She bit her lip. She didn't know whether to reach for him or leave him be. Crossing her arms, she held tight to her elbows.

"I was held back from fighting the fire. But even as they restrained me, I promised her I'd do something. Something to conquer fire. And that's when the idea for automatic sprinklers came to me. It was as if my mother paused on her way to heaven and offered a parting suggestion. A dying wish, if you will." For the first time, his voice wavered. He looked down. "What she failed to mention was what to do if I invented such a thing but no one wanted it."

Uncrossing her arms, she grabbed his hand. "Oh, Cullen. Even if no one places an order, you've done your part. You've offered the fruit of your hands. No one would ask you for more. Not your mother, not God, not anyone."

He gave her a self-deprecating smile. "I would. I would ask for more."

STEAM FIRE ENGINE

COLUMBIAN GUARDS

"The park was practically deserted,
the atmosphere subdued."

CHAPTER 24

After dropping Della safely at her room, Cullen went upstairs, changed into the denim work trousers he'd worn on the train from home, and headed straight back to the disaster site. He might not have been allowed to clean up the mill fire, but he could certainly help clean up this one. John and the other twenty-plus men needed to be given a proper burial. But first they needed to be found.

The park was practically deserted, the atmosphere subdued. Many flags had already been lowered to half-mast. The heap of ruins still smoldered, producing steaming heat—some pockets worse than others. Marines from foreign countries and sailors from the caravels now joined firefighters and men from the crowd who'd flung aside their jackets and plunged into the smoking mound.

Without waiting for direction, Cullen clambered over twisted pipes and charred beams in an effort to reach the most likely location for the bodies. The stink of smoke and scorched rubble overwhelmed him. He took a deep breath, then regretted it immediately, as particles lodged in his throat, causing him to choke and cough. Grabbing a blackened piece of metal, he jerked back his hand as the heat singed his palm.

"Here!" a man from the perimeter shouted.

Cullen turned. A fireman sat in an oil coat, knees bent, catching his breath. He held up a pair of work gloves.

With care, Cullen traversed the pile like a tightrope walker. "Don't you need those?"

"We're taking shifts. It's too hot to stay in there for long." With a face covered in black soot, he peeled off his coat. "Take this too. When it becomes too much, come on back, and I'll relieve you."

"Thanks."

While he put on the protective gear, he studied the pile more carefully. Removing the debris would be every bit as delicate as when he and Wanda used to drop a handful of wheat stalks on the ground, then attempt to remove them one by one without allowing the mound to collapse. But here, if a mound collapsed, lives were at stake.

He hauled tangles of wire, shards of glass, and bits of chandelier to a nearby garbage cart. With each trip, layer upon layer of soggy wet soot caked his boots and trousers. Ash particles stung his eyes. Dust filled his lungs. Soot coated the inside of his mouth.

Still, he continued. He wanted to find the bodies—yet at the same time, he hoped it was someone else who found them. He lifted the frame of a window. Underneath, a pocket of charred timbers burst into flames. He jumped back, dropping the frame, then stomped out the fire with his boot.

From a tunnel-like passageway to his right, a god-awful smell caused him to whip his head to the side. And that's when he saw it. A charred stump. And though it bore no resemblance to a human form, he knew what it was.

Bile rushed up his throat, souring his mouth and nose before he could force it back down. His stomach convulsed. His eyes watered.

Oh, Lord. Oh, Lord, he thought.

Lifting his head, he searched the area. Some men shoveled, the clinks of their spades just now registering. Others worked in units hauling off the larger pieces. Another picked up an ice skate that had somehow made it through the conflagration intact.

Cullen's gaze snagged and connected with the man on the sidelines whose equipment he wore.

The man's slumped posture began to straighten one vertebra at a time. He pushed to his feet. "Chief?" he called, not looking anywhere other than at Cullen.

"What is it, Gray?"

The man named Gray pointed to Cullen.

Cullen scanned the area, quickly spotting the white-helmeted chief who'd been consulting with two infantrymen. The chief handed his pad and pencil to the men beside him, then headed toward

Cullen with long strides that quickly turned into jogs.

The shovels stopped. Those hauling rubble paused. All movement suspended as the chief climbed over hills and vales to reach Cullen's side.

When he did, Cullen pointed.

The chief's drooping mustache looked as if a frozen frown had been painted on his face. He pinched the bridge of his nose.

"I'm so sorry," Cullen rasped, tears streaking his cheeks.

The chief looked at him. "What's your name, son?"

"Cullen McNamara. I work in the booth next to John Ransom."

"Are you the one with the automatic sprinkler?"

Cullen blinked. "Yes, sir."

The chief nodded. "John went on and on about that thing. I've been meaning to go over and see it. I just haven't had the time."

Cullen had no words. He had no idea John had mentioned him or his exhibit. Looking away, he swiped his nose with his sleeve.

The chief placed a steadying hand on Cullen's shoulder. "There's no need for you to do this."

"Please, sir. I want to help."

After a brief hesitation, he nodded, then turned to the ambulance corps and signaled for them to bring a stretcher.

Fifteen minutes later, another body was found. More turned up at frequent intervals until eight more were recovered. When nightfall came, the chief called a halt to all work and was met with protest.

"It's too dangerous," he said. "I'll not risk any more injury. We need to wait until it's light."

Much of the volunteer help tapered off after that day, but Cullen reported to the disaster site at first light morning after morning. He'd been working from can-see to can't-see his entire life, much of that time with closed airways and swollen eyes. He figured that pretty well qualified him for the job.

"Don't you have an exhibit to man?" the chief had asked. "Seems to me after a big fire like this, you'd garner a lot of interest in that sprinkler of yours."

Whether the chief was right or not, Cullen would never know, because for now, he knew the support these men needed. As much as he'd wanted to help with the mill fire, he couldn't fathom having to wonder if the bones he uncovered were those of his beloved mother. Yet in a way, that's what these men had been asked to do, and he wouldn't leave it to them alone. It was his one opportunity to pay tribute to those who had done this task for him so many years ago. If it meant a missed opportunity in Machinery Hall, so be it.

Still, the task was the most difficult he'd ever faced. Yet as is often the case, an unexpected blessing came with it. He became close to a fraternity of men who risked their lives every day for people they'd never met and would likely never see again. And though Cullen wasn't one of them, they welcomed him into their brotherhood nonetheless.

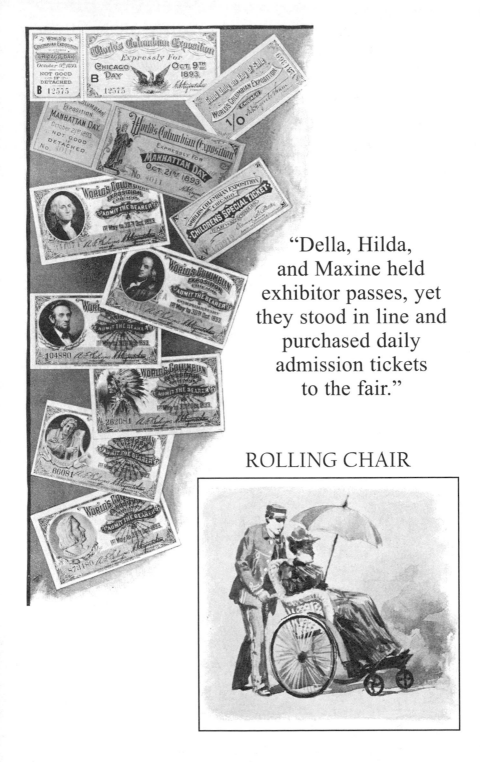

"Della, Hilda, and Maxine held exhibitor passes, yet they stood in line and purchased daily admission tickets to the fair."

ROLLING CHAIR

CHAPTER 25

Della, Hilda, and Maxine held exhibitor passes, yet they stood in line and purchased daily admission tickets to the fair, for today had been designated as a memorial for the men who perished in the fire. As part of Firemen's Sunday, all receipts at the gates were to be added to an ongoing relief fund for the families of the victims.

Della had reverted to touring the fair with her coworkers ever since Cullen began volunteering at the disaster site. She wondered if the men would take a break from their labors today or if they'd continue to work. Either way, Cullen had not made any attempt to take up his lessons again. He'd slipped a note under her door saying he didn't know how long cleanup would take and he'd let her know when they were finished.

"Was there anything in particular you two planned to see?" Della asked, the constant clicking of the turnstile sounding like a watchman's rattle.

Hilda consulted her notes, her body listing from side to side, her ankles swollen from all the touring she'd done over the past couple of months. Her white hair and labored steps reminded Della of how old her friend was. Funny, but Della had never thought of Hilda as old. But then she'd never done much socializing with her either. Not here, nor at home.

"I believe we'd agreed to eat at the Roof Garden in the Woman's Building, didn't we?" Hilda tucked her notes back into her reticule. "A large percentage of their proceeds today are to be added to the relief fund."

"Yes, you're quite right," Maxine agreed, her black hair carefully tucked inside an old-fashioned snood.

Della cleared her throat. "If it's all right, I'd like to stop by one of the firehouses and pay my respects. Do we have time to work that in, do you think?"

Maxine shrugged, her black gown stark against her fair skin. "It's too early for supper just yet, so what if we do that first? Do you know where one is?"

"There are several," Della answered. "But I'd like to go to the one by the Government Building."

"What's so special about that one?" Hilda asked.

Della hesitated. She hated to bring up Cullen. It had become a sore spot between her and Maxine. Her coworker felt Cullen was taking advantage of Della by not paying her, and, worse, Maxine had made some not-so-subtle admonishments about how late Della stayed out every night with a strange man. But then, anyone who stayed out past eight o'clock was "up to no good" by Maxine's standard.

Still, she'd done nothing wrong. "One of the men who perished was a friend of the man I tutor," Della answered. "His name was Mr. Ransom, and he was a member of the company that works out of that particular firehouse."

Maxine flattened her lips. "Not your 'pupil' again."

"Oh, hush." Hilda tapped Maxine's arm with her fan. "For heaven's sake, he just might be our Della's Prince Charming. Then what will you say to our girl after all the disagreeable things you've said about him?"

Della felt herself flush. She wasn't sure which was worse. Maxine's disapproval or Hilda's romantic inclinations. Thank goodness they didn't know Cullen was staying at Harvell House. Nor did they even know his name. He was an early riser and had long since left before she and the others even made it down to breakfast. And since she and Cullen were usually the last to arrive, her coworkers had never met him, nor had they made the connection between his name on the nightly list and hers.

Maxine lifted her chin. "Well, I for one am glad you've come to your senses about him and started spending your time with us. As you well know, I have disliked the way he abused your sense of goodwill. Imagine. All those lessons and not a dime to show for it."

She sighed. She hadn't told them why she and Cullen were taking a break, only that they were. "It's only temporary. I plan to complete what we started in very short order."

"Well, of course you will." Hilda gave her a conspiratorial wink.

Maxine pushed her spectacles up the bridge of her nose. "I wish you wouldn't. It's unseemly."

"Nonsense." Hilda dabbed her neck with a black handkerchief. "It's the most natural thing in the world."

While the women continued to belabor the point, Della directed them toward Fire and Guard Station One. An afternoon thunderstorm had emptied the park and left the serene beauty of the fair beneath a somber pall. The gay banners above the White City's domes hung limp at half-mast. Crepe dripped in drooping festoons across the buildings, emitting a less-than-pleasant odor.

Picking their way over mud as gray as paint and nearly as sticky, they skirted the lagoon. Deserted gondolas bobbed in protected nooks, their bronzed masters lolling under canopies and singing soft operatic tunes of their homeland. The occasional visitor strolled about statues and monuments as if wandering through a graveyard, their silence contagious. Even the poppies turned their weeping faces to the ground.

When they finally arrived at the firehouse, a brisk wind from the west flapped the crepe draped across its oversized door. Dark streamers hung on all the apparatus inside. A roughened helmet rested atop the hook-and-ladder's seat, causing Della to miss a step as she wondered if it belonged to the man who'd tossed his helmet from the burning tower. The wagon's horse gave a long blow, shaking black and white rosettes fastened to its harness.

The guard station held a mere fraction of the company, since most of its members had perished during the ordeal. She'd heard it was not uncommon for survivors of such tragedies to struggle with guilt for having survived when they were no more worthy than the fallen men. She wished she could take their pain and bear it herself, but the most she could do was pray for the men and offer her heartfelt sympathy.

A fireman approached. His cheeks were hollow, his brown hair flat, his eyes as black as the scarf tied over his fatigue uniform. "Thank you for coming."

She swallowed. "I'm so sorry for your losses."

His red-rimmed eyes took on a sheen. "Thank you."

"The rain won't stop people from coming." Hilda patted his arm with affection.

As if affirming her pronouncement, the wind lapped up the remaining clouds, pushing them out over the lake. Sun burst through in splendid radiance, casting its rays on the White City.

They conversed for a few more minutes, offered their condolences to the other firemen, then dropped donations into a box.

The visit put an end to the gentle bickering between Hilda and Maxine and greatly curbed their usual bent for gossiping.

Within an hour, the turnstiles at every entrance brought in people by the pairs, then by tens, and finally by flocks until guests stacked up against the pay gates.

On the Wooded Island, drenched ducks came out from the protection of the bushes. Peacocks spread their feathers in the sun to dry.

After supper on the roof of the Woman's Building, they made their way to the ruins of the Cold Storage Building. The dark mass lay in tangled confusion among the white temples around it, its high beauty of six days ago nothing more than a surreal memory. The smell of scorched timbers mixed with the aroma of rain.

Some men labored with shovels, others with gloved hands. Della scanned them, easily spotting Cullen, though he didn't see her. She was somewhat surprised to see him in shirtsleeves and denims. He looked so different. Only once had she seen him without a jacket. But this was neither the time nor the place to ruminate about that.

She couldn't help but note, however, how the early evening sun silhouetted his handsome physique as he bent over, grasped a shovel low, scooped up a load of ashes, then carried them to a garbage cart.

Somewhere in those ashes and embers were Mr. Ransom's remains and those of countless others. According to the papers, only a few bodies had been recovered so far. The reason, they said, was that the explosion—caused by large amounts of ammonia stored within the building—left no traces of the victims it had claimed. She couldn't imagine the horror of the task Cullen and the other men faced.

After depositing his load in the cart, Cullen turned and saw her. His steps slowed, then halted altogether. He was on the opposite side of the rubble, and out of respect for the dead, no one was talking. To hail him or even wave would have been inappropriate. And truth be told, she didn't want Maxine to meet him. For once she did, his name would jump off the list of boarders and she'd never hear the end of it.

Still, she wished she could at least greet him. Ask him how he was holding up. Tell him he needn't worry about practicing his words right now. Tell him she missed him.

She knew of a way. She had but to hold her hands next to her waist and make some subtle movements. But to do so was forbidden. So she simply held his gaze, wondering what he was thinking and if he missed her too.

Blowing into a handkerchief, Hilda sniffled. "Are the two of you ready?"

Della forced her attention to her friend. "Whenever you are."

"Then let's go," Maxine said, her voice somber.

Della glanced back, but Cullen had already returned to the rubble, his focus on his work.

She strolled to the Court of Honor alongside Hilda and Maxine feeling bereft and somehow abandoned. They gathered about the Music Hall's outdoor pavilion. Under the lull of fountains and the lash of waves against the sea wall, musicians played home melodies, moving hymns, and "The Vacant Chair."

At concert's end, the fountains flashed crimson, a reminder of the fire's fury, then purple—the color of royalty, dignity, and heroes.

Someone in the crowd began to sing "Amazing Grace," his tenor voice pure and true. Della, Hilda, Maxine, and the others added their voices until all five verses had been sung a capella. After the last refrain, silence descended.

Gulls wheeled along the shoreline, their squawks drowning out the fountain's raindrops. The moon made an early appearance in the still-lit sky. The faint rumble of distant machinery assured that life would go on.

GOVERNMENT BUILDING

"Cullen exited the Government Building
in his denims and sat on the top step of the
wide, marble-like entrance."

CHAPTER 26

Two weeks after the fire, Cullen received another letter from home. He exited the Government Building in his denims and sat on the top step of the wide, marble-like entrance. Dad hadn't paid the principal on his merchant credit for two years, and had racked up a total debt of six hundred dollars, not two hundred. So his interest rate had jumped to fifty percent. *Fifty percent.*

And if that weren't bad enough, he had lied about the cushion. There was no cushion. Not now, not ever. The three hundred dollars he gave to Cullen was part of that thousand he'd borrowed. And now it was gone. Used to pay Mrs. Harvell and the rest of Cullen's fair expenses. The only money they would have would be the three to four hundred dollars from the crop.

But outgoing, they'd have their mounting merchant debt, plus interest, plus the mortgage, plus seed and supplies, plus property taxes, plus the Dewey boys Dad had hired, plus extraneous expenses.

Propping his elbows on his knees, Cullen pressed the butts of his hands against his forehead. He needed to make at least six hundred dollars. How the devil would he do that when he'd not had so much as a nibble in almost three months, even with Vaughn's carrot?

He supposed he could go back home and hire on at one of the mills, but it would take almost three years to earn six hundred dollars, and that didn't include living expenses—not to mention the duress his body would be put under in those closed-up, fiber-filled mills. No, he'd write back and have Dad see if the Building and Loan would float them for one more year. If they said no . . . he didn't even want to think about that. Instead, he'd once again concentrate on selling some sprinklers and selling them now.

Pushing himself up off the steps, he headed toward the disaster site to tell the boys he needed to return to Machinery Hall. It'd be a good while before the site was completely cleared, but they had recovered as many bodies as they were going to and were now working in a rotation of shifts between the ruins and the fire stations. They would understand that saving the farm needed to take precedence.

Cleaning up the debris had allowed him plenty of time to think. Too much time. He was stunned and not a little concerned at how often his thoughts drifted to Della. At how much he missed their lessons. At how much he missed her.

With a determined effort, he redirected his attention to John and the fire. And the more he considered it, the surer he was. His sprinkler would have put out the fire in the cupola, alleviating any reason for John and his battalion to have even climbed up there. A manual sprinkler system wouldn't have worked, for in order to turn it on, someone would have needed to climb those stairs.

Same thing for the fire beneath, which had triggered the explosion. If it had been subdued immediately, the explosion might never have happened.

Entering Machinery Hall, Cullen admitted it felt good to be back in his suit and it felt good to have a plan of attack. John had asked him to do a demonstration from the first day they met. And by all that was holy, he was going to do one. If folks could see how his system worked, then maybe they wouldn't be so skeptical.

First item on the agenda was to write to the fair's director-general. He suspected it would take a good deal of persuasion to convince the commission he needed to set a shed on fire in the middle of the fair grounds, but he was determined.

As he approached his booth, his steps slowed. Someone else stood where John was supposed to be. It wasn't any of the boys from the brigade, but instead a tall, gangly man with thinning hair and a receding hairline. As different from John as you could possibly get.

Emotion clogged his throat.

"Mr. McNamara." One of the women with the Crowne Pen Company stepped from behind her counter. "We heard you were helping with the aftermath of the fire." Her eyes watered. "I'm so sorry for your loss. John spoke of you often."

She'd used John's Christian name. This must have been the woman John had referred to. The one he'd pointed out that long-ago day as being someone "mighty special" and more recently as one whom he was becoming quite serious about. He racked his brain, but could not for the life of him remember her name.

"Thank you, Miss . . . ?"

"Carpenter. Greta Carpenter." She had a classic beauty, like paintings of the Madonna.

Disregarding protocol, he slipped his hand into hers and left it there. "I'm so very glad to meet you. John spoke of you with great warmth and admiration."

Her lips trembled. "And I of him."

"I'm so sorry. We will all miss him."

"Yes, and thank you." She touched two fingers to the corners of her eyes.

A machine behind them began to transform solid bars of steel into wire netting.

He glanced at it. "I'd best head on to my booth."

She gave his hand a long squeeze. "Good luck with your *sprnklrs*. John thought they were a wonderful invention."

Swallowing, he nodded. "Thank you, Miss Carpenter."

ILLUMINATION SHOW

"From all parts, a chorus of *oohs* and *ahhs* came forth. Below, gondoliers bent to their oars, each stroke breaking the Basin's reflections into a thousand glistening fragments."

CHAPTER 27

Allowing Della to go first, Cullen followed her through the massive portal of the grandiose Manufactures Building. They'd spend a good deal of time on tonight's lesson in order to leave room for the premiere of the fair's illumination show. Dr. Bell had given Della two tickets for the Otis elevator, running to the highest roof promenade in the world, and she'd decided she wanted to use them tonight so they could watch the show from there.

"We'd better get moving," he said, "or we'll be late. The elevator is in the center aisle on the northern side."

Every booth they passed was a work of art. Gilded domes, glittering minarets, mosques, palaces, kiosks, and pavilions all produced a magical miniature city roofed in with a dome of glass. Instead of aisles, it held avenues complete with electric lampposts. Laid out like a grid, the roads divided the rectangular edifice into four quadrants. People strolled along each avenue, adding to the profusion of sound, color, and movement.

Della pulled him to stop. To her right, a little shaver in short trousers and velvet jacket leaned on his closed umbrella with one hip cocked. In his ears were two hard-rubber tubes hooked up to

261

a graphophone. A smile began to form on his face, spreading wider and wider until his mouth opened and he giggled aloud. Then giggled again. Finally, he closed his eyes and guffawed with unadulterated joy.

Della dug inside her chatelaine purse and extracted a nickel. "Well, I don't know about you, but I have to see what's so amusing."

He followed her to the machines, wishing he could offer to pay. But more than ever before, he had to save every penny. He'd spent the last week collecting throwaway lumber from the fair's carpenter's shop and lumberyard behind Terminal Station. He'd rounded up piping from the machine shop behind his building, and cajoled the blacksmith next to it into letting him use his workshop in the wee hours before the fair opened. All he needed now was approval from the commission. Once he had that, he'd be ready to assemble his shed and do a demonstration.

Della dropped a nickel into the box and placed the rubber tubes in her ears. She had the same reaction as the boy, her delighted eyes finding Cullen's.

Taking out one of the tubes, she handed it to him.

A comic singer's voice gave a lively rendition of "The Cat Came Back," and Cullen felt himself grinning. Listening to the childish song while sharing the tubes with Della gave him a sense of well-being. Of coming home. She was a lovely woman, laughed easily, and took joy in the little things.

He tried to recall experiencing those feelings with Wanda, and the most he could drum up were memories from their childhood. Nothing from recent years. The thought did not sit well.

She hung the tubes back up. "That was wonderful. Definitely worth the stop, don't you think?"

"Wouldn't have missed it. But no more, or we'll be late for the illumination show."

The elevator was a jail-like affair, with wooden bars on all four sides. They followed a dozen other passengers into the cage. Being the last ones in ended up giving them the best view. The operator secured two collapsible doors, then pressed a button. The upward journey treated them to an ever-expanding view of the vast interior of the building.

As they ascended past the upper gallery, Cullen pointed through the cage's bars to some small compartments on the second floor. "Look there. It has periodical rooms. That would be an excellent place for our lessons if the weather were ever to take a turn."

When he got no response, he glanced at her. Her face was stark white and frozen. He followed her gaze straight down to the immense depth below. Tiny figures now moved noiselessly about. He knew the elevator was not going to fall, but for the briefest of moments he felt himself shrinking before the enormity of the space.

Slipping an arm about her, he pressed her head against his chest. "Close your eyes," he whispered.

Had he taken a dive into a vat of roses, the scent couldn't have been more powerful. He closed his own eyes, savoring the stolen moment. And stolen it was.

He told himself he'd have comforted anyone in such a circumstance. But Della wasn't just anyone. Far from it.

The gate opened, and he could feel her hesitation to step onto the bridge leading to the roof.

"Come on, now. I've got you." He kept her tucked against him as they slowly made their way across the gangway, passing others who stopped at their leisure to look down on the building's interior. Finally, they reached a widow's walk running along the perimeter of the roof.

He guided her to a bench and eased them both down.

Full dark had set in, with a sky of clouds blotting out all evidence of stars. The blackness allowed them anonymity and a sense of privacy.

He removed his arm from around her. "Are you all right?"

"It was the height." Her voice sounded strained.

"You're afraid of heights?"

"I don't know. I've never been two hundred feet in the air before."

"Me neither. It certainly made me realize what a monster building this is. Reading about it in the guidebooks is quite a bit different from experiencing it firsthand. Are you all right?"

"Better. And a little embarrassed. I think I'll be fine going back down. I just wasn't prepared."

He wished he could see her eyes. Wished he were free to take her hand, hold her close . . . kiss her lips. A heaviness settled around him. He needed to take a very close look at his feelings for Wanda. Would they be as strong if she were the one sitting here?

He'd want to comfort Wanda, certainly. But make love to her? Probably not. The consequence of that admission was too chilling to contemplate.

"Oooooh." The crowd about them murmured.

He glanced at the rail. "It's starting. Would you like to see, or would you rather stay here?"

"I want to see." There was no hesitation in her voice.

Stalling her with his hand, he kept her from rising. "I'm happy to sit here or even go back." And he found he meant it. The show held no attraction if he couldn't share it with her.

"I'm fine. Really. It was just a shock. That's all."

"Well, if you become uncomfortable at the railing, simply say the word. Do you promise?"

"I promise."

Helping her to her feet, he guided her to a chain-link barrier, careful to place her on his left so he could better hear. A crisp breeze whistled between them. Tempted as he was to keep her warm, he forced himself to grasp the handrail.

The entire Court of Honor spread out before them. To their right, the Electricity and Mines Buildings. Catty-corner, the Administration Building and Machinery Hall. Directly across the way, the Agricultural Building, the waters of the Grand Basin separating their two structures and leading to the peristyle, then out to the great lake.

White globes of light glittered around the perimeter of the Grand Basin, crossing and recrossing one another over its rippling waters. The avenues of the court still held its normal street lamps, throwing pools of light on a crowd gathered for the spectacle. Beyond them, stretching away for miles, a hundred thousand sparks of gold revealed that the great city of Chicago was still awake.

"It's beautiful," Della whispered.

"Yes."

Snippets from the gondoliers' songs echoed off the walls of the palaces and bounced up to them.

Without warning, a yellow light flickered and grew bright on the peak of the Administration Building's dome. Like shooting stars, lines of light swept from it, dividing the dome into sections, then encircling its base in a wheel of light. Light then began to creep around the building's ground floor until it looked as if it were surrounded with a band of liquid fire. Electricity shot along the upper floor, a second band of light encircling its facade.

Thinking the show was over, Cullen whistled, while those about and below applauded. But between the upper facade and the base of the dome, a man rose from a gallery. A great flame shot upward from the top of a pipe beside him. Man after man rose. Flame after flame ignited until the whole looked like ancient warriors standing on the parapet of a besieged castle, about to hurl firebrands at its enemy below. He hoped they were careful with those flames. The last thing he wanted was to witness another disaster.

From within the building, light burst from every window, wrapping its tentacles around grand statues and giant pillars. A yellow ribbon of light skittered across the top of the peristyle, drawing Cullen's attention. Before he had time to absorb its beauty, a huge searchlight struck the statue of Diana frozen on one foot atop the Agricultural Building, her bow bent, her arrow ready to fly. Vanishing as quickly as it appeared, it was replaced by yet another. This one was crimson and centered on a statuary of Columbus's mystic caravel, the figures of handmaidens straining at its oars.

From all parts, a chorus of *oohs* and *ahhs* came forth. Below, gondoliers bent to their oars, each stroke breaking the Basin's reflections into a thousand glistening fragments.

Green, purple, and scarlet searchlights flashed from spire to dome, from statue to statue. Two primary-colored streams crossed their rays, producing a mass of secondary color midair. Smoke from a passing locomotive curled into its path, transforming it into a swirling, colored cloud.

When that light vanished, another replaced it. It landed full force on a gondola, catching a young man snuggling with a woman. Both straightened hastily, but the crowd saw it and whistled. Cullen couldn't help but feel for the fellow.

Just as the lights refocused on the huge gilded statue of the Republic, an orchestra burst into strains of "America." Cullen, Della, and all those present stood straight, cheering and applauding, then sang every verse and every chorus. Patriotism filled the court and Cullen's entire being. He was proud of his country, his countrymen, and this miraculous White City.

The last note lingered. One by one the lights turned out, the fairyland faded. The grounds returned to normal and the roof of the Manufactures Building became shrouded in darkness. The thick black sky offered not so much as a twinkle of star. People shuffled behind them, expressing to one another their delight in the show and their eagerness to beat the crowd.

Neither he nor Della moved. He kept his eyes on the court, watching the ebb and flow of humanity moving with the regularity of ocean waves. But every nerve in his body was attuned to the woman beside him. He couldn't see her, but he could smell her, picture her. His pulse beat too fast. His chest tightened in his effort to restrain himself.

"If it's okay," she said, "I'd like to wait up here until the crowd in the Court of Honor thins a bit."

"Of course."

It was an innocent enough request, considering what she'd experienced on opening day. Still, those who'd been on the roof with them were being whisked away by the elevator. He wasn't sure how long he'd last alone with her in the dark.

"Would you like to go back down the elevator and look at some of the exhibits inside the Manufactures Building while we wait?" he asked.

"Not really. I don't want to mar the mood and beauty of tonight's spectacle." She shifted, turning toward him. "What about you?"

"I'm fine to stay up here." He placed his elbows on the rail, squeezing his hands together. "You're not cold? It's a bit windy."

"I'm fine."

"Not frightened of the height?"

"Not at all. I just wasn't prepared for that ride. I don't know why."

"It would be a shock to anyone, I think."

"Was it to you?"

"It was." He looked at her then. He could make out only her silhouette, but his mind colored in every feature, every nuance. His breathing grew thick. His muscles tensed.

Straightening, he moved to the bench opposite the chain-link fence and sat. Thankfully, she stayed where she was, placing her back to him and watching the crowd below.

"How's your *xhbi* going?"

He cocked his ear. "I'm sorry?"

She turned around, leaning against the barrier and hooking a heel on one of its links. "Your exhibit. How's it going?"

"I've gathered some materials, and I'll soon be giving a demonstration. Lord willing, that will generate interest."

"How will it work?"

"I'm going to set a wooden shed on fire, then step back and wait for my sprinklers to put it out."

"The fair officials are going to allow you to do that?"

"I'm still waiting to hear back."

Silence descended once more. Light from below filtered up, outlining a sparking couple a ways down the promenade. The woman stood much like Della did, with her back against the barrier. The man moved in front of her, boxing her in with his arms. He leaned in.

Cullen turned away. Della hadn't noticed. Was still looking straight at him.

"A representative from the National Association of the Deaf came to my classroom today," she said.

"He did? And what did he think?"

"He was deaf and said I was denying the children their free mental growth."

He frowned. "Did he say why?"

"No, he *signed* why."

"In your classroom? In front of the children?"

She smoothed a tendril of hair from her face. "No. Fortunately, they'd left to play on the roof, so it was just the two of us."

"Did you sign back?"

"I did. I felt it would be impolite not to."

He shifted to a more comfortable position. "So why did he think you were denying the children?"

"He'd been forced to go to a hearing school as a child and lip-read. He said all the hearing children came into class chattering about the spelling bee or what their mothers packed for lunch." Looking down, she traced the outline of her gloved fingers. "All but him. He was neither speaking nor listening. He was deaf and completely isolated because of it."

Distant laughter filtered up from the crowd below.

"That must have been difficult."

She crossed her arms, her chin still down. "My children don't banter when they come into the classroom. Nor when we eat lunch. Nor, I imagine, when they go to the playground."

He said nothing.

"Part of that, of course, is because they can't articulate well enough to read each others' lips." She looked at him then, her voice impassioned. "If they knew sign language, I wonder if then they'd use it to chatter until they became proficient at lip-reading."

For the umpteenth time, he wished her face weren't in the shadows. "I loved our sign-language lesson," he said. "I wish it were taught to everyone, not just the deaf."

She tilted her head. "What a lovely thought. Shall we start a crusade?"

He chuckled. "And I suppose you'd expect me to be Joan of Arc to your Charles VII?"

"Either way, it'd be a tragic tale, I'm afraid." She lifted her face to the heavens. He pictured her with her eyes closed. Then he pictured her lifting her face to him.

He cleared his throat. "Tired?"

"A little." Straightening, she looked over her shoulder. "It's probably all right to head back if you'd like."

He stood

They'd taken no more than two steps toward the bridge when she hesitated. There was no mistaking the passionate embrace at the other end of the promenade. The couple was oblivious to all else and must have assumed they were alone.

Placing a firm hand against the small of Della's back, he compelled her to continue. Crossing the bridge into the brightness of the Manufactures Building, she cleared her throat, fiddled with her bodice buttons, then withdrew a handkerchief from her sleeve and patted her neck.

Other than the elevator man, they were the only two in the cage. Cullen expected her to retreat to its center, but as soon as the gates closed, she grasped a bar and took in the magnificence she'd missed the first time. He took in the magnificence of her.

Neither spoke for the rest of the walk home. He concentrated on protecting her from the crowd. She concentrated on putting one foot in front of the other.

He kept his eyes forward at all times. She stole surreptitious glances at his profile.

He tried to recall everything about Wanda he liked. She started to speak, then stopped.

Finally, they reached the boardinghouse. All names had been marked through except his and Della's.

Picking up a pencil, he crossed out their names,

lit a taper, then turned off the lamp. The stairs creaked as they ascended to the second floor. He held up the light while she fished a key from her chatelaine bag, inserted it into her lock, and twisted. A loud click ricocheted off the walls.

She turned. "Thank you for tonight. I'm so glad we weren't late for the show."

Her dark pupils picked up the flickering flame, reflecting it back to him.

"Thank you for the lessons," he managed.

"You're doing quite well, considering what little time we've had. And . . . I've enjoyed them."

He tried to swallow. "Yes. Me too."

She moved her gaze to his lips. His mouth went dry.

Finally, she placed a gloved hand on her doorknob. "Good night, Cullen."

"Good night, Della."

She slipped inside her room, shutting the door softly behind her. It was a long time before he turned and found his way to his own room.

MIEHLE PRINTING PRESS

FIRST PRINTING PRESS IN NEW HAMPSHIRE

TYPESETTING MACHINE

SELF-CLAMPING PAPER CUTTING MACHINE

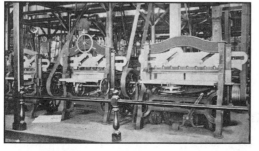

"Printing Press Row had shut down for the day, and many others were beginning to follow suit."

CHAPTER 28

The commission denied Cullen's request. Too dangerous, the letter said. But he wasn't going to take no for an answer. He couldn't. He'd draft an appeal tonight and request an audience with the director-general himself.

Printing Press Row had shut down for the day, and many others were beginning to follow suit. He'd just picked up his hat when a gentleman in Bulenberg's booth noticed he was leaving. The man stopped Bulenberg midsentence, excused himself, and made a hasty retreat, going straight from Bulenberg to Cullen. Bulenberg's face suffused with red.

"Orville Grasty," the man said, offering a hand to Cullen.

The first things Cullen noticed were his expensive black suit and his teeth. The man had a lot of teeth, and he was not afraid of showing them off with an overly bright smile.

Cullen took his outstretched hand. "How do you do, Mr. Grasty."

"I have a *nwsppr* printing works here in Chicago and several more along the east coast. Mr. Tisdale thought I might be *intrstd* in your product."

"Tisdale?" The name sounded familiar, but Cullen had met so many people.

Grasty lifted his cane and pointed. "He runs my letterpress *rght* over there."

The automatic platen press. Of course. "Yes, sir. That's a beauty of a machine."

Another big smile. "Thank you. She's a special one, that's for *crtn*. Now what do we have here?"

Cullen began his now-rote explanation. From the corner of his eye, he saw Bulenberg snatch up his hat and storm past them toward the exit. But Cullen had no time to ruminate on it, for Grasty peppered him with question after question. It was clear the man had a good grasp of mechanics and Cullen found himself talking about much more than just the sprinkler.

When Cullen finally looked at his watch, he realized he was running out of time if he wanted to swing by the fire station before his lessons.

Snapping his watch closed, he held out his hand. "Thank you for stopping by, sir. It was a pleasure."

"I'm intrigued, McNamara. Let me contact my insurance *cmpny* and see what they *thnk*. But the fact that the system is unproven will be a stumbling *blck*. I'd heard something about a demonstration?"

Cullen didn't even hesitate. "I'm working on that and will let you know when I have a specific date. Also, if your insurance company doesn't provide you with the answer you're seeking, don't forget about Vaughn Mutual. I'd be glad to put you in contact with its owner. In the meanwhile, would you like me to take a look at your Chicago location while I'm in town?"

"I certainly would. What about two weeks from today? Monday, the twenty-first?"

"Perfect, sir. I'll be there."

As Grasty walked away, Cullen wondered exactly how many printer works he had in all. However many it was, he needed that demonstration.

Inside Fire and Guard Station One, a hook and ladder waited in readiness, its horse flicking a fly with its tail. Firefighters lounged about benches in red shirts, while others played cards at a long table.

"Well, if it isn't Gulliver traveling our way," one of them shouted.

Cullen smiled at the nickname they'd given him because of his height. "Hello, Spud, Fish, fellows. How've you been?"

They regaled him with the tale of two little shavers who'd rigged up a raft from an old packing crate behind the Government Building, then tested it out on the lagoon, fell in, and had to be rescued. They teased Fish for being afraid of the water. Then they asked Cullen for his news and became indignant when they discovered the commission had denied his request.

"Want us to go egg the director-general's house?" Spud asked.

Cullen laughed. "Not just yet. I can appeal it. Let me try that first."

After disappointed groans, they agreed to wait.

"I was hoping to talk to the chief, though. Is he here?"

"Right behind you, son."

Cullen whirled around, then pumped the man's hand. "Good to see you, sir."

Murphy ran a thumb and finger down his mustache. "I keep meaning to come by and see your system. I'm sorry I haven't."

"I'd really like to show it to you. I'm there every day until the supper hour."

"What happens at the supper hour?"

"He turns into a pumpkin," one of the boys yelled.

Cullen lifted his hands in a what-can-I-say gesture, then slowly sobered. "I heard the donations from Fireman's Sunday were tallied, divided, and ready to be sent."

Murphy nodded.

Pulling a letter from inside his jacket, Cullen handed it to him. "When you send a donation to John's family, would you mind including this?"

In his letter, Cullen offered his sympathy and shared as many memories as he could so the Ransoms would know John's last days were full ones.

"I'd be happy to. Thank you." Murphy squeezed Cullen's shoulder. "It'll mean a lot to them."

279

MIDWAY PLAISANCE

"Ferris's enormous wheel took up the middle of the Plaisance. Each screened-in box car creaked and swung from the wheel's spokes."

CHAPTER 29

Cullen and Della passed beneath a viaduct and entered the mile-long Midway Plaisance. Nothing since the tower of Babel held such a confusion of tongues in one place. His concern about this section of the fair, though, was that most exhibits required an admission fee. A fee he couldn't afford to pay. But Della wanted to see it, so see it they would.

"Look at the balloon." She pointed to a hydrogen balloon taking off from behind a walled-off park. Placing a hand on the crown of her hat, she watched its ascent. "Oh my soul, it's so huge. I had no idea." She'd hooked the purple netting from a peach-colored hat underneath her chin, then tied it in a saucy bow just below her right ear.

"I know there's a lot to see," he said, "but I'd really like to get started with our lessons."

She gathered herself. "Sorry. There's just so much. Good heavens, are those ostriches?"

Lifting his hat, he replaced it on his head. It had become increasingly difficult to stay on task during their excursions, but that was his fault as much as hers.

"What are we working on today?" he asked.

Opening the chatelaine bag hanging from her belt, she extracted a folded piece of paper and handed it to him. "I'm going to ask you questions throughout the evening. Those are hints to help you lip-read my queries."

The paper held numbered phrases. *Hot chocolate. Gondola. Grover Cleveland. Investor. Helen Keller. Brilliantine. Tree trunks. Harvell House.*

After scanning all twenty-five, he nodded. "All right. I'm ready."

But she was no longer beside him. Instead, she conversed with an Italian man attired in the uniform of a Vatican Guard and armed accordingly. Behind him stood a miniature replica of St. Peter's Cathedral. "Miniature" was a bit of a stretch, however, for though it was about one-sixteenth the size of the original in Rome, it was still a good thirty feet long and fifteen feet wide.

Smiling, she looked at Cullen over her shoulder and pointed to the exhibit. The wide brim of her hat reflected the peach color of her cheeks. *Let's go in here.*

He'd read it. He'd read the entire sentence.

"The guard said it's an exact replica, down to the minutest details," she said as he approached.

"You go ahead. I'll wait here."

"You sure?"

"Positive."

She captured his gaze. *Who's the president of the United States?*

Blinking, he hesitated, then smiled. "Grover Cleveland."

"Very good." She handed a coin to the ticket taker and entered the exhibit.

Cullen watched her peek inside the intricately carved wooden structure coated with a stucco-like substance. Long pleats formed a V in both the back and front of her peach and purple bodice, drawing his eye to her slender waist and curvy hips. Turning, she swept to the other corners of the exhibit, where miniatures of the Cathedral of Milan, the Piombino Palace, and the Pantheon were displayed.

Returning to him, she thanked the guard and proceeded back onto the Plaisance. "Oh, Cullen. They had minuscule portraits of the popes and papal coats of arms inside the cathedral."

He glanced again at the display, wishing he could have seen it as well.

They passed the Irish Village. Behind its turreted stone keep, bagpipes squeezed out rousing tunes, their notes obliterating all chances of conversation.

What kind of boats are on the lllnnn?

He glanced at his paper. "Must be gondola. That's the only boat on my list. But I missed the last word you said."

You're doing very ball.

No. She must have said *well*. You're doing very *well*.

"Only with you," he said. "Your lips aren't difficult to decipher. But some people mumble or barely move their lips, and I have a terrible time interpreting their words."

You'll get *rrrr.*

"I'll get what?"

Bet-ter.

He nodded. Up ahead, Ferris's enormous wheel took up the middle of the Plaisance. Each screened-in box car creaked and swung from the wheel's spokes. A long line of fairgoers awaiting their turns twisted past the Vienna Café and the Indian Bazaar.

Della stopped, once again holding her hat as she surveyed Ferris's monstrosity. She looked at a painted sign above the ticket booth, then winced. Fifty cents per person.

Vendors walked up and down the line bawling, shouting, and hawking their wares. "Cigarettes! Ver' sheap! Two for five!"

"Step forward! Ferris wheel souvenirs! Two nickels! One dime!"

Della ground to a halt, an exhibit on her left capturing her full attention.

What's that? she mouthed.

Towering above a fence, an old-fashioned double-ripper whipped passenger-filled toboggans through a winding course, its occupants screaming with a mixture of fear and delight. A rumbling machine kept the chute's surface slick and coated with ice.

Della dug into her chatelaine bag. "Imagine,

sliding on ice in the summertime and without a coat. I can't wait to write my brothers back in Philadelphia. They'll never believe it." Extracting a dime, she squeezed it in her palm. "Go with me?"

He glanced at the ride. Most of the riders were boys and men, but he simply couldn't spend the dime. "You go ahead."

"But it's no fun by myself." Biting her cheek, she gave him a speculative look. "I won't get any hot cocoa for two days, and right after the ride, we'll sit down and work on our lessons for the rest of the evening."

That alone was worth the dime. Still, he paid for her cup of cocoa every day before their lessons. It was five cents a cup and the least he could do to compensate her. If she went without for two days, though, and he went on this ride, then he'd come out even.

He pulled on his ear. "Well, I suppose. Just this once."

The smile she gave him produced both dimples and hit him right in the gut. Before he could recover, she was already flying toward the sleds, calling for him to follow.

At the entrance platform, the cars passed them once, whooshing by in a blur. The boys inside held their arms high in the air, screaming like a bunch of girls. The smile on her face grew even bigger.

Again the cars passed. Della shifted from foot to foot. Finally the ride halted in front of them. As soon as their sled vacated, she scrambled inside. He slipped in the seat behind her. Each section held three seats, but they were the only two in their car.

Twisting around, she lifted her shoulders, her grin wide. "Scared?"

"Hardly."

She cocked an eyebrow. "You going to hold on?"

"I hadn't really thought about it." His eyes widened. "Are you?"

"Of course not."

He scowled. "Don't be ridiculous, Della. You need to hold the handles. Do you understand me?"

"Don't worry, Cullen. I won't tell anyone if you hold on."

"That's not it. You need to hold on. You're scared of heights, for crying out loud."

"I'm not. I told you, I just wasn't prepared before."

The sledge jerked and she faced forward, her laugh tumbling back to him. Starting slowly, the sled gradually increased its speed, ruffling the plum feathers in her hat.

As it approached an incline, the sledge slowed considerably, and wouldn't have made it to the top except a cable gripped it and hauled it to the peak of the hill.

Della clapped her hands.

"Hold on," he barked.

She grabbed the handles. But as soon as the cable released the sled, one of her hands went to her hat, the other shot into the air. They dove down with great speed, then whipped around a curve.

She jerked to the left, her body hanging halfway out the side. Her squeal propelled him forward. Reaching around her seat, he grabbed her belt and skirt, dragging her back in. She swatted his hand, but he didn't let go until they righted themselves, only to repeat the process on the other side when they rounded the next curve. The tails of her bow slapped his face and caught in his mouth.

How could someone who was afraid of an elevator have no compunction about a toboggan ride?

Three times they sailed through the loop. Three times she refused to hold on. By the time they reached the end, he was furious.

The minute they climbed out of the car, he spun her around. "What the deuce were you thinking up there? Are you out of your mind?"

Her lips fell open. "It was all in fun, Cullen. I've been tobogganing since I was a child. My brothers and I never held on."

"I have never in my entire life seen a lady behave with such abandon. You scared the living daylights out of me. What if you'd fallen?"

"I wasn't going to fall."

"Because I made sure you wouldn't."

Her face began to harden. "All you did is risk tearing my gown, not to mention squeezing me so hard I'll probably be black-and-blue."

An attendant stepped forward. "Time to move on, folks," he said, gently.

She jerked her arm out of Cullen's grasp. "It most certainly is."

Storming off the platform, she stomped down the steps, her skirts whipping side to side in time with her hips.

He told his pulse to slow, but it wouldn't. He told himself to calm down, but he couldn't. He told himself she wasn't his problem, but it made no difference.

Taking large strides, he began to follow her. The last thing he needed was to lose her, leaving her alone and defenseless in a crowd this size.

She made a beeline for the Vienna Café at the west end of the Ferris wheel. A place she knew good and well he couldn't afford. The ornamental structure served hot meals on the first floor, while the upper floor devoted itself to cold meals and beer tables.

He hadn't told her of his financial woes, and she never asked. But she knew he didn't have enough funds to pay for her lessons, nor did he ever buy himself hot chocolate or concessions, and he didn't go to any of the paying exhibits.

She must have drawn her own conclusions from there.

She paused long enough to read a sign outside the entrance, then made her way up the outdoor staircase leading to the café's second story. She neither waited for him nor looked over her shoulder to see where he was.

Weaving through the crowd, he watched as she disappeared behind the café door.

Unreasonable woman. What did she expect? That he'd let her plunge to her death while he sat there and did nothing? Anger sluiced through him once again. Wanda was looking more attractive by the minute. She'd never have done such a fool thing.

VIENNA CAFÉ

"She made a beeline for the Vienna Café
at the west end of the Ferris wheel. A place she
knew good and well he couldn't afford."

CHAPTER 30

Della followed a pretty young woman in a blue Austrian dirndl and white pinafore. The girl's sash wrapped around her back and tied at the front on her left side, indicating she was unmarried. Ornate screens decorated the room while an orchestra's concerto filtered up from downstairs.

The waitress led her to a corner table far away from a boisterous group of beer-drinking men.

"Thank you." Smoothing her skirt beneath her, she scooted up the chair.

"Vould you like someting to drink, Fraulein?"

"Do you have hot chocolate?"

"Ya. I vill be back."

Removing her gloves, Della tucked them inside her chatelaine bag. She probably shouldn't have run off, but sometimes he made her so angry.

So she had left, searching out a place where she could catch her breath and sort out her thoughts. But the more she sorted, the more guilty she felt.

You scared the living daylights out of me.

She hadn't meant to do that. They probably didn't get much snow in Charlotte, if any. She wondered if he'd ever even been on a toboggan.

Her remorse increased. Perhaps she should go look for him. She glanced toward the kitchen where the waitress had disappeared, then to the front entrance.

He stood just inside the door, scanning the patrons. His gaze snagged on hers. Relief, guilt, and a tiny thrill shot through her in quick succession. She drank in the fine cut of his suit, his towering height, and his marvelous chest, which had sheltered her on more than one occasion.

She was falling in love with him, she admitted.

It wasn't a hard thing to do. From the moment he'd rescued her on opening day, she'd been infatuated. But the game was up when he told her of his inventions and his mother's tragedy, comforted her in the elevator, and cried in her arms during the fire. It had just taken a while for her to acknowledge it.

She knew he had feelings for her as well, though he'd not yet reconciled himself to them. But that was all right. She would wait. He had the rest of the fair to figure it out.

He stopped in front of her table.

"Hello." His voice was deep, soft.

"Hello."

"I'm sorry I yelled."

"I'm sorry I scared you."

He nodded. "May I sit down?"

"Of course." She patted the spot to her left. "Sit here and we'll work on your lessons."

"That's my bad side." He reached for the chair across from her.

She patted the spot again. "That's why you need to sit there. I want you to practice hearing people who are on your right."

He hesitated, eyeing the proximity of the two chairs.

She tried not to smile. Why did he fight it so hard?

"What's so funny?" He took the place she indicated, his voice gruff.

What is my favorite drink? she mouthed.

"Hot chocolate. And don't change the subject."

"Very good. I've already ordered mine. I didn't know you were coming. How did you find me?"

"You were never out of my sight." He twisted around, looking for the waitress.

But she was already heading in their direction with Della's steaming cocoa in hand. Her daring décolletage was accentuated by the cinched-up dirndl beneath her breasts. Della tried not to notice Cullen noticing, but notice he did.

Della studied him as he ordered a glass of water, trying to imagine what he'd look like when he was old and gray. She'd bet Father Time would only enhance his attractiveness.

Finally, the waitress left. Soft strains from the orchestra downstairs filtered over to their corner.

She blew on her cocoa, making an indentation in the dollop of whipped cream floating on top. "It's not heights I'm afraid of."

Leaning his chair back on two legs, he regarded her. "But you are afraid of . . . ?"

"Closed-in spaces. That's why I was so distraught on opening day." He was the first person she'd ever told. But since he'd told her about his hearing, she figured it was only fair.

Crossing his arms, he took his time responding. "Have you felt that way since birth?"

"No, I was four, maybe five. I went into my grandfather's wheat field. I wanted to see if I could hear the wheat grow."

A hint of a smile touched his lips.

"Anyway, I was small for my age back then, and the stalks were much taller than I was. I became thoroughly lost among them. I'm not really sure how long I wandered scared, confused, and crying out for Grandpapa. I do remember Grand-mamma was making dumplings for supper that night because they were my favorite. I was devastated that I'd never be able to eat them or see my grandparents or family again. I truly thought I was going to die in that field."

"What ended up happening?" His voice was low, soft.

She ran a finger along the rim of her cup. "I eventually cried myself to sleep."

"But you found your way out."

Shaking her head, she hooked a finger in the handle, then took a sip. "Grandpapa's clear booming voice woke me. When I answered, he told mc to stay still and to sing 'Jesus Loves Me' as loud as I could. I wasn't even through the first chorus before he found me, scooped me up, and carried me home."

A group of men across the room clinked their glasses together and sang a drinking song in German, drowning out the orchestra downstairs.

"You must have been beside yourself in the crowd on opening day," he said.

"It wasn't nearly so dense when I arrived. By the time I realized how thick it was going to get, there was no escaping it." She took a deep breath. "I was singing 'Jesus Loves Me' to myself when you suddenly appeared in front of me."

"Had you gotten through the first chorus?"

She lifted her gaze, her throat thickening. "No."

His jaw worked. His chair legs came down with a quiet thud.

"Thank you for that," she said. "For rescuing me."

He slowly uncrossed his arms, his Adam's apple bobbing. "You're welcome."

She smoothed the napkin in her lap. "Did you have grandparents growing up?"

They spent the next several hours talking, laughing, and learning. He spoke not only of his grandfather but also of his growing up on a farm. Told her he'd sat on a nest of hen's eggs to see if he could get them to hatch. That he'd eaten a concoction of mashed-up worms like the birds so that he too could fly. That he'd driven his dad crazy taking anything and everything apart, only to put it back together again, not always correctly.

"I remember being sorry I hadn't been around for poor old Humpty Dumpty. I felt sure I'd have been able to fix him up."

The table had been cleared, the orchestra had retired, and the sun had long since set.

Placing her elbows on the table, she rested her chin in her clasped hands. "Your father must be so proud of you."

"His dreams for me are a bit lofty, I'm afraid."

Reaching over, she squeezed his arm. "I wouldn't be so sure. I think he might have the right of it. Your invention is remarkable. It's only a matter of time before others recognize the brilliance of it, of you."

His muscle twitched beneath her palm. Waiters in traditional Austrian costume began to stack chairs upside down on the empty tables, while their female counterparts swept the floor.

She squeezed him once more, then brought her hand to her lap. *The Forestry Building has pillars made of what?*

Narrowing his eyes, he zeroed in on her lips. "Which building again?"

The For-es-try.

"Tree trunks."

She smiled. *Where do we board?*

"The Harvell House."

What is Cullen looking for?

He took so long to answer, she wasn't sure he understood the question.

Finally, he lifted his hip and withdrew the answer sheet from his pocket. "Investors."

Whom did Della meet at Jastrow's demonstration?

"At what?"

Jas-trow's. Dem-on-stra-tion.

"Still didn't get it."

"Try the last word." *De. Mon. Stra—*

"Demonstration."

She nodded.

He gave her a sheepish look. "I've forgotten the question."

Finished with their tasks, the restaurant staff retreated to the kitchen, leaving them alone in the corner, partially hidden by topsy-turvy chairs.

Whom did Della meet at Jastrow's demonstration?

He looked at his list. "Helen Keller?"

"Yes."

Cullen rubbed his jaw. "I still can't figure out how Miss Keller uses her hand to 'hear' what you're saying." He splayed a hand across his own cheek and throat, his brows furrowed in confusion.

"I'll show you." Sitting up, she untied her hat, removed the pin securing it, then placed them both on the chair beside her. "She places her hand like . . ." She tried to arrange her hand on her own throat the way Helen did, but couldn't twist herself about. "Here, like this."

Reaching over, she took his hand, startled again at how much bigger it was than hers. And rougher. And warmer. "Put your thumb on my throat, directly atop the larynx."

She positioned his thumb, then maneuvered his index finger. "The first finger goes right over the lips."

She rested his finger across her mouth, then sucked in a breath. Sensations ricocheted through her body. Her gaze snapped to his.

His eyes turned dark, unreadable. "And the other fingers?"

She swallowed. "The third finger lies against the nostril." With each word, her lips caught against his callused finger. She positioned his middle one. "The rest of the hand relaxes against the cheek."

He bent his elbow at an awkward angle.

"It's easier if you sit a little closer—more side by side."

After a slight hesitation, he removed his hand and scooted over. Placing his left arm against the table in front of her, he leaned in, then rested his right hand against her larynx, lips, nose, and cheek. Mint from his hair tonic filled her.

"Now what?" His words were barely above a whisper.

"Well . . ." She cleared her throat. "You use your thumb to feel the hard consonants, like *g*. *Guh*."

His eyes brightened. "I feel it."

"And *k*. *Kuh*."

He made tiny circular motions with his thumb.

Grabbing his thumb, she held it still. "Don't move it around. Just hold steady."

"All right." He crooked his index finger, brushing it back and forth across her lips. "And what are these used for?"

Every nerve she had was at attention, some at the most startling places. "Those, um, those are for sounds like *b, v,* and *puh*."

"*Bee, vee, puh*." His breath fluttered across her eyelashes. "I definitely feel them."

She started to moisten her lips, then immediately pulled back. Good heavens. "The third finger is, um, um . . ."

"For the nose?" His voice teased.

"Correct. The nasal sounds. You know, *nnn* or *mmm*."

"*Mmmmmmmmmm*."

She swallowed. "The first word she learned was *it*."

"You used your lips for that one." But he wasn't looking at her. He was looking at her lips, much like the statue of the bobcat she passed on her way to the Children's Building—as if it were going to spring at any second.

"Yes," she managed. "Miss Sullivan made the *ih* sound, then the *tuh*. Helen put the two together and formed the word."

"What was her first sentence?" His breath ruffled her hair.

She shivered. "Her what?"

"Sentence. Helen's first sentence."

Her eyes drifted closed. "I."

"I," he repeated.

"Am."

"Am."

"Not."

"Not."

"Dumb."

"Dumb."

"Now."

"Now."

The silence between them stretched. Clinks from the kitchen along with muffled German voices drifted into their sanctuary.

He drew his fingers together so that they moved across her cheek.

Her pulse hammered. Her chest tightened.

The door to the kitchen slammed.

She opened her eyes.

He looked toward the sound.

"Ve are closed for zee night. Time to go."

Nodding, he turned his attention back to her, his gaze traveling over her hair, eyes, nose, cheeks, and lips.

Her mouth parted.

"Time to go," he said, scooting back. He stood, then pulled out her chair, his knuckles barely grazing her.

After a charged moment, she rose as well.

CHAPTER 31

Staring at his bedroom ceiling, Cullen wiggled a foot free of the covers. A far-off train whistle disrupted the quiet but not his thoughts.

His control was at the breaking point. He'd come so close to kissing her. He threw an arm over his eyes. What had happened exactly? Why had it spiraled so out of control?

Touching her while learning about Helen Keller had been the spark that ignited the fuse, of course, but why tonight? Why not before? It wasn't as if he'd never been tempted.

It didn't take him long to sort out the reason. Other than the obvious, Della's continued, unquestioning belief in his work had moved him. Deeply.

It was the one thing Wanda hadn't understood, even when they were children. She'd teased him about it then, but the year she put up her hair was the year he moved to Boston, and she'd been livid.

When he returned, everyone, including Wanda, assumed it was for her. But the truth was, if that piano factory hadn't burned down, he'd never have returned. He would still be there now.

But it had burned, and he had moved back. For good. And that was that. He was a farmer, just like his dad, his granddad, and his great-granddad. With that came Wanda. He'd never pictured it any other way.

Until now.

He sighed. Was he making excuses for his attraction to Della? Trying to justify his thoughts and urges?

Maybe. But the fact remained, misplaced or not, Della saw something in him that Wanda never had. The same thing his father did. The same thing his mother had.

Rolling onto his side, he burrowed a hand beneath his pillow and clasped the letter underneath it. With great tenderness, he removed it from its coveted place and laid it on his night table.

Tonight, he was going to give himself permission to dream about whatever and whomever he wanted. Just this once.

ADMINISTRATION BUILDING

"Cullen glanced at the Administration Building directly across from him, then squinted against the brightness of its golden dome. Inside resided the directive power of the exposition, and from what he'd read, no expense had been spared to make it glitter, dazzle, and intimidate."

CHAPTER 32

Descending the wide steps of Machinery Hall, Cullen glanced at the Administration Building directly across from him, then squinted against the brightness of its golden dome. Inside resided the directive power of the exposition, and from what he'd read, no expense had been spared to make it glitter, dazzle, and intimidate.

Cullen had difficulty reconciling that with the economic perils facing the country, for this edifice, more than any other structure on the grounds, gave no apologies for its grandiose opulence. Through it, foreigners would plainly see America didn't need kings or nobility when it had railroad barons, oil tycoons, and a director-general who had the power to approve or disapprove every activity on the fairgrounds—including Cullen's fire demonstration. He tried not to let all the trappings cow him.

Talk and laughter reached his ears as visitors moved from building to building, crossing bridges, admiring sculptures, and stopping at concessionaires. A few feet away, a farmer in a rusty black suit and collarless shirt placed a hand atop his broad-brimmed hat and bent back his head, a dazed expression on his face as he tried to take in the frescos and groups of statuary.

Cullen wondered what his dad would have

thought had he been the one standing there. Passing the man, Cullen pushed through the south entrance. If the exterior was grandiose, the interior was downright ostentatious. Neither gold leaf nor gold dollars had been spared in the decorating of it. Crossing the rotunda, he headed toward the northeast corner of the building, his boots clicking against the stone floor. Gilded, frescoed walls rose like mercury in a thermometer, then sloped in, meeting around a center skylight that looked like a giant cyclopean eye. At every turn, gilded moldings, gilt slates, and gilded letters served as a backdrop for innumerable sculptures and paintings.

He skirted a miniature rendition of Washington, D.C.'s Treasury House made solely with Columbian Exposition half-dollars.

A guard at the bottom of a curved mahogany staircase stopped him. "Do you have a permit?"

Cullen handed him his appointment card. "I'm to see Mr. Davis at noon."

As if confirming his statement, the replicated Liberty Bell began to toll the midday hour. Its bell was composed of gold and silver heirlooms contributed by people from all over the world.

The guard nodded. "Follow me."

They took two steps per chime, and Cullen found himself counting the tread. In the balustraded inner balcony, he had an unrestricted view of the painted mural gracing the dome.

Apollo sat on a lofty throne conferring honors on leaders in science and art. Cullen's gaze skittered away from the list of early discoverers and inventors recorded below it.

"Wait here," the guard said, stepping behind an oversized door with cut-glass inserts. A moment later, he returned, indicated Cullen enter, then pulled the door shut behind him.

Surely Grover Cleveland's office couldn't be more sumptuously appointed. Decorative molding, gilt-framed paintings, an electric chandelier, and wall-to-wall carpet in varying shades of purple bespoke the man's importance. He'd not only overseen the administration of the entire fair, but also appointed the heads of its departments. He sat at a rolltop desk jutting out from the wall, and if his white hair and goatee were any indication, he looked to be in his sixties. With one leg crossed over the other, he gently rocked his swivel chair while one arm rested along the armrest and his other held the paper he perused.

Cullen's stomach tightened. What was he doing here? He was a nobody, his exhibit child's play compared with all the other great displays he'd seen. What made him think even for a second this man would listen to his appeal? Only desperation held him in place.

Finally, Director-General Davis put down his paper and leaned back in his chair. "You must be

McNamara." He indicated the spindle chair beside his desk. "Have a seat."

"Thank you." Cullen eased into the chair and tucked his long legs out of the way.

"I understand you want to set a shed on fire and endanger the entire park." Davis's voice was calm and matter-of-fact, but his steely gray eyes looked Cullen square on.

Scooting back in the seat, Cullen straightened his spine. "I'd never endanger the park, sir. If I thought my demonstration would do that, I wouldn't be here."

"But you do want to set a shed on fire?"

"Yes, sir. Just temporarily. My sprinklers will put it out within three minutes."

Davis placed his elbows on the armrests and threaded his fingers together over his stomach. "You sound very sure of yourself."

"I am." Slipping a hand into his coat pocket, Cullen removed a sprinkler head. "If I may?"

Davis nodded. "Go ahead."

Cullen showed him where the solder joint would be and what would happen when it melted. "Water pressure on the diaphragm keeps water away from the moving parts, protecting, the device from corrosion. But the moment the solder melts, the diaphragm bursts, the valve opens up, and water gushes through."

Davis tapped his thumbs together. "What happens if it's a windy day? Heaven knows we get plenty of those up here. It would take much less than three minutes for sparks to fly from your shed to a neighboring building. And these buildings are highly flammable."

"That's why I recommend we do this in an out-of-the-way place. Maybe in the back corner of the park by the trash furnace?"

Davis shook his head. "It smells back there, especially with the sewage cleaning works right next door. I wouldn't want any guests over there."

"What about over by the terminal tracks, then? You know, behind Machinery Hall's annex? That's fairly deserted. Or maybe at the end of the north pier?"

"I don't know. I just don't see the benefit outweighing the risk."

Clasping his hands together, Cullen leaned forward. "Sir, this automatic sprinkler can save lives. Not just a few, but hundreds, thousands of them. Think of any fire you've ever been a part of." He knew the man wouldn't be able to help but think of the Cold Storage fire. "If the home or building you're thinking of had had automatic sprinklers installed, they would have released water at the first sign of trouble. In most cases, the sprinklers would put the fire out completely. If nothing else, they would at least help control it until the occupants could escape and the brigade could arrive. But none will ever be installed unless business owners see it work

309

with their own eyes. And for that I need a demonstration."

"I appreciate that, son, but I simply can't take that kind of risk. Not after the Cold Storage tragedy."

He scrambled for a compromise. "What if we had a company of firemen at my demonstration ready with hose carriage and water tower? At the first sign of trouble, they could douse the whole thing."

Davis rubbed his eyes. "There wouldn't be any signs of trouble if we didn't do the demonstration at all."

"Please, sir."

"I'm sorry. I just can't approve this."

Cullen's breaths became shallow. "Could you talk with Chief Murphy about it? See what he thinks?"

Uncrossing his legs, Davis put both feet down and rolled his chair back to his desk. "It would take more than that, I'm afraid. I'd also have to speak with Colonel Rice of the Columbian Guards, the president of the commission, the Council of Administration." He shook his head. "The list goes on and on. I'm sure you can appreciate the difficulty in receiving a unified response, not to mention the time spent in tracking everyone down."

"What if I speak to them? What if I track them down?"

Davis shrugged and picked up a pen from its holder. "If you like. Be my guest."

"May I tell them you sent me?"

"Fine, fine. Now, if you'll excuse me?" He dipped his pen in the ink.

Cullen stood. "Yes, sir. Thank you for your time."

Instead of returning to Machinery Hall, he wandered through the upper-floor corridors, reading the nameplates at each door, and knocking on the ones that held the decision makers.

NURSERY IN THE CHILDREN'S BUILDING

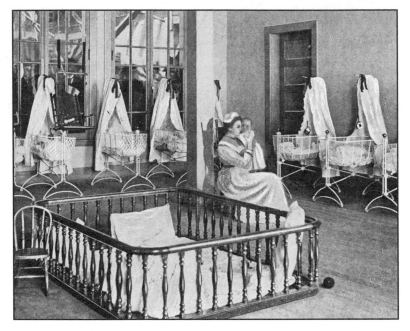

"Of all the attractions at the fair, Cullen couldn't think of any he'd rather skip more than the Children's Building. What possible interest would he have in looking in on a bunch of kiddies whose parents had checked them at the door?"

CHAPTER 33

Della arranged fifteen toys on a pallet in front of the children, then returned to her seat. The school didn't require uniforms for the students. Instead, the girls wore homemade smocks in a variety of colors, while the boys dressed in brown or navy short pants and miniature neck scarves.

She gave their semicircle a sweeping glance. "Who can show me where the baby doll is?"

Eight little hands shot into the air. Vivienne waved hers above her head in a large arch. Edgar wiggled all five fingers. Theo rocked back and forth. Kitty gave her an imploring look. Boyce sat slumped with his arms crossed. Julia Jo sat prim and proper.

"Julia Jo."

She bounced off her chair and ran straight to the doll, hugging it fiercely to her breast. "The *daaa* is *riii he-yore.*"

" 'The doll is right here.' Very good, Julia Jo."

Kitty's face crumbled, her eyes watering.

Della quickly moved to the next object. "Who can spy the woolly lamb?"

It didn't matter who else raised a hand. Della knew she'd pick Kitty. The doll and stuffed lamb were her very favorites. Next to those, any type of instrument that would allow her to play house—whether it was a broom, a washboard and a pail,

313

or a collection of miniature pots and pans. But in order to give all the other girls a chance to play with the doll and stuffed lamb, Kitty had gone without for almost a week.

"Kitty."

Blinking away her tears, Kitty slid from her chair, her tightly coiled blond curls bouncing, then went immediately to the lamb. *"Hiss* is a *wulley am."*

" 'This is a woolly lamb' is correct."

A group of visitors shuffled in, but Della paid them no mind as she continued the drill until all children had a toy to play with.

"You did an excellent job." She clapped her hands in approval, the visitors following suit. Then she checked the watch pin on her blouse. "You may have twenty minutes for playtime."

The tourists began to shuffle out.

"Mama!" Kitty screeched, dropping the woolly lamb and rushing to a fashionable woman who crouched down with open arms.

The adults stopped. The children froze. Della sucked in her breath.

Mrs. Kruger clasped Kitty to her much like Julia Jo had the baby doll, then stood without letting go. Both mother and daughter cried and hugged and kissed. Mr. Kruger, a young, affluent man in a tailored silk suit, placed one hand at his wife's waist and the other on Kitty's back.

Della clasped her hands, then caught the tour

314

guide's eye and indicated with a slant of her head that she take her group from the room.

"Right this way, please. Our next stop is the roof." Giving parting glances to the touching scene behind them, all but the Krugers left.

But no good could come from this. There were strict rules about visitations.

She glanced at her students. They loved playtime. She made a point to rotate the toys so they never became old. Boyce had a box of ten-pin blocks. Vivienne had a Cinderella coach with blocks illustrating the story. Edgar had a bucket of toy soldiers.

Yet none of them were playing. All watched with stricken expressions, wishing it were their parents at the door.

Della approached the couple.

Mr. Kruger glanced up. "Please forgive us, Miss Wentworth. We'd come to the fair and wanted only to have a glimpse of her. We didn't intend for her to see us."

"Mr. Kruger, you know there are rules about this. Just look at the other children. And now, Kitty. She'll be morose for who knows how long, knowing you are here yet not understanding why she can't go with you."

Mrs. Kruger tucked Kitty against her shoulder. Kitty stuck a thumb in her mouth and ran her other hand along the fringe of her mother's collar.

"Why can't she go with us?" the woman asked.

"What would it hurt? We could take her to see so many things. Has she even been out of this building? Or is she imprisoned here so the curious can come look at her, as if she were no more than an animal in the zoo?"

Della's lips parted. "That's not at all what it's like. We are allowing the public to come in so they can see how critical it is for us to teach the children to lip-read at as early an age as possible. To show them these children are equal to the task just as the hearing are. That is our purpose here."

"Has she seen any of the fair?" Mr. Kruger asked.

"Well, no, sir. We have school all day, then supper and bedtime."

His lips narrowed. "I cannot imagine being in this amazing White City and not taking the children on regular outings. The only reason I can think of for such an oversight is so you can put on this little show." He swept his arm to encompass the other children.

"No, sir. It's not like that at all."

"Isn't it?"

Mrs. Kruger lifted her chin. "We're taking her with us."

Della's eyes widened. "You cannot."

"Just for a few hours." The woman's eyes filled. "Please. She's gotten so big. And she feels so good. It would be such an educational experience for her and a healing one for us."

Della's throat began to fill. "You know I'm not allowed. The temptation to use hand gestures to communicate with her would be too strong."

"Would it really set her back that much?" she asked.

"It would," Della said, but deep inside, she wasn't so sure.

Mr. Kruger lowered his voice. "Don't you think the benefits of spending a few hours with her parents at the World's Fair would outweigh any perceived drawbacks were we to accidentally use a hand gesture?"

She bit her lip. "It's not my decision. I don't have the authority to grant you permission."

"Then go get someone who does," he barked.

"I cannot leave the children."

"Please," Mrs. Kruger begged, her blue eyes so much like Kitty's. "Please. She hasn't been home since she was two. Not for Christmas, not for her birthday, not for Thanksgiving. We just want an hour outside a school setting. Please."

Della's heart squeezed. This wasn't right. She'd never questioned the rule until now, but clearly keeping children from their parents was unnatural.

The door burst open. Her director stood in its threshold, eyes narrowed, lips pinched. "What is the meaning of this?"

In her midthirties, she dressed in dark, sedate colors, her saddle-brown hair pulled back into a bun. A continuous row of short hair curling over like a sausage framed an extremely high forehead.

Mr. Kruger straightened to his full height. "We're taking Kitty to tour the fair with us for a couple of hours. We'll be back before supper."

"You will do no such thing. Put her down immediately, and we'll discuss this in my office."

"No." Mrs. Kruger held her daughter more tightly. Kitty's lips trembled. Della's other students whimpered.

"You are upsetting the entire class," the director said. "Have a care. We have an extremely long waiting list for students. You knew what the rules were when you enrolled her. You gave us your word you would abide by them." She seared Mr. Kruger with her gaze. "Is your word worth nothing?"

Her students might not be able to hear, but they could feel the tension and heartbreak. Della didn't know whether to go to them or stay close to Kitty.

Finally, Mr. Kruger thrust his chin forward. "Give her to me, Pam."

"No, Howard. Please, no." The woman shook her head, curly blond wisps escaping her coif. Still, she released her daughter into her husband's hands.

Cradling Kitty in his arms, he touched her chin and looked into her eyes. "I love you."

He did everything he wasn't supposed to. He spoke slowly, and he exaggerated his lips. A single tear rolled down his cheek.

"I *wuv ooo.*" Her cherubic voice trembling, Kitty brushed the tear from her father's face.

Leaning over, he kissed her on the forehead. "Say bye-bye to Mama."

Kitty's mouth fell open. "No, Papa. No."

Mrs. Kruger clasped Kitty's hand and brought it to her lips. "We'll be back, sweet girl. Mama loves you."

He leaned over to set her down, but she wouldn't let go. She screamed, she cried, she crushed his silk jacket in her fists.

Della didn't even know she was crying until she tasted the salt on her lips. Squatting down, she forced Kitty's fingers from her father's lapels.

"No!" She kicked, she swung her fists, her blond curls springing in every direction.

Finally, Della had her and tucked her against her chest. But Kitty fought, flinging herself toward her parents.

"Quickly," the director said.

Pulling his sobbing wife against him, Mr. Kruger did as he was instructed.

FERRIS WHEEL

"The wheel is going to be to this fair what the Eiffel Tower was to the Paris Exposition."

CHAPTER 34

Cullen stared at the official-looking piece of paper with disbelief. All the legwork, all the knocking on doors had actually paid off. His appeal had been granted. The commission had said yes—*if* he had a fire wagon and *if* he held the demonstration behind Terminal Station where there weren't any buildings. The commission hadn't asked him how much time he needed but simply scheduled the demonstration for this coming Monday. He couldn't wait to tell Della, but first he had things to attend to.

He asked Tisdale if he would print up some invitations on the platen press from scrap paper. Then he took a morning train out to Grasty's printing works. Cullen had already promised he'd come by and give an estimate. He couldn't afford to cancel that.

Though Grasty Printing Works was a pre-existing building, it was a simple one. Four sides, one ceiling. What fascinated him most were the printing presses that chugged beneath that ceiling. He stood before them, marveling at the constant motion of man and machine.

Grasty joined him, his toothy grin intact as he indicated Cullen follow him to a partitioned-off corner. Tucked behind a paneled screen were a bookshelf and a desk with rolled papers crammed inside its pigeonholes and others strewn across its surface.

"Have a seat," Grasty shouted over the noise.

Wondering if he'd ever have a client with a quiet office, Cullen lowered himself into a spindly chair, then caught his balance when its uneven legs shifted.

"So, what's *yr* estimate?" Grasty asked, hooking eyeglasses over his ears.

"I should be able to do the entire job for eighty."

"Eighty dollars?"

"Yes, sir."

Grasty's smile grew even larger. "Excellent. That's great news. When can you start?"

Cullen's jaw slackened. He hadn't expected to close the deal, particularly on an unproven system. "Well, I . . ." He shrugged. "Let's see, the fair ends the thirty-first of October, which is a Tuesday, I believe. Then I'll need time to tie up everything, gather the materials, and make the sprinkler heads. So how does the first week in December sound?"

Turning to a wall calendar beside him, Grasty lifted some sheets, then penciled in *SPRINKLER* on December fourth.

Euphoria shot through Cullen. "I'll need fifty percent down, then fifty percent on completion."

"I'll bring the money to you this week. Will that suffice?"

Smiling, Cullen started to rise. "Yes, sir. Thank you, sir."

Grasty held up a hand. "Not quite so fast, son. We're not done."

Cullen lowered himself back into the flimsy chair.

"We haven't talked about my other printing works. They're spread all along the eastern seaboard. Will you need to see those, or can you give me an estimate from architectural drawings?"

"It depends on the drawings."

For the next thirty minutes, they perused several drawings and discussed options. And with each building, the quote mounted. It was currently at fifteen hundred dollars and Grasty hadn't so much as batted an eye.

Cullen had been figuring in a fifty percent markup, plus another ten percent for wiggle room, since looking at drawings was a lot different from looking at the actual structures. Still, at this rate, he'd be able to pay off the farm's debts and have enough left over to live off of. For the first time in a long, long while, a spark of hope flared inside him.

The longer they talked, though, the more Cullen struggled to hear. Between the background noise and Grasty's tendency toward smiling, lip-reading was next to impossible. And worse, he was on Cullen's right. Cullen had asked the man to repeat himself several times, and with each subsequent request Grasty became more agitated.

Finally, he whipped off his glasses. "Is there a problem, McNamara?"

Taking a deep breath, Cullen quelled his sudden nervousness. The man had asked him outright if there was a problem. And there was only one way to answer that truthfully.

"I'm sorry, sir," he said. "But I'm hard of hearing. If you could just speak a little more slowly and loudly, I should be able to hear just fine."

Steepling his fingers against the table, Grasty pierced Cullen with his gaze. "Hard of *hrng*? What do you mean hard of *hrng*?"

Again. A direct question requiring a direct and honest answer. He swallowed. "I can barely hear with my right ear, but my left one works fairly well."

Grasty slowly straightened, his face blotching. "You're deaf? You *nvr* mentioned you were *df*."

"I'm not deaf. I'm hard of hearing. But it doesn't affect my work."

"This is very *trblsm* news, McNamara. You should have *tld* me this long ago. Why haven't you mentioned it *bfr*?"

"It, um, never came up."

"Never came up?" He shook his head. "I'm sorry, Mr. McNamara. But I'm sure you understand Grasty Printing Works is not in the business of *cntrctng* with the deaf and dumb."

Cullen tensed. "Do I appear dumb to you, sir?"

He spoke calmly, his voice almost too even. "Do not be *imprtnt* with me. For our own protection, we can't hire *smone* like you. It would put the whole *plnt* at risk."

"I'm sorry?" It was out before he could call it back. It didn't really matter what Grasty had said. Cullen should have just nodded and kept his mouth shut.

Grasty narrowed his eyes. "How about this. Our. Deal. Is. Off. Did you hear *tht*?"

Panic assailed him. "Please, sir. I do excellent work. I'm fast. And my prices are very reasonable."

Grabbing one end of the architectural plans, Grasty began rolling them up. "I'm no longer interested. There was another exhibitor right beside you who didn't have one foot in the madhouse."

Cullen whipped himself up to his full hcight. "There's nothing wrong with my faculties, sir."

Grasty eyed him with displeasure. "Hearing is a faculty, McNamara. I'm not *aboot* to spend this kind of money on a man I can't rely on."

"But you can rely on me. Besides, Bulenberg's sprinkler system doesn't even compare. It's manual. It's antiquated. And someone would have to be there to pull a lever for it to work. Mine is one-of-a-kind and will work night or day no matter who is or isn't there."

"I've said what I had to say." Grasty's breathing grew deep. "I believe you've wasted enough of my time. You know the way out."

Ten minutes later, Cullen sat on the train back to Jackson Park, watching Chicago whiz by his window. Typical. Everything he touched turned to stone. Well, lesson learned. No one, but no one, could learn he was going deaf. He only hoped Grasty didn't spread the word before Cullen's demonstration on Monday.

Della saw Cullen before he saw her. He sat at their table in Blooker's cradling his chin in his hand, staring into space.

Her own heart heavy, she approached. "Hello."

Rousing himself, he rose to hold out her chair. "Hello."

"Are you all right?" she asked.

"I was just going to ask you the same thing." He pushed in her chair.

"I had a horrible day."

His brows drew together. "What happened?"

"Some parents came to class and tried to whisk one of my students away for a few hours."

He motioned for Miss Zonderkop to bring a cup of cocoa.

"And that's bad?" he asked.

She rubbed her temples. "Yes. The students are supposed to stay with us for an uninterrupted six-year period."

"What does 'uninterrupted' mean?"

"It means they never go home."

He studied her. "Not even for Christmas?"

"Not even for Christmas."

"Doesn't that seem a bit excessive to you?"

She sighed. "The parents are allowed scheduled visits as often as they'd like, they just aren't allowed to take the children off the property."

"Why?"

"The directors are fearful the parents will use hand gestures during vacation and will undo all our hard work. But you should have seen these parents, Cullen." Her nostrils flared as she tried to swallow the hurt. "They just wanted to take Kitty out and show her the fair for a few hours. A few hours. I just don't see the harm in that."

"I don't either. Did you let them?"

Her hot chocolate arrived, but she didn't touch it. "No. Our director came to the classroom and made me tear the child out of her parents' arms." She fumbled with the napkin in her lap. "It was awful. Awful."

"I'm sorry."

She shook her head. "Hearing people use hand gestures all the time. We wave, we point, we cross our arms, we stomp our feet. We do all manner of things."

"So you think signing should be taught instead?"

"No. Lip-reading is very important. My question is, Why can't we teach both?"

"Why don't you ask?"

She looked at him. "Maybe I will." Swiping her eyes, she sniffed and gave him a watery smile. "So how was your day?"

"Not as bad as yours, but not one of my favorites. Still, there was one bright spot."

She took a sip of cocoa, its warmth soothing her raw throat. "Oh, I would love to hear about something bright."

"Well then, guess who came by my booth just now?"

"Who?"

"Mr. Ferris."

She blinked. "*The* Mr. Ferris?"

"Yes. We talked extensively. He's an engineer, of course, and takes great interest in all things mechanical. Anyway, he gave me some tickets as a token of good luck for my demonstration." He reached inside his jacket and withdrew two tickets.

Taking one, she turned it over in her hand. On one side an "F" in fancy calligraphy had been set against ornate scroll designs. On the back, *THE FERRIS WHEEL* had been printed in a wave-like pattern across the top. Along the bottom, *ONE RIDE*. "Oh, my goodness. Why did he give them to you, again?"

"As a token of good luck for my demonstration."

"What demonstration?"

A dimple began to form. His eyes took on a

shine. "The director-general said yes. A demonstration of my automatic sprinkler is scheduled for a week from today."

"Oh, Cullen. That is a very bright spot." She smiled, her heart lifting. "Congratulations. I'm so proud of you and pleased. You must be ecstatic."

He gave a shrug. "Relieved would be more accurate. At least I can do something other than stand in my booth all day."

She took another sip. "And how did the meeting go with the printing works man?"

Unbuttoning his suit jacket, he allowed it to fall open a bit. "He passed."

She slowly set down her cup. "I'm sorry."

"It was no surprise, really. I should never have gotten my hopes up."

"It's his loss, Cullen. Not yours."

He lifted one shoulder.

Straightening, she tapped the Ferris wheel ticket with her hand. "What do you say we forget about our troubles for now and instead celebrate the commission's decision with a ride on this. Everyone has said the wheel is going to be to this fair what the Eiffel Tower was to the Paris Exposition. And I, for one, can't wait to ride it."

FERRIS WHEEL CAR

" 'Forty people to a car!'
A ticket taker let the appropriate number
past the wheel's barricade, which separated
them from its loading platforms."

CHAPTER 35

The line to the Ferris wheel wound clear down to the German Village, but she hardly noticed it. Shoving her situation at work aside, she placed all her focus on Cullen as he told her of his plans for the demonstration and all the preparation it would require.

An Egyptian woman with a hooped nose ring beat her drum in a strange rhythm, momentarily drawing their attention to the Cairo theater. Della would love to see the show, but she knew Cullen wouldn't want to spend the money, and she'd do well to save hers too.

"Forty people to a car!" A ticket taker let the appropriate number past the wheel's barricade, which separated them from its loading platforms. The enormous iron spiderweb gave a creak and rumble as excited voices rose all around them.

The line surged forward, but before they could reach the front, the barrier was replaced. Still, they were close enough to watch passengers load the cars. Once full, those began to ascend while six more cars settled along the bottom. Sliding doors opened, allowing riders to unload.

Cullen gave her a sharp glance. "Is the height of this going to bother you?"

"No, no. I told you, I wasn't prepared before. I'll be fine."

Calling for more people, the ticket taker let them through.

Anticipation built inside her. She wondered if this would be as thrilling as the toboggan ride. Placing a hand on her hat, she looked up, but the brightness of the sky made her squint and kept her from seeing the height of Mr. Ferris's engineering marvel.

Someone bumped her from behind, while another man crowded her on the side. Taking her elbow, Cullen tucked her close and guided her toward the middle coach. At its door, she stopped short. Her breath hitched. People swarmed by on either side like a stream rerouting around a stone.

The cage was about the size of a passenger car on a train and held five huge wire screens on opposite sides. Numerous revolving stools were nailed to the floor.

"Della?" Cullen looked down at her, a question in his voice.

Her stomach gave a small objection.

"Is everything all right?" He bent slightly to see below the rim of her hat. "Do you want to turn around?"

It reminded her of the elevator, only bigger.

You're being silly, she told herself. *Start walking. You conquered the elevator. You can conquer this. It's Cullen's celebration for receiving the commission's blessing. Don't ruin it.*

"No, no." She forced a smile. "I'm fine."

Someone again bumped her from behind, pushing her forward. She placed one foot in front of the other, her stomach graduating from an unpleasant tickle to a rumbling, nauseating sensation.

The door behind them slid shut with a distinctive click. An attendant dropped a bar across it.

A new tingling danced atop the nausea. That hadn't happened in the elevator.

"It doesn't look like there are any two seats together anymore." Cullen's voice came to her as if through a long tunnel.

She wanted to turn around. She wanted to run.

The wheel jerked and began an upward descent. She slung an arm out to steady herself.

"Come on." Cullen guided her toward a vacant stool.

The upward motion was noiseless, like a balloon flying away in the sky.

Her oxygen supply shut off. She stumbled, trying to suck in air, but couldn't get enough. The tingling turned into a prickling and rose from her stomach to her chest. What was happening?

Cullen slipped an arm around her and helped her into a seat. "You're pale as a ghost. Are you all right?"

Don't leave me, she thought. But she was afraid to speak. She didn't have enough air to spare. The prickling continued to rise, now from her chest on up to her throat. Its rate of ascent matched that of the wheel's.

Those on the stools around her nudged Cullen with their knees and shoulders. He stepped away to find himself a seat.

She felt boxed in. Her nausea increased. *Look out the window. Look at all that open space.*

And when she did, she made the mistake of looking down. The earth was sinking away, slowly, quietly, and at a great distance. The racetrack beyond the park held throngs of carriages and swarming crowds, while little horses galloped in a circle. They were so small it looked as if she could pick the whole thing up and watch the race on the palm of her hand.

The prickling filled her face, spreading out like arms of an octopus. She touched her cheek. It was numb. Her face was *numb.*

She gasped for air, able to catch only tiny snatches. Just enough to tease her. Just enough to keep her alive.

But for how long?

The whole fair spread out before her—its buildings, lagoons, green turf, and trees. Old Vienna and its bandstand were surrounded by tiny tables with microscopic people drinking beer. And beyond the fair were prairies. Endless prairies.

She sucked in, but no air reached her lungs. No

air at all. Oh, Lord. She was dying. She was actually going to die. Right here on the Ferris wheel.

The woman next to her *oohed* and pointed at something she saw. Her son pressed his face against the strong wire mesh and looked down.

Della bit her lips together to hold back the nausea but had to quickly open them again for air.

Her fingers began to curl of their own volition. Tighter and tighter, they froze into a fist until they too were numb. Why was this happening?

Terror sent shivers through her. Her heart pounded with such speed it would surely leap clear out of her chest. Was her heart failing? Would it cease altogether, or would she instead suffocate in slow agony?

Pulling in snatches of air, she scanned the crowd. Where was Cullen? Where was he?

Then she saw him, weaving through the stools to get to her, his face filled with concern.

What is it? he asked, knowing she could read his lips.

Take me to the hospital.

He didn't understand, but she couldn't sign by alphabet because her fists were frozen shut. Still, she stacked her fists, stretched them in front of her and pulled them into her chest. *Help me.*

His eyes widened. He practically leaped over the last few stools. There was no room for his large body. She shrank back. She needed space. More space.

Scooping her up, he sat on her stool and cradled her in his lap. "What is it?"

She touched her collar with fisted hands, gasping, gasping. "Air," she croaked. "I need air."

Cullen thumbed open the buttons at her neck, loosening her collar, spreading her blouse open.

The boy who'd been pressed against the window pointed at her, then cupped his hand over his mouth and said something to his mother. The woman twisted around. One by one, those around them began to stare, having no idea she could read every word they whispered.

What's wrong with that woman?

She's sitting on that man's lap and he's, he's undressing her!

Shocking. I never . . .

She averted her gaze. The view the occupants had paid precious money for was no longer as interesting as watching her die. For there was no question now, she was going to die.

Tears rushed to her eyes.

Where was the bright light? The one everyone said you see just before you die? She began to sing "Jesus Loves Me" to herself.

It's an attack, a man said. *She's having an attack.*

Is it contagious? Will we get it?

What's a woman like that even doing here? Her kind are to be locked up.

That little boy next to her will have nightmares for months.

Quick, cover little Shirley's eyes.

Della closed her own eyes, but the dark made her dizzy.

She finished the chorus of her song. *Just take me, Lord,* she thought. *Just take me.*

Instead, she found the next breath a bit easier. And then the next. Feeling reentered her fingers, a thousand pinpricks stung her skin. She took a tremulous breath, her first real one since she'd stepped into the car.

At some point, Cullen had removed her hat, for she saw it on the floor next to their stool.

Her fingers relaxed. She slowly unfurled them.

Tears rushed up again. It had passed. Whatever it was had passed.

Cullen placed his hand against her face and tucked her head beneath his chin. He swayed from side to side, his arms around her, one hand rubbing her back.

She took deep, healing breaths. Nausea still held her captive, but she could breathe. And she wasn't numb.

Her heart slowed to match his, which beat with reassuring steadiness against her ear.

"I want off," she murmured.

"My lap?" he whispered.

"The wheel."

"It won't be long now. You're better?"

337

She gave a slight nod against his chest, too weak to do more.

The wheel lurched to a stop with a slight creak and a grumble.

She tensed.

Cullen rubbed his lips against her forehead. "Shhh. It's all right. They're letting passengers off. There are two more groups after them, then it will be our turn."

"What if something gives way?" She heard the fear in her voice.

He gave her a gentle squeeze. "The machine is solid. The weight of two thousand people would mean no more to it than a fly on the back of your hand. And we've only forty in here."

She closed her eyes, willing away the image of dangling at the top of the wheel's cycle. "Did you see the axle at its hub? It's barely the width of my finger."

"It's at least three feet in diameter. It's the distance that makes it look so small."

The wheel lurched again, along with her stomach. The second group began to disembark.

After a bit, he smoothed the hair away from her face. "Do you feel like sitting up? We'll be getting off soon, and I thought you might want to repair your shirtwaist first."

Placing a hand against his chest, she pushed herself to a sitting position, then tried to remove her glove but was too weak.

He steadied her on his lap, then pulled the fabric of her blouse together and buttoned it, his knuckles and fingers grazing her skin. It had been a long time since anyone fussed over her. She barely recalled the last time her mother had performed such a task.

It felt much different when he did it.

She studied the side part in his hair, tempted to run her hand through it. Tempted to rest her nose against it. Tempted to breathe in his scent.

But air was still too precious and the patrons of the car were shocked enough as it was, so she stayed put.

Lifting her chin, she allowed him to secure the last few buttons. Though she made eye contact with no one, stares pierced her from all around. She wondered if this was how her students felt when people realized they were deaf.

Her eyes widened. They could lip-read. Those sweet, precious children would be able to see every ugly thing people whispered about them.

Cullen lowered his hands to her waist, bracing her for the next lurch. It wasn't long in coming.

When they stopped again, he scratched his thumbnail against her waist. "We'll be next."

She braved a glance over his shoulder. Men eyed her with lasciviousness. Women eyed her with disgust.

For the first time, she experienced what it was like to be "different." What her students experienced, through no fault of their own, every single day. This was what she had been trying to protect them from. For if they used sign language in public, it would garner every bit as much attention as she had.

Yet deafness didn't make them inferior any more than her inability to breathe made her inferior. She was still the same person she'd always been.

"I'm sorry," Cullen said. "I should have known better. I don't know what I was thinking."

"It's my fault. I didn't expect it to bother me." She wondered if the entire episode had stemmed from a fear of being closed in or launched up into the air.

"You're okay, though?"

"For now, I think. My stomach is still upset and my limbs are weak, but the rest has gone away."

He nodded. "Your color looks much better."

"I still want off this thing and don't ever want back on."

"I don't blame you. I'm sorry for all the chatter in here. I know you saw it."

She swallowed, having forgotten he could lip-read enough to garner the gist of the conversations around them. "I think I'd have been more prepared for their comments if I'd known I was going to become so frightened. The whole thing took me by surprise."

"There's still no cause for what they said."

"They didn't know we'd 'hear' them."

"They knew God would."

She gave him a slight smile, wanting to rest against him again. To thank him for his fierce protectiveness. It was the same protectiveness she felt for her students.

But she couldn't be with them forever. At some point, they'd have to face the world and its prejudices. And when they did, would lip-reading be enough? The man from the National Association of the Deaf didn't think so, and if she were completely honest with herself, she didn't think so either.

No, her students would need as many tools as they could garner, including sign language. For sign language was not only a tool, it was one of the most critical. As was spending time with their parents. She'd been so tied up in her quest to make the children "normal" she ended up making them abnormal. For what could be more unnatural than being wrenched from their parents' loving arms when they were barely old enough to dress themselves? And then being separated from them for another five years?

She shook her head. She'd been hindering these children for years, all under the guise of benevolence.

She needed to speak with her director. There was no question the school and other deaf advocates had the children's best interests at heart. The problem was, those who supported sign language accepted difference, while those who supported lip-reading sought equality. What she'd just begun to grasp was the deaf were not one or the other; they were both different *and* equal.

ENTRANCE TO THE WOMAN'S BUILDING

"A chattering group of women
entered the building, a gust of wind
filling their skirts like bells until the large
wooden door clicked shut behind them."

CHAPTER 36

Cullen paced outside an infirmary just off the vestibule in the Woman's Building, then sat on a bench provided by the Board of Lady Managers, then went back to pacing. The intricate tapestry draping one of the soaring walls depicted episodes in William the Conqueror's rule. It seemed oddly out of place in this building until he read a plaque stating the original had been fashioned by William's wife. Still, the piece held his interest for no more than a moment before his concern for Della returned.

"Is everything all right, sir?"

A Columbian Guard approached. He looked much like the others Cullen had seen—tall, fit, and serious. Except this one wore cowpuncher boots.

"You've been circling this foyer like a squirrel in a cage," the man said. "Is there somethin' I can help you with?"

"No, I'm sorry. I have a . . ." A what? A tutor? A friend? Neither of those came close to what Della had become to him. "The lady I'm with is in the infirmary."

The guard smiled—not a polite smile but a full-fledged grin. "Is that right? Well, don't you worry about a thing. The doc in there's the best of the best."

"He is?" Cullen glanced at the door. "He's trained, then?"

"Graduated cum laude from the University of Michigan." The man puffed up as if he'd been the one to receive the diploma. "And it's a she, not a he."

Cullen frowned. "Who's a she?"

"The doc."

He took a step back. "He's a *she?* Do you mean to tell me my lady isn't seeing a real doctor?"

The guard narrowed his eyes. "She's real. And before you say anything else, you probably ought to know she's my woman." He looked at the door, pride and affection replacing his irritation.

Cullen tried to process the idea of a female doctor. The guard didn't seem to notice, though. He simply clapped Cullen's shoulder and told him again not to worry.

Cullen wasn't sure that was possible. Della had been weak as a babe. He hoped her distress in the Ferris wheel had been just that—distress. If it was anything more serious, he figured the doc would know. Still, a lady doctor. That was going to take some getting used to.

The guard disappeared around the corner, leaving Cullen alone with his thoughts. He called himself ten kinds of a fool for taking Della to the wheel to begin with. He'd seen what happened in the elevator. The wheel was a hundred times worse. He didn't know what he'd been thinking.

But he did know that when she turned from white to gray to white, his heart had dropped to his stomach. Every protective instinct he had kicked in. He wanted to shield her from the intrusive eyes of others, from the terror she was experiencing, from the helplessness she felt at not being able to capture enough air. And he wanted to do it for the rest of his life.

A chattering group of women entered the building, a gust of wind filling their skirts like bells until the large wooden door clicked shut behind them.

"I want to be sure to go to the Violet Booth," one of them said, fluffing her skirt. "It has a little booklet called *The Story of the Woman's Building*, but it's been adapted from *Three Girls in a Flat*."

"Has it? How very clever."

Cullen stopped his pacing and let the women pass, then sought out the bench once more. He stared at the door of the infirmary, his mind finally accepting what his heart had been screaming these last three months. He wasn't ever going to fall in love with Wanda. And he wasn't doing her or himself any good by promising to marry her when he was in love with someone else.

Didn't matter that they'd set a date. Didn't matter that everyone expected it. What mattered was, he wanted to spend the rest of his life with Della.

He'd waited for those exact same feelings to surface with Wanda and had fully expected them to come. But now he knew better. If they hadn't shown up by now, they weren't going to show up at all.

If he and Wanda had already been married, that would be different. But they weren't. And after the scare of losing Della, he knew beyond a shadow of a doubt. It was time to be honest about his love for her and his sorrow for having tied Wanda up when he shouldn't have.

Wanda would be heartbroken. Her mother would be livid. Her father . . . he didn't even want to think about her father. His own family would be shocked as well. Should he write a letter? Wait until he returned home?

But he didn't want to wait. He wanted to express his feelings now. He wanted to have the freedom to love without guilt.

Della stepped out of the infirmary and into the vestibule.

Leaping off the bench, he strode to her. "What did the doc say? Are you all right?"

She pulled on her gloves. "The doctor was a woman."

"So I heard."

"There wasn't a single man in there at all. Everyone, from the secretary to the nurses to the doctor, is female."

He glanced at the door, still a bit befuddled.

347

She touched his arm. "I liked her, Cullen. She was, well, she was wonderful."

He rubbed his eyes. "So, what was the diagnosis, then?"

"I'm fine. Embarrassed, but fine."

"You've no call to be embarrassed. Did the . . . the doctor say anything else?"

"I'm to stay away from closed-in spaces that soar high above the ground."

He grimaced. "I'm sorry, Della. I can't believe I took you up there."

"It's not your fault. Neither one of us expected that to happen." She dusted nonexistent dirt from her skirt. "And I am embarrassed. While we were up there, I made my brain tell my body to quit being ridiculous, but it refused to listen. It just went right ahead and did whatever it pleased."

"Well, I suggest we heed its warnings. In the meanwhile, I say we call it an early night." He offered his elbow.

And though they usually talked nonstop, they headed toward Harvell House in silence, both caught up in their own thoughts.

CHILDREN'S BUILDING

"Della hovered at the threshold of
her director's office on the second floor
of the Children's Building."

CHAPTER 37

Della hovered at the threshold of her director's office on the second floor of the Children's Building. Seascapes decorated the walls, while a smattering of chairs from different centuries sat about the floor in a haphazard arrangement, no two together or facing one another.

"May I come in?" she asked, tapping her knuckles on the door.

Miss Garrett sat at an oak table, papers spread out, her hair in a tight bun. "Certainly. Come, have a seat."

Crossing the room, Della joined her at the table.

"Is everything all right?" Miss Garrett asked, setting down her pencil. "You've not been your typical sunny self."

Della forced a smile. "I've been a bit troubled, I'm afraid."

All night she'd wrestled with herself. Sympathizing with someone who was "different" was not at all the same as experiencing it herself. And now that she had, she could no longer sit still and say nothing. At the same time, advocating sign language was heresy within these walls. Questioning the exclusion of it could very well put her job in jeopardy. And if she lost her job, she'd never see Kitty or any of her other students again. And how could she help them if she never saw them?

"What is it that's troubling you, dear?" Miss Garrett asked, threading her hands and setting them on the table.

Della moistened her lips. "Yes. Well, I was wondering if there is a particular reason we don't teach both lip-reading and sign language?"

Miss Garrett sat back in her chair, studying her. "You're upset about the Krugers."

"I am."

She nodded. "It was an awful scene. Very insensitive of Kitty's parents to put her through that."

Della blinked. It wasn't the Krugers who were being insensitive. But she'd best tackle only one thing at a time.

Miss Garrett tilted her head. "And now you're trying to figure out a way to work around the visitation rules. You think the most logical thing would be to teach sign language. Then there would be no reason the children couldn't go home on holidays. Am I correct?"

"Partly. It's more than that, though. It's also the exclusivity of teaching lip-reading only. What will happen when our students leave school and try to interact with other deaf people who know only sign language?" She shook her head. "The more I think on it, the more convinced I become. They should be taught both."

Miss Garrett's jaw began to tick. "The use of sign language sets the children apart, Miss Wentworth. You know that. It makes them the target of scorn. Why would you willingly set them up for that when they can function as readily as hearing children if they read lips?"

"I'm not sure they can function *exactly* like hearing children. Have you ever noticed our students don't chatter before class starts or during mealtimes? Don't you think that's unnatural?"

Miss Garrett straightened. "Of all the ridiculous things. We are doing everything we can to make these children as normal as possible. We treat them as if they could hear. We speak to them as we would hearing children. We avoid unnatural movements of the mouth or anything else that would single them out as different." She gripped the armrests of her chair. "As a matter of fact, we even try to forget that they are deaf at all. Now how, might I ask, is that unnatural?"

Della rubbed her watch pin between her fingers. Nothing she could say would persuade Miss Garrett, or Dr. Bell for that matter, to think any differently than they already did. If she didn't like it, then she was teaching at the wrong school.

Letting out a slow breath, Miss Garrett placed a hand on Della's arm. "If it were your loved one who was deaf, what would you want for him?"

"I'd want whatever was best."

"Exactly." She sat back, a satisfied look on her face. "Now we'd best wrap this up. I have an appointment in a few minutes."

GOVERNMENT BUILDING

"Finding a spot on the front steps
of the Government Building,
Cullen opened the letter and sat down."

1. Government Building
2. Manufactures Building

CHAPTER 38

Almost a week had passed since Cullen posted a letter to Wanda ending their engagement, but he'd yet to hear back. The only letter waiting for him this morning was from his dad. Finding a spot on the front steps of the Government Building, he opened the letter and sat down. He used to look forward to hearing from home, but now he dreaded it.

Every day he'd kept up with the headlines, each newspaper report worse than the day before. Bank reserves had fallen $20 million last month and $21 million the month before. Even the banks in New York were struggling. He only hoped their own Building and Loan still had its doors open.

He skimmed Dad's letter with a sinking heart, then went back and read it more slowly. Dad couldn't afford to pay the Dewey boys, so he took on a sharecropper. The bank was quick to point out, however, that it's against the law to give a sharecropper part of the harvest's profit since the crop was now mortgaged, along with the farm buildings, the horses, the milk cows, the oxen, the cattle, the sheep, and the pigs. Dad had to let the sharecropper go. Which left no one to help him bring in the harvest.

He said there wasn't any point in Cullen coming home to help, though, because he now owed the merchants seven hundred dollars. And because of the thousand dollars he'd borrowed, their mortgage payment had doubled. The Building and Loan wouldn't lend him any more since he didn't have the collateral, and even if he had, the run on the banks had dried them up and they didn't have money to lend.

Cullen felt his throat begin to close. Even if he were to sell six hundred dollars worth of sprinklers, it wouldn't be enough. With the doubled mortgage, the merchant debt, the interest, and the bank refusing to lend, there wouldn't be enough money to pay down the debt, much less buy next year's seed.

Come the end of the year, the two hundred fifty acres his grandparents bought in 1847 when they'd left Ireland on a coffin ship, the farm that had been raided and burned during the War, then put back together with blood and sweat, would be taken by a bank. A bank that, in this economic climate, wouldn't be able to find an investor and would end up with land, animals, and buildings that weren't worth any more to them than a pail of hot spit.

But they meant something to his dad. And they meant something to Cullen. They might play havoc with his lungs and his skin, but they were home. And this downhill spiral had all started when Dad gambled three hundred dollars on Cullen's invention.

He had to do something. He had to make it work. His demonstration was set for tomorrow. The shed he planned to burn sat assembled behind Terminal Station, ready to go. All that remained was putting it to flame and letting his sprinklers do the rest.

Cullen's display in Machinery Hall lay at an awkward angle on the ground, its latticed roof ripped off, its pipes knocked askew, and one of its spigots snapped in half. He'd arrived well before the noise started and well before other exhibitors. All except for Bulenberg, that is, who usually didn't saunter in until a good thirty minutes after the gates opened.

Slowly turning toward him, Cullen drilled Bulenberg with his gaze. "What do you know about this?"

With a smug expression, Bulenberg lifted a scrawny shoulder. "Can't say I know *anythng*. It was like that when I arrived."

"Well, it didn't just fall over by itself. Something or somebody knocked it over."

"Like I said, it was already on its side when I got here."

In four long strides, Cullen crossed to Bulenberg's booth. "What about last night?"

"What about it?"

"Was it still standing when you left?"

"I can't say that I take much notice of your

exhibit, McNamara." He crossed his arms. "Of course, nobody else takes notice either, do they? Who knows, maybe this will be just the thing to draw some attention to your pathetic little display. Heaven knows your demonstration won't."

Cullen opened and closed his fists. "What's that supposed to mean?"

Dropping his pose, Bulenberg thrust his chin forward. "If you think you're going to steal my customers with some pitiful little sideshow, well think again. Nobody's interested in risking his money on a contraption that hasn't been proven. And putting out a fire in something hardly bigger than an outhouse is far from indisputable proof of reliability."

"You know nothing about it." He forced himself to take a deep breath. "And I'm not trying to steal your customers or anyone else's. I'm simply giving them a glimpse of what's next on the horizon. Some will pass, others will hop on board."

"We'll see *abut tht*," he mumbled.

Cullen cocked his left ear toward Bulenberg. "What's that?"

"Nothing." He made a jerky gesture toward Cullen's booth. "Go clean up your mess. It's bad enough for the rest of us to be seen with your poor excuse for a display. The least you can do is make it presentable."

It took every bit of restraint he had to walk away, but walk away he did. Bulenberg wasn't worth the trouble it would cause were Cullen to retaliate. Besides, he had no proof Bulenberg was behind the deliberate destruction of his exhibit, only suspicion. A mighty big dose of suspicion.

But steal his customers? Bulenberg thought he was stealing customers? Cullen shook his head. What absurdity. Bending over, he picked up his hinged wall and began to repair the damage as best he could.

As the day progressed and Cullen cooled off a bit, he considered Bulenberg's fear. And the more he did, the more encouraged he felt. If Bulenberg was worried about tomorrow's success, then maybe this demonstration would be his golden egg after all.

"Della scurried past the
east entrance of Machinery Hall."

CHAPTER 39

Della hurried in the direction of Terminal Station, past the broad pediment over the east entrance of Machinery Hall. Fire, Water, Air, and Earth stood side by side. Fire grasped lightning in one hand, a torch in the other. Water held a dolphin spurting like a fountain. Cullen's invention encompassed both.

Rounding the corner, she circumvented the building, then passed its annex and a blacksmith's shop before reaching an open area beside the incoming railroad tracks. A large crowd of men and a few women gathered about a wooden shed. A white and gold fire carriage stood to its right. Though the engine could be outfitted with parade reels and wheels, it held more serviceable ones today.

A dozen members of Company Eight stood at attention in red shirts and black trousers. An oversized numeral eight emblazoned on each black helmet and each silver belt buckle reflected off the sunlight.

She leaned to the left to see better. Cullen's hair had been carefully brilliantined beneath his jaunty derby hat, his gray suit showed off his physique, and his silk bow tie drooped against his shirt with the artful indifference so many men were now affecting. Smiling, he laughed at something one of the men in the front row said, giving no sign of nervousness or concern.

It was good to see him in his element. Something had changed since her episode on the Ferris wheel. She couldn't put her finger on it exactly, but Cullen was different somehow. His moods were more intense, his concentration more keen.

"The problem with current sprinklers is three-fold." His voice projected confidence and conviction as he held up three fingers, then ticked off each of his concerns. "The perforated iron piping is prone to clogging from oxidation. The pipes discharge water over the entire building, which often causes more damage than the actual fire. And most important, the current sprinklers are manually activated. This means they can't be activated at night when so many highly destructive fires occur."

Members of the crowd murmured, nodding their heads in agreement.

"My system is completely automatic." Removing a sprinkler head from his coat pocket, he held it aloft. "It's a valve with deflectors and is set into operation when temperatures reach a predetermined heat level. The solder around this cap melts, then the cap falls off, exposing the diaphragm beneath it." He pointed to a cap covering the sides and bottom of the sprinkler head. "When the diaphragm is exposed, the pressure causes it to burst, allowing water to gush out and extinguish the fire. As you can see, each sprinkler activates independently according to when the heat level is reached. So the entire building will not be deluged, only the part on fire."

She glanced about the audience, pleased to see he had captured their full attention.

"Beside me, I have a twelve-by-twelve foot shed. Inside I have strewn the floor with a mass of chips, shavings, tallow, cask shavings, barrels, cotton, and a decrepit old loom, fully threaded."

Her eyes widened at each subsequent mention of combustible material. How on earth would that tiny spigot put out all that?

"I've fitted the shed with water pipes and three of my sprinklers. Once the fire takes hold, I expect the first sprinkler to open within a minute and the entire conflagration to be extinguished within three."

Skeptical glances were exchanged. Men swapped bills surreptitiously, making bets on the outcome. But the firemen gave one another knowing looks, as if they had no doubt the system would do just as Cullen claimed.

Still, her stomach began to tense. She wished he hadn't made such an impossible prediction. It would have been better to light the fire, then let the sprinklers do their job in whatever amount of time they needed.

"The contents of the shed have been saturated with paraffin oil," he continued. "Fire Marshal Murphy, chief of the Fourteenth Battalion of the Chicago fire brigade and in command here at Jackson Park, will light the shed in two places."

Cullen stepped aside. Murphy, in a white chief's helmet, struck a match, then tossed it and one other inside two strategically placed openings. Within seconds, huge, dense flames burst forth with a roar.

The crowd stumbled back several yards. The blaze gained complete mastery of the shed, licking its sides and sending up billows of smoke.

Heat stung Della's face and pressed against her. Holding a handkerchief to her nose, she continued to fall back, along with everyone else. One minute passed.

The fire on one side of the shed began to falter and fade. But the other portions continued to burn. Two minutes passed. Then, three.

Cullen's brows began to crinkle. His body tensed.

Hose men reached for the nozzle at the end of their reel. They looked to their chief.

The chief held up his hand, stalling his men.

Four minutes. Cullen turned to Murphy and gave him a nod. The brigade opened their hoses and doused the fire.

The crowd stood still and quiet.

Cullen turned to them, his face grave. "I'd like

to thank Company Eight for standing at the ready for us."

A smattering of applause. Money exchanged hands.

"As you can see, their help saved the day. I apologize. I don't know what happened, but will do a thorough investigation and get back to you as soon as I can." The color had all but drained from his face. "Thank you for coming."

Amid murmuring, most of the crowd dispersed and left. A few gentlemen approached Cullen, as did the fire chief. A fireman squeezed Cullen's shoulder, then joined his comrades as they made sure all hot spots were extinguished.

A woman stood back and to the side. Della kept her distance as well, her heart breaking for him.

MOVABLE SIDEWALK

"The movable sidewalk traveled around and around in a stretched-out oval from one end of the pier to the other. Its rows of benches, wide enough for four people, reminded her of pews."

CHAPTER 40

Noise bombarded Cullen from every side. The fire brigade's shovels clinked against buckets as they scooped up the remains of his shed. Railway cars screeched to a stop on the tracks to his left. And voices layered one over the other like bricks building a wall to shut him out.

He tried to pay attention, to hear, to lip-read, but his mind whirled. What had happened? Why hadn't his sprinklers opened?

It didn't really matter, though. Not now. He'd failed. Again. And even if he were to do another demonstration successfully, this would be the one they'd remember.

Mr. Ferris shook his head. "I'm *pzzld*. The design looked as if it *shld* work. I'm *srry* it didn't."

Cullen concentrated on breathing in and out. "Thank you. And thank you again for those tickets."

Another man approached. Cullen muddled through the rest of the conversations, nodding, trying to reassure people he would find and correct the problem, but he received only looks of sympathy by way of response. He may as well pack up and go home.

"Something isn't right," Vaughn said, leaning on his cane. "You look through the debris very carefully. Let me know what you find."

"Thank you, sir. I'll do just that." Cullen spotted Della hanging back. In a rush, he realized he had nothing to offer her. Not even a farm. He might as well—

"I'm sorry, McNamara." The chief squeezed Cullen's shoulder. "I was really hoping everything would work out."

"Thank you for your help, sir. I'm sorry I let you down. I'll clean this up. I know you and the boys have other things to do."

"Nonsense. We'll help you with it."

"Thank you. I—" He stopped, his train of thought completely shot. For there, not thirty yards away, was Wanda all fancied up in her Sunday blue skirt and shirtwaist.

Waggling her fingers, she headed toward him.

Murphy glanced between the two. "I'll leave you to it, then."

Cullen gawked at her. "What are you doing here?"

Cocking her head, she propped her hands on her waist. "Now is that any way to greet yer *fee-on-say?*"

He immediately swung his attention to Della.

She stumbled back, her eyes wide, her lips parting. She looked from him to Wanda, then back to him.

His chest squeezed. He opened his mouth to explain, but what could he say? That yes, Wanda was his fiancée, but he didn't love her—at least

368

not the way he loved Della? That he'd written Wanda a letter ending the engagement?

He swallowed. He couldn't. Wouldn't. Not with Wanda standing right there. He respected her too much, loved her too much to act in such a thoughtless way. So he closed his mouth and said nothing.

Whirling around, Della ran past the blacksmith's and Westinghouse Company's offices, her hands holding up her skirts, her hat bobbing from side to side.

Die and be doomed. He looked to see if Wanda had noticed. It would have been hard to miss.

All flirtatiousness had fallen from her stance. In its place were limp arms, a stricken face, and a world of hurt. "What's goin' on, Cullen?"

He rubbed his forehead. "Did you get my letter?"

"The letter about ya changin' yer mind?" Her voice rose. "The letter Thomas Hodge read to me?" She walked up and walloped him as hard as she could with her traveling bag.

The boys shoveling behind him paused for the merest second, then continued.

He stepped to the side, holding his arm out. "Is there any chance we can do this later?"

Her eyes took on a moist sheen as she drew her satchel back again.

He caught it one-handed, then yanked it free from her grasp. "What are you doing here?"

"What do ya think I'm a-doin' here? Thomas reads me some letter about how ya changed yer mind all of a sudden, outta the big blue sky. That after being together fer fifteen years, ya wanna call it quits. And yer wonderin' what I'm doin' here? Didn't all them books ya read teach ya nothin'?"

"How long have you been calling Hodge by his Christian name?"

She narrowed her eyes. "How long ya been callin' *her* by her Christian name?" She pointed in the direction Della had fled.

He wanted to say that was different. He was in love with Della. But now probably wasn't the best time. "You and I haven't been together for fifteen years."

"I was seven when we started, and I'm two-and-twenty now." She held up her fingers, giving them a quick count while she whispered the numbers, then jerked up her head. "Fifteen. I'm still countin' fifteen."

"How long since I asked you to marry me?"

"Now how am I supposed to remember that?"

His anger began to bubble. "I remember. Zero. It's been zero years because I never asked you, did I?"

She jerked back as if she'd been slapped.

His shoulders slumped. "I'm sorry. I shouldn't have said that. This is just a bad time, is all."

Tears filled her eyes. "Well, I'm sorry to have

called at a bad time. Why don't ya tell me when a good time is and I'll see if I can arrange it."

With every last ounce of control he had, he reined in his temper. "Where are you staying, Wanda?"

"I have no i-deer. I just got off the train this mornin' and it took me all the live-long day ta find ya in this god-awful city. They wouldn't even let me through them gates unless I paid 'em fifty cents. *Fifty cents.* I done told 'em you and me was gettin' hitched and how exactly were we supposed to do that when yer in here and I'm out there. They congratulated me on our weddin', then still made me pay." She blew a strand of hair from her face. "Guess ya cain't expect much more from a bunch o' Yankees. Anyway, I figured we'd marry up now and then I'd stay with you."

He studied her brown eyes. Eyes he knew almost as well as his own—or at least he thought he did. "Are you telling me you came all the way to Chicago alone?"

Lifting her chin, she gave her shoulders a little shake. "I shore did."

"Do your folks know where you are?"

"I told Thomas ta tell 'em. I give him strict instructions to let me have a good six-hour start."

Hodge. That idiot. Wait until he got his hands on that sawney.

Dragging a hand through his hair, he handed her the traveling bag and pointed to an empty orange crate. "Sit there and don't move. I need to clean up my mess over there."

"Cullen?"

Looking back over his shoulder, he pulled off his jacket.

"I'm sorry yer cowshed burnt down just now. I done told ya before ya left that this was a bad i-deer. Will ya come home now?"

Home. That was a laugh. He didn't have a home anymore. Yet it wasn't the farm or the disastrous demonstration or Wanda's unexpected appearance that weighed most heavily on his mind. It was Della. He couldn't imagine what she was thinking. He needed to talk to her.

But he couldn't do that yet.

"It wasn't a cowshed," he said, then he folded his jacket and set it aside.

STATUE OF THE REPUBLIC WITH THE PERISTYLE IN BACKGROUND

"Passing the giant golden statue of the Republic, Della turned into the peristyle's Roman-looking colonnade with its double rows of forty-eight columns, one for each state."

ELEVATED TRAIN

"The elevated railway rumbled above her."

CHAPTER 41

Della stumbled around the corner and into the Court of Honor, her throat clogged, her eyes burning. She was surrounded by a multitude of people, yet never had she felt so alone.

Tears rose like an incoming tide, but she stemmed them, having no desire to succumb here. She needed somewhere to go, though. Touring the buildings held no appeal, and it was too early to retire to the boardinghouse. Returning at this hour would produce too much curiosity in Mrs. Harvell, and she was in no mood to field questions from that quarter.

Hilda and Maxine would be at some restaurant or other, but she had no appetite and no wish to unburden herself on them. Maxine would be full of I-told-you-sos, and Hilda would be downright crushed.

The elevated railway rumbled above her. She could ride in its electric cars as they circled round the fair, but she'd have to spend twenty cents for each revolution. The gondolas promised escape, but she'd have to disembark after just one pass. The Wooded Island beckoned, but it was out of the question. She had no desire to face its benches. Its statues. Or the rose garden's pathways occasioned by lovers.

She needed somewhere quiet, somewhere free,

and somewhere that didn't hold memories of him. Of its own volition, her body turned toward the lake. She passed people from every walk of life. A farmer jostled elbows with a banker. Both smiled and apologized. Brothers and sisters from the rural districts skipped side by side in harmony. The high and the low sat together at outdoor café tables beneath covered passage-ways. Uniformed waiters wove between them balancing piles of plates and glasses.

All the while, her entire world had unraveled.

She walked the length of the Grand Basin only because her legs knew what to do. Gondoliers paddled by, singing ballads to young lovers within their boats. Tuning them out, she focused on the peristyle, its center looking like the Arc de Triomphe.

Almost there, she told herself.

Passing the giant golden statue of the Republic, she turned into the peristyle's Roman-looking colonnade with its double rows of forty-four columns, one for each state.

A young woman squatted down, tucking a young boy into her side. "Look, David. Here's ours."

Della didn't read the name of the state carved at its base. She had no interest in it, nor in finding the one with Pennsylvania's name. For she didn't want to inadvertently see North Carolina's.

Finally, she made it to the pier. The wind off the

lake whipped her hat, lifting its brim. She forged ahead, her target in sight. The movable sidewalk traveled around and around in a stretched-out oval from one end of the pier to the other. Its rows of benches, wide enough for four people, reminded her of pews.

A ticket taker stopped her from approaching. "Five cents, miss."

Digging in her chatelaine bag, she pinched a nickel between her fingers, then handed it to him. Lifting a corner of her skirt, she stepped from the stationary platform onto a slow-moving one, then from there onto a swifter one with seats. The benches weren't crowded, and she managed to claim one all to herself.

Settling onto its wooden slats, she raised her arms, pulled the pins from her hat, then set it on her lap. A brisk breeze blew against her. She closed her eyes, allowing a sense of freedom to overtake her.

And with the freedom came her tears. Silent, quiet, unobtrusive. She made no noise, nor gave away her distress with shaking shoulders. She simply let the tears pour from beneath closed eyes.

Is that any way to greet yer fee-on-say?

The fire chief had been speaking to him, but Cullen's attention was on the woman. Her simple navy ensemble and straw hat held a country-like charm, as did her accent.

What seared into her consciousness most, though, was Cullen's expression when he'd turned to Della. No denial of the woman's claims formed on his lips, only an expression of distress.

A new rush of tears added to the ones already coursing down her cheeks. He was to be married. Had, from all indications, been engaged this entire time. The thought was so repugnant, her stomach began to roil.

Eavesdropping was one of the drawbacks of lip-reading. It wasn't something she ever did on purpose, just something that happened accidentally. She and Hilda jokingly called it "eyesdropping." But she hadn't had to lip-read the young woman's pronouncement. Her voice had easily carried to Della's ears.

Is that any way to greet yer fee-on-say?

She pressed a fist against her mouth, holding in the sobs. It explained so much. His strict adherence to propriety when he was with her. But no, someone adhering to the rules of propriety would never have removed his shirt in front of a lady. Even if the lady had insisted. Even if it was the only way to prove he was who he said he was.

Someone adhering to the rules wouldn't have held her close under the guise of protectiveness. Someone adhering to the rules wouldn't have pulled her into his lap, no matter what the circumstances. Someone adhering to the rules would have told her he was promised to someone else.

Her father was right. Men were devious creatures.

Gulls squawked, reminding her where she was. She drew in a shaky breath, allowing the smell of fish and the sound of waves to soothe her. But she kept her eyes closed, her head down.

Did his fiancée know about Cullen's hearing? About his lessons? She began to straighten, her eyes slowly opening. Was that the real reason he hadn't wanted anyone to know about his lip-reading? Because his fiancée might find out?

The sun began to set, putting on a glorious show, but she took no joy in it. Just continued to ride round and round in a circle, always traveling but never arriving anywhere. When she finally stepped off the machine, darkness had long since taken hold, and the emptiness inside her still loomed, pressing against her rib cage, her chest, and her heart.

She pushed back new tears welling up. Whether the woman knew about them or not, Cullen's lessons were over. Finished. Through.

She told herself to drive him from her mind, to not give him another thought. But she knew it would be a long time before she'd be able to accomplish such a task.

COURT OF HONOR AS VIEWED FROM THE ADMINISTRATION BUILDING

1. Manufactures Building
2. Peristyle
3. Agricultural Building

CHAPTER 42

Cullen should have been up-front with Della from the very beginning. He knew that now. Would even admit he knew it earlier. And because he hadn't, she'd found out he was engaged in the most deplorable of ways.

Desperate as he was to go to her, soothe her, confess to her, he couldn't abandon Wanda. Not when she had no place to stay, no place to go.

He thought of his bleak future. Did he even have a right to ask Della to share it? He had nothing. No investors. No farm. No prospects. No money.

He knew beyond a shadow of a doubt that Wanda would stick by him. Maybe she was right. Maybe he was just a farmer. Fancy clothes and a make-believe city had not only failed him, but also played a big part in losing the farm.

He looked at Wanda sitting with her elbow on her knees, her face in her hand, her eyes closed, her straw hat crooked. The sight warmed his heart. He truly did love her. But could he live the rest of his life with her? Farm on her father's land, if nothing else? Could he go a lifetime without Della?

The answer was no. No to all of the above. No to the farming. No to Wanda. No to a life without Della.

He might not have much of a future, but he had God. A God who, according to Scriptures, had a plan. A really good plan. And though Cullen hadn't spent much time lately praying, maybe it was time to do so now. Heaven knew, God sure had a better view of things than he did.

Turning back to the soot and debris, he stripped off his shirt and undershirt, regardless of Wanda's presence. The firefighters eyed him curiously but said nothing. They had no way of knowing she had come upon him plowing the fields countless times, or that he couldn't afford to ruin his clothes. But it didn't matter. At this point, he just wanted to recover those sprinkler heads before the sun fully set. They should have worked. Not just one of them, all of them.

He absently noted the bronze on his skin had almost completely faded. It was a good thing he didn't need to prove himself a farmer now, for though the suspender lines were there, they were barely discernible.

They found the first sprinkler head pretty quickly. It had opened and worked exactly as it should have. The other two, however, were nowhere to be seen.

After a while, the boys had to leave. They shook his hand. Squeezed his shoulder. Clapped his back. If he needed anything, anything at all, all he had to do was ask.

Keeping his emotions in check, Cullen thanked them again, then continued to work.

The sun dipped farther toward the horizon. Finally, he found one. Wiping soggy soot from the spigot, he turned it over and frowned, then angled himself so the greatest amount of fading light shone on the piece.

It wasn't his sprinkler head. But that didn't make a bit of sense. Surely someone hadn't replaced his with a manual device. Yet what other explanation was there?

Dropping his hand by his side, he looked into the distance, reviewing in his mind the last time he'd physically touched the sprinkler heads. It had been two days ago, when he lined up the ceiling boards with holes that his spigots popped through.

Anyone could have come out here at any time, jimmied them off, replaced the heads, then nailed the boards back up. As secluded as the spot was, they could have easily done what they needed to without ever being detected.

Would Bulenberg go to such lengths? Was the man really that scared? That desperate? Cullen couldn't fathom it being anyone else.

"Are ya finally done?" Wanda asked. "I'm near starved to death over here."

He glanced at her. "Almost. Give me another few minutes."

Setting the faulty head down, he pushed aside

his disbelief and mounting anger, concentrating instead on finding the third. The light was barely hanging on when he found it. Though it was too dark to see the details, he could tell by the weight and feel of it that this one wasn't his either.

FISHERIES BUILDING

"The detail on the Fisheries Building was lost in the night's shadows, but the central part of the building had plenty of artificial light."

CHAPTER 43

Cullen sat Wanda down in his booth with his boxed supper. After noting Bulenberg was nowhere to be seen, he walked over to the Crowne Pen Company exhibit.

Miss Carpenter recognized him immediately and smiled. "Hello, Mr. McNamara. Would you like to watch how a piece of alloy and gold is turned into a fountain pen? Or perhaps purchase a pen as a souvenir?"

"Not today. I'm afraid my request is of a more personal nature."

"Oh?" Her eyes and hair were the color of a newly born fawn, her skin so smooth and fresh it looked as if she'd stepped out of a painting. It didn't take much to realize why John had been drawn to her.

"A young lady from my hometown arrived in Chicago without a place to stay or enough money to secure a room," he said. "I wondered if there was any way she could share quarters with you tonight?"

Miss Carpenter glanced at his booth. "Is that her?"

"Yes. Miss Wanda Sappington. I know this is an imposition, I just didn't know who else to—"

"You tell her we'll be glad to welcome her in,

though she might have to make do with the floor. Will that be all right?"

"That would be wonderful." A great load lifted. "Thank you so much."

"My pleasure. Just have her back here by nine-thirty. That's when the girls and I finish up."

He nodded. "Yes, ma'am. I'll make sure. And thank you again."

As he returned to his booth, Wanda set the empty supper box by her feet. "That was good. I hadn't had nothin' to eat since I left."

Sighing, he held out his hand. "Well, come on. Let's find us somewhere to talk."

She eyed him with suspicion. "I don't wanna talk. I wanna find a preacher."

"You know as well as I do that we aren't getting married."

"Tonight, ya mean. We ain't gettin' married tonight."

Ever. But he held his tongue. "Come on."

They walked across the Court of Honor and toward the Fisheries Building, the only exhibit he felt wouldn't completely overwhelm her.

"Them machines is noisy in that place ya work."

"That was with half of them turned off. You should hear it during the day. It's been a nightmare."

The temperature cooled. Notes from Sousa's concert in the bandstand floated on the breeze, bringing bits and pieces of "After the Ball."

She peeked up at him. "Ya finished bein' mad?"

"I don't have the luxury of being mad. There's too much to do."

"Ya gonna tell me about her?"

"I'm going to show you some sea creatures."

The detail on the Fisheries Building was lost in the night's shadows, but the central part of the building had plenty of artificial lights. Those impressed Wanda almost as much as the aquariums with fish, eels, crabs, and sea anemones.

"Look at them bubbles," she said, pointing.

A stream of fresh air pumping into the water produced millions of silver bubbles that flew to the surface and exploded. Schools of colorful fish swam among the shoals as if they had but one mind for the entire number.

Cullen pointed to a stingray hiding in the sand at the bottom, its two protruding eyes giving it away. After examining every tank in the central circular room, he checked his watch, then guided her outside to a bench facing the lake.

"Some o' them gave me the willie-wobbles." She shivered. "I hope I don't have nightmares."

Angling himself so he could see her, he took a deep breath. "You got my letter, then."

She looked down at her lap. "I got it."

"I'm sorry you had to hear it from Hodge."

"I'm not. He was very sweet about it. Didn't make one ugly comment about ya that time."

Lifting her chin, she turned to him. "But I'd a-rather heard it from you. Why'd ya have to write it down like that when ya knew I wouldn't be able to read it?"

Breakers splashed against the bulkhead as if punctuating her words. There was some comfort in knowing a person as well as he knew her. And just as always, she didn't fool around, just cut right to the quick.

"I wrestled about that," he confessed. "I didn't like it any better than you, but I needed to tell you. And I needed to do it sooner rather than later. Even if it meant Hodge had to read it to you."

"Yer either not bein' honest with me or not bein' honest with yerself. Maybe both. 'Cause two more months wouldn't have made a lick of difference, and ya know it."

He almost smiled, for not only did she go straight to the point, she was usually spot-on. Better than he knew himself sometimes. "You're right. I guess I'm not being completely honest with either one of us."

"That's why I'm here. That's why I told Thomas to tell our folks that yer letter said ya couldn't wait no more. That ya had to marry me right away. And that inside the letter was a train ticket to Chicagy."

He slid his eyes shut. "Oh, Wanda. I wish you hadn't done that."

"Well, what was I supposed to do?" She threw

her hands up in an exasperated gesture. "Write ya back and say, 'Okay. If that's the way ya feel. We'll just break off our engagement. Just like that.'" She snapped her fingers, then leaned in toward him. "Well, that ain't gonna happen. I figured it was some city gal trying to turn yer head, and I'm here to stake my claim. I had ya first, and I'll sure as shootin' have ya last. I ain't givin' ya up. Not without a fight, anyway."

Even if the splash of light from the lamppost hadn't revealed her expression, he'd have been able to easily imagine it. He'd seen it many times before.

Taking one of her hands into his, he covered it with his other one. "I'm sorry, Wanda. I'm so sorry, but I'm in love with her."

She snatched her hand back, her voice quivering. "Now yer talkin' crazy. Ya hadn't known her long enough. You've only been gone, what, four months? That ain't nothin' compared to us. Wc been together fifteen years."

He dragged a hand down his face. "We've known each other for fifteen years, we've been engaged for only . . . what?"

"Ya got back from Boston six years ago. That's when all the weddin' talk started up."

"And we didn't set a date until this April."

"That's got nothin' to do with nothin'."

"Now who's not being honest?"

She jumped to her feet, pacing in front of him.

"I don't believe it. How can . . ." She stopped. "How can ya love her when ya love me? 'Cause I know ya do. You'll never convince me ya don't."

Taking her hand, he gently tugged her back to the bench. "Come here."

She plopped down beside him. Close beside him.

Leaning forward, he rested his elbows on his knees, scrambling for a way to explain it to her. "You know in the Bible where God tells one of the churches He'd rather they be cold or hot than lukewarm? But since they were lukewarm, He was going to spew them out of His mouth?"

She gave him a baffled look. "I reckon. I think the reverend sermonized about it once or twice."

He nodded, then picked at his thumbnails. "I never understood that verse. I mean, you'd think He would rather have someone lukewarm than cold, right?"

"I reckon." Caution entered her voice.

"Well, I figured out what was so detestable about being lukewarm. It was when I realized you deserved a man who was passionate for you. One who was completely sold out for you and only you." Lifting his head, he searched her eyes. "But a man who is lukewarm is not worthy of you."

She shook her head, over and over. "No, Cullen. Ya ain't lukewarm. And even if ya was, I'd never spew ya out. Never." Her chin quivered. "Please don't ask me to."

He swallowed. "I love you, Wanda. But I'm not *in* love with you."

She covered her mouth, her eyes filling.

His throat worked. "I'm sorry."

She shook her head. "No. No. You cain't mean that. I shouldn't have made ya set a date. I'm sorry. We can change it. Lots of fellers get cold feet. I was just—"

"It has nothing to do with setting a date. And I don't have cold feet. I've been questioning this for a while now."

Wrapping her arms around her waist, she began to rock. "How long?"

"Since arriving at the fair. Maybe before."

Her chin quivered. "'Cause of her? Is she the one what made ya question it?"

"Partly."

The tears that had been hovering slipped free. "And yer not . . . lukewarm fer her?"

His throat clogged. He shook his head.

She doubled over, covering her face. "No, no. You cain't mean it. I came all the way from home. I cain't go back. I'll be ruined fer sure."

"You're going to have to go back. You knew what my letter said before you ever left."

"I didn't know what it said. Not fer sure, anyway. I mean, Thomas, he started gettin' feelings fer me. Sometimes I wondered if he was readin' the letters the way ya really wrote 'em. 'Cause they didn't sound like ya. They sounded . . .

391

funny. And when he read me that last one, well, I started screechin' like a plucked jaybird. Said all manner of awful things to him." She sucked in a breath. "Then I told him I was comin' after ya. And when I came back I was gonna have me a ring on my finger and a new name to go along with it. I told him that. Right to his face. So, don't ya see? Ya cain't send me back. We got to get married."

He stared at her, the breeze ruffling his trouser legs. "Have you, have you fallen in love with Hodge?"

"No!" She surged to her feet. "Where'd ya get a fool thought like that?"

He said nothing.

She started pacing again, giving another soliloquy and making sweeping gestures with her arms. He let her rant and pace and rant some more.

Finally she ran out of steam and squatted down in front of him, placing her hands on his knees. "Please, Cullen." Tears poured down her face. "Please marry me. I'm beggin' ya."

"You really do love him." Cullen still couldn't quite wrap his mind around it.

"I don't. I don't love him at all. I love you. I've loved ya my whole life."

Rather than argue, he brushed his knuckles down her cheek. "And I've loved you, you silly woman."

"But yer not gonna marry me?" Her voice sounded pathetic.

"I'm not going to marry you."

A quiet moan came from the back of her throat. Sitting back on her feet, she covered her face and cried.

Lifting his hip, he retrieved a handkerchief and tucked it in her hand.

Finally, she began to wind down. She blew her nose. Then blew it again, and again before finally wiping it clean.

She raised her face. "Will ya, will ya at least kiss me one last time?"

Tears of his own surged to the surface. He forced them down. "No, Wanda. We've done all the kissing we're ever going to do."

After a tremulous sigh, she turned her head away, looking at everything but him.

Taking her by the elbows, he helped her stand. "Come on. I have to get you back to Machinery Hall. You're going to be staying the night with a nice lady from the Crowne Pen Company. In the morning, come back to my booth, then I'll walk you to the train station and buy you a ticket home."

She hiccupped, then cried some more. Placing his arm around her, he pulled her into his side and walked her back. When they approached the Hall's entrance, he stopped, took her by both shoulders, then leaned in and placed a gentle kiss on her forehead. "I do love you, Wanda."

Her eyes filled. "I know. I was sorta hopin' fer the other kind of kiss, though."

He smoothed her hair back with his hand. "Those kisses are to be saved and closely guarded. You must promise me you will not ever, *ever* let a man kiss you like that—not even Hodge—until he's put a very handsome ring on your finger."

"Ya must be crazy if ya think I'd make a promise like that. Those kisses are clearly the very best kind. They put the others to shame."

He frowned. "I'm serious."

"So am I."

Squeezing her by the shoulders, he propped her up like a child. "He will misunderstand. And will think you offer him more than you mean to. I really do want you to—"

She placed a finger against his lips. "I promise to try really hard not to let anyone kiss me like that."

"Not good enough."

She wiped her eyes with the palms of her hand, then tucked the well-used handkerchief into her sleeve. "I don't suppose you want that back?"

"No. And don't change the subject."

Bracketing his face, she ran her thumb against his cheek. "I'm tired, and I'm ready to go to bed." Her eyes filled. "If ya change yer mind?"

Placing his hands over hers, he gently moved

them to her sides and gave them a squeeze. "My mind is made up, I'm afraid."

"You might—"

This time, he put his finger against her lips. "Good-bye, Wanda."

She kissed his finger, even while tears streamed silently down her face. "Good-bye."

He helped her to the door, then walked her to the Crowne Pen Company's booth.

The moment Miss Carpenter saw them, she took in Wanda's distress, then scrambled from behind the counter.

Cullen gave a nod of his head. "This is Miss Wanda Sappington, the young lady I told you about. Wanda, this is Miss Greta Carpenter."

Reaching for Wanda's hand, Miss Carpenter took it in hers. "Is everything all right, honey?"

Though she nodded, Wanda's eyes filled again.

Miss Carpenter glanced at Cullen, then hooked her hand around Wanda's arm and pulled her close. "Well, come meet the girls. We were just getting ready to go get some ice cream from the concessionaire."

Miss Carpenter gave a brief look over her shoulder.

Cullen's throat worked. *Thank you,* he mouthed. And then he left them.

NEAR VIEW OF MOVABLE SIDEWALK

"When she finally stepped off the machine,
darkness had long since taken hold."

CHAPTER 44

Cullen paced the walkway outside Harvell House. The steady stream of fairgoers leaving the park had dwindled down to an occasional carriage passing by. Where the devil was Della? Every boarder's name had been marked off the list except for hers. He'd gone straight from Machinery Hall to the Children's Building, then to Blooker's. But she was nowhere.

It was well past dark. The fair would be closing soon, and she'd have to walk these streets alone. She was every bit as upset as Wanda and every bit as vulnerable. What was she thinking?

Had she been hurt? Was she, at this very moment, lying alone in some hospital with no one to look in on her? To check and make sure she was receiving the best of care? What if she'd wandered into a tightly packed crowd and become frightened? What if she'd conked her head and couldn't remember who she was? He wondered how many hospitals Chicago had and how long it would take to visit them all.

He called up newspaper articles buried in the back sections of the paper. Short mentions of women who'd arrived at the fair from out of town, then simply vanished into thin air. In the advertisement section, desperate families had descriptions of their loved ones and appeals for information. Every woman described had been young, beautiful, and on her own.

He tried to stem the flow of his imagination, but horrific possibilities continued to bombard him. He cursed. He prayed. He willed her home with his thoughts. Yet still she did not appear.

Flipping open his pocket watch, he decided to give her thirty more minutes. If she wasn't home in thirty minutes, he was involving the police.

Sitting on the steps, he held his head in his hands. He hoped Wanda was all right. At least he knew she was being well taken care of.

His mind then wandered to the replaced sprinkler heads. It had to be Bulenberg. Who else would have done such a thing? He had no enemies that he knew of. The only person who'd demonstrated opposition of any kind had been Bulenberg.

The irony was Cullen hadn't made a single sale, so it wasn't as if Bulenberg had all that much to worry about unless he really felt Cullen's demonstration would have tipped the scales. And if the demonstration had worked, it very well might have.

Propping his elbows on his knees, he rested his mouth against his fists. Maybe he needed to take a closer look at those sprinkler heads. It shouldn't be too hard to figure out who the manufacturer was.

A train whistle pierced the silence, momentarily

interrupting the crickets' songs. Then all stilled again, and the night creatures resumed their concert. He checked his watch. She had fifteen more minutes.

As for his demonstration, he had no prayer of getting the director-general's permission again. And even if he did, no one would come to watch it. No, he had to do something else. Something big and dramatic that would put away all doubts but wouldn't jeopardize the fair in any way. And he'd have to do it in secret, so neither Bulenberg nor anyone else would have an opportunity to sabotage it.

He snapped his watch closed. Time up. Standing, he squinted down the walkway. Splashes of light from the street lamps offered a spot of illumination between stretches of darkness. Where *was* she?

He started to head toward town, then stopped. What if he made it to the police station, only to discover she'd returned to the boardinghouse while he was gone? Should-I-go and should-I-wait played tug-of-war within him as time seemed to slow to a standstill. Finally, he spotted her. At first it was just a woman, then it was Della. Relief lasted a mere second, then anger wrapped itself around him like a boa constrictor. She was in no rush whatsoever, but shuffled down the walk as if she were a century old.

By the time she reached him, he was shaking with fury. "Where the devil have you been?"

She looked at him as if he were no more than a passing acquaintance. "Good evening, Mr. McNamara. I trust you had a fine day. Would you excuse me, please?" She made to skirt around him.

He stepped into her path. "I have been waiting for you for hours. Where have you been?"

For the first time since he'd known her, she kept her emotions beneath a carefully controlled mask and didn't so much as twitch. "I don't believe I'm your concern. Now, if you'll—"

"Don't play games with me. I've been out of my mind with worry."

She lifted her brows. "I'm surprised you had room in your mind for anything other than your fiancée."

All the bluster left him in a whoosh. "Della—"

"Miss Wentworth. I think, under the circumstances, a more formal address is in order."

He'd leave an address out altogether before he'd revert to Miss Wentworth. "We need to talk."

"There's nothing to discuss."

"There's a mountain of things to discuss. And it will start with an apology from me. For lying to you by omission."

Her mask cracked. A searing hurt flashed across her face.

His chest caught. "I'm sorry. I never meant to hurt you."

"Who is she?"

"She's a woman from home whom I'd planned to marry." He took a fortifying breath. "Until I met you."

Shaking her head in denial, she wrapped a fist around a brooch at her neck. "Why didn't you tell me you were engaged?"

"I should have. I have no excuse."

"I don't understand."

"Then let me explain. I wrote to her and ended our engagement. That's why she came. To confirm it. But she'll be returning home on tomorrow's train."

"When did you write her?"

Not nearly soon enough, he thought, swallowing. "Last week."

She tightened her lips. "I'm not a fool, Cullen. I've heard about men who travel from town to town, preying on unsuspecting women. Well, I may have been unsuspecting before, but I'm not so gullible as to believe you broke off an engagement last week just like that." She snapped her fingers.

"You know good and well I don't travel from town to town luring women like some spider with a web full of flies."

"I know nothing of the sort. All I know is what you've told me. And if today is any indication, there's quite a bit you've left out." Her voice cracked. "I need to go inside."

"Not yet. Can we talk about it, first?"

She shook her head, barely holding on to her composure. "No amount of talk will change the fact that you are not who you say you are."

"I'm exactly who I say I am," he barked. "If I could peel off my shirt and prove it, I would. But that would accomplish nothing this time."

"Hush!" she hissed, indicating the brownstone's windows above them. "People can hear."

He took a step toward her. "Let them hear. I don't care. I broke off my engagement. I did it because I am in love with someone else. You." He gentled his voice. "I'm in love with you, Della."

She closed her eyes. "Let me pass, Cullen."

"You don't believe me? You really think I'd say something like that and not mean it?"

"I don't know what to think anymore."

"What can I do to prove it to you? Would you like to talk to Wanda? She's staying with a woman from the Crowne Pen Company tonight, but she'll be at Machinery Hall first thing in the morning because I'll be taking her to the train station." His face hardened. "It would be incredibly cruel to flaunt yourself in front of her, but if that's what it takes, by all means, come by in the morning."

"A very safe offer, considering you know good and well I have class in the morning."

"Quiet, down there!"

Cullen looked up at the windows, trying to

determine who had shouted. He opened his mouth to tell them exactly what he thought, but Della jerked his sleeve.

"Hush," she hissed. "They're absolutely right. I'm going to bed. Good night."

She stomped up the steps, him right behind her. She didn't even stop to cross out her name or light the taper.

He tightened his jaw. If she could find her way in the dark, so could he. He doused the light. Everything went pitch-black. The sound of her footsteps stopped.

He put his hands in front of him, looking for the stairs. She continued up them, albeit more cautiously. He followed the sound and quickly caught up to her.

"Della, please," he whispered. "Stop this nonsense."

She made it to the landing and took hesitant steps.

He reached for her hand but captured an arm instead. "Here, follow me."

She tried to pull away, but he didn't let loose.

"I don't want you tumbling down the stairs." He kept his voice low.

"Let go."

"Give me your key."

"I can do it."

"Give. Me. Your. Key."

She gave him the key.

Releasing her, he found the door, then the door-knob, then the keyhole. After several attempts, he unlocked the door.

"Where's your candle?" he asked.

"You are not going in my room," she hissed. "Now give me the key back."

He handed it to her. "I'm not leaving until you have some light." His eyes adjusted to the dark, and he could see her faint outline.

"Fine." She followed the wall with her hand and hit something. *"Ooof."* Then continued.

"Do you need any help?" he asked.

"No. Now keep your voice down." A flame flared bright. She touched the match to a candle, then turned to face him. Her eyes were wary. Her chest lifted and fell with quick breaths. Her hand held the smoking match.

Standing at the threshold, he made a quick scan of her room. A tidily made bed. Her brush-and-comb set on the washstand. Her extra pair of stockings hanging over a peg in the wall.

Finally, he returned his attention to her. "I love you, Della. And rather than proving it by taking off my shirt, I'm going to prove it by leaving it on. Because it is out of great love and respect for you that I leave you in this room untouched and unkissed."

She gave no indication as to her thoughts. Just stood stiffly by her bedside table.

Stepping back, he paused. "It's just like mine."

A beat of silence.

"What is?" she asked.

"Your room." He pointed to the third floor. "Mine's right above yours."

Lips parting, her gaze shot to the ceiling.

"Good night." He crossed the hall to the stairs, leaving the door for her to close.

CHAPTER 45

Della lay in her bed, covers to her chin, thanking the good Lord that the room Hilda and Maxine occupied faced the back of the house. If they'd been facing the front and had heard Cullen and her, the game would have been up for certain.

She studied the ceiling. Every creak and scrape told of his movements. He'd said their rooms were exactly the same, so she knew when he crossed to the washstand. When he undressed and hung his clothes on the pegs. When he crawled into bed. When he tossed and turned.

When all had settled, she moved her attention to the window. Was he asleep, or was he looking at the full moon?

I'm in love with you, Della.

He'd finally said it. The one thing she'd longed to hear. Until she found out he had a fiancée.

Raising an arm, she laid it beside her on the pillow and ran her other hand down her braid. Her father had told her of men who had multiple wives living in multiple towns, none aware of the others. She hadn't believed him. Had thought he was exaggerating. Now she wasn't so sure. It would be much easier to do than she'd suspected.

Wanda. Her name was Wanda. She'd wondered.

She also wondered how long this Wanda had known him. And how often her fiancé traveled out of town.

He'd said she could question Wanda, then quickly followed it up with an admonition of how insensitive that would be. Was it because his concern for Wanda's feelings was real or because he didn't want Della to find out the truth?

He'd discouraged her from trying to discover the truth once before, but she'd insisted. And he'd not been lying. But was that enough to exempt him now?

She didn't know. She wanted to believe him. Oh, how she wanted to believe him. But her father had said blind trust was for fools. The way a person earned trust was to check on what they said. To demand proof.

But if she confronted his fiancée and she confirmed Cullen had been telling the truth, well, that would be awful. Horrific. She couldn't imagine subjecting any woman to such a thing.

And even if Cullen was telling the truth, would that excuse him for failing to mention his fiancée? They'd talked for hours and hours over the past four months about everything—their homes, their lives, their jobs. He'd had plenty of opportunities to bring it up. Yet he hadn't. And that was nothing short of outright dishonesty. And he knew it. Had apologized for it. So, did that make it okay?

Not by a long shot.

Frustrated, confused, and exhausted, she curled into a ball and tried to find solace in sleep that would not come.

CHAPTER 46

Della refused to give Cullen any more lessons and had been deft at avoiding him. He'd parked himself outside her classroom, but the Board of Lady Managers ran him off. He tried to wait for her in front of Harvell House, but she'd had her name removed from the list. He had no way of knowing if she was there or not.

And aside from all that, time was running out. He needed to make one last push to win customers, and he had to do it now. So if worse came to worst, he'd follow Della back to the Pennsylvania Home for the Training in Speech of Deaf Children Before They Are of School Age and try to woo her there.

In the meanwhile, he stepped into Chief Murphy's office at the Fire and Guard Station, closing the door behind him. Unlike Grasty, who had a habit of strewing papers everywhere when he worked, Murphy kept everything so clean it made him wonder if the man ever did any paperwork at all. Then again, maybe it was the only part of his job he could control and keep in an orderly fashion.

Running his thumb and finger down his bushy brown mustache, Murphy indicated a ladder-back chair with his head. "The boys said you *sspct* foul play."

"No suspecting about it." Cullen deposited the three sprinkler heads, now cleaned, on the desk. "Two of my automatic heads were replaced with manual ones."

Murphy examined them, reached for his magnifying glass, then examined them again. "Do you know who?"

Though he had his suspicions, they were just that. And he was loath to name Bulenberg on nothing more than conjecture. Giving his trouser legs a tug, he lowered himself into the chair. "The manufacturer's mark was sanded off, and I wouldn't even begin to know how to investigate such a thing."

"Did you *notfy* the police?"

"I told the commandant of the Columbian Guards. He took my report, but I'm sure there are many more pressing matters for him to see to."

Murphy set down the magnifying glass. "What do you intend to do?"

"About the culprit? Nothing for now. Mainly because a second demonstration is more pressing. Still, I can't afford for anyone to tamper with it again."

Leaning back, Murphy tapped his fingers together. "Even if this *scnd* demonstration is successful, it won't make people forget the last one."

Cullen pulled on his ear. "What if I had three separate sheds? And all three were lit one right after the other, then all three were doused at the same time?"

Murphy shook his head. "I don't *thk* you'll be able to draw the audience you'd need. Not after that last demonstration."

"I thought of that, and that's why I'm here."

Murphy pursed his lips. "I'm listening."

"I saw in the fair's daily bulletin that Fireman's Week was coming up. I was wondering if I could be part of it."

A hum of voices dipped and swelled in the hallway behind them.

"That's *sppsd* to be a tournament between firefighters," Murphy said.

"It's also been billed as a competition to see which engines and apparatus do the best work. I don't need to be a contender for a medal. I'd just like to do a demonstration of my apparatus. That way I wouldn't need to get approval from the director-general. I'd only need to be added to the slate by you."

Leaning forward, Murphy put his arms on his desk, his chair squeaking. "The tournament starts in ten days. Do you have enough time to build three sheds and three systems?"

Cullen nodded. "If I don't man my exhibit, which shouldn't be a problem since no one will come by now anyway."

"What about materials?"

"I saw your battalions answered a call a few

days ago when the Lincoln Hotel's fire threatened to blow sparks into the Midway."

Murphy nodded.

"Do you think I could collect some lumber from the ruins of the Lincoln?"

"I don't see why not. You'd be doing them a favor to haul off *whtvr* you can." Opening a drawer, he pulled out a piece of paper. "I'll write Marshal Green a note saying as much. He's in charge of the *Chcgo* battalion that answered the call."

"Then you'll do it? You'll let me be a part of Fireman's Week?" He held his breath.

"Of course." Dipping his pen in ink, Murphy began to scratch a message across the paper. "It's going to be *dffclt* to keep three sheds a secret, though."

Euphoria shot through him. "We won't have to keep them a secret. They could simply be sheds for the upcoming competition. No one need know there are sprinklers inside."

Murphy looked up. "Clever. Where do you plan to build them?"

"I'll build right on the lakefront where the competition is to be held."

Murphy blotted the paper, blew on it, then folded it in thirds. "We'll give her a try, McNamara. I'll have my own *bttln* standing by, just like last time."

Taking the memorandum, Cullen slipped it into

his jacket, then extended his hand. "Thank you, sir. I, I don't know what to say."

"No thanks are necessary." Murphy held their handshake. "I only wish I could do more. If you ever decide you *wnt* to be a firefighter, you let me know."

Releasing him, Cullen gave a wry grin. "If this demonstration doesn't work, you may find me on your doorstep."

"Not to worry, son. I've every faith that your *sprnklrs* will work."

Smiling, Cullen placed his hat on his head, then swiped his fingers down its rim. "Yes, sir. I believe they will."

CROWNE PEN COMPANY EXHIBIT

"Della stepped up to Crowne's counter.
Glass cases displayed fountain pens,
along with pearl, ebony, and silver holders
nestling inside plush cases."

CHAPTER 47

For the last month, Della had not been herself. She'd been in no mood to spend her evenings with Hilda and Maxine, so had not even told them she wasn't tutoring Cullen anymore. Instead, she simply walked through the fair's buildings alone, with only her feelings for company. And those feelings had continued to fluctuate from shock to disbelief to lethargy to anger.

Today she was angry. Angry with her father for being an alarmist. Angry with Cullen for lying to her. Angry with herself for falling in love with him. But when she snapped at sweet little Vivienne, whose sole purpose in life was to please her teacher, Della knew it was time either to do something about her situation with Cullen or let him go.

She loved him and always would. And though she was extremely upset about his subterfuge, was standing on the high ground the route she really wanted to take? For he'd not been the starry-eyed one. She had. And the first time he'd ever shown any overt feelings of attraction for her was after the toboggan ride.

Assuming he hadn't been attempting to lead a dual life, as it were, she couldn't imagine the inner turmoil he must have experienced being engaged to one woman, then suddenly finding himself falling in love with another.

If that was the case and he promised to be completely honest and up-front now and forever-more, was she willing to risk it? Willing to give their love a chance?

It didn't take her long to decide. She was. She absolutely was. But first, she needed to find out if he was telling the truth. If he really had broken it off with Wanda.

She had no idea how to contact Wanda. The only thing she knew was Wanda had stayed with someone from the Crowne Pen Company. So after work, she headed to Machinery Hall.

Every place she passed contained a memory of Cullen. The lagoon on her left. The Manufactures Building beyond that. The Ferris wheel reigning over it all.

She wondered if she'd see him in Machinery Hall or if he'd see her. His booth was just a few exhibits down from Crowne's. What would she do if he approached? What would she do if he didn't?

Fairgoers buzzed about her, chatting, laughing, pointing, and exclaiming, having no idea she wasn't part of the fun. Having no idea she'd shored up her nerves to find out the truth. And that the answers to her questions would determine whether she'd be with or without the person she loved above all others.

The whirling wheels of a rolling chair warned her to move aside or be run over. A popper over hot coals set corn kernels dancing. Their crackle and snap along with their poignant aroma filled the area. It immediately brought to mind the bag of Cracker Jacks she had shared with Cullen, both marveling at the new concoction and agreeing that regular popcorn would never taste the same again.

Crossing the Court of Honor, she approached Cullen's building, her nerves jangling. But he wasn't inside. His booth was empty of everything but his tiny display. Relief and disappointment warred for dominance.

She stepped up to Crowne's counter. Glass cases displayed fountain pens, along with pearl, ebony, and silver holders nestling inside plush cases.

A woman in a smart taupe suit greeted her with a smile. "Good afternoon. Might I show you to a seat in our amphitheater?" She gestured toward a horseshoe of seats behind her that faced several machines. "You can watch crude materials such as gold and alloy transform into finished pens right before your eyes and then, perhaps, take a souvenir home with you. Our next show is just about to start."

Della clasped and unclasped her hands. "Actually I was hoping one of you could help me with a more personal matter."

417

The woman's face changed from that of a salesperson to a person of concern who shared a common bond with those of her sex. "I'll do my best. What is it you wished?"

"I was hoping to speak to the lady who opened her quarters to a Miss Wanda a couple of weeks ago."

The woman's eyes became wary, her tone cautious. "I know Miss Sappington."

Sappington. Wanda Sappington. Somehow, knowing her full name made it worse. Della took a deep breath. "Is she still here, by any chance?"

"Who's asking, if you don't mind?"

"Oh, of course. I'm sorry. I should have done that first. I'm Adelaide Wentworth of Philadelphia, but everyone calls me Della."

"And you have business with Miss Sappington?" The woman's tone flattened.

Della swallowed. "I believe we're both in love with the same man."

A stocky gentleman stepped onto the stage area of the amphitheater and began to address a smattering of spectators, his voice loud in order to be heard over the noise in the Hall.

The saleswoman threaded her hands together and rested them on the counter. "I see. Yet I'm still unsure of your purpose."

Della tugged at her gloves. "This is very awkward."

"You're welcome to leave at any time."

Oh, dear. The woman must have liked Wanda Sappington.

Della cleared her throat. "I had just wanted to ask her a very quick question."

"And what might that be?"

She darted her gaze from the amphitheater to the other salesladies, then back to the one before her, who had yet to introduce herself. "I was, um, simply wondering how long she had known Mr. McNamara."

The woman studied her, her spine as straight as one of the fountain pens inside the display case. "Since they were children."

Della's lips parted. "Are you certain?"

"That was my understanding."

"Do you know if Mr. McNamara traveled extensively?"

The woman drew her brows together. "What is your purpose, Miss Wentworth?"

She rubbed her forehead, then took a fortifying breath. "I'm terribly sorry to be so forward. It's just, my father has put the fear of God in me ever since he discovered I was coming to the fair. One of the things he cautioned me about was men who lead dual lives, if you will, with one wife and family in the East and another in the West. I know it sounds preposterous, but I am just trying to confirm exactly what manner of man Mr. McNamara is."

The more she spoke, the more the saleslady's posture relaxed. "You're here alone?"

"I'm here with my school. We teach deaf students at the Children's Building."

Her eyes lit in recognition. "I've heard much about your exhibit. You're teaching them to lip-read?"

"Yes."

Biting the inside of her cheek, she thrummed her fingers on the counter, then blew out a soft breath. "Mr. McNamara is a very conscientious man. I have no way of knowing his travel schedule, but from what Wanda told me, he lives on a farm in North Carolina with his father and has lived there always. He and Wanda were childhood sweethearts—or so she thought until quite recently."

"Then they are no longer engaged to marry?"

"They are not."

Della nodded, a spark of hope coming to life. "Thank you. Thank you so much." She glanced at Cullen's booth. "Do you know where he is?"

"He hasn't manned his booth since his demonstration."

"Do you know where I can find him?"

Again, the woman took a long time in answering. "I'm sorry."

Her throat began to close. "Please, I must see him."

"Does he know where to find you?"

420

"He does."

"Then I'll tell him if I see him again."

"If?" Her pulse began to hammer. "You're not certain if you'll see him again?"

"I have no idea."

Biting her lip, Della stepped back from the counter. "Well, thank you for your help, and good day."

She questioned the men whose booths bracketed Cullen's. But no one knew where he was or where he'd been.

With drooping shoulders, she left Machinery Hall and headed to the place she'd found succor these past several weeks—the revolving side-walk.

AGRICULTURAL BUILDING AND THE GRAND BASIN

"The boulevard between the Grand Basin and the Agricultural Building held a typical crowd—those who strolled leisurely down its walk, those who studied maps, and those who tried to impress upon their children the importance of what they were seeing."

CHAPTER 48

Following her now familiar route, Della crossed the Court of Honor, then headed toward the pier, allowing the harmonious strength of the White City to soothe her raw emotions. Cullen was who he said he was. He'd known Wanda Sappington virtually his whole life, and she'd known him. It stood to reason, therefore, that he wasn't living a life of duplicity.

Relief, happiness, and guilt washed over her in succession. Relief that he'd told the truth about ending his engagement. Happiness that she could declare her love to him if he promised not to hold any secrets from her. And guilt that she'd caused him pain by refusing to believe him in the first place.

Still, he wasn't completely blameless. He should have told her about Miss Sappington. He certainly had ample opportunity.

That didn't explain his absence from his booth, though. Was he ill? Surely she'd have heard him puttering about his room if that were the case.

She squared her shoulders. Whatever the reason, she'd wait for him tonight on the steps of Harvell House just as he'd waited for her. No matter how long it took.

Decision made, she began to take in her surroundings. The bricked boulevard between the

Grand Basin and the Agricultural Building held a typical crowd—those who strolled leisurely down its walk, those who studied maps, and those who tried to impress upon their children the importance of what they were seeing.

But the ones who fascinated her most were those who made a duty out of touring the fair. Loaded down with guidebooks, pads, pencils, and bags, they were easy to spot. Today it was a family of five. Like a duck with a line of ducklings, their leader walked at a brisk pace, a specific destination in his mind.

The piercing voices of juveniles in red toggery carried over the hum of the crowd. "This way for your World's Fair catalogue!" they cried, striving for dominance over the boys in blue who sold official guides and cried out attractions not listed in the book.

A line of guards hurried down both sides of the Basin, urging folks to the edges of the boulevard. "Clear the track! Clear the track!"

A clanging gong sounded, causing her to jump out of the way. Fire engines belching out smoke and sparks galloped by, one on each side of the Basin, as if they were in a race. Rattling hook-and-ladder trucks followed closely on their heels.

Tremors ran through her body as memories of the Cold Storage Building assailed her, but she could see no fire.

The drivers, encouraged by shouts of the crowd,

urged their panting teams into speedier action. When the first engine reached the shore, it pulled to a stop, the driver of the truck lifting his arms in the air like a pugilist winner. Cheers from an assembly of fairgoers met their arrival.

Still, she could see no fire. Half of her wanted to turn around and go in the opposite direction. The other half wanted to make sure all was well.

"Company Seven of Boston beat them by a hair!" a young man shouted. Those around him passed the information to those behind them until all were informed, and another roar of approval rose forth.

Of Boston? she thought. *What in the world?*

Foreigners, unaccustomed to such displays, had hurriedly retreated into the Agricultural Building. Little by little, they crept out of hiding and back onto the boulevard, as drawn to the spectacle as everyone else.

"Fireman's Week!" a lad in blue shouted, holding up a pamphlet. "Puffing, blowing, and throwing of water by the engines! Hook-and-ladder maneuvers! Get your schedule here!"

She let out a slow breath. Of course. It was only a demonstration. A contest between firemen from most every state, eager to show off their skills and earn a Fireman's Week medal. The fair had designated so many "special" days—Irish Day, Miller's Day, Confectioner's Day, Poor Children's Day—that she had long since quit trying to keep up with them all. Still, she wondered if perhaps Cullen might be at this one cheering for his friends.

Weaving through the crowd, she wandered along the shoreline looking for him in the crowd, then paused to examine an antiquated hand engine as an old-timer in dark clothing, an over-sized hat, and an engraved white belt explained the difference between fire equipment of long ago and that of today.

Firemen in scuffed-up red shirts swapped friendly insults beside a pile of smoldering ruins, its stench bringing flashes of horror from the Cold Storage fire. Up ahead, a large crowd gathered around three wooden structures. But the crowd was too dense for her liking and she had no wish to see the competition. She already knew of the bravery and skill these firemen displayed. She'd just have to wait and see if she could catch Cullen tonight when he arrived at Harvell House.

Turning, she'd taken only a few steps when a crier announced a demonstration of an automatic sprinkler system.

"You've heard of a horseless carriage. Now you'll see a fireman-less extinguisher! Three burning sheds will be snuffed out in three short minutes without any help from man or beast!"

Whirling back, she hurried to the edge of the crowd, trying to skirt around it. The sheds ignited like tinderboxes. The crowd fell back and spilled around her. Heat from the blaze scorched her face.

Pushing down the panic from being in a crush of people, she focused instead on reaching Cullen, for it had to be him. When the crowd took a step back, she leaned in and took a step forward. Squeezing her eyes shut, she concentrated on pleasant things.

She pictured Cullen laughing in the cocoa shop. One step forward. She pictured him cheering during the illumination show. Two steps forward. She pictured him handing her a rose in the Wooded Island. Three steps forward.

She sang "Jesus Loves Me." She opened her eyes and found that the flames on the first shed had begun to falter and fade. Then on the one in the middle. And finally on the one on the right. When she broke through to the front of the crowd, not a vestige of flame remained.

A man beside her popped open his timepiece. "Less than three minutes."

The crowd thundered their approval with applause and exclamation. A smile broke across Cullen's face, taking her breath away in a rush. The fire chief stepped forward and shook his hand, clapping him on the shoulder. The firemen who'd stood in readiness punched their fists in the air and roared in celebration.

Spectators quickly shared what they'd seen,

their stories being told and retold until all who had gathered heard of the sprinklers that put out fires without any human help.

The firefighters swarmed Cullen, then lifted him up onto their shoulders. Laughing, he balanced himself with his hands on their heads. And then he saw her.

Pride and love swelled within her.

I'm sorry, she signed. *I love you.*

If possible, his smile grew even wider. And right there, regardless of who could see his hand gestures, and even though he knew she could read his lips, he pointed to himself, then crossed his fisted hands over his chest, and ended by pointing at her. *I love you, D-E-L-L-A.*

The moment the firefighters put him down, businessmen swarmed him. She stayed back, emotion clogging her throat. A moment later, an extended arm was raised above the huddle.

W-A-I-T. F-O-R. M-E.

Warmth flooded her. And though she doubted he could see it, she raised on tiptoes and held her arm high.

I'll wait, she signed alphabetically.

When the crowd thinned, he scanned the periphery until he spotted her, then gave her a searing look that sent tiny bumps straight up her arms before he focused once again on the men. His jacket hugged his shoulders, his hat sat a bit off-kilter.

Finally, he shook hands with the last person. The man had taken no more than one step away when Cullen moved the full force of his attention to her. No smile, no laugh lines, but a world of promise. With each step he took, her knees weakened a bit more.

Cullen couldn't believe she was there. Couldn't believe she'd forgiven him and loved him. Couldn't believe he could look his fill with a completely clear conscience. And look he did. From the tip of her dainty brown hat to the toes of her black boots and all the way back up again.

Her cheeks pinked. "Congratulations."

He flexed his hands in an effort to keep from reaching for her. "Thank you."

"Were those men interested in placing orders?"

"Yes, but I don't want to talk about them right now." Taking a step closer, he lowered his voice. "You're beautiful. I've thought it for the longest time. But I've never been free to say it."

The pink cheeks turned to red. "Thank you."

"Your eyes are the purest blue I've ever seen in my life. Especially in the sunshine. Your pupils get really small, and that blue—it's, it's like nothing I've ever seen. And your nose is so elegant. And your lips . . ." His breathing became labored. "Your lips are . . ."

Dragging his gaze away, he scanned the area.

There were people everywhere. Not a single private spot in sight.

He grabbed her hand. "Come on."

"What are you—" She slapped a hand over her hat, scurrying to keep up with him.

He dragged her down the shoreline, into the east entrance of the Manufactures Building, then down the first aisle. People chattered, exhibitors called out, babies cried. Finally, they reached the corner of the building, where two sets of stairs led to the second floor.

Without wasting another moment, he opened a door under the eaves, ducked inside, propelled her into his arms, and kissed her. Not as thoroughly as he'd like, but enough to learn her texture, her special scent, and any little sounds she made while he showed her the depth of his feelings.

She was so tall. And tiny. And wonderful.

Angling his head to the other side, he kissed her again, not wanting to waste a single moment.

She mewed.

Desire surged through him. Peeling his lips from hers, he bracketed her face, kissing every inch. So soft. So smooth. So delectable.

"I've been wanting to do that since our very first lesson," he murmured.

She tilted her head, giving him access to her jaw and throat. "Even back then?"

"Your lips drove me crazy. I thought I'd go mad

trying to read them when what I really wanted was to taste them." He cradled her head and crushed his mouth to hers once again.

It took a moment before he realized she was trying to shift to the side.

He pulled back, bumping his head on the slanted ceiling. "What is it?"

"There's a broom or mop—"

For the first time, he noted the smell of lemon with a tiny touch of vinegar. Reaching behind her, he tried to move the mops out of the way, lost his footing, and almost fell out the door.

She squeaked, grabbed him, then giggled.

When he finally regained his balance, he braced his feet wide, pulled her in for another kiss, then reluctantly loosened his hold. "I love you."

"I love you too."

"How did you find me?" he asked.

"I was at the exhibition and heard one of the criers mention a fireman-less extinguisher."

Moving his palms up and down her sides, he gloried in the feel of her. "I'm glad you did."

"Me too."

"Do you believe I'm not a philanderer?"

"I do, but you must promise to be completely open and up-front about everything from now on."

He let out a sigh. "I will, Della. I will. I'm sorry I wasn't before." He sealed his vow with another fierce kiss before finally pulling back. "Much as

I'd like to stay in here, my neck can't take this closet much longer. Would you like to go back to the exhibition?"

Smoothing her hands beneath his lapels, she tugged his jacket into place. "I'd love to."

STATE STREET, CHICAGO

"Cullen stood in the waiting area of Vaughn Mutual Insurance in Chicago, hat in hand."

CHAPTER 49

Cullen stood in the waiting area of Vaughn Mutual Insurance of Chicago, hat in hand. Walnut-stained wood covered every surface of the room—floor, walls, and ceiling. The wooden seats of two bentwood chairs had faded from constant use. Across from them, a modest desk held a matronly woman with a soft white bun at her nape and a pleasant disposition.

But what intrigued him the most was the speaking tube on her desk. It appeared as if a tube ran from it to the wall and into what he assumed was Vaughn's office.

As he stared, it whistled. The secretary pushed a lever to one side, then spoke into the tube. "Yes, sir?"

"Send Mr. McNamara in, Miss Forsythe."

Fascinating, he thought.

Standing, Miss Forsythe circled her desk. Her back bowed out, giving her a permanent slouch. "Right this way, Mr. McNamara."

Opening the door, she waved him in. Piles of papers formed a castle-like wall on Vaughn's desk, while other papers had been plopped atop books in a bookshelf and overflowed onto the floor. Fire hazards if he'd ever seen any.

Vaughn rose and indicated an upholstered seat across from him. Above the ring of his cropped white hair, the man's head was slick and shiny.

"Sit down, *McNmra*," he said. "That was quite a demonstration you had at Fireman's *Wk*."

"Thank you, sir."

"I'm almost afraid to ask how much *bsnss* it generated."

Cullen lifted a corner of his mouth. "Even more than I'd hoped. Once a few companies signed up, they told their acquaintances, who then told theirs, and, well, so far, I have commitments from cotton, woolen, corn, and saw mills. From biscuit works, sugar refineries, rubber works, drapers' shops, calico printers, linoleum works, ware—"

Chuckling, Vaughn held up a hand. "I get the picture."

Cullen handed him a paper listing all his clients.

Setting his spectacles on his nose, Vaughn took several moments to peruse it. "This is very good, *McNmra*. Very good. Did any of them *cmmt* with a down payment?"

"Yes, sir. I required a fifty percent deposit." He delineated which ones had already paid.

With part of the advances, he'd sent money home to pay for the Dewey boys' help. Between the harvest money and the upcoming installs, he'd be able to buy down enough debts to keep the farm for at least another year—more if his dad was careful and if Cullen's business continued to grow.

Vaughn settled back in his chair, his vest

buttons straining against his portly belly. "I'm *assming* you're here to find out how much I'll reduce their premiums?"

"Yes, sir."

He tapped his thumb against the armrest. "I wasn't *expcting* you to do so well, *prtclrly* in light of our current economic *cndtn*."

Cullen gave him a wry grin. "Forgive me if I don't apologize. And I told them of Vaughn Mutual. I know many of them hope to recoup much of their investment by signing policies with you."

Vaughn returned his grin. "Excellent."

A clock on the wall ticked in the ensuing silence.

Drawing in a large breath, Vaughn sat up and leaned on his desk. "Let me take this to the board. Our *intntn* is to offer a premium discount to any of our current policyholders who adopt your *sprnklrs* and to, of course, garner new *clnts* from this list of yours. In the long run, their *rdcd prmms* will be well *wrth* the *cst* of your *systms*."

Even in the quiet of the room, Cullen had trouble grasping what had been said. He knew that if Vaughn pulled out, he'd lose some clients—maybe not all, but certainly enough to put the farm back in jeopardy. Still, Vaughn was not a one-time install job. He'd be working with him and his company for at least a year, maybe more if things went well.

Trying to hide his hearing loss would be not only almost impossible, but also dishonest. And that was a road he didn't care to take again.

With a quick prayer, he mustered up some courage. "I'm terribly sorry, sir, but I'm hard of hearing and didn't catch those last two sentences."

Vaughn's eyes widened behind his glasses. "Hard of *hrng*? Is this *smthng* new? I've never noticed it before."

"I've been gradually losing my hearing over the past year. It's become much worse since arriving at the fair. As you know, though, I've been taking private lip-reading lessons from one of the teachers of the deaf."

Vaughn pushed himself straight in his chair. "I thought that was because of the noise in Machinery *Hll*. I had no idea your actual hearing was a problem. Who else knows *abt* this?"

"My family, my, uh, teacher, and a former customer."

"What do you mean, 'a former customer'?"

"I had a printing-works man who withdrew his orders once he found out I had difficulty hearing."

"Well, I'm not the least bit *surprsed*. Do not under any circumstances tell anyone else. It could very well jeopardize all of *ths*. People have very definite opinions about that sort of thing."

"Don't you think that would be dishonest?"

Vaughn ran a hand over his head. "Absolutely not. Having a *hring* problem does not mean you have to run *arnd* with a scarlet letter pinned to your chest."

Cullen frowned. He hadn't thought of it quite like that. "I wasn't planning to tell every person I met on the street, but clients are a bit different, don't you think?"

"Will this hearing *prblm* affect your work? Your *sprnklr* systems?"

"Not at all."

"Then the clients don't need to know *abt* it."

Cullen shifted positions in the chair. "What if I knew a particular client would clearly object to working with someone subject to a deficiency of this kind?"

Vaughn shook his head. "Your ability to hear— or not hear—has no impact on the reliability or effectiveness of your product any more than your looks, personality, weight, or height would. Therefore, you are *undr* no obligation to share it."

"Don't you think that would be lying by omission?"

"Lying by omission would be installing a product that was faulty. *That* is relevant to the relationship. *That* is lying by omission."

Cullen tapped a fist against his lips. Partial deafness might not affect his equipment, but it would have an impact on his relationship with a buyer who held strong prejudices. Still, what

Vaughn said made sense. He supposed he'd have to take it one client at a time and simply do as his conscience dictated.

"There's nothing wrong with my product," he said.

"Of course not." Rising to his feet, Vaughn tapped Cullen's list of clients. "Would you mind if I kept this for now?"

Cullen held out a hand. "I made that copy for you."

Vaughn gave him a firm shake. "I'll let the board know. We should have a proposal for your clients by the end of the fair."

GONDOLA ON THE LAGOON

"A golden-skinned gondolier wearing an embroidered purple jacket took his position on the dancing bow, his long oar secured across a twisted lock. His partner, in crimson and white, balanced on tiptoe in the narrow stern."

CHAPTER 50

Della had become so accustomed to groups of tourists entering her classroom that she hardly gave them a second glance. But at the back of this particular group stood Cullen, as antsy and full of excitement as a young boy on Christmas morning. His eyes danced, a barely checked smile hovered at his lips, his weight shifted from one foot to the other.

What on earth?

With difficulty, she forced her attention back to the children. Lifting a small plate with cake, she held it in the air. "What is this?"

Idanell raised her hand. "*Caag.*"

"Very good, Idanell. Now, everyone together . . . 'Cake.' "

"*Caag.*"

One by one, the children identified a bottle of wine, some wildflowers, a red cap, and a drawing of a wolf.

"Excellent. Now we are ready for story time."

She told them of Little Red Cap's instructions from her mother, her meeting with the wolf, and the sly plot the wolf had. Whenever one of their vocabulary words was used, she held the object in the air and the children chorused that part.

Although they'd heard the story a thousand times, they still sat breathless during the telling.

The scene with the disguised wolf was Della's favorite.

She put the red cap on her head. "Oh, Grandmother, what big . . ." She pointed to her ear.

"*Eeyyoos.*"

". . . you have. And the wolf said . . ." She held up a drawing of the wolf.

"*All dddd bbbedddr to heee you wid.*"

"Oh, Grandmother, what big . . ."

"*Iiiiz.*"

". . . you have. And the wolf said . . ."

"*All dddd bbbedddr to zeee you wid.*"

"Oh, Grandmother, what big . . ."

"*Haaandz.*"

". . . you have. And the wolf said . . ."

"*All dddd bbbedddr to gwabbb you wid.*"

"Oh, Grandmother, what a horribly big . . ."

"*Mow-f.*"

". . . you have. And the wolf said . . ."

"*All dddd bbbedddr to eeed you wid!*"

"And he jumped from the bed and ate up poor Little Red Cap."

Kitty's eyes widened. She covered her mouth and shook her head, her blond ringlets bouncing every which way. Della quickly brought in the huntsman who cut the wolf open with his ax and saved Little Red Cap and her grandmother.

The applause from the tourists gave her a start. She'd forgotten all about them. Her gaze connected with Cullen's.

His grin was wide and his shoulders shook.

Heat rushing into her cheeks, she snatched the red cap from her head, then turned back to the children. "What did you learn?"

Vivienne bounced off her chair, jumped up and down, and waved her hand in the air.

Della gave her a gentle frown. "Ladylike manners, please, Vivienne."

The girl scrambled back to the chair, bottom up, arm still waving.

Della bit her cheek. "Go ahead."

"*Doo whaad your mudder sezzz.*"

"Do what your mother says. You are exactly right."

Edgar raised his hand, his feet swinging back and forth in the chair.

"Edgar."

"*Do nod lizzn tooo woooves.*"

The tourists chuckled.

She nodded. "Do not listen to wolves or . . . ?"

Julia Jo raised her hand.

"Julia Jo."

"*Or peeeble ooo dell you do braag de ruuuz.*"

"Or people who tell you to break the rules. Excellent. Shall we close with a prayer?" Putting her hands together, she led them in prayer, then released them for playtime on the roof.

The tourists followed them out, talking quietly among themselves. At last they were gone.

Closing the door behind them, Cullen leaned

against it, ankles crossed. "They understood you very well."

"It took me months and months to teach the story to them the first time. Now the repetition reinforces the words on my lips and makes them more recognizable when I use them out of context."

He nodded. "That was the final lesson of the day, wasn't it?"

"It was. What are you doing taking a tour of the building?"

"It was the only way I could get in here before school was over."

"Has something happened?"

His smile grew huge.

She felt her own begin. "Oh, Mr. McNamara. What a big smile you have."

Pushing away from the door, he grabbed a chair and wedged it beneath the doorknob.

"Cullen," she scolded. "What are you doing?"

He took a step forward.

She took a step back. "Oh, Mr. McNamara. What mischievous eyes you have."

He winked. "The better to see you with."

He made a swipe.

She jumped out of the way, giggling. "Oh, Mr. McNamara. What big hands you have."

"The better to grab you with." This time he was ready for her and snagged her arm, then pulled her close.

She squeaked. "What if someone tries to come in?"

"No one is coming in." His wicked smile engaged laugh lines and dimples.

She bit her lip. "Oh, Mr. McNamara. What a horribly big mouth you have."

He splayed his hands across her back. "The better to kiss you with."

She stiffened. "Not here!"

But it was too late. His head descended, and she was lost. By the time he'd finished, she was on her tiptoes, her arms around his neck and her breath coming in short spurts.

He rested his forehead and nose against hers. "Guess what?"

"What?"

"My sprinkler system won a medal."

She pulled back. "What!"

Releasing her, he slipped a hand into his coat pocket and withdrew a shiny silver filigree case.

Excitement and awe bubbled up inside her. She clasped her hands behind her back. "You open it."

His big, virile hands pressed the spring-loaded button. Inside, a bronze coin nestled against a black velvet lining.

"Oh, Cullen. This isn't a medal from the Fireman's Week competitions. It's a medal from the *fair*." She looked up. "Can I touch it?"

Grinning, he nodded.

She ran her fingers along a figure of Columbus

stepping ashore onto the New World. "It's gorgeous."

"Look at the other side."

Placing one hand beneath his, she picked up the coin with her other and turned it over. A cartouche with a commemorative inscription was flanked by torches on either side, two winged females and a globe on the top, and a large sailing ship along the bottom.

"Read it," he urged.

" 'World's Columbian Exposition. In commemoration of the four-hundredth anniversary of the landing of Columbus. 1892–1893. To . . .' " Gasping, she glanced at him again. "They engraved your name on it."

His smile grew wider. "Can you believe it?"

She ran her finger across the C. B. McNamara. "What's the B for?"

"Berneen. After my father."

Returning it to its case, she rotated it just so. "It's beautiful. I'm so proud of you. This should help garner even more orders, don't you think?"

"It already has."

She bracketed his cheeks and gave him another kiss. "Congratulations."

"Want to celebrate?"

She lifted a brow. "Will it involve heights and closed-in spaces?"

"Nary a one."

"What did you have in mind?"

"A gondola ride."

Her lips parted. "Really? Do you mean it?"

"I've been dying to see the fair from that vantage point. Haven't you?"

She nodded, remembering the many times she'd admired the elegant vessels.

He glanced at her table. "Think Red Cap's granny would mind if I swiped her bottle of wine?"

Giggling, she shook her finger back and forth. "You wouldn't believe the difficulty I had in convincing the director I needed it. But it's right there in the story, so what could I do? Anyway, 'Granny' would most definitely miss it if it disappeared. And I'm already persona non grata around here."

"Why?"

"Because I've been asking why we can't teach both sign language and lip-reading. She is not pleased."

"Well, tonight we're going to forget all about that. So get your things in order, Miss Wentworth, and let's go."

GREAT WHITE HORSE INN

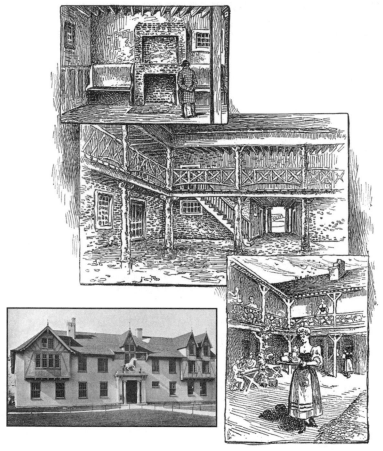

"It was an exact reproduction of
the famous English inn described in
Dickens's *Pickwick Papers*, right down to
the statue of a horse over its entrance."

CHAPTER 51

Eager as Della was to ride the gondola, Cullen first surprised her by taking her to one of the fair's restaurants. He chose the Great White Horse Inn, directly across from Blooker's. It was an exact reproduction of the famous English inn described in Dickens's *Pickwick Papers*, right down to the statue of a horse over its entrance.

Removing her gloves, she felt as if she'd stepped back in time to the fifteenth century. Brick walls, wooden rafters, and oriental carpets in turbulent fields of green, pink, and maroon had her imagining the passengers who'd been entertained within the original inn's rustic walls while waiting for a coach to London. Even the picture frames were made of braided straw and tied with ribbon.

"This is much more cheerful than the way Dickens described it," she said, raising her voice over the noise.

Cullen nodded, but from the angling of his head with his left ear close, she could tell he had difficulty understanding her.

She scanned the boisterous crowd for a vacant table. "Will you be able to hear in here?"

"I might have to make an intent study of your lips, but I'll somehow manage," he said, winking.

Flushing, she followed a young barmaid in a

black gown, a white kirtle, and an old-timey caplet to a table by a crackling fireplace.

The noise ended up being more than Cullen could conquer. They tried sign language, but she hadn't taught him enough without a lot of spelling. She'd have to do something about that.

Still, she enjoyed the atmosphere even without conversation. Their supper of potage, quail, and short-crust pie was served in old stewpans and wooden trenchers. Because forks had been rare during that era, they were given only spoons and one knife, which they shared.

Cullen broke off a bite of quail, jabbed it with the knife, then held it out. She reached for it, but he pulled back and shook his head. "Open up."

Glancing about, she opened her mouth. He placed the bite inside, then drew the knife from her closed lips, watching her chew.

He took a bite of his own, still eyeing her lips.

She shifted in her chair.

He continued, breaking the bread and offering it to her, his hand gliding over hers, feeding her occasional bites of figs and cheese, his fingers brushing her lips.

By the time supper was over, her face stayed red, her body hot, her breath uneven. When they stepped back outside, it was all she could do not to drag him to the corner stairwell in the Manufactures Building.

Neither spoke. His hand rode low along the

small of her back, his fingers stroking. With each caress, her abdomen clinched tighter and tighter.

Finally, they reached a set of wide steps leading down to a collection of gondolas with dragons rampant on their prows. Blue, yellow, green, and purple bows bobbed against the Basin's landing. While Cullen secured tickets, she drank in the red and orange streaks of twilight and tried to steady her nerves. It was no use. The moment he took her elbow and helped her onto one of the blue, crescent-shaped boats, her insides became all jumbled again.

The vessel swayed. She gripped his arm.

"Easy there." His voice ran across her skin, followed by a rush of goose bumps.

He settled her into a velvet-covered bench, its seat and back cushioned with plush golden pillows trimmed in purple. With a quick stroke, he swept her skirts to the side, his hand swishing down her thigh so swiftly, he'd already sat before she had a chance to react. His long, muscular legs fell open, the left one pressing against her.

A golden-skinned gondolier wearing an embroidered purple jacket took his position on the dancing bow, his long oar secured across a twisted lock. His partner, in crimson and white, balanced on tiptoe in the narrow stern, leaning forward.

They backed up with practiced ease, then pushed on their oars. The boat shot forward like a released arrow, continuing on in one smooth glide. No command passed between them, yet they acted in harmony with each other, cutting around the base of the huge golden statue of the Republic, then moving down the center of the Basin and swinging under a bridge to the expansive walkway between the Manufactures and Electricity Buildings.

The rhythmic sound of their oars merged with the ripple of waves against the craft. A subdued murmur from people passing on the banks added to the refrain. Untamed plants along the edges of the channel juxtaposed with the sweep of architectural wonders reaching heavenward on either side.

She glanced at Cullen to see his reaction to the nooks of the park that could not be seen from land.

But his eyes were not on the vista. They were on her.

The soft breeze caused by the boat loosened tendrils of her hair, spinning them across her face. A wisp stuck to the corner of her mouth. Before she could release it, he hooked it with his finger, pulling it free.

I want to kiss you, he mouthed.

Her stomach bounced. With an iron will, she pulled her gaze away. The gondoliers crossed the calm water and traveled beneath a bridge. As they emerged on the opposite side, the Wooded Island came into view. She drew in her breath. From this perspective, it rose like a crown jewel set amid the silvery lagoon.

Lily leaves floated about its edges, framing an embankment trimmed with every specimen of flower imaginable on reeds, climbers, ornamentals, and trees. It was as if the brilliance of the blooms reflected a hundred prisms hung in the clouds.

Along the magnificent promenade, people stopped to point at their gondola. Did they not see the soft zephyrs, the fragile sweet peas, and the immense hydrangea bushes with delicate blossoms blessing every branch? All of which were diminishing in the rapid loss of sunlight?

A crowd continued to collect, all congregating along the path and looking out at them—some staring, some smiling.

Shaking her head, she turned to share her exasperation with Cullen, but he was no longer at her side. He was on the bottom of the boat, one knee bent.

Her eyes widened. "What . . . ?"

He opened a black velvet box. Nestled inside was a ring with five luminous gray diamonds encircling a sixth and making a flower-like shape. "Would you do me the great honor of becoming my wife?"

She covered her mouth, her gaze zigzagging between him and the ring. A combination of disbelief and euphoria exploded inside her. Having no power to speak, she simply nodded.

He smiled. "May I see your hand?"

Lowering her hands, she pulled off her left glove.

He slid the ring onto her finger. The group of spectators clapped.

"It's beautiful," she whispered.

"It was my grandmother's."

Her breath caught. "Oh, Cullen."

Grasping the back of the bench, he bracketed her with his arms, then leaned in and kissed her. Their audience cheered and whistled. She felt him smile against her lips.

"Can we elope?" he asked, pulling back just enough to whisper the question.

She pushed into the pillow to better see him. "Are you being serious?"

"I am."

The thought of waiting for the fair to end only to then have the delay of planning a wedding held no more appeal to her than it obviously did to him. "All right. When did you have in mind?"

"How about tomorrow?"

A nervous laugh wiggled its way up from the back of her throat. "Well, maybe not tomorrow."

"Then when?"

"Soon." She tugged at his sleeve. "Come back up here."

This time she swept her own skirt aside.

Settling next to her, he laid his arm along the bench behind her, his brown eyes ardent and impassioned. "I love you."

Her heart filled. "I love you too."

He toyed with a tendril of hair at the back of her neck, twining it round and round his finger. Every part of her wanted to launch herself into his arms.

His eyes darkened as if he'd read her thoughts.

They drifted beneath another bridge. Within its dark shadows, the gondoliers flattened their oars, bringing the boat to a stop. Waves gently rocked them from side to side.

Cullen gathered her into his arms. She had no time for protest, for his kiss commanded all her attention. It was the kiss not of a courting man but of a lover.

Every nerve, every impulse, every fiber in her being magnified a hundred times. She pressed herself against him. He tried to draw her closer, but the bench was awkward. The pillows slipped and the boat swayed.

He broke their kiss, his chest heaving. "Marry me tomorrow."

Yes, her insides screamed, but her mind held on to some semblance of sanity. "Not tomorrow."

"The day after?" He nipped her ear, nuzzled her neck.

She gently pushed against his chest. "The gondoliers," she whispered.

He stilled, then slowly straightened. When

they'd righted themselves, the boatmen guided the gondola toward the wings of the Art Gallery. The channel curved and wandered, now narrow, now wide. Now straight, now crooked.

Darkness crept upon them, welcoming the man in the moon, who smiled at them. Cullen returned his arm to the back of the bench, his fingers making circles along her arm. They passed the Wooded Island again, strings of green Japanese lanterns bobbing in the breeze, a medley of sweet odors wafting across the waters. As they reentered the Grand Basin, the vessel glided to its center, then floated about as they gloried in the illumination show. The resplendent glow of lights made her feel as if they'd drifted into an enchanted land.

Snuggling into the crook of Cullen's arm, she laid her head against his shoulder and turned her betrothal ring about her finger. She couldn't wait to look at it more closely. She wondered which grandmother it had belonged to—his father's mother or his mother's mother. His mother's wedding ring had most likely been lost in the fire.

She fisted her hand, pledging to take great care of this one. She still couldn't believe he'd proposed. But he'd obviously planned to do so for some time, because he'd had to send for the ring.

She worried her lip. What had his father's reaction been? Especially since it wasn't Wanda

Cullen planned to marry. Had his father been close to Wanda?

The colored spotlights captured her attention as they began to highlight different parts of the Court of Honor. The brilliance of the electric lights along with the featured statues and fountains captivated, enthralled, and mesmerized. Perhaps it was enchanted, this White City.

Even still, she looked forward to the show's finale. For then Cullen would walk her home. She felt sure he'd find a spot to try to convince her once more to set as early a wedding date as possible.

She had no intention of marrying him tomorrow. All the same, she looked forward to the convincing.

WOODED ISLAND

"In the morning the Wooded Island was
blessed by heaven and held no rivals.
Not even a rainbow could compete."

CHAPTER 52

DO NOT MARRY UNTIL I HAVE MET HIM. STOP. I MEAN IT. STOP. ON MY WAY NOW. STOP.

Della smiled as she thought again of her father's curt response to her news. He and Mama had taken the next train to Chicago and arrived within a day.

Cullen had tried to explain that eloping meant saying the vows and *then* telling her parents. But Della had refused. It would hurt their feelings, and she had no intention of starting married life off on the wrong foot.

Still, Papa hadn't been easy to pacify. He had harangued and blustered and then beseeched Mama for help. But Mama was so thrilled Della had a groom, she didn't care who he was or how quickly they married.

Now that the moment had come, though, Della experienced her first rush of nervousness. They received special permission to allow her parents into the park while the sun had just begun its journey into the sky, for in the morning, the Wooded Island was blessed by heaven and held no rivals. Not even a rainbow could compete.

They crossed the bridge where the sculpture of the half-naked Indian reminded her of her first visit to the island with Cullen. This time, he'd be waiting for her inside the rose garden with the intent of making her his wife.

Despite Papa's stern countenance, he agreed to purchase an exquisite new dress for her. The gown of rose silk faille and houndstooth had a matching hat, complete with netting that covered her eyes like a bridal veil. Never had she owned something so nice.

As they crossed to the inner part of the island, a green flowery fence beckoned. As she stepped through its gates, the sweet aroma of thousands of blooms enveloped her. In front of a wall of roses, Cullen stood in his gray suit with his hands in his pockets, talking with Chief Murphy. An entire battalion of firemen in full regalia visited with Hilda and Maxine.

Sensing her presence, Cullen turned and slowly pulled his hands free, then straightened his white collar and silver necktie. The men formed a group on one side of him, her friends on the other.

She took both her mother's and father's arms and walked toward them. Never had a church been more beautifully appointed. The cool, scented garden was their nave, the blue cloudless sky their high roof. Even the gentle breeze stirred vines and flowers, making them a soft-voiced choir.

Cullen nipped a pink rose from a bush behind him, then snapped its thorns from the stem.

When they reached him, he extended it to her.

"You look lovely." His voice held awe and reverence.

Warmth surged through her. Releasing her mother's arm, she accepted the rose, then touched it to her nose. "Thank you."

Murphy cleared his throat and opened his Bible. "Who giveth this woman to be married to this man?"

Her father searched her gaze, a silent message that it wasn't too late to change her mind.

Smiling, she leaned over and kissed him on the cheek.

With a heavy sigh, he offered her hand to the chief, then stepped back.

With his right hand, Cullen took hers from Murphy.

"Repeat after me," Murphy said. "I, Cullen Berneen McNamara, take thee, Adelaide Rosalind Wentworth . . ."

Cullen gave his troth, his voice strong and full of conviction. She then took his right hand and repeated her vows, emotion rising and causing her words to wobble.

Cullen gave her a reassuring squeeze, then once again slid the same ring she'd worn since their engagement onto her left finger and pledged to her all his worldly goods.

Murphy said the Lord's Prayer, joined their hands, and clasped them with his. "Those whom God hath joined together, let no man put

461

asunder." He offered a blessing and pronounced them man and wife.

Though the firemen whistled and whooped, the wedding kiss was chaste and simple. But Cullen's ardent look made promise of a more rousing one in private.

CHAPTER 53

Cullen thought night would never come. Della's parents had stuck by their side the entire day as the four of them toured the fair. Della was clearly close to them and enjoyed their company. Mr. Wentworth, however, had enjoyed thwarting Cullen. The man knew good and well Cullen had wanted a moment alone with his bride, but made sure no opportunity arose.

Now, however, the illumination show was over and the park was closing. Mr. and Mrs. Wentworth had no choice but to leave. In the Court of Honor, they hugged Della good-bye and Mr. Wentworth shook Cullen's hand—squeezing so hard Cullen struggled to keep his fingers from overlapping.

Still, a surge of satisfaction swept through him, for Della was his and carried his last name to prove it.

The exiting crowd swallowed up her parents.

He captured Della's hand and brought it to his lips. "Did you have fun?"

A lamppost picked up the sparkles in her eyes. "I did. I hadn't realized how much I missed them until now."

"Are you sorry they're leaving tomorrow?"

She tilted her head. "Yes and no. Yes, because there was so much more I wanted to show them.

And no, because . . ." She bit her lip. ". . . Because I sort of wished we'd been alone."

He tucked her hand into his elbow. "Well, we're alone now, Mrs. McNamara."

He started toward the South Canal.

Her brows lifted. "Are you taking me to a hidden staircase?"

Chuckling, he shook his head. "We are man and wife. No need to search out eaves and alcoves anymore."

"Then why are we heading in the wrong direction?"

"You didn't think we'd spend our wedding night in Harvell House, did you?"

A bit of panic crossed her face. "Well, yes. That's where all my things are."

"Your mother packed a bag for you and had it delivered to our destination."

Her shoulders relaxed. "And what is our destination?"

Bed. "Oh, over that way." He whirled his hand in a southeasterly direction.

"We're staying on the fairgrounds?"

"We are."

She glanced toward the Agricultural Building. "Where? 'Over that way' could mean yards or it could mean miles."

"Farther than yards, shorter than miles."

She cocked a brow but said nothing. Her smile began to stretch when he brought her to the threshold of Blooker's Dutch Cocoa Company.

"We're having some hot chocolate?" she asked.

"We are." Pushing open the large wooden door, a rich chocolate aroma enveloped them. Della removed her gloves.

A rosy-cheeked Dutch maiden wearing wooden shoes and a gaudy dress greeted them.

Cullen smiled. "We'll have two cups, Miss Zonderkop."

She curtseyed, then hurried into the kitchen.

Placing a hand on Della's back, he guided her around a few dozen tables with chairs turned upside down on their tops, then into an old-fashioned parlor, sitting room, and kitchen.

Two dining chairs and a side table faced a cheery fire popping inside a brick fireplace. Drop leaf tables, holding the vases of roses he'd requested, graced the north and east walls. A geometric carpet offered cushion for their weary feet.

"I don't understand," she said. "Are we going to tour it again?"

"We're going to honeymoon here."

Stunned, Della widened her eyes. "But, how—"

A knock interrupted her.

Turning toward the open door, Cullen accepted a tray from Miss Zonderkop. "That will be all for tonight. Thank you for staying late."

She curtseyed again, her cheeks pink, then skittered away.

Cullen set the tray on one of the tables, closed the thick wooden door, and secured the latch. The sound of the lock sliding into place made her stomach jump.

She never expected a bridal suite, and certainly not one inside the gates of the fair. She couldn't imagine the trouble he must have gone to.

"Would you like some cocoa?" His brown eyes were warm, patient.

A wave of shyness spilled over her. "Please."

He settled her into one of the armless dining chairs in front of the fire, then brought a cup of hot chocolate to her. She held the mug with both hands, finding comfort in its warmth and familiar smell.

"Are you hungry?" he asked. "There are some fritters."

She shook her head, unsure if she'd be able to eat. "The cocoa is perfect."

He moved his chair next to hers, leaving the table on her left, then retrieved his cup and joined her. "It feels good to sit down."

"It does." She covered one toe of her shoe with the other.

Finishing his cup, he reached across her to set it on the table, then angled himself toward her. She took another sip, trying not to squirm under his scrutiny.

With a great deal of gentleness, he gathered the wisps of hair tickling her collar and brushed his fingers along her neck. "Would you mind if I took your hat off? I'd like to see your eyes without the netting in front of them."

She started to set down her cup, but he stalled her.

"I'll do it." Searching the trim, he found her hat pin and drew it out.

"There's another in the back." She tucked her chin down.

He removed that one too, then placed the hat and pins next to his feet. Tracing the lip of her cup with her finger, she kept her head down.

He rubbed her neck.

Her body relaxed, her eyes sliding shut. "That feels wonderful."

He said nothing but continued to rub with one hand while tugging her hairpins free with the other. Bit by bit, strands of hair spilled free, forming a curtain around her.

He lifted a strand to his nose. "Heaven," he whispered.

Tingles shot throughout her body. She raised her face.

He tunneled his fingers into her hair, dislodging the last of the hairpins, then leaned in and kissed her as he'd done in the gondola and many times since.

She gripped her cup, wishing her hands were free. The longer he kissed, the limper she became.

He pulled away. "I'm so glad you're my wife." He started to descend again.

"My cup . . . it's—"

Taking the mug from her hands, he reached across her and set it next to his. Before he could straighten, she captured him within her arms.

He slid her from her chair and onto his lap, his kisses becoming more ardent. His hands were everywhere. Each place he touched sent new sensations ricocheting through her.

She curled her legs up, trying to get closer. Her skirts fell across his knees and his hand found her stockings.

Stiffening, she broke their kiss.

He searched her eyes, but left his hand where it was.

Her heart thrummed.

Hooking a finger through her garter, he whisked it off, his knuckle running the full course of her leg. Then with slow, careful strokes, he rolled her stocking down over her knee and to her ankle. Blindly, he unlaced her shoe and let it drop to the floor with a thunk. The stocking followed. His hand gripped the arch of her foot and retraced its previous path.

She held her breath. Her stomach squeezed.

"Will you be my wife?" His voice was hoarse, gravelly.

Love for him overflowed from inside. "Yes. For the rest of our lives, yes."

His eyes darkened. Placing a soft kiss on her forehead, he scooped her up and carried her to the bedchamber.

Epilogue

Cullen slipped into the back of a classroom in McNamara's School for the Deaf. Though there wasn't a lot of noise, there was certainly a lot of chatter. Standing to the right of a fireman in full uniform, a volunteer parent signed while he spoke.

At the moment, the children were marveling at the big ax he carried and signed among themselves in their excitement.

"Who'd like to try on my helmet?" he asked.

All thirty hands shot into the air.

"What about you, young lady?" He pointed to a girl in the second row.

Jumping to her feet, Kitty scurried to the front, her wild hair tamed with braids.

"And what's your name?" the fireman asked.

"Kitty Kruger." Her voice was nasal but easily understandable.

At the back of the room, Della squatted to remind two of the students to quit "talking" and pay attention to the presentation on the dangers of fire.

Her light brown hair was silky and in a soft twist. Her neck, long and slender.

She stood. Up, up, up she went. Her green

469

skirt and white shirtwaist showed off a slender figure with curves in all the places they should be.

Creeping up behind her, Cullen poked her in the waist.

Squeaking, she whirled around.

Mrs. Anderson and the fireman glanced at them, but none of the students heard.

Della shooed him out the door and followed him into the hall. "When did you get back?"

"Just now." Hooking an arm around her waist, he pulled her close.

She swatted at him. "Stop that. What if one of the students comes out?"

"Then they'll know that being hard of hearing doesn't mean they can't live a full and rewarding life."

"But I'm the director. And I—"

He leaned in for a kiss, but he had no wish to be caught either, so he kept it short. "Did you miss me?"

"You know I did. How did it go?"

Smiling, he let her go, took a step back and spread his arms wide. "You are now looking at a charter member of the National Fire Protection Association."

She brought her hands together in a clasp. "It happened?"

"It happened. The other members are Vaughn and four more insurance men."

"Congratulations." Taking his hand, she squeezed it. "Did you cable your father?"

"I did. He and Alice sent congratulations and a special hello to you."

"What did the association think of your new glass-disc sprinkler?" She spoke and signed at the same time to make sure he heard.

"They loved it and agreed it would eliminate the problem of built-up dirt clogging the system. But they brought up something else I want to look into."

"What's that?"

"An automatic fire alarm system. I need to figure out a way for the fire to trigger some chimes or bells and alert anyone in the building of the danger."

She propped her fists on her hips. "I thought these glass discs perfected the system."

"They perfected the part that puts out the fire. The chimes will be an added feature."

Shaking her head, she looped her arm around his. "Well, I'm glad you're home. Were you able to make it through the meetings without too much trouble?"

"More or less." They walked down the corridor toward the front of the building and her office. His hearing loss had leveled out over the past year, but Machinery Hall had taken its toll. He was completely deaf in his right ear. "I could definitely use some more practice. One of the men had an accent. Those are always hard to read."

"What kind was it? Perhaps I should start speaking with an accent."

"I have a better idea." He veered toward the broom closet, opened the door, and nudged her inside.

"What are you doing?" she whispered, her tone a bit frantic.

Closing the door behind them, he gathered her into his arms, her rose water mixing with the closet's smell of lemon and vinegar.

"What do you think I'm doing?" he murmured, as his mouth descended. "I'm practicing my lip-reading."

AUTHOR'S NOTE

Now it's confession time. Though I did extensive research and depicted things as accurately as I could, I did take a bit of creative license here and there. To help you discern between fact and fiction, here's a summary.

All characters in the book are fictional other than historical figures, such as President Cleveland, Alexander Graham Bell, Helen Keller, Ann Sullivan, Fire Marshal Murphy, and Miss Garrett (the director of the school for the deaf). I obviously put fictional words in the mouths of all but Cleveland. His dialogue was taken from excerpts of his actual speech.

When I started my research on the Chicago World's Fair, I had no idea how comprehensive the resources were, how much I'd fall in love with it, and how important the fair was to our country. It set our standard for architecture in the upcoming century; it introduced foreign cultures to our amazed population; it wowed the world with our scientific innovations; and it gave women their first official board position recognized and approved by an act of Congress (all before we had the right to vote). But it was technology that claimed the day as it nipped at the heels of horses, buggies, and man-powered tools. I wish I could have camped on all that, but this novel is character driven rather than information driven. So you'll have to go uncover those delicious details from more scholarly sources.

The opening ceremony was based on fact—the size and crush of the crowd, the trampling at the front and all its ripple effects, the description of what happened when Cleveland pushed the button, and the carrying of a woman over the heads of three muscular men (though I don't know the nationality of the men, nor who the woman was). When I read that account, however, I immediately knew how Cullen and Della would meet. It was just too much fun to pass up. It was also a bit over the top (no pun intended)—so much so that I made up Della's hurt ankle to justify her being carried above the men's heads. I am also the one who made Cleveland see them, though I'd bet money that in real life he probably did.

I took a ton of creative license with the time line of the fair. The only dates I didn't touch were opening day (May 1, 1893), the Cold Storage fire (July 10, 1893), and closing day (October 31, 1893). Everything else I tweaked to accommodate the needs of my story line. For those who are curious, here are some of the more blatant events I flip-flopped around.

The fair wasn't completely built nor were all exhibits installed until mid-June. In this book, that's not the case. For example, one report had the water fountains working on opening day; numerous others said they weren't. I wanted you to "see" the fountains, so I have them working on opening day. The Children's Building wasn't finished until June 2nd; I have it open in May. The Ferris wheel wasn't finished until June 21; in all my descriptions, it is in full operation regardless of the date. The illumination show started running at the beginning of May; I have it beginning in August. Cullen borrows wood from the Lincoln Hotel's fire in September, but that fire actually occurred a couple of days before the Cold Storage fire in July. Fireman's Week (the contest) was the last week in August; I have it toward the end of September. See what I mean? So, don't trust the time line.

Same thing with the economic crisis. Cullen read headline news about things that absolutely happened, but they might have happened a few weeks earlier or a few weeks later. What you can rely on is that America was experiencing the worst depression it had ever seen up to that point; farmers, banks, and railroads were in trouble, and Europe was in a recession. In that year alone, 158 banks failed. Of these, 153 were in the West and the South. The depression lasted four years. More than fifteen thousand businesses failed, and five hundred railroads went bankrupt. In 1895, Cleveland had to borrow $65 million in gold from J. P. Morgan. Ouch.

Something I didn't take creative license with was the structures and the displays within them. Every building at the fair was enthralling, each containing an endless number of captivating exhibits. You have no idea how difficult it was for me to pick only a few buildings and a smattering of exhibits. But even if I'd only been able to show one, I would have been hard-pressed to leave out the Children's Building. Can you believe they had a kitchen garden for training future house-wives? I about died. And that library—I'd have loved to have seen that library. In the middle of the Children's Building was a gigantic gym with ropes, pommel horses, parallel bars, and a Jacob's ladder. Loved that building. But I loved all the other ones too, like the Administration Building.

It was the one that had an operational post office, but since we visit this building when Cullen sees the director-general, I decided instead to turn a postal counter in the Government Building (which was only a display) into an operational post office. Totally my doing. I wanted to give y'all a peek at some of the fun exhibits over there.

Every single resource pronounced the Wooded Island as nothing short of amazing. I did want to clarify that though some described the rose garden as labyrinthal, it was not a maze in the true sense of the word.

As for Machinery Hall, it was in fact the power

source for the entire fair, and it also had a ton of its own machines chugging away simultaneously. Its noise level wasn't widely reported, but it was mentioned. Since it worked so well with Cullen's issues, I exploited it. How much? I'm not sure. All I know is it was supposed to be incredibly noisy, and the din did affect the crowds to some degree.

Where I strayed most was with the floor plan of Machinery Hall. The fire apparatus was exhibited in the far left corner of the building, but I have no idea if the exhibit included a sprinkler system. I also have no idea where the Crowne Pen Company had its booth. But their "lovely salesladies" were too fun to pass up, so I put them close to Cullen. The printing presses were not next to the fire apparatus. I moved them there in order to make more noise for Cullen. And as a side note, due to fire-hazard concerns, the fair didn't allow the match factory to dip matches in an igniting solution. It dipped them in nothing. So for their show-and-tell, they cut and boxed 12 million unusable matches per day.

I depicted the rest of the exhibits in the novel as accurately as I could, though I had to leave out a TON of detail in order to keep the pace moving. I didn't come anywhere close to describing even the tip of the iceberg. There were hundreds of thousands of them—all wonderful, interesting, and fascinating. The novel would have been a bazillion pages long if I'd tried to squeeze them all in. Still, I absolutely *hated* leaving them out. ☹

The outsides of the buildings were as fantastic as the interiors. I didn't come close to doing them justice. Again, it would have taken pages and pages. So unless I say so here in this note, you can assume that the exhibits, statues, boating vessels, buildings, elevators, restaurants, and everything else that our characters saw or interacted with were in fact the way they reportedly were at the actual fair—though some of them were even more extravagant than how I portrayed them.

I admit to being a bit concerned about giving those less familiar with the Columbian Exposition the wrong impression about its purpose. Cullen was exhibiting in order to make sales, but I feel the need to stress that the World's Fair was not a trade show. It was designed to illustrate the development of the United States and the progress we'd made in four hundred years as compared with all participating nations, which were, for the most part, hundreds upon hundreds of years old. In other words, it was, for all practical purposes, just one big show-and-tell. ☺ Many of the exhibitors, however, promoted their brand and sold products as souvenirs (as the Crowne Pen Company did). Others sold their product the way Cullen did—just not the majority of them.

The Columbian Exposition made a huge impression on all its visitors—everyone from royalty to the most common of people. A few of the famous visitors we'd recognize were Walt Disney's father (think Epcot); L. Frank Baum, author of *The Wizard of Oz* (think Emerald City); Henry Ford; and Frank Lloyd Wright, to name a few. Those who had exhibits were also there, such as Edison and Bell. (I have no idea if their names were carved on Machinery Hall's statuary. My resources never said. I put Bell's there because it served my purposes.) Mark Twain managed to make it to Chicago, then became ill and never actually attended the fair. Can you believe that? I would have so loved to have seen what kind of literary work it would have inspired in him. Such a loss. I bet he kicked himself for not staying long enough to see it.

Helen Keller too was at the fair, with Ann Sullivan and Alexander Graham Bell as her escorts. She would have been thirteen at the time. She was the only guest who received special permission to touch fair exhibits. The African diamonds were just one of many displays she was able to "see." The tests Dr. Jastrow executed in this novel are a fraction of those he actually performed. All tests were done in front of an audience. What a sport Helen was!

Though the tests took place in the Anthropological Building, you might have noticed I was a bit vague with Helen's location in the novel. That's because I needed the fire wagons to come racing by, and there weren't any fire stations in that corner of the park. I fudged a little bit on that part.

Though the fire was real and everything that happened on that ledge is exactly how it was reported to have happened, John Ransom was a fictional character. However, the firemen really did throw their helmets off the ledge in an appeal for help. The men hugged and said good-bye, though, to my knowledge, none were brothers. I added that detail. The firemen on the roof below them made a makeshift net with their clothing. And the last man standing threw his wallet, shook his own hand, and pounded his heart before going down the rope right as the tower fell.

Captain Fitzgerald and the men in Companies One and Two were the ones who climbed to the top of the tower and subsequently lost their lives. Chief Fire Marshal Murphy headed up the battalions that day, though he was second in command to Chief Swenie.

As for the conflagration itself, there was much more than what I actually included. The biggest gap in description was what happened after the tower collapsed. The heat building up inside the remaining structure made the roof that Chief Murphy and his men stood on so hot that it began to bubble and threatened to collapse. There was another scene of intense drama as the men all scrambled to get off the roof. The soldiers, sailors, and marines of other countries came out of the crowd to help contain the gathered multitude. Many of those same men, along with volunteers from the crowd, stayed to help recover bodies. And as I depicted in the novel, the Sunday after the fire was indeed designated as a memorial for the firemen. All ticket sales, as well as a percentage of the proceeds of many of the concessionaires, went to the families of the fallen and wounded.*

I never could confirm where the Fireman's Week competition (which occurred toward the end of my novel and well after the Cold Storage fire) actually took place. I do know fair officials were considering a few options, including the shoreline. I chose the shoreline because I liked that better than some far-removed corner of the fair. (I can't imagine them putting it on the

---

*After *It Happened at the Fair* had already gone into publication, I discovered that the statue of Columbus the firemen pulled down so they could better fight the Cold Storage Building fire actually survived. It was originally placed in front of Engine Company 51's firehouse, because it was Battalion Headquarters and the chief there was a veteran of the Cold Storage fire; today, you can see it in all its glory at the Fire Museum of Greater Chicago.

shoreline, though, especially not with the way the wind whips off the lake. But who knows.)

I took a shameful amount of creative license with the historical time line of automatic sprinkler systems and twisted it in all sorts of ways in order to make Cullen's plight more dramatic. My reasoning was that it was more in keeping with the fair to have his sprinkler new and cutting-edge than to simply be new and improved. But the truth is that the automatic fire sprinkler was first conceived in 1806 by John Carey. It became much more practical when it was improved in the 1870s and 1880s by George Parmelee and Fredrick Grinnell. The National Fire Protection Association (NFPA) was formed in 1895, but obviously Cullen and Vaughn weren't founding members. So to all of those fire sprinkler history buffs—sorry! Forgive me?

As long as I'm asking for forgiveness, I ought to mention the animal treadmill Cowboy (my family's beloved border collie who makes a cameo appearance) hopped onto at the beginning of the book. Again, this wasn't a new invention. It was patented by Nicholas Potter in 1881. I had Cullen "rig one up" in order to show readers his mechanical genius. The treadmill was for dogs and sheep to run on while powering butter churns, cream separators, early washing machines, or whatever.

The Columbian Exposition was a fair of firsts,

not just in its size and grandeur but in products that debuted there. Several became household names, many of which we still recognize today. Among them are Cracker Jack (though it wasn't called that until after 1900), hamburgers, picture postcards, the Ferris wheel, chili con carne, Aunt Jemima, and shredded wheat.

The medals awarded at the Columbian Exposition were noncompetitive, a change from previous fairs. All bronze and all exactly alike, they were awarded to articles that indicated some independent and essential excellence and also denoted improvement in the condition of the art or industry they represented. I have no idea if any of the sprinkler systems exhibited were awarded medals.

The official fair medals should not be confused with souvenir medals. There were a plethora of those in all sizes, shapes, and colors and with all manner of engravings. You didn't earn those; you paid for them.

Something I regrettably was forced to overlook were the designated days and weeks of celebration. The fair had a Children's Week, German Day, Miller's Day, Chicago Day, Irish Day, and many more. The only one I managed to work in was Fireman's Week.

The Pennsylvania Home for the Training in Speech of Deaf Children Before They Are of School Age, which became known as Bala Home, did transport the school to the fair as an official exhibit. I could find no record of how many teachers and pupils there were, nor where they all boarded, so I took complete creative license there.

Neither was I able to discover how they taught lip-reading back in the day. I found a lot of information about why it was taught, but I couldn't find a thing on how it was taught. So I used one of today's methods. If I made mistakes—and I'm sure I did—it wasn't for lack of trying. I just couldn't find the resources I needed.

The same thing with sign language. At the time of the World's Fair, if I'm not mistaken, America was using a French-based sign language. In my novel, however, I have Della teaching Cullen American Sign Language (ASL). Again, it wasn't for lack of trying, I just couldn't find the resources I needed concerning sign language in 1893.

What I did find plenty of material on was the heated debate the country was having about whether sign language should be taught or used. The advocates of lip-reading were called "oralists," and the advocates of sign language, "manualists." The debate represented a much bigger issue, however: the one where society was so busy striving to make everyone the same that it failed to look at a person's character and integrity and instead concerned itself only with the superficial surfaces.

Alexander Graham Bell was a purist when it came to oralism. His wife was in fact deaf, so I firmly believe his heart was in the right place, as was everyone else's. The manualism versus oralism topic is still a sensitive one. It is my deepest desire that I have not hurt any feelings or stepped on any toes. If I did, I apologize and ask for your forgiveness.

You might have wondered why I didn't end the book with the closing ceremonies on October 31. They were to be as magnificent as the opening, but two days before the fair ended, the mayor of Chicago was murdered. So tragic. He was, of course, a major player in the success of the fair, so the closing ceremonies ended up becoming a funeral dirge. Not exactly the tone I wanted to end the book on.

As for weddings and honeymoons, I found reports of people wanting to say their vows on the Ferris wheel and such, but official permission was always denied, so it is my guess that Cullen and Della would not have been allowed to get married on the Wooded Island. Still, there are folks today who had grandparents or other relatives who claimed to have married on the grounds. I did find confirmation of a couple who honeymooned inside the fair. It was a specially prepared bridal chamber in one of the bastions of the miniature Fort Marion in the Florida State Building. Since neither of my characters was from Florida, I decided to use Blooker's as a substitute.

Just as Della mourned the temporariness of the Columbian Exposition, so do I. Its buildings were burned to the ground the following year by union members involved in the Pullman strike. Only the Art Building survives today. Because of all the masterpieces it displayed, it was the only build-to-last structure of the fair. Its walls were brick based, its floor and roof, iron. It was also the only fireproofed building. It is now the Chicago Museum of Science and Industry and still looks out over the north end of the lagoon in Jackson Park.

Other evidence of the fair can be seen by driving on one of Chicago's highways that runs along the shore, roughly on the same route as the elevated train. The Plaisance is now in the middle of the University of Chicago's campus. It's still called the Midway Plaisance, and the Chicago Bears are called the "Monsters of the Midway."

I'm an avid scrapbooker and save every piece of memorabilia imaginable from every trip our family takes. Evidently there were more than a few of us back in 1893 too. Because of it, we can find souvenirs of the fair here and there—some more expensive than others. For example, you can find a picture postcard from the fair for a few dollars on eBay. While in 2011, Coca Cola's soda fountain from the fair was auctioned off for $4.5 million. I'd love to hear from you if you have a piece of the fair or if you know of one. E-mail me from my Web site, IWantHerBook.com.

Well, my friends, it was great fun to research and write this book. I cannot tell you how much it means that you came along for the ride with me.

Many blessings,

PERISTYLE DESTROYED

"The fair's buildings were burned to
the ground the following year by union
members involved in the Pullman strike.
Only the Art Building survives today."

READING GROUP GUIDE

Introduction

Cullen McNamara didn't set out to be an inventor. He had long ago settled on a life of farming, but his debilitating allergies to cotton—and a tragic history with his mother—continued to steer him toward his idea for inventing an automatic fire sprinkler system. With the support of his father, Cullen attends the 1893 Chicago World's Fair and finds more than just a platform for his invention. A beautiful lip-reading teacher quickly turns his world upside down, and everything he thought he knew about himself—and life—changes.

Discussion Questions

1. In *It Happened at the Fair*, we are introduced to a hard-of-hearing farmer with severe allergic reactions to his crops. What are your first impressions of Cullen McNamara? Why do you think he was so resigned to a life of farming, even though it made him miserable?

2. Cullen's father manages to persuade Cullen to attend the fair after confessing he has paid the nonrefundable money for Cullen's travel expenses and fair fees. Despite Cullen's protests, do you think he was privately happy about this? Why or why not?

3. Describe Cullen and Wanda's relationship. How does he view his girlfriend? Why is he hesitant to set a date for their wedding?

4. Adelaide Wentworth, the beautiful lip-reading teacher at the fair, is hesitant to trust Cullen at first. Even when he proves his loyalty, she suspects he is lying. What makes her so distrusting? How do you think that defined her character?

5. Della is forbidden from teaching sign language to her pupils because if they were

to engage in it, they would be branded as different and therefore less than. How do you feel about that stigma? How has the stigma changed since the 1890s?

6. One of the overarching themes of the culture of America during the World's Fair appeared to be assimilation—if you weren't one of us, you were against us. Beyond the sign-language stigma, in what other ways did this culture manifest?

7. Wanda accused Cullen of not being honest when he wrote the letter to break their engagement. She said he should have done it in person and that two more months wouldn't have mattered. Did Cullen do the right thing in writing Wanda to break off their engagement? Should he have waited and done it in person? Should he have written earlier? What else could he have done?

8. The backdrop of the World's Fair adds a certain ethereal magic to Cullen and Della's relationship. How do you think things would have developed under different circum-stances?

9. Cullen refuses to retaliate against or reprimand the manual sprinkler salesman,

even though he feels certain Bulenberg sabotaged his shed demonstration. How would you have reacted in Cullen's position? Why do you think he refused to address it?

10. Why do you think Cullen chose not to tell Della when he met her that he was engaged? Do you think he had feelings for her from the very beginning?

11. If someone had lied to you about having a fiancée, would you forgive him under the right circumstances?

12. Vaughn advised Cullen that he should not disclose his loss of hearing to potential clients since it had no bearing on the reliability of his sprinkler system. Yet Cullen felt this might be lying by omission, especially if he knew the client would object to working with someone with a disability. Who was right—Vaughn or Cullen? Why?

13. Discuss the author's note. Had you wondered if her descriptions were real? Is the Chicago World's Fair an event you wish you had been able to attend?

14. What were your favorite descriptions from the fair?

Enhance Your Book Club

1. The Chicago World's Fair wasn't just about celebrating inventions—it was about celebrating America and its innovations. Choose a local museum to attend with your book club, preferably one focusing on North American history. If there are multiple museums in your area, make a day of it.

2. Pick three buildings as themes and ask everyone to bring something fun or unique, old or new, that would have gone in one of the "buildings." Set up three tables and label each with its "building" name and have everyone put their items on the tables as they arrive. For example, "Art Palace" would have paintings, sculpture, music, etc. The "Woman's Building" would have cooking, lace and tableware, shoes and clothing, and household items. "Horticulture" would have plants, seeds, gardening tools, etc. Be sure to make time for everyone to share why they chose the items they brought.

3. Give each person a card with one of these words written on it: eat, love, hurt, help, more, please, thank you, daddy, mommy, cheese, meat, banana, cereal, cookie, drink,

juice, milk, hot, cold, all done. Have them make up a sign for their word and try to communicate it to the group. If the group is a little shy, this can be less intimidating if done in pairs, but it is hilarious when done as a group. If there is someone who knows sign language, have that person demonstrate the real signs afterward. If not, here's a link to an animation of each sign: http://www.labelandlearn.com/signgamecolor.swf. Sign demonstrations can also be found on YouTube, so feel free to make up your own list of words to play with.

4. In honor of Cullen and Della's romance, have your book club make their favorite hot cocoa recipes for your next meeting. If the weather is warm, experiment with frozen hot chocolate instead!

Center Point Large Print
600 Brooks Road / PO Box 1
Thorndike ME 04986-0001 USA

(207) 568-3717

US & Canada:
1 800 929-9108
www.centerpointlargeprint.com